Eleanor Bailey is a writer and journalist. She lives in Japan. She has recently been selected as one of twenty-one women writers in the Orange Futures promotion, highlighting the writers to watch in the twenty-first century. Her first novel, *Idioglossia*, is also published by Black Swan.

Acclaim for *Idioglossia*:

'Highly original and beautifully written . . . a brilliant imagination and genuine psychological insights'
Sunday Telegraph

'Relentlessly building beneath an entertaining and well-written story, the reader is made aware of the relationships which bind us, not only to our family but one being to another'
Daily Mail

'[Bailey's] unsentimental but sympathetic language penetrates the private world of the emotions in an impressive way'
The Times

'A brilliant, accomplished début . . . slick and clever, heartfelt and deep . . . Bailey's observations are startling and fresh . . . the sort of read which haunts you for weeks afterwards'
Sunday Express

'Bailey is an intelligent writer, eloquent about memory and women's stories. Her grip on poetic language is an assured one . . . an ambitious first novel'
Independent on Sunday

'Hugely entertaining . . . a clever dramatic read'
Margaret Forster

'Eleanor Bailey's exuberant novel plays with the fate of characters struggling with the tension between inner and outer reality . . . Funny and sad and full of human sympathy'
Jill Paton Walsh

Also by Eleanor Bailey
IDIOGLOSSIA
and published by Black Swan

MARLENE DIETRICH LIVED HERE

Eleanor Bailey

BLACK SWAN

MARLENE DIETRICH LIVED HERE
A BLACK SWAN BOOK : 0 552 99863 X

Originally published in Great Britain by Doubleday,
a division of Transworld Publishers

PRINTING HISTORY
Doubleday edition published 2002
Black Swan edition published 2003

1 3 5 7 9 10 8 6 4 2

Set in 11/13pt Sabon by
Kestrel Data, Exeter, Devon.

Black Swan Books are published by Transworld Publishers,
61–63 Uxbridge Road, London W5 5SA,
a division of The Random House Group Ltd,
in Australia by Random House Australia (Pty) Ltd,
20 Alfred Street, Milsons Point, Sydney, NSW 2061, Australia,
in New Zealand by Random House New Zealand Ltd,
18 Poland Road, Glenfield, Auckland 10, New Zealand
and in South Africa by Random House (Pty) Ltd,
Endulini, 5a Jubilee Road, Parktown 2193, South Africa.

Printed and bound in Great Britain by
Clays Ltd, St Ives plc.

To SMW

Sculpture: Untitled, 1999
White fibreglass, wood and laminated newspaper

I have no name. But I firmly believe that from every
tragedy comes good – in my case, unencumbered by
parental bad taste: I got to choose. I call myself
Potsdamer Man. Obvious, but then
I was never troubled by excessive imagination.

I live alone, four metres above the ground. It's the
modern urban way, you know, scratching the clouds,
ganz allein. Better than eighty years ago, when people
were crammed six to a room. You don't have to tell me. I
know all about the history of housing, its relation to social
theory and the growth of a middle class. I'm not
complaining. I'm explaining.

I could wish for more privacy. It's hard with tourists
pointing and taking photos. Berliners no longer see me.
That hurts too.

Potsdamer Platz used to be the busiest transport
interchange in Europe. Sixty-seven Underground routes,
twenty-six tramlines and five buses. How impressive is
that? It doesn't move me. We can all resort to hyperbole.

I must be the highest fibreglass sculpture suspended
on a wooden plank; self-swinging; in white overalls. Don't
laugh. We all need to feel special. It creates a sense of
self. It makes us real. Doesn't every citizen – even a
fibreglass one – have a right to self-determination?

I know my existence is temporary, that one day I'll be

thrown in the incinerator. And that the day of reckoning will come all the sooner if I don't keep myself pretty. I have at most a couple of years before I'm swallowed up into the burning firmament.

If I sound overly dramatic, I tell you, round here it's nothing. There's this ad hoarding, over there, way up towards the Brandenburg Gate. She's a perfectly ordinary rectangle, but, man, does she shout. 'TEN YEARS TALKING IS ENOUGH! HONOUR THE JEWISH DEAD!' Just that, all day. Annoying, but at least she's saying *something*. And I have to admire the sacrifice. The minute they give her what she's shouting for, she'll be ripped down, never to turn the head of a passing motorist again. That's commitment.

I don't know what my message is. I'm convinced I have something to say; I just haven't articulated it yet. I may look merely decorative but I swear I'm a mass of unanswered questions. What am I doing here? Was I created by a higher being or passed by committee? The fundamental things.

Right now, I just sit and swing. It's a good show. The erstwhile busiest interchange in Europe is now the biggest building site. A forty-year wasteland transformed into a rather obvious combination of office, residential and entertainment buildings. Shining edifices to international modernism. An architectural squid pasta. It's everywhere.

I'd have thought this living adventure playground would be excitement enough. The people can clamber over planks, peer through ring-wire fencing and thrill to the noise of the pneumatic drill and the sight of the crane that swings (with no thought of its personal safety) way above their heads. Its long-necked elegance, very Audrey Hepburn, keeps me riveted (that and the steel screws in my arse).

I find the journey more interesting than the destination. But people want more. They built the multiplex cinema so the human population can flee this rubble. I guess they like to be distracted, but I never grasped this urge to

8

be somewhere else. My one aim is to stay put, in perpetuity.

Here's a superlative. In the last hundred years Berlin has transplanted more statues than any other Western city. That's what I heard and I can believe it. They are forever carting one lot off, the offending faces covered in sheets, just to bring another lot in. And they won't last. Oh how we stony-faces laughed when we heard that Friedrich II of Prussia was coming back. If they could only remember the effort it took to get rid of him.

We live for the most part in closed rooms . . . If we want our culture to rise to a higher level, we are obliged, for better or worse, to change our architecture. And this only becomes possible if we take away the closed character from the rooms in which we live. We can only do that by introducing glass architecture, which lets in the light of the sun, the moon and the stars, not merely through a few windows, but through every possible wall, which will be made entirely of glass.

PAUL SCHEERBART, *Glass Architecture*, Berlin, 1914

In his forty-five years Erich can say he has learned two things. One: urinary urgency is less traumatic, long-term, than visiting a Belgian public lavatory. Two: he never should have let Ursula meet his younger brother.

After emptying his bladder at the autobahn service station on the German border, he can hold on, through Belgium, all the way to England, all the way to Max. He is proud of this talent, unreasonably, like those who boast of skin that tans. He knows that his strong continence, along with a youthful face and still thick hair, is luck. That all anyone can lay claim to is acquired wisdom.

He presses for a black coffee at the automatic machine

and buys a pack of madeleines, since they are out of fresh bread. He walks past eleven bare-breast magazine covers on his way to the till, where the boy behind the counter is alarmed by his distracted, edgy mien and holds his finger over the emergency button until Erich leaves the room.

Oblivious, he returns to his denim-blue Seventies Beetle, which he drives partly out of a weakness for old-fashioned style, but mainly because he cannot afford a new one. Erich feels safe driving. He likes to be alone, surrounded by glass, and for no-one to know exactly where he is. Though he read that the pollution count inside is higher than out. And, right now, it's even worse inside his head.

They had already agreed to split when Ursula confessed. After a week of monosyllables and the baggy, sludge-green tracksuit bottoms he had always detested, she came to him in the evening, to the computer where he was working, wearing her tight blue dress.

He looked at her. Tantalizing, now she was forbidden. Her black hair shone; cut sharply under the chin, it exposed her delicate neck. And the dress dropped from her shoulders in a low circle, revealing skin creamy and somehow softer than before. When she smiled, her blue eyes were misty.

'There's something I have to tell you.'

Intimacy; the first time she'd looked him in the eye for months. He knew what she was going to say. He'd been waiting his adult life for this.

'It began the night you broke the window.'

He grimaced. 'Uh-huh.'

Her voice was low in recollection. That voice. Once directed at him. 'After you stormed out, I stayed with Max in the gallery.' She raised her chin, and the skin on her neck and her collarbone tautened. She breathed.

12

'And?'

'We were both hyped up after what had happened. We had to sort the window out, of course. And while we were waiting for the glazier, we talked.'

'What about?'

'About you, mainly.'

'What did he say?'

'He said he wished he knew you better.'

'Doesn't sound like Max.'

'Not the Max you know, maybe. But then, you don't sound like you when you're talking to *him*.'

'Tell me what happened.'

She smiled softly and swayed, unconsciously leaning towards him so her small stomach bulged forward. Through the thin silk of the dress he saw the outline of her belly button. He remembered her, the mother of his second child. The many guises of Ursula. Betrayer now, but other roles were still a part of what he saw. He could not hate her, nor fully let go.

'Nothing . . . then. But, as we talked I was watching him. There's something about him. His eyes. He looks so self-contained. He looks like he knows everything. I just knew I wanted to be with him.'

Yes. The less Max encouraged attention, the more he attracted it. He had been that way at six years old.

'I couldn't sleep that night. I was still upset. Eventually I got up to go to the loo.'

Ursula, Erich notes cheerfully, has no talent for muscle control.

The car passes lines of fields punctuated with industrialization, cylinders and squat, square buildings emitting billows of smoke.

*

'And Max was in the kitchen, drinking wine.'

'Why did *you* go into the kitchen?'

'I was restless. I wanted a glass of water. It was dark, but I was immediately aware of him. I switched on the light, but he asked me to switch it off again. He was sitting at the table by the window and his face was lit from the light in the yard. I asked him why he was sitting there. He said he was thinking. I asked what about and he dismissed it with some joke. The funny thing is, in that light he looked so like you – the dark features and the sandy hair, the cheekbones. He smells like you too: sweet skin. I love that smell.'

'So why didn't you just do it with me?' Erich could take small pleasure from this irony.

She watched his eyes fall into familiar folds of amusement. The lines around his eyes showed a face that smiled a lot.

She laughed too, her eyes glittered, then she looked serious. 'He's like you, only . . .' Erich's brown eyes widened quizzically. He was interested. While Ursula was thinking, she moistened her lips with her tongue. '. . . Only, he knew what I wanted. And I knew that he would. We didn't communicate verbally. It probably sounds terrible now, but at the time it just felt . . . right, you know?'

'Yeah, sure, it's natural. I screw your sister every time she visits.'

She touched his arm and smiled fondly. If he closed his eyes he could imagine that the story she was telling was some small tale of her day – a student spilling oil on her clothes, Otto asking a child's imponderable question about the nature of infinity – not the end of the relationship and Ursula letting out secrets, since there was no longer anything to hide.

There was pleasure in Ursula's pale face as she told him.

14

For a moment Erich grasped at a retort with which to shock *her*; a table-top fling with a former waitress maybe, himself pinned to the coffee machine by a narrow-waisted, long-limbed, pert-breasted, twenty-year-old, precociously talented hussy, hiding their cries of ecstasy from the customers in the steaming blasts of the cappuccino machine. Good. That would kill Ursula, particularly the mention of long limbs. But she wouldn't believe him. His lies always ring hollow unless *he* believes them.

'We walked back to the gallery. I remember the silence and the darkness and the feel of his hand on the small of my back. I was nervous and fumbled with the keys, but Max took my hand and the lock gave instantly. We had barely got inside when, well, he threw me down on the floor.'

'But it's made of stone!'

'I didn't feel it. I was too excited. I felt totally sexual. I was—'

Heavy sarcasm. 'On fire?'

Astonishment. 'How did you know?'

He sighed. 'You used to admire me.'

Ursula's eyelids flickered. He stared at her while she said slowly, 'I know what you're thinking.'

He blinked with irritation. 'You do.'

She nodded. Her hand on his arm was calm. 'Don't worry. Sex with you was great. Very reliable. We worked together to make the experience good.' Now her fingers luxuriated through her straight, bowl-cut hair. 'It's just that with Max I didn't have to try. There was something . . . universal about it.' She paused; her smile was crooked. 'It changed everything afterwards. My painting was better.'

Erich balked. 'Because of him?'

Her voice trembled. 'He used his brush to paint me inside.'

'Oh, don't.'

She looked defensive. 'Can you blame me? That night, he didn't have to touch me at all. I didn't want it. It was incredibly erotic just as it was, to be an object of pure desire. Oh God,' Ursula was running her hands now across her chest, 'I still dream about it.'

When Erich covered his ears with his hands, Ursula pushed her hair back, leaned her head on one side and said, only half abashed, 'Oh, hell, Erich, we're bohemians, aren't we? We're *supposed* to explore our dark sides. It's a perk of the job – a rare one.' She pulled at his shirt and struck a portentous finger in the air. 'You were the one who talked about choosing one moment of exquisite ecstasy over a lifetime of mediocrity.'

'That was hypothetical,' Erich growled. 'And three in the morning.'

'All hypotheses must have the potential to come true.'

'What do you know about hypotheses?'

'About as much as you do.'

'Nothing, then.'

Ursula pulled his hands across the table and gripped them. He still liked the feel of her hands. Soft and warm, never clammy. 'Look, this doesn't decry you. You know how much we all admire you.'

Erich didn't want to hear it. He shook his head and rubbed an imaginary mark on the corner of the table, his head bowed.

Ursula became exasperated. 'Oh, don't look like that. It shows how close *we* are that I still want you to know.'

He tutted at this perfidy. The rationalization must sound so good in her head. Had he been so sympathetic that she truly believed he would listen to this information, clucking like a best friend? Perhaps he had. The empathetic veneer was easy. 'Why didn't it carry on if it was so good?'

She flushed and looked away. 'You know Max. Can't think of anyone who isn't in the same room.'

'I don't know Max.'

There were tears in her eyes. He felt sorry for her.

That was the summer Christo wrapped the Reichstag. He shrouded the folly in silk. This showed that Berlin had changed. The city could take a joke. It was fun again. Mario Vargas Llosa wrote that, after a century of different oppressions, Berlin in the Nineties had the vitality of Paris in the Sixties. It was vibrating with change. With ripper-toothed bulldozers and pneumatic drills. They built a shining luxury shopping mall off Unter den Linden, filled with American designer clothes and black-and-white décor, where German rap stars filmed opulent music videos. Luxury-car showrooms with gleaming windows appeared near the Aeroflot building and the white hotels at Pariser Platz were restored to their former glory. Except that few people could afford to stay there. Not long afterwards the city went bust, the fountains were switched off and office building faltered for lack of business. And as the parliament moved back to Berlin, into the Reichstag, they found cocaine in the toilets and ghosts in the lives of the politicians.

*   *   *

Max and Erich have not met in the six years since. After their parents died, they barely saw one another. They have lived in different countries so long. Erich moved back to Berlin in his early twenties. Max rarely left London. There are few reasons to meet. Time passes. It never seems to matter enough.

When he was a teenager Erich, seven years older, would pretend that Max was his, relishing the reflected glory of a human being who was so beautiful and so sharp that, even at seven, he was still stopping strangers in the street. Max hated it and spat at rose-lipped old women. The time and the place have changed and Max's impossible questions: 'Why don't men wear dresses?' are replaced by Otto's, Erich's real son, in Berlin, who will ask: 'What is that man *doing* in a dress?' Max doesn't ask questions now.

The Belgian countryside is flat and featureless, flicking past like the pages of a book he has lost interest in – anonymous clusters of houses, iron fences painted in blue and yellow, flashing advertising hoardings.

Erich drove west early this morning from his home in central Berlin, past Hanover, Cologne and the border at Aachen. After two decades in the city and twelve years since the Wall came down, he still thinks, every time, that one different turn would take him east into Poland. He never drove the wrong way. But he needs to know that he could.

Max did not cause the break-up – Ursula and Erich managed fine on their own, four years later, in a dreary free-fall of communication. It was hard to remember when the colour started fading. Erich never confronted Max about Ursula. They don't talk like that.

Five times in one week! When Erich was pleased to notch up twice a month. Max was better. Better in bed, apparently, but much more than that. He is more talented, better-looking, *seven years* younger at a time when it's just beginning to make a difference, more successful, more attractive to people (on his confirmation day, from the slouching line of pimple-faced adolescents the bishop singled out apple-smooth Max for a solitary smile), and, of course, Max is much better off. In fact,

Erich muses, to the sound of the moving tyres, in fact, killing himself is probably the first thing that Max has ever failed to do.

*   *   *

Max was deafened even by the opening of the door. In forty-eight hours he had become completely accustomed to these four cream walls, as if this was the only way he had ever lived. He resented every intrusion.

'Max.'

When did nurses start using first names?

'Max!'

Even now he knew she was smiling at him.

'Max!'

He turned his face round. He saw a clock; it said five thirty. Evening, then. 'Yes?'

'Max,' the word rolled pleasurably from her lips, 'M-a-x, your brother is here.'

Max's lax face stiffened.

Erich walked in, with dread on his face. He looked at his brother and breathed again. The face was white, drained of life, and his eyes were red in contrast, but it was still Max. Erich had expected Max to be lost. The character, the mind, the soul, or whatever it was that shone out from his brother's face to make it more than a collection of nose, mouth and eyes – Erich had thought this would be gone. But Max was there; something still emitted from his eyes. He looked apologetic. Erich offered his hand. They always shook hands. Max's grip was cold and feeble.

The nurse hovered, kicking her toe against the floor. 'Max, love, I'll bring you some of those butter cookies in a bit.' She smiled broadly and turned and patted Erich on the elbow. She saw the familial similarity. Their faces were held together by the same pronounced bone structure, which would have been too sharp but for the soft, almost feminine smile. Max's had charm.

'Go easy on him.'

Erich nodded, pursing his lips. The nurse backed off, closing the door.

Max looked wan. Erich's eyes narrowed. He mimicked her cooing voice: '"Butter cookies"?'

Max shrugged. 'I didn't say a word.'

'You smiled at her.'

'I can't smile. I was grimacing.'

Erich's lips were narrow and when he smiled there was a flash of well-constructed white teeth. He pulled out the wooden chair and sat on it. He looked down at his hands, then up, inhaling. 'Well, I won't ask you how you feel.'

Max's lips moved imperceptibly. 'I feel bloody awful.'

Erich exhaled exasperation and stretched to pick up an empty cola can from the floor. 'I'm fixing the coffee, it's an ordinary day. Then the phone rings and some complete stranger's telling me my only brother has taken an overdose and is lying unconscious in hospital. Christ, Max.'

The faintest flame coloured his cheeks. 'Who said overdose? It wasn't an overdose. I just, uh, you know, miscounted.'

Erich looked at him sceptically. 'Yeah and I bet Marilyn Monroe was planning on saying the same thing when she picked up that telephone receiver. Christ. Somebody needs to whack some sense into you.'

The shock was too great for him to act differently. He could only be as he always was with his brother. He had a prescribed role. With his brother, and with everyone. It was a symptom of maturity. Lately Erich was beginning to feel like a parody, a pantomime version of himself, whose audience demanded a favourite catchphrase, *every* time. Children, particularly, had done this to him; they needed to be sure of who he was. Who they *thought* he was. Which may just be what he'd become.

'Funny,' said Max, who would have been more disturbed if Erich showed up dripping sentiment. 'That's what the doctor said.'

Erich looked at him. 'Really?'

Max winced as he tried to drag his body further up the pillow. 'No, not really. Look, I know it looks bad, but I just wanted to sleep.'

'Max, they pumped your stomach.'

'I was desperate. You don't know what it's like. You get hysterical. People who sleep don't realize.'

Erich gazed into his brother's eyes. 'You think I sleep?'

Max said nothing. Erich shook his head and looked away. Uneaten breakfast was curling on a trolley beside the bed. Tissues and unidentified wrappers were spreading centrifugally. Even unconscious, Max made mess. He had a more forceful personality.

'Nice room,' said Erich. 'Does your insurance cover self-harm?'

'Don't know, don't care.' Max smiled weakly. 'Thanks for coming.'

Erich grunted. He massaged his temples. 'Look.' He breathed tightly, leaning forward, clutching his fists. He had been preparing to say this the whole journey. It was difficult. 'Look, Max, where are you going to go?'

Max's face was blank. 'Back home, I guess.'

'Is Maria going to look after you?'

Max blinked. 'Maria?' He looked confused. 'Oh. Yeah. I meant to tell you. Maria left.'

Erich bit his lip. He frowned. Hesitated. 'Uh. Sorry. Still, you weren't with her long.'

'Three years. Not bad for me.'

'Oh . . . sorry.'

Other people's lives passed more quickly. Though Erich hated people thinking Nina was still a child, he too was culpable. Erich had never met this woman. He had long ago lost count of, and interest in, the stream of companions in his brother's life. They were invariably beautiful, intelligent and tall. A Salman Rushdie choice of Stepford wife.

'No, that's OK.'

'Is that why . . . ?'

'I told you' – strength was gathering in Max's voice – 'I was having trouble sleeping.'

'Oh, right. Yeah.'

Max closed his eyes. 'I don't miss Maria. She was worse than Nicola.'

'Christ.'

'You'd have hated her. She's a model. Even though she never ate, she cried when I couldn't get her favourite table at The Ivy.'

Erich smiled. 'So who's going to look after you, then?'

'Look after me?'

Erich leaned forward, his voice soft but insistent. 'I think you ought to come back to Berlin.'

Max shifted in the bed. His lips parted. Straight brows knotted. 'Berlin?'

Erich nodded. 'Just for a while, until . . . while you sort out that sleeping problem.' He flailed a hand in Max's direction.

'No, really. I don't think . . .'

Erich looked serious. 'Is there something in London you can't leave behind?'

'No.' Max considered. 'No. I couldn't say that.'

*　　*　　*

Max is an ideal travelling companion. He offers no better routes, no preferred speeds. He doesn't comment on the scenery, the sudden acceleration in continental Europe. The flatness. He doesn't care when it starts raining. He expresses no surprise when the rain slows down. Nor when they pass through and the sun almost appears.

Erich plays a tape of something loud and atonal. Max is rubbing sweat from his hands. His black leather coat is not absorbent.

Erich blinks at the falling rain on the windscreen. Euphoria in the hospital room to see his brother alive is being overtaken, days later, by discomfort. Resentment too, compounded by guilt for feeling it. Not the sex, after four years: that wound has eased. Who could blame them? No-strings ecstasy does not come often, not these days – not to Erich, at least. No, what is bothering him, though he hates the way it sounds, is that it is Max who tried to kill himself.

Erich has been disappointed. For twenty years, Erich has tried and failed. He should be allowed this drama. Not Max, who has breezed through everything.

Max half raises an eyelid. 'Christ, Erich, what is that noise?'

'Schoenberg,' shouts Erich and turns the volume up.

Max pulls his coat, which is draped across his lap, up over his head. An exquisitely cut, black, soft leather coat, Erich can smell its luxury.

He has to concentrate as they pass through Liège. It's a complicated interchange and the signs are written in Flemish, French and German, but never, it seems, all three together. Confusion when different languages say the same thing.

*   *   *

They are back over the German border and Erich pulls up at a quiet service station. A non-place. He is buying thin coffee and paprika chips from a woman with fingerless gloves. Max's unused legs buckle as he leaves the car and urinates into the dusk.

Erich's mouth twitches. 'I take the trouble to deposit you at a decent German toilet and still you slash in the bushes.'

Max walks the few steps back, doing up his flies. 'I like pissing out of doors. It's real.'

'Right.' Erich smirks. 'There's a plastic bowl under your seat. Katrina bought it eighteen years ago for Nina to be sick into. That's the reality of this car. Why don't you use that?'

Max pulls a face, puts his hands back into his pockets and inhales the fresh petrol-infused air.

Erich pushes a beige plastic cup of hot tacky liquid onto the roof of the car in front of him. 'Have some fake coffee.' They both lean sideways against the vehicle.

Max pushes his feet against the tarmac, hunting for feeling in his toes.

'You all right?' Erich asks. Every minute he needs to check that Max is still alive. He is forty-five. He does not yet accept that people die. 'All right?' he repeats, more loudly. It is like watching his first child, newborn. So fragile, every silence scares him.

Eventually Max replies, 'Oh sure. Just tired.'

Erich nods, relieved that his brother's lips are moving again. 'Well, you've had a hard week. You're the only suicide survivor I ever met who was soliciting nurses from his hospital bed.'

Max looks aggrieved. 'I'm not a suicide survivor and I wasn't soliciting nurses . . . Besides, just how many have you *met*?'

24

Erich wants to stoke this energy, this sarcasm. To have Max normal. 'Nurses or suicide survivors?'

'The latter.' There is a subtle difference in Max's monotony. He is grudgingly amused.

Erich is encouraged. 'Ursula teaches all those frustrated adolescents. As it dawns on them that they're not Van Gogh, half of them try and top themselves.'

'You're exaggerating.'

'Yes.'

As he rejoins the autobahn Erich accelerates into the fast lane. The aged Beetle isn't happy. Erich shouts above the sound of the engine. 'By the way, you ought to know, I'm not with Ursula any more.'

'Oh . . . dear.'

Max is a good person to tell. He resists reactions. There is no recognition in his eyes. If he believes he had a role in the split, he does not show it.

'Yeah, a couple of years ago. My getaway was not clean. I still see her every day. We share the café and gallery financially and she and Otto live five minutes away. I can't wait for you to see Otto. He remembers you. He's amazing. Eight years old and more bilingual than we are. I've even started him on a bit of Russian. And brilliant with figures, which is inexplicable – but then, I read that most gifted children come from two mediocre parents. We've entered him into a special educational programme for the summer. It's only when he gets bored he can be . . . difficult. Now,' Erich is warming up to quotidian patter, 'you may not see much of Nina. She's earning ten times as much as I am, she was arrested last year for public indecency and will soon be more famous than Jesus – well, more famous than Zlatko anyway. Nina definitely takes after her mother. Speaking of whom . . . Katrina, Katrina, what can I tell you about her? Inexplicably, in the last five years her interior-design

25

business has exploded. But then, I guess the ex-husband is unlikely to be a fair judge of his ex-wife's talents. But as far as I can see she had one idea and puts it everywhere. Every new bar in Berlin, she paints orange. That's it, unless you count a few frosted-glass tables and uncomfortable steel chairs. And, frankly, I don't. Still, no doubt you'll hear all about it, you know how she adores you. I couldn't persuade her to stay away. Your best chance is if she brings Dirk with her. That's her new husband – some kind of Belgian aristocrat. Great guy; he's really rude to her. Oh, and I'd better tell you before somebody else twists it: I'm seeing a woman nearby. She lives in Mitte. I keep it very separate from the rest of the menagerie. Well, it's the way she wants it. She's a very private person, but you might be interested to— Max? Max, are you all right?'

Max has fallen asleep. Erich's mouth drops open. Outside, the moon is wrapped in gauzy cloud. He sees no beauty against the buzz of the engine and the heavy breathing that now accompanies the rise and fall of his brother's chest. Erich shakes his head. 'I thought you were a bloody insomniac,' he murmurs.

II

The propaganda exercises on free love at the cabaret that seek to be informing are taken very seriously, but, in spite of the lecturer's assurance, it is extremely difficult to understand how a man can really find delight in the thought of his wife's unfaithfulness.

QUERSCHNITT magazine, Berlin, 1929

The flowers in the entranceway of her tiny flat were dying. Red tulips almost a week old, the yellow tongues inside panting in the dry air and peeling slowly outwards.

Ursula looked again into the mirror. Old. Invisible, probably, to others, she could see new lines and the skin of her cheeks losing elasticity. In her face these days she could see her mother, who would have no sympathy. Her mother did not believe in self-pity and said so. Ursula told her you did not need to believe in it. It just showed up every so often, like the rain. There was rarely understanding between her mother's generation, brought up with the guilt of *their* parents and hers, which was sick of it. Ursula did not want to feel sorry any more.

She wore the loose black dress that hung so well. Huge, black brushed cotton. Sleeves to the elbow, loose at the

27

waist, falling to just above the ankle. There was room for someone else inside.

Ursula flushed deeply, a red wine stain spreading down her neck. Like a trail, she thought, flashing the path into her dress.

She wanted him to see the new paintings. Those she had made since they met last. The paintings he had inspired. She would hold out the pictures one by one. Pictures of Ursula in greens. Green because she cannot see her own colour, she sees straight through. But the body is hers and he is looking at it. The glacial expression was not hers, but one she wished she had.

She thought. 'Tell me about your photos. Tell me about beautiful bodies.'

She could hear his response as if he was standing in front of her. 'It's business. I take photos for money.'

'No,' she said. 'When I had Otto, there was a man who did the scan, who takes pictures of women for a living. He turns them into a black screen of ovaries and tubes. You don't do that. You don't reduce us to science.'

As with many women, Ursula's art was personal. She drew from inside. She felt she had sucked herself dry. When other women her age were fighting flab, Ursula stayed bone thin.

She pulled out a box of acrylics from a drawer in her desk. The desk was tiny. Her flat was too small to breathe. Even the bed folded away.

Ursula opened a pot of green gold, wet her fingers in her mouth and rubbed them against the paint. She dragged her fingers across her forehead and down her nose. The paint had a mildly acrid scent. Across the soft down of her upper lip and across at an angle to behind her ear, then down her neck, so that the colour bled.

She pulled her dress to expose her bare shoulder and drew a circle. Perhaps like a bruise. She did not look. It was always better in her imagination. She had forgotten the beginning of her trail by the end of it.

She stared through her window. From this high point she could see the top of the Axel Springer building – where Western journalists used to watch the high-rise flats across the Wall, wondering how the occupants earned their view of the West. Now the building had a new glass tower block, a celebration of the new Berlin. Everything was built of glass – the revamped railway stations, the new library, the thirty-six-metre bulb on top of the Reichstag. People wanted to see through the city.

Ursula wiped her mouth. She stretched over to the phone. One advantage of living in miniature, she need never move.

The receiver was picked up after only two rings. A crisp voice. '*Ja*, Flinkerhof.'

'Hey, Barbara, I'm getting morose. Come save me?'

There was a pause at the end of the line. 'Treasure, I'm busy. Can't you hear the intimate oiling of the naked masseur I hired?' Another pause. 'I'll be right over.'

Walking through the door, Barbara shrieked. 'Ursula, honey, you're green.'

'Oh,' Ursula swung her hand casually through her hair, 'this is my real colour. I want to be ready in case my people ever come to take me home.'

'What?'

Ursula let out a low moan. 'Nothing. Have a drink.'

There was a half-drunk bottle of schnapps on the narrow kitchen table. Ursula swung herself heavily into the chair. She was sweating. Barbara took a shot and eased into the chair opposite. It was difficult, it fitted so tight against the wall.

'So,' Barbara raised her glass, '*Prost, Liebling*.'

Ursula drank. She rested her glass on the arm of the chair and pointed into the air with her free hand. 'I wouldn't say this if I weren't drunk already. But don't you sometimes think, Barbara, how wonderful it would be to be a muse? Nothing but a dumb sacrificial body for some great male talent? Just to keep house during the day and yield to his needs in the evening? To give everything up and let someone else look after you?'

Barbara looked at her incredulously. 'You want to be slapped around by Picasso?'

Ursula pursed her lips. 'Oh, any minor little talent would do, as long as he made enough money to stop me having to paint or work ever again. It could be a woman, for all I care.'

'Ursula.'

She frowned. 'I know, and you must not repeat a word of this. Tomorrow morning I return to the struggle, I promise. Just tonight, let me enjoy the thought of being completely looked after. Kept. Not a word, OK?' She leaned towards Barbara with her index finger vertical, to rest it against her mouth. The sleeve of the voluminous black dress stroked the side of her glass where it stood on the table. It teetered and smashed to the ground.

Barbara squealed, an incongruous noise from such a robust body. She crouched down to examine the damage. 'Hey, Ursula, you know what? I think the schnapps is lifting the stains from your floor . . . Hey, what's the matter?'

Ursula sat fixed, staring at the shards of glass. Only her eyes shifted around their edges. Monotone. 'Did I tell you about the time Erich broke the window?'

Barbara shook her head.

Ursula's eyes glistened. 'The last time Max was here.'

Barbara swept wavy blonde hair away from her face. 'Let me tidy this up. Where's the brush?'

'Leave it. I like looking at the jagged edges. Reach me down another glass.'

Barbara swivelled round and passed the wineglass to her. 'Uh, OK. I see. Is that what this is all about, Max again?'

Ursula hated that phrase. Nothing is 'all about' anything. She wished she *could* distil her behaviour into one convenient motive.

Barbara patted her arm. 'Tell me.'

Ursula held her head up. Staccato. 'Because Max had just arrived, we ate in the gallery and the lights in there are too bright, so we used candles. I can't remember what we ate, but Erich cooked.'

'Oh God.'

'Exactly. In the dim light everything looked brown. I made some joke about how we should have candles in the café as well, so that the customers wouldn't know what they were eating. I apologized, I don't know why.' She stopped. 'Maybe I *do*. I was apologizing to Erich for what was going through my head. And Erich was suspicious. He didn't want me to meet Max in the first place. He said that everybody who did fell in love with him.' Ursula smiled.

'Does he look like Erich?' asked Barbara, using her practical mind to try to picture the face that would appeal to everyone. Someone who did not exist. Even Cary Grant said he dreamed of being Cary Grant.

'Yes. They both have that dark sand hair. What Erich described as a mix of yellow ochre and burnt umber.' At this Barbara snorted but Ursula ignored her. 'Max is slightly taller. He could be stronger but . . . let's say, he obviously doesn't work out much.'

'He's let himself go?'

Ursula laughed. 'Some men are too clean.'

'Mm.'

'Anyway, when I apologized, Max thought I was talking to him, about the darkness. And he was being polite, so he agreed with me, even though I was talking nonsense. He said that seeing too much was bad. Catching his face in one of those magnifying shaving mirrors in a hotel bathroom recently had terrified him.' She let out a half laugh. 'I didn't tell him we never stay in hotels.'

Barbara poured more schnapps. Ursula grabbed at her glass. She drank and then, putting the glass down, her fingers came together with such force that Barbara jumped.

'There was a huge noise against the window. Relentless thudding, knocking the pane. Bang. Bang. Bang.' She clasped her ears. 'It echoed all round the gallery. So loud, it was frightening. And Erich ran outside, just frantic, shouting. We followed of course, but slower.'

Barbara was attentive now. Ursula drank more. Outside, a dog barked painfully and her flat was consumed by the sound.

'On the street outside there was a boy with a brick. He was probably twelve years old but looked older because he was so fat. He was grotesque, disgusting to look at. His eyes were tiny. His chin melted into his neck, and he had huge legs in jeans that hung halfway down his buttocks, and a massive jellied stomach barely held in by a dirty T-shirt with the word "Defiance!" scrawled across it.'

'Defiance?'

Ursula raised her eyebrows. 'Erich was livid. He stormed up to the boy and pushed him, but it made no impact. None. The fat just wobbled. Then the boy put the brick down and walked away. Whistling.'

'And the window was broken?'

'No. Erich spent ages looking across the glass for damage, but there wasn't a scratch on it.'

'But I thought you said—'

Ursula held up her hand. 'Wait. I said Erich broke the window.'

Barbara sat back in her seat. Ursula drank some more.

'So Erich, always the die-hard sixty-eighter, was holding his hands in the air, ranting about how he threw bricks in protest, but now people do it in boredom.'

'Of course.'

'Yeah. Erich was really angry. Max was trying to make light of it – as always – but this time it just made things worse. Max started telling this story of a time when he was in Moscow with a Russian friend who saw a British woman wearing a T-shirt with Russian on which apparently meant "I'm an ignorant Western pig". And the British woman had no idea that her T-shirt was a joke at her expense. When Max told this story, he started laughing. He doesn't laugh much, but when he does, you believe it. So I laughed too. I couldn't stop. We laughed until at some point Erich started to think we were laughing at him. Like the whole story was against him. Max saw it was happening, but the only means he had to deal with it was to get louder. I could see Erich was exploding. Max just couldn't stop. Erich stood up and Max was silent. Erich stormed outside, took the brick and flung it through the window. The crack whipped through the room. I covered my eyes. When I looked back the floor was covered in glittering smithereens and Erich was gone.'

Barbara's eyes widened. 'Why?'

Ursula looked at her friend with slightly drunken incredulity. 'I never knew anyone see his brother so rarely yet think about him so much.' She paused. 'That was the night I first slept with Max. And it was Erich's fault.'

Barbara smirked.

'No, I mean it. He built Max up. I think he wanted me

to sleep with him, to prove his point. That Max always wins.'

'But why did you?'

'After Erich left, Max pulled out a phone and just called someone to come and mend the window. He had it at the tip of his fingers, the power to sort everything out.'

'You banged him because he had a mobile phone?'

'It wasn't what he had, it was what he did with it.' Ursula clinked her glass against Barbara's and winked. 'His eyes are much darker than Erich's. So dark, the pupil and iris merge. You can't read them. You can't tell what he's thinking.'

'Don't you want to know what he's thinking?'

'Of course not. He probably doesn't think anything, like the rest of us, but I don't want to know that.'

Barbara put her hands over her ears. 'OK, that's enough. You live in a dream world.'

Ursula accepted this sadly. 'I'm worse than that. I'm a completely selfish pig. I haven't even told you why Erich's bringing him over here.'

Barbara pulled at several kitchen-cupboard doors before successfully locating a broom. She began brushing up the pieces of the broken bottle. Ursula was kicking her right leg idly into the air.

'He took an overdose.'

Barbara stopped sweeping.

Ursula was nonchalant. 'I'm in denial. But apparently he is too. He says it was an accident.' She smiled, her lips in a bow. 'You see? We'd be perfect for each other.'

'Horrible.' Barbara swallowed. She heard a bus go by. The walls shook. She put the pieces of glass into a plastic bag and looked out of the window, unnerved. She did not like to feel this way. She shook her head and looked back to Ursula. 'Hey, I was going to tell you. Some guy came

34

up outside the supermarket with a clipboard today trying to recruit me for a dating agency.'

Ursula looked at her without comprehension.

Barbara stamped the floor with her heavy shoes. 'I mean, is it that obvious that I'm available? Does it smell? God, I hate this city.'

Ursula smiled and bent forward shakily to where her friend crouched on the floor. Her voice was amused but she was sincere. 'Be strong, Barbara. You are an artist. You need to suffer.'

Barbara stood up, taking Ursula's hand. 'That's what I told him.'

'And?'

Barbara was solemn. 'He wouldn't leave me alone, so I gave him your details.'

'*What!*'

Barbara smiled. 'Yeah.'

Ursula sighed. 'Thanks, Barbara.'

'Any time.'

III

After the October revolution, architects drew up plans for the 'proletarian coffee shop'. Constructionist ideology, practical beauty – smooth lines of wood and glass, magazines and books lined up on simple shelves – in the new society, anyone could access a world of knowledge and ideas for the price of a hot drink.

UTE RIESTSCHE, historian

Had he succeeded, Max would have killed himself on the same day as Hannelore Kohl. Their father died in the same week as Rudolf Hess. The first time Erich felt the loss was when he couldn't share this fact. Heinrich would have loved it. Even more with the rumour, years later, that the old man rotting away in Spandau probably wasn't Rudolf Hess and never had been – and why didn't anyone guess since Hess was teetotal and this guy loved expensive Scotch? Especially as he grew older, what their father loved above all was to discover the deep twist in each apparent truth. Age, wisdom, brought irony, and he liked it confirmed.

It was past midnight when they pulled into the city. Through the sparse traffic on the West side, through the high-rise blocks, the old-fashioned neon signs. Small, squat, pink letters advertising a flower shop, a family-run bar, an Italian restaurant. Like a 1960s postcard still flaunting modernity way past the sell-by date. A few people, mainly small groups of young Turk males, sauntered along the wide asphalt.

Adrenalin surged through Erich whenever he arrived in Berlin at night. An inarticulate thrill, a smell, something he could never have committed to paper. After twenty years, he was still enchanted.

Max stopped differentiating places and signs for towns he didn't know, lit and unlit buildings, a blurred kaleidoscope passing across his eyes. He had not spoken for the last hour. Maybe he slept. They stopped at traffic lights and Erich turned to his brother. The stilled engine stirred Max; he opened his eyes.

'You all right?' Erich spoke softly.

Max stretched his neck, twisting to the left and right, up and down. 'I'm very tired.'

The voices and music from the café were audible from the parked car. Erich looked at his watch. 'We don't close until two and Fridays are always busy. Sorry.'

Max had a resigned smile. 'Oh, you know I can always put on a good show.'

＊　　＊　　＊

The café had changed little since 'ninety-five. Brightly coloured collage constructed by different hands swamped the walls. Styles, bodies and abstraction as a backdrop to the crowded room, it was almost impossible to see. The air was smoky and the illustrations merged with real people who sat alongside them, almost as animated. Maybe forty people, in small groups clustered round glass-topped tables, were talking, laughing, drinking. Similar scenes play out in every time zone. The slow evening hours. The quantity of shocking copper hair and painted eyebrows made it Berlin. And the gesticulations, expansive but rugged. Max could see a person speaking German long before he heard the words.

The long bar stood opposite the door – a line of shining steel and glass dotted with bottles and white cups. Dominant, in the centre of the bar, against the wall, sat the red coffee machine.

Before Max had time to take it all in, someone was tugging at his sleeve. He blinked and looked down at a sharp-faced woman with a chocolate bob. He stared at her without seeing.

Her mouth opened; she was trembling. 'Max . . . it's me . . . Ursula.'

At first he seemed unsure. She stared at him until she saw focus in his eyes and a broad smile.

'Ursula! How are you?'

'Oh, fine. How are you?' She blushed at her mistake.

He coughed and said loudly, 'Thank God for a civilized country with no licence restrictions. Can I get myself a drink?'

The German language lay within him, like a chronic illness, flaring up, under stress. Both brothers were brought up bilingual, speaking German to their father and English to their mother, in line with a carefully constructed plan by parents passionate about education and communication as weapons against the insidious evil of ignorance. Max was not sure it made any difference. It depended on the education and with whom one communicated.

She gripped his arm. 'Sure, what would you like? Are you hungry? Do you want something to eat?'

He saw Erich watching them with his hands engaged in opening a bottle of red wine. Max mimed the raising of a glass to his lips. Erich caught the action and smiled. He came over, glass in hand.

'Priority delivery for Max Brandt.'

'Where do I sign?'

There was a rhythm to their conversation, a skimming patter that had developed over years.

Erich patted him on the back. 'Don't worry. "No pain lasts for ever." So I tell myself five times a day.'

Max looked interested. 'Good. Where d'you get that from?'

Erich poured a glass for himself and allowed his finger to mop up the drip that ran down the side. 'My yoga teacher.'

'And how does he know?'

'*She* used to teach physics.'

Max looked perplexed. 'Does that mean she proved it scientifically or she's just lived through hell?'

'Both, I think.'

'Wonderful. I love triumph over tragedy. Gives us all a reason for living.' Erich's eyes widened in such alarm that Max added: 'Metaphorically speaking, of course.'

With violent auburn hair that licked her cheeks like severed feathers the face of a second woman stormed up, searing across his vision. Her voice was scorched, deep and arresting. 'Max! Wonderful to see you!' The new hair, the round gold spectacles, bloodstained lips almost disguised her, until she laughed a horsy snort, revealing disproportionately big teeth.

He smiled almost convincingly. 'Katrina, darling.'

'Max.' She kissed him extravagantly and held him till he gasped for air. She stood back, holding onto his hands. The tips of her steeply manicured nails dug into his palms. She scrutinized him. 'Max. So many years and still my gorgeous boy. Why haven't you got any older, you naughty thing?'

'And is it possible, Katrina, that you have got younger?'

She giggled and shifted sideways with her hands on her hips, delaying only slightly to pinch the buttock of her former husband, who stood impotently next to them. She turned back to Max. 'Thinner?' She smoothed her hands over her stomach and hung her mouth open, waiting.

Max nodded. 'A positive rake.'

She beamed. 'Dirk says my renovations worked from top down. Got the hair done first,' she stifled a burp with the back of her hand, 'chopped off that awful hippie mop, then moved on to the body. I left the socialists and joined a gym. My membership to the real world.' She smirked. 'For my forty-third birthday Dirk built me a gym. Erich was outraged, weren't you, Erich?'

Erich was counting the heads in the room.

Max smiled. 'Was annoying my brother part of the plan?'

'Call it a happy by-product.' Katrina grinned. 'Erich takes it all a bit seriously. He needs shaking up, don't you, darling?' She poked Erich until he must either pay her attention or bleed.

He turned back. 'And you do such a fine job, Katrina.'

A couple of tables had been pushed loosely together in the far corner of the room, around which Ursula, Katrina and the taciturn Dirk, beaming good-naturedly across his cloudy wheat beer, had been sitting before the travellers' arrival, and to which they now returned. Extraordinary turnout, Max reflected; what were they doing here, the ex-wife, the ex-girlfriend, the son with the ex-girlfriend and the ex-wife's new husband? Erich left no-one behind. Amazed, Max stood watching his brother move round them.

His thoughts were interrupted. Across the room, two dark-haired men, dressed in black, eating olives and small fish with forks, spoke in unnaturally raised voices.

'Art should be protest, but Berlin is just another shrine

to capitalism, a party city. That guy, what was his name, that guy who ties up city centres with police tape, what's his name?'

Sucking oily fingers, the other man shook his head, his brow furrowed. 'I don't know.'

His friend banged his fist. 'Yeah, you know. We saw him at the young art exhibition last year.'

'I wasn't there.'

'Yes, you were. You saw that film of him tying up Tokyo and Berlin. In Tokyo he got arrested, the crowd was moved on and total normality resumed in fifteen minutes. You know what happened in Berlin?'

'I don't know. I wasn't there.'

'You *were* there. In Berlin, a taxi driver stuck in the middle turned his stereo up full volume and there was a party. I think the police joined in.'

The other man was lost. 'But surely that's a good thing?'

'If an artist has nothing to fight against, if the police applaud him, well, what's to be done? What is there left to do? The artist is obsolete, like the mountaineer who has to repeat routes without oxygen because there's nothing new left.' As he talked, his voice grew louder and louder against the buzz in the room. 'Now when Dostoevsky brooded over *Crime and Punishment*, he was imprisoned in Siberia. If he hadn't had four years' hard labour for sedition there is little doubt the book would never have been produced. I quote: "I was thinking of it while I lay on my bunk in prison, at a time of great mental suffering and self-analysis." Do you not see?'

The other sneered. 'You read that on the back of the book. I have the same edition.'

'Does that make it invalid?'

'I think it's invalid to have an opinion on *Crime and Punishment* unless you've read it.'

'That's a very old-fashioned point of view. I don't have to read the words to despair that nineteenth-century Siberia inspired *Crime and Punishment*, while post-Wall Germany inspires the number-one hit "It's cool to be an arsehole".'

Max was unaware that he was absorbed by this conversation until he was shaken from it by a man whispering in his ear, 'Ignore them.' Max turned.

The man, middle-aged with a sleek silver beard, intense grey eyes and self-consciously expensive clothing, stood too close. He smiled unctuously. 'Scrounging students; Erich gives a discount to people engaged in "genuine artistic conversation". They only talk like that when he's here. I call them the Brothers Dostoevsky – just a little joke of mine, hey.' He looked serious. 'But we don't tell Erich it's a con.'

'Why not?'

He held out his hand. 'Mex!' The German was afflicted with mid-Atlantic vowels. 'Mex, I'm so glad to meet you.'

'I'm sorry, I don't—'

The man smiled. 'It's all right. You don't know me, but I know you.'

Max narrowed his eyes.

The man clasped his hands together; his voice was breathless. 'That fabulous exhibition of yours here a few years ago. We have a poster in our living room. It's one of yours. The girl in the McDonald's queue in St Petersburg. That lust in her eyes. Fantastic. The simplest image to say so much about East and West, our problems, our desires.' He stopped. 'Visitors always comment on it.'

'Oh.' Max was reluctant. He looked back at his ill-fitting family sitting down, the spaces disappearing. 'Thanks.'

The man held a card between his fingers. 'Professor

Lucas Froniel. I run a psycho-linguistic institute near here. I'd love to talk to you about your work.'

Max stepped backwards and hit against a table. 'Oh no, that was a one-off. I was just helping out a friend. I'm just a hack; there's nothing to see.'

The man's smile was undinting. 'We *should* talk. I'd love to commission some pictures for our offices. You have such a penetrating eye.' The man's own eyes widened and gleamed.

Max was now desperate to sit down. His delay had left him with the last seat, between Ursula and Katrina. He slunk in and stared at the laid table: ashtrays, wine bottles, baskets of bread and bowls of olives; the ubiquitous bottle set of olive oil and balsamic vinegar that Max only noticed when it was missing. A safe place to let his gaze fall.

Two waitresses were working the tables. A blonde German, who introduced herself as Barbara, kissed him energetically on both cheeks. When she reached past him to collect empty plates, her big breasts were enlarged further by deliberate protrusion and compensatory arching of her back. The other was a darker, quieter girl named Éva. Max only learned her name when Erich called for more wine.

Katrina put her napkin down. 'So. Max. Erich tells me you tried to kill yourself.'

'Katrina!' Erich shouted across the table.

'What?' She turned round, to acknowledge the gaze of eyes. 'Why be coy? Aren't we supposed to be open and honest these days? Didn't *Stern* magazine dare to suggest that Hannelore Kohl's suicide might not be accounted for by her troublesome light allergy but because her Helmut had been "seeing" his assistant for twenty years? Do we Berliners not believe in boldness above all?'

'Which Berliners would these be, honey?' said Erich.

'I'm looking round the table and I don't see many. Ursula's from Cologne, Dirk's Belgian, Max and I are half English and you're from Chemnitz, which is close, I suppose – if you didn't live in Poland half the week as a tax dodge.'

Katrina was airy. 'The best Berliners have always come from somewhere else.'

Max lifted his glass exuberantly, his eyes glowing. 'Well said, Katrina. Honesty in all things, that's my philosophy. And honestly my little mishap was not nearly so dramatic as you imagine. It was an accident. I'm very embarrassed about it. From now on I shall stick to alcohol and philosophy when I'm trying to get to sleep.' He smiled broadly.

Silence. With a rushed voice, Ursula broke in. 'And our very own Chad is involved in the campaign to out closeted gay politicians who are speaking against gay marriage. He doesn't have time to clean up for us any more; he's too busy taking pictures of important people in fag bars.'

'But he's American,' Erich objected. 'You can't count him as a bold Berliner. Americans tell everybody everything.'

Ursula patted Max on the arm. 'Hey, Max, maybe you could go with Chad and take some photos too. That would be a good thing to do.'

'Yeah,' said Erich, turning to him. 'Did you bring your camera?'

'No.' Max smiled. 'Too heavy.'

Ursula laughed. 'But you came by car!'

Max looked pained. 'It's just clutter. I want a lighter life. From now on I want to rent possessions by the day.'

Ursula's light laughter stopped abruptly when she saw he was serious.

'But where is Chad?' said Katrina. 'I haven't seen him.'

'He's been visiting some old relatives in Florida. There are at least six great-aunts and they all seem to be sick.'

'My aunt died.' Dirk spoke so rarely that his words commanded complete attention; it was assumed he must have something really important to say. He had a deep, sad, slow voice. 'She died three years ago, but I found out only last week. Nobody told me. What's going on, huh?'

Max thought the talk would never end. He saw he might have to abandon conversation as well in his quest for lightness.

At the bar, Barbara was cleaning up since the last customers had left and the café was closed. The other girl, Éva, had slipped out earlier, unnoticed. As Ursula passed, Barbara pulled at her shirt.

Ursula jumped. 'What?' She looked round the room.

Barbara was lighting a cigarette. 'Why are you so nervous?' Ursula started stacking ashtrays. Barbara persisted. 'Are you avoiding him?'

Ursula's teeth were clenched. 'Not at all.'

'This is not what we promised, remember? This is not seizing every opportunity, is it?' She was staring at Ursula, who held her eyes firmly down.

'Christ, Barbara, he's only just arrived. I haven't seen him for six years.'

Barbara leaned towards her ear. 'And he barely recognized you, did he?'

Ursula pushed herself free. 'I'm going back. Otto is about to play. Put all the dishes away before you go, will you?'

The eight-year-old boy combined Ursula's straight dark hair and pale-blue eyes with Erich's aquiline cheekbones and thin, sad lips. He had olive skin and a slight body, but it was the sour expression on his face, that perfected the vision of intense gloom, that most impressed Max.

A table had been shunted into the corner. The small

case, mouth open, rested on a chair. Otto stood in front of the group, legs clad in grey combat trousers, with a violin drooping from his chin, extending his frown.

The adults sat opposite him, smiling encouragement. Otto shivered at this wall of open mouths and bared teeth – although his disquiet may have been exacerbated by the wine he had drunk (he had topped up the permitted spirit glass of wine, unnoticed, six times).

He growled, 'Shall I start, then?'

Ursula, easing back into the chair, nodded.

Squeaky Bach – the undersized violin was mainly to blame – but fluent. He played from memory. His eyes were closed. There was more feeling than Max would have expected and, though the piece was quite complex, every note was in the right place. But Max found the *Weltschmerz* on Otto's face more arresting. It struck him for the first time that the boy was related to him.

The sounds magnified in the quiet night. At the end, Otto tossed the violin back into its box and withdrew, scowling, to his seat.

Katrina led the applause, banging her hands together and emitting an exultant 'Ah!' She turned to Ursula. 'A talented child is such a joy. Of course these days Nina is a little beyond family performances.'

Ursula bit her tongue. 'Where is she tonight?'

'Oh! I'd be the last to know. Something big, I think. But whatever and wherever it is, one can always be sure that it will be— uh, Otto honey, what are you doing?'

The small boy looked up at Katrina with big eyes, thin white paper rolling between his fingers. 'Uncle Dirk's been teaching me to roll spliffs.'

Hearing his name, Dirk waved across the table. Katrina blew him a silent kiss, then turned back to the child with a frown.

'Now, Otto, what have I said about not calling Dirk "Uncle"?'

'Sorry.'

Erich put a hand on Max's shoulder. 'More wine?'

Max pointed at Otto, who was now singeing a knob of hash with a lighter. 'I didn't know you—'

Erich tutted. 'Oh, I don't, it's Ursula. She thinks it makes her more creative. I've tried telling her that only a loser relies on props.'

'Hey!' Ursula shouted across the table. 'So says the alcoholic. I've seen you with your double cognac before you walk into the studio.'

Erich raised his hands. 'But I am a loser! I never denied it.'

Ursula conceded the point with a gracious smile. Through the squeals of laughter that Erich's remark provoked, Otto, knocking on the table, whined: 'Mama, I'm tired. Can I go to bed?'

She looked across, bleary-eyed. 'Sure, do you have the key?'

'I'm staying upstairs. Erich says it's OK.'

'Oh, OK. Just make sure you're back in time for school.'

Max looked up. 'Would it be completely unacceptable for me to turn in too?'

'Don't be silly. You must be exhausted.' Ursula's voice sounded forced.

Erich sat up. 'I'll show you the room.'

'No, don't worry. I remember.' He had stayed before.

As Max walked away he could still hear Katrina's raucous laughter and Erich's rebuffs. Ursula had slumped, her head in her hands.

The staircase led up, in darkness, from behind the bar. Max groped for a handrail. His steps felt so heavy. At the landing there was a window grazed on the outside by

47

the leaves of a tree in the courtyard below. Though the filtered moonlight was dappled, Max could still see a small figure sitting on the windowseat. 'Otto?'

'I've got something for you.' The boy held out a small pile of paper, held together by a string tag.

Max took it and read the title page. He struggled in the darkness and his voice faltered. ' "The Memoirs of Gerte Mela"?'

'I thought you'd like it.'

'What is it?'

'It's something Erich's working on. He translates sometimes, you know.'

'No, I didn't.'

Otto shrugged. 'You need something to read. It's about Berlin. What could be better? I'm doing you a favour.'

'Why do you think I need something to read?'

'I looked through your bag.'

'You did?'

'There's nothing in it.'

'Ah.' Max looked at the boy in silence. 'You know, you're very different from what I expected.'

Otto's glassy green eyes were painfully penetrative. There was intention behind his eyes. Max felt the script between his fingers and when he looked up Otto was already gone.

Sleep felt far away. Max sat in the room, it was small and square, with something institutional about the neat but ageing decorations: the almost dirty cream walls; the thinning rug over the dark wood floor; the old single bed that gave with a twang under his weight. His prison sentence. He liked the feel of that.

He took off his clothes, opened the window and inhaled the air of Berlin. Different from London, sweeter. He lay on the bed and started to read.

48

IV

The Memoirs of Gerte Mela, 1903–84

Translated from the original German by Erich Brandt

Introduction

Gerte Mela was a minor figure of the Expressionist movement. Her relevance is historical rather than artistic –
in particular, her unique hybrid view, thanks to her
strange friendship with Nikolai Poltonov, of two artistic
communities – the Russian and the German – who though
living together in the same city had little or nothing to do
with one another.

Her timing was ominously potent. She arrived in Berlin,
aged eighteen, shortly after the First World War. It is
impossible not to equate her personal evolution during
these years with that of the city itself: at first energy and
radicalism, which, diluted with experience, grew into confusion and increasing disillusionment. Equally, the change
in her mirrored the growing torpor of art. During this period
the Expressionist dream turned sour. Political purpose
evolved into narcissism and apolitical romanticism.

It is perhaps saying too much that she herself drew a parallel between her own life and that of the city around her. But there is little doubt that she hoped that her words would one day be made public – in a way that her painting failed to do. It was not just vanity. She belonged and remained attached to the earlier school of Expressionism – if such a disparate mix of artists, architects, poets and thinkers can reasonably be grouped together. For Mela, art remained synonymous with utopianism and internationalism, with anarchism and socialism. Art had a duty to influence for the good. No matter that as the 1920s progressed Expressionism was used by non-artists of both the left and the right as proof of the degeneracy of the other.

Mela never fulfilled her painting ambitions. Her vision lacked the edge of her better-known contemporaries. Nor, much as she would have wanted it, will history ever pay homage to a Russian artist whose considerable potential was tragically frustrated through disability. Mela was very aware that Poltonov had a gift that she did not. She did not resent him for this. She more resented the fate that left Poltonov crippled. In fact, it is clear that these writings are less about her and more a lament for what Poltonov should have been.

The memoir is incomplete. She gives no explanation. Perhaps she never intended to finish it. Perhaps fragments are a fitting testament to the time and way in which she lived.

Wolfgang Elsen
December 2000, Berlin

50

The Memoirs of Gerte Mela (I)

This is not my story. So it does not matter that when I was a child I wanted to be a painter. Nor that an early dim need was clarified at twelve years old on the occasion of my confirmation. That on that day I travelled by train with my parents from our small town in the East to the cathedral. That while the other white-dressed girls were rapt, open-mouthed, hanging on the words of the bishop, I heard nothing. That instead my eyes were fixed on a window. That in that window I saw an unknown figure and that the figure was dressed in a robe of deepest violet. That the day outside was so dark it barely grazed the colours of the window, but that the darkness, the missing light, intensified the depth of the colour itself. I saw it darkened from inside, by the fumes of incense. That at that moment I knew what I wanted. That is not important. I no longer want to describe what happened to me that day because I now know I cannot. I cannot paint that colour. I cannot communicate that feeling. And since I cannot, that I saw the glass at all is also irrelevant.

The colour I have seen in my life was shown to me by my friend Nikolai Poltonov. As I learned to know him I lost interest in myself, certainly as a painter. It did not happen at once. At first, I still had desire. The desire remained long after the realization that I would never achieve my dreams. Gradually I came to understand and, later, accept my mediocrity. I had to. Understanding was all that remained to me. If I could not paint, I could, at least, see.

Gerte Mela, 1983

For the first six months of our acquaintance, Poltonov believed I was a boy. He believed this because I told him so. The deception was deliberate. I was desperate for money and too young to fear or even imagine the consequences. There, it is so easy to say now. Months of fear can now be reduced to a comical opening. But the fear was important. And it grew. What was at first just fear of discovery became fear of loss. Of losing, if unveiled, the precious chink of understanding that Poltonov had already given me. Not to mention the promise of more. It is strange now, looking back, to remember the deception. Stranger still to think that the greatest love affair of my life survived despite my femininity not because of it. I cannot speak for him.

The Volksfeld Art Academy is famous for its superb eighteenth-century façade. But the amber stone of the outside columns and the sublimely proportioned white marble staircase that leads to the grandiose doorway is a barely adequate answer to the mosaic of black-and-white tiles of the floor inside. A pattern of perfect symmetry, there is something bigger about it, something spiritual in the weaving circles that seem to follow like an eye as a visitor walks across the space.

Yet I did not like it. It made me aware of my own inadequacy. That I would never produce a work good enough to walk on. It reminded me of the barb of fate that had left me financially desperate and personally humiliated. But without which, it turned out, I should never have met Nikolai Poltonov.

When I walked into the entrance hall in October 1921 I kept my eyes on small things, as I had every day for the past month. The hushed groups of students clad in black smocks. The rude commissar posted inside a glass booth to the left of the doorway, the plain corridor, which turned to the right at the end of the hall. The shabby noticeboard on the left-hand wall in that corridor, on which students and professors could post their small barters: violin tuition; easel for sale; lodgings in return for English lessons. At this I stood, as I had done daily since my arrival for no other reason than that it was there and allowed the possibility of hope. Even though the transactions were invariably one-sided. Always to sell, never to buy.

On this day, however, I was struck by the sound of an approach. I listened because I recognized the noise, a heavy ringing on a stone floor. It was the sound of shoes falling apart, of nails coming through the heels.

I turned round. A young girl wrapped in an ageing winter coat several sizes too large walked to the board. From a leather bag she pulled out a piece of paper. She found space on the board and pinned her message to it with a tack. She performed her task with great care. She concentrated so minutely, made the message seem so important, that I felt an immediate and irresistible urge to read it.

The girl, who I afterwards knew as the daughter of Poltonov's housemaid, Anna, was wasting her time. Seconds later, as soon as my scanty reading revealed there was money on offer for honest work, the note was in my pocket, where it remained, unseen by a wider public.

The note was pompous but clear. A young man was sought to walk the dog of an incapacitated gentleman. Individuals seeking this post should be prepared to undertake the task with absolute reliability, morning and evening, seven days a week. A more important requirement than punctuality, however (and this next part was written in bold), was that the aspiring youth should possess a genuine sympathy for animals.

Securing employment at that time was more a matter

of cunning than suitability. Regular hours were not a problem. My canine fondness was well described when I say that it felt more of an obstacle than my gender failure.

But none of this held me back. A thousand less-deserving others would have snatched the paper from me. It so happened that I got there first. Any guilt I might have felt was overcome by desperation.

I had come to Berlin to take up a scholarship I had won to Volksfeld – one of the best colleges in the country. I could scarcely believe my good fortune. I was convinced that it would prove to be a terrible mistake. Mutti stroked the fears from my face. 'You are going to be a very great artist, Liebling. It is natural that you should be afraid, but you will overcome it.' It turned out, however, that, not for the last time, I was right.

'Gerte Mela?' The commissar barked like the Cerberus he was. He ran his finger down a list of names. 'No, no, you are mistaken. We have a Grete Milach but she arrived yesterday.'

I showed him the letter confirming my place. The typed words, which had once looked so definite, were now a little smudged from their time in my hands.

He scanned the lines, muttering. The words were punctuated with small pungent belches. An artist sees beauty in strange places. I saw the partly digested meal inside him as a swathe of ochre mustard.

Ochre is a painful colour. The colour of rotting straw. Ludwig Meidner wrote that painting Berlin needed only three colours – ultramarine, umber and ochre. I saw them now: the angry blue of the eyes of the commissar, his desk of dark brown wood and the smell of wurst and mustard.

'You have made a mistake,' he said coldly, holding the register so close to my face I could hardly read it. The name Grete Milach was scratched in thick black ink, the signature of the dark pretender.

He looked up at me with an absolute intransigence that, with experience, I would now read as self-doubt. But in those days I was convinced. My mouth trembled and tears swelled. I turned and ran back down those magnificent steps, a retreat that seemed to take for ever, now that I was running in shame.

No place at the academy meant no stipend, which meant that I had no money for my rent.

I returned from the academy unable to hide my tears. Frau Kellermann, my landlady and my mother's cousin, clucked at my story as if she had known it was going to happen all along. She passed me coffee, into which she poured a liberal quantity of cognac. (Her son, Georg, could get hold of anything.)

'I shouldn't worry about it,' she said, screwing up her face with stoicism. 'There are opportunities here for an attractive girl who doesn't mind hard work. Mind you,' she added, 'the conditions in Berlin are very bad at the moment.'

Dumbly, for I was afraid that opening my mouth would bring more tears, I passed her the note I had stolen from the board. She snatched it from my hands and her hawk eyes read. Then she smiled and looked up at me. 'You see, the Lord gives as well as takes away.'

Berlin then has been described as like living in a dream. The normal contained the extraordinary.

So onto a streetcar filled with winter-clad, grim-faced travellers, a man climbed with a live penguin. I blinked and wondered for a moment. An elderly lady, previously silent, would say out of the corner of her mouth, in a deep, assured voice, 'For the naked dance troupe.' The crowd nodded at this and returned, curiosity satisfied, to its stupor.

In a dream we accept the impossible. Frau Kellermann assured me, or maybe herself, 'Oh, don't fret. The old boy will never notice. You know how dingy those big places are. Likely he's half-blind anyway. Anyhow,' she kept talking to win me over, 'it's quite the thing. There are girls who do this for pleasure and there are men that want them too.' She sniffed long and hard. Her pointed nose had a noise for every need. This sniff was certain, solid.

She led me, still talking, to Georg's bedroom. Before the war he had shared it with his elder brother. Though Heinrich had been dead for more than four years, the evidence of him endured as if he was expected back at any time. His clothes continued to take an equal share of space in the wardrobe.

Frau Kellermann pulled the hangers apart without emotion. The collection maintained a strong sense of its owner: heavy wool and tweeds that smelt sourly masculine. A winter coat, jackets, a patched suit, white and cream shirts with their detached collars wrapped around the hanger necks.

She pulled out a tidy jacket of flecked dark grey. The arms bent a little at the elbows, as if Heinrich had taken it off only hours before. It was large. The dead son was evidently a broader and far superior specimen to the one who had survived solely, I believed, to torment me.

I was just eighteen; my body was still boyish. With limitless ingenuity, Frau Kellermann found bandages to bind my breasts and, from somewhere, a theatrical moustache. At least I knew that it came from her wardrobe; what I didn't know was *why*. She oiled my short hair back with some of Georg's hair wax. I hated to smell of him but it was undeniably effective. I examined myself in the mirror; I looked like a boy who was trying to be a man.

The transformation had taken just fifteen minutes. To me, it was shocking. I had never put on a disguise before. That my own self could be so quickly and completely hidden alarmed me. Frau Kellermann was entirely un-concerned. She was only anxious that the effect should be convincing. Once the outfit satisfied her, she went downstairs. I was left looking at the stiff vision in the mirror.

The address I was given was just off the Kurfürstendamm, a narrow strip of bourgeois wealth that lay next to a strip of tenement poverty. I passed both in the three-minute walk from the tram stop. The contrast was shocking, the change abrupt and unsignalled.

The door betrayed money. The knocker shone gold and the paintwork gleamed. Someone had time to look after it. I rang the bell.

Almost immediately, this was answered with the approach of scratching toenails and the sound of four feet slipping on a polished surface, accompanied by mid-pitch barks.

The door opened. A slim, pleasant-faced woman, dressed in a tunic dress protected by a white pinafore, stood behind the excited animal. The dog, a mongrel, far smaller than its noise, scrabbled through the woman's legs to me. Even through my stockings and the thick male trousers over them, I felt the rough warmth of the dog's tongue.

I spoke, my voice urgent in an effort to hide my distaste. 'I've come about the dog, about the job. I rang this morning. My name's Gerhard Mela. I have an appointment at three.'

'Yes, yes.' She smiled at my anxiety. 'Come in.'

Inside it was, as Frau Kellermann had predicted, dark and gloomy. But as I hesitated, I realized that within the darkness was a hum of purple. There was no immediate reason. The hall was wood-panelled. The wooden floor was a dark brown. The purple was coming from a room off the hall. To this, the maid led me.

57

'Wait outside,' she said as she knocked on the heavy carved door. She did not wait for an answer. The dog stayed with me and sniffed the floor around my feet. It was an ugly dog, black and brown, with loose matted fur. I looked at it and wondered how to pretend sympathy.

The sound of muted conversation from inside was followed by the return of the woman. She ushered me in. The purple light grew stronger as the door opened. I walked through, as though from day into night.

Purple curtains were closed to the sun pushing violently from behind. Purple fabric covered the furniture, but my eyes, while drawn to this vision of stifled luxury, were distracted by the man himself.

He sat in a bath chair, a wooden-wheeled relic of the last century. His face was hard to make out as my eyes were still adjusting to the purple darkness, but I could see that his body was incomplete. Where his right arm should have been the sleeve was stitched up. His legs were bandaged. I looked away, not through disgust but because I felt uncomfortable staring. He was not so sensitive. I felt his eyes tearing at me. He did not like what he saw. I held my breath.

He barked: 'Raskolnikov needs to be exercised twice a day.'

A wretched, stringy hound, Raskolnikov barely reached my knee.

Poltonov read my thoughts. 'A young lad like you will not yet appreciate the benefits of regular exercise – but I assure you, despite the obstacles, I will not allow Raskolnikov to end up a cripple.' With a crescendo, he slammed his good fist down against the chair. The exertion left him red and coughing.

I stood awkwardly.

'So you're a student of art,' he said at last.

'Yes.' I held my head high. I did not want to complicate

my deception with an accidental truth. Better that the whole story be false. It was purity of a sort. Only later did I learn that the truth and the lie, like art and life, could and must mingle hopelessly together.

He looked at me piteously. 'What a damn waste of time!' The words came out with a force that left his lips vibrating and my heart beating fearfully.

I held my composure or pretended to. 'I'm afraid I don't quite understand.'

He closed his lips and examined me, if it were possible, more closely, with even greater suspicion.

I continued speaking, I could think of nothing else to do. 'Do you mean, sir, that being a student of art is a waste of time or art itself is a waste of time and so being a student of it is a waste as well?'

He looked almost angry. I felt afraid. The helpless body seemed to give his words and his persona more power. It was more than a minute before he said anything and the colour in his cheek rose again. 'I meant, why study?' He coughed and spoke more softly. 'But the question was ambiguous. Why study . . .' he trailed off into a weary sigh. Then his handless sleeve waved in the air. 'But then again, why art? It's a fair question, but not one spoken in this city.'

His eyes rolled upwards. 'After all those years when only painting the Kaiser's military glory was allowed, the new freedom has undoubtedly gone to people's heads. You can't leave the house without falling over the latest group of layabouts parading themselves as an artistic movement. It's abominable. Yet one can scarcely blame them.' He shuddered. 'Those interminable pictures of officers with their absurd moustaches, plump uniformed legs astride horses, whose nobility was ever indicated by flaring nostrils and stamping feet . . . My God, how one longed for a little weakness and disease.' He had forgotten me and stared sadly into space. 'And now one has it.'

Raskolnikov woke him. The noise from the courtyard of men shouting, negotiating loudly, and the sound of wood falling on wood disturbed the dog and he responded with aggressive yaps. Poltonov looked distressed and clutched the arm of his bath chair in obvious pain.

I saw my chance and crouched down to the wet-lipped mutt. I put my hand on its dishevelled head and stroked the warm body.

'*Beruhigen Sie sich,*' I whispered unctuously, struggling to keep my tone huskily male, 'calm yourself.' To my surprise the dog responded. Its strained body relaxed. The eyes in the pointed face, which had been tensed up to the window, shifted their gaze and looked about the room. It padded disinterestedly across the floor to its master and curled up by his feet.

I stood up again. I cannot say why the dog responded to me. Normally I had no feeling for animals unless they were served on a plate. They say dogs have an intuitive understanding. Maybe Raskolnikov realized I had no time for his fancies. Maybe he realized I needed the money and took pity on me. Whatever it was, it worked – better than anything I could have done.

I looked up and saw Poltonov examining me with new interest. His broad, flat face turned sideways. It was the size of a small dinner plate.

'Extraordinary,' he said, breathing erratically. 'My dog is the best judge of character I know. I was entirely unconvinced by the pathetic specimen I saw before me. Your feeble frame and childish demeanour gave me every reason to believe you were an individual entirely unworthy. It appears my dog thinks otherwise. I trust him more than I trust myself. The job is yours.'

I stared and mustered thanks, which he ignored. He

was concentrating entirely on the dog. Raskolnikov lay beside his master and sharpened his toenails noisily on the wooden floor. Poltonov stared affectionately at the ugly animal.

I stood still, wondering how he could not see that the feeble male specimen before him was in fact a female one. How could he fail to notice that behind the quivering moustache lay the nervous face of a young girl? Moreover, one who hoped to be a painter not an actress.

He looked up some minutes later, surprised that I was still there. 'You can go,' he said aggressively. 'Come tomorrow morning at six.'

V

The taste of espresso is bittersweet, with an initial impression of acidity. With your first sip, the aroma is intense and explosive. Afterward you are left with a very pleasurable coffee taste that can last half an hour. The predominant flavors are caramel, flowers (including jasmine), fruit, chocolate, honey and toast – but only if you do everything exactly right. One false step and you are totally doomed.

JEFFREY STEINGARTEN, American *Vogue*, 2000

Max fell asleep eventually. He must have done, because at some later point he woke up, in pain, exhausted, angry with the sound of a vacuum cleaner downstairs and the sporadic buzz of a drill outside.

At night he could not sleep because of the silence; during the day he could not rest because of the noise. Not even in his London flat, high above the ground, with what estate agents called 'panoramic views' of the river, from the Houses of Parliament to Chelsea Bridge. Even there, where the cars below were smaller than Meccano toys, he was plagued – inside, by neighbours. A fashionable crowd who held parties during the day – scraping heels through the ceiling – and started work at one in the morning, with drum kits and several shifts of furniture. Each year, the noise increased and his tolerance dwindled.

Pictures of the transvestite, the crippled Russian and his perceptive dog filled his visual mind. He wished there was more of it, for that would be a reason to stay in bed. As it was, the room was bare of entertainment and he must get up. Though he did not want to be with other people, he could not stay on his own.

He rose and dressed in a single movement. Yesterday's clothes, which waited for him on the floor. He did not notice, as he grabbed at them, that he pulled a kink in the rug that lay, perfectly positioned, in the middle of the bare boards. Now flawed.

He walked out and stopped briefly outside Erich's bedroom to peer through the gap between the door and the wall. Cool air whistled through a partly opened window. He saw a writing desk and a free-standing wardrobe. Ironed bed linen.

He walked down the dark stairs, along a broad passageway, empty but for a bureau, and into the café. Barbara sat behind the till. She leaned forward, stout legs open, facing the room, at a proprietorial angle. The other girl, Éva, would not have grasped his hand. Her hand would not be clammy, like this one, with a grip so strong it almost hurt. He had some kind of homing instinct for women who left him alone. But it did no good, for the cool ones made it too easy for him to be dragged into the lives of women who never let up.

The smell of coffee, the warmth of escaping steam, the floor that trembled from traffic on the street – since returning to consciousness, every sensation was stronger. As he sat down, his fingers grated against the wooden table. The detergent clean floor stung his nose. The smell of eggs on a plate across the room turned his stomach and the noises hammered against his brain. He felt a rush of dislike for spring and its open windows. Even the café door this morning was propped wide against the wall and the street sounds romped in. He sat, stunned by the buzz of scooters, the moaning of cars. The heels and laughter of pedestrians. The drivers revving, the ravers pumping music through wide-open sunroofs, the beepers and the drillers, the un-oiled squeaks, the farts of engines choking, vying to be heard.

Then a sound rang like somebody dropping a ton of chainmail from ten metres onto a hollow glass floor. He jumped. 'What the hell's that? And why doesn't it drive you crazy?'

Barbara was surrounded by an unflappable solidity. She shrugged. 'Building works? Oh you get used to it. And this is nothing. I used to live in the East. There was so much going on there, I learned to lip-read the TV. Lucky they all talk the same, huh?' There was a cloth in her hand and a smile on her face; she was out of breath. 'So. Do you want a coffee?'

'Yeah, that'd be great.'

'Cappuccino?'

'No.' He shrank back. 'Far too much effort.'

She started. 'But it doesn't take a minute.'

He smiled. 'I meant for me. Wading through all that foam.'

'Oh.' She looked confused. 'OK.'

In a wooden rack by the stairs leading to the WCs were a range of newspapers: *Le Figaro, La Gazzetta Dello Sport, Berlin Tip, Zitty, Kunst, Der Künstler* and a range of impenetrable artistic journals with matt murky covers. He sat down and began reading a long feature about the American college professor forced to resign over his falsified Vietnam War record. He flicked to the photo montage overleaf. The man was one of many. Twenty years ago no American had fought in Vietnam; now they all had. Real fighting experience – albeit fabricated – lent gravitas, which sold more memoirs. Not so much lying as a publicity tool.

Barbara brought coffee, her tread solid. The cup thudded onto the table and coffee slopped over the rim. She was mopping rigorously before he could fight her off. Now she smiled down at him, her hands on her hips. She wore a tight top. Its too-short arms exposed thick, inelegant wrists. From this angle her breasts loomed even larger. He veered backwards.

She stopped again at his side, planting one buttock on the edge of the table. The round tray carrying a sugar dispenser and coffee-stained cups rested familiarly on her hip. 'Oh, by the way, Erich said sorry, he's out seeing some guy's portfolio.'

Anxiety lit Max's face. 'He keeps himself busy.'

'Sure does.'

She hovered. But Max was good at conversation. Like the quiz-show host who makes every greasy-haired contestant think he wants to take them home. When in reality he hates them for what they represent: his own limitations.

'Tell me, who is Zlatko?'

Barbara looked at him. 'Huh?'

'On the way over here, Erich said his daughter Nina was more famous than Zlatko. Who is Zlatko?'

Barbara laughed briefly. 'Oh God. *Big Brother*: it's a show, you know—?'

'Yes, yes.'

'Yeah, OK. Well, Zlatko was a Macedonian immigrant – or maybe Montenegrin or Moldavian, I don't know: one of those places. He made it really big because he hadn't heard of Shakespeare. He had a number one and now I think he presents Shakespeare on TV.' She leaned intimately across the table and said with pleasure, 'Erich loathes him.'

'And what do you think?'

She smiled, charmed. She said quietly, 'I'd rather see Zlatko on TV than Nina.'

'Nina? Why, what's wrong with her?'

She broke their collusion by her shock of his ignorance. 'I thought you were reading the paper! Take a look.' She leaned across him and he smelt her scent – a melon tang he recognized but could not name. She snatched a tabloid from the table and riffled aggressively through its pages. 'Look! Just look!' She pointed to a picture of a slender naked woman being led away from a building site. '"Naked Nina to reveal new project on live TV".'

Max peered at the image. 'That's her?'

Barbara nodded. 'Can you imagine how it makes Erich feel with his daughter whoring on the streets of Berlin for fame and fortune?'

Max was both uncomfortable and riveted by this florescent woman's body; his niece, who six years ago had been a fully covered-up child. He stared at Barbara. 'Whoring? I thought she was an artist.'

'Artist, whoring, what's the difference in her case?'

A man in a sheepskin jacket walked in, shaking a carton of strawberry milk.

'Or, indeed, in anybody's,' Max added.

Barbara did not appear to take this in. She smacked the paper with contempt. 'That picture's not even new; they always print it with any story about her.'

'Mm. I suppose they would.'

She snatched it from his hands and ripped the paper in half. 'It's disgusting. She doesn't give a damn about how Erich feels. She just goes right ahead and takes what she wants. And Erich doesn't even complain. He just laughs it off, but you know how hurt he must be inside. After years of hard work, his whore daughter steals in and hits the headlines in two years. Can you imagine how it makes him feel?'

Max could not. He did not want success and he had never wanted a daughter. He could smell Barbara's hands. Her nails were ingrained black. He asked because she wanted him to. 'Do *you* paint?'

'Well, you know . . .' She broke into a smile and lit a confidential cigarette. 'Yeah, Erich is so supportive. He lets me hang my stuff in here. I'm good, I'm damn good, but of course people who come in here are artists themselves, or students. They have no money either.'

'You must show me some of your stuff.'

She flicked back dismissive cynicism. 'Don't. Erich told me you're not interested in art.'

He murmured. 'Oh no, art's OK. Though most of it's bullshit. No, it's artists I can't bear.'

If he did not like art it was because it made sense, drew conclusions where none existed. Even in the sophisticated ambiguity of modern work it still presumed to know the questions. It isolated one aspect of life and dismissed the rest. Just as people judged others from so little information then wedged it to fit. It blistered.

In a restaurant, new people took his hand. 'Maria's told me *so* much about you.'

Maria loathed his overreaction. 'What's the problem? What are you so afraid of?' Indignant, the nostrils of her thin nose flared. 'What am I going to tell them? What did you do? If you murdered someone, I don't know about it.'

His faint smile infuriated her as efficiently as her nostrils riled him. 'I didn't murder anyone.'

'Why would I say anything bad about you? We're

supposed to be on the same side. I'm going to want my friends to like you, aren't I?'

'What friends? I met them this evening and now I've known them nearly as long as you have.'

She threw her hands into the air. 'You're so paranoid, Max. You act so cool, but really you're the most paranoid person I know.'

Pain on his face. She spoke like a teenager. Now she was gone, he realized how she had infected him.

'I'm not paranoid. I just don't like being talked about.'

'Isn't that the same thing?' Her eyebrow was raised, quivering. She thought she had him, had caught him in her cleverness. In a way she had; to engage, to crush her illogic, easy though it would be, meant he took it seriously.

'Not remotely.' He yawned. 'I'm going out.'

Maria could not live like that.

Max looked back at Barbara, who had her head on one side, a little shocked, to see if he was joking. He had said he hated artists. She was an artist.

Barbara said sharply, 'If you don't like artists, you've come to the wrong city.'

This much was true. Berlin is like Hollywood, but life without money is almost possible. Every waitress is waiting for her first exhibition. Every waiter is a DJ and into concept TV. Cheap, plentiful white walls give a noble background in the city's raw wounds. Maybe there is room to breathe. Twelve years on, the strange deserts are only slowly disappearing. Scaffolding and rubble feels dynamic compared with the concrete establishments in Munich or Cologne. There are fifteen thousand artists. Soon there will be more painters than people, and more cameras than real lives.

When Max returned from the toilet Erich was back and

fiddling with the coffee machine. The mirror behind the bar magnified its chrome and steel. Max stared at him.

Barbara put a finger to her lips and spoke in a whisper. 'He has to check it after he's been away. He doesn't trust us.'

'But wha—'

'Sshh!' she hissed. 'He doesn't realize he does it in front of other people.'

Max watched as his brother stroked the steel wand tenderly and examined the filter, its holder and the spouts, feeling around the sprays and gaskets for any clinging grain. The machine was always warm, even at night, when it hummed the gentlest vibration, discernible only to a sensitive palm spread against its flank, when it was visible only by the single orange light that gleamed through the darkness. It was his best worker.

'How curious,' was all Max could say.

Barbara twisted her lips. 'Frankly, that machine seems to offer a more satisfying relationship than that sick old woman he hangs out with.' She stacked dirty cutlery with unnecessary force.

Erich swivelled round. 'Max!'

'Erich! Uh, great . . . coffee machine.'

Erich breathed again. 'Thanks. Only had it six months.' He glanced round the room. 'The grinder has tapered blades.'

'Oh yes?'

'Mm-hmm. Much more control over the smoothness of the grind. And, of course, the blades last longer.' He checked himself. His chin fell. 'Uh, did you sleep well?'

'Fantastic. Must be the German air.'

'Well, you've come home, brother.'

'Mm-hmm.'

Through his irony emerged Erich's truth. Berlin had

69

always been home. When the family left in 'sixty-one, Erich was five years old and Berlin was already inside him – or so he came to believe. He moved back at the earliest opportunity, in the late Seventies. Catching a wave of blond punk hedonism. West Berlin was so easy then.

'Uh, where's Ursula today?'

Erich's eyes narrowed. He said suspiciously, 'I don't know. Why?'

Max shrank back into his seat.

'Hey, Chad's back! Hey, Chad!' Barbara was calling across the room to a figure staggering through the doorway with a plastic crate filled with unwrapped salad and vegetables. Tall, skinny and lightly tanned, he was something under thirty, with a Dallas baseball cap pulled down over dark, doe eyes, and his tight jeans gripping a substantial lump between his legs. She bounced over to him. As he drew closer Max could see a hair's-breadth beard split the man's chin.

'Hey! Pumpkin! My, Babsi, you're looking *pert* today. Is this new?' The man pinched between his fingers the material covering her breasts.

Barbara looked down, blushing with the half-hearted pleasure of a reluctantly single woman who only receives male attention when it's gay. 'Yes. Mama sent it to me.'

'Your mother is a treasure. Tell her to get one for me. But in khaki . . . The military brings out the green in my eyes.'

Chad put his hand into a carrier bag on top of the vegetables, pulled out a plastic bottle, strode up to Erich – who, since the man's arrival, had sat at the bar apparently intent – and poked him in the back, waving the bottle vigorously. 'Erich, I told you not to get this bullshit stuff!' The German sounded strange with the strong American accent.

70

Erich was ready. 'And I told you, that bullshit stuff happens to be biodegradable and phosphate-free. The label too, since that's the thing that matters to you.'

Chad rolled his eyes. 'Yeah, right, and tap water's just as good as Evian, I know, *I know*. I'm a capitalist shit, you told me before. But you know what? *I* can tell the difference. Maybe you're just not as discerning as I am.' As he spoke, he held Erich's face in his hands, clasping his cheeks at the corners of the mouth, so that he could not respond if he wanted to. With a sigh, he released him, running his finger along Erich's jaw. Then he whistled. 'I *never* knew a straight guy get so smooth.' He looked around at the others. 'Isn't he a treasure?'

Barbara's round face dimpled.

Erich's smile was reptilian. 'How was your trip?'

Chad smiled. 'Oh God. Nothing but bags. Uncle Walt has a colostomy bag, fitted after his operation last fall. Aunt Betty has excess bile. Randy has prostate cancer. Darianne has something, I don't even know what. I think they gave her a bag since she got too fat to walk and can't make the bathroom any more. Everybody had a bag, apart from me. I felt left out.'

Erich shook his head: 'Uh, Chad, my brother Max. Max, this is Chad. He cleans for us when he's not pursuing his political agenda or his social life.'

Chad swept round, threw out his hand, lowered his voice. 'Oh, *hey*. I didn't know you were visiting. Are you on vacation?'

'Well,' drawled Max, 'I guess, kinda.'

Erich perked up. 'You know, you should think of this as a holiday. You should look around. It's very exciting. The city changes by the day.'

Barbara smacked him on the shoulder. 'Oh, don't be so sentimental. The place is miserable. Financial ruin. The worst unemployment in Germany. The streets are full of

71

shit. Cafés close, taxes go up, the pollution is terrible. The place is a sewer.'

'I could go see the Panoptikum,' said Max with a glimmer of enthusiasm. 'The hall of grotesquerie, where was it, Ku'damm? I enjoyed that last time. Nothing like someone else's syphilitic genitals to put things in perspective.'

Barbara smirked. 'You can't. It closed down.' She turned to Chad and, in a little-girl voice, said, 'Come and talk to me, over here.' As she dragged him by the elbow into the corner, his feet took exaggerated little steps.

Max sighed and said to no-one, 'Well, I'll go and buy some clothes, then. I can't wear these for the rest of my life. I'm too hot already.' Limpid, he pulled his body from its slump and dragged himself away, without turning back.

Erich watched him go, marvelling at the sudden departure and yet the slowness of the actual movement. And the fact that he still recognized this walk. Max had always limped. As a child he did it, Erich thought, to elicit sympathy. Maybe that was how it started but it suited him. He was always reluctant.

'Does he have one leg shorter than the other?' Chad had a disarming practical streak with which he skimmed over other people's suffering with his happy paintbrush.

Erich shook his head. 'It was at its most pronounced on those Saturday evenings when we got taken to classical-music concerts by our parents. He was bored to tears. Only came, he said, for ice cream in the interval. One time, in the foyer was a display of the work of local artists. Max and I were arguing over which was the very worst – in terms of content as well as execution – and we came up with this vile sailing boat, the mast bigger than the river, the two people on board like turds in a bowl.

Max was talking loudly, gesticulating wildly, in praise of its soaring mediocrity.'

Chad and Barbara listened with pained anticipation.

'Of course, the artist was behind us. A fat pepper-bearded guy, in navy smock and beret. Only an amateur would wear that . . .'

'So what happened?'

'Max thrust a pointing finger at the appalled man's face and said in a really loud voice, "I've come from the hospital. I have very little control over my body. But that doesn't make your painting any less execrable." Then he turned and walked off with such a limp, his knee was almost scraping the floor.'

'How old was he?'

'Oh, about eight, I suppose.'

'Didn't someone just smack him?' No-one doubted that Barbara had been brought up tough.

Erich smiled. 'I was much more compliant. If someone told me this painting was worthwhile I would believe them. I liked the order of things. But there was always a part of me that admired Max, for ruining everything. It was thrilling. It was terrifying.'

VI

A city is itself a medium; it strengthens the impulses one has within oneself, yet it also shows one's weaknesses.

THORSTEN SCHILLING
Co-founder of the media and cultural
collective mikro e.V mikro *Children of Berlin*

What else was there to do in a city but look at it?

The café stood opposite a cemetery, with the gallery a few doors down. Max passed a stonemason's, the window full of stone-carved fictions; a dusty food co-operative with handwritten posters on the door; a kindergarten where twenty cross-legged, open-mouthed children stared at the words 'quality not quantity' written on a board. Another art gallery lay twenty metres from Erich's. Inside was a display of bent and rusty coat hangers. Closed.

When Erich moved here, until reunification came Kreuzberg was the desirable slum against the West side of the Wall. A hole in the middle of the city, home of punks, squatters, immigrants, anarchists, drug dealers, pop stars and other social outcasts. Erich could hang out with the Maoists, Trotskyists, vegans and Stalinists in Café X, where they planned the new world order and overlooked their differences for the financial expediency of sharing the copy of *Spektrum* magazine. Kreuzberg had the biggest social problems, the highest percentage of young people and the best places to hang out at two in the morning. Since reunification, real anarchists moved to cheaper, rougher Friedrichshain and snuggled up with the neo-Nazis. Those that stayed could not hide the grey in their shaven heads. They ate at the Tex-Mex chain that used to be a local bar.

At that time, Erich said that the tension in Berlin complemented the questions within him. Sprawling south London choked him. One of the first things Max ever knew was that he was different.

Badges against the Vietnam War emblazoned Erich's canvas haversack. He joined Artists for Socialism; he marched for CND. Cold air swept through the front door as he stomped in and out in his Doc Martens. Max shivered from his cosy spot next to the TV. The only mass meeting Max ever attended was a Jethro Tull concert. And that put him off for life.

Max walked past a shop of old clocks and second-hand books in floor-to-ceiling piles. He was searching for a cashpoint machine. This was a purpose.

He passed high-rise flats, crummy despite their pastel paint, and turned into Friedrichstrasse and Checkpoint Charlie – or, at least, what *had been*, for this, now, was only a model, an attraction. An imitative sign read 'You are leaving the American sector' in Russian, French, English and German. A huge poster of a border guard in green uniform, blond, with chiselled Benetton cheek-bones, hung above the street.

Tourists swarmed round the Café Adler, but Max was picturing the building as it was when the Wall still stood. A boarded-up chemist's with Gothic façade, decaying windows and broken blinds. Even this memory no longer seemed real. More like a film, an interactive tourist experience. Like everything. That people were shot climbing over a wall seemed, on reflection, too perfectly mythic. The escapees, including so many East German border guards, were just Hollywood. Brad Pitt in the lead, playing the blond bastard, Robin Williams in the role of the improbably hairy anti-Establishment hero.

From a rack outside the Checkpoint Charlie museum, a fat man pulled out a T-shirt imprinted with the image of Brezhnev and Honecker locked mouth to mouth. He looked to his woman for approval.

She shook her head and let out an American drawl like pipe smoke from the side of her mouth. 'That's gross. I like the Pope smoking hashish. Get that one.'

He looked at her incredulously. '*Dope*. The Pope smokes *dope*. It's a poem. Can't you see that? You can get those *anywhere*. I've seen them loads of places. This Commie one's something special.'

Her face was squashed up with disgust, as though she was about to sneeze. 'You gonna wear that in Iowa? Are you crazy? There's two guys kissing there!'

'OK, OK, how about I get the tank? Huh? The tank?' His voice was getting louder. He walked to the next rack and pulled out the T-shirt picturing a Russian and American tank nose to nose.

She looked unimpressed. 'I don't think that's very funny.'

He was not amused either. 'What, you reckon these two tanks are frenching too, huh? Shay, huh? Jesus.'

Like a braking lorry: 'Whaddya wanna go round wearing a tank on your fat belly for? You're crazy. I bought you that South Park one and you never wear it.'

Max moved away, gathering speed and distress, scouring the street, the lines of grey buildings. Was Berlin so foreign or was he?

In the past, he had travelled, unmindful, all over the world, turning up at two in the morning in tin-shack airports where men closed in on him, pressing the only words of English they needed, 'You wan' money? Taxi? Fucky?' and he dealt with it, no problem. In totally alien environments, he felt at home, he thrived. But here, now, in Berlin, he was lost, surrounded by weirdos.

Then, at last, he spotted a cashpoint blinking across the street. Oasis. He crawled gratefully, falling against it, almost embracing the machine. As the card was swallowed and he waited, drumming elegant fingers, he scanned the metal frame. One particular piece of graffiti caught his eye. Scratched in black were the words: '*Du bist ein Sklave.*' 'You are a slave.'

This arrant truth stabbed him like a knife. He felt its pain in his chest. His hands started shaking. The money took a lifetime. He aged while he waited, his heart pounding. Then he staggered back across the street, ran a few steps and collapsed into a bar. It was small, dark, smoky and tourist-free.

As he walked in, the laughter stopped. The dense air was stale and prohibitive. The barmaid cocked her head at him. 'What do you want?' She spoke in a thick Berlin accent.

'A beer.'

Her voice was sarcastic. 'Oh yeah, what kind of beer?'

He tried to peer at the bar, but she shifted her head in his way as he moved and eyed him with suspicion.

'Pils?' he whispered.

She tossed her head contemptuously at his safety game. 'Siddown. I'll bring it over.'

A group of construction workers in dusty uniforms sat a few tables away. Eyes followed him to his seat. Their voices were loud and harsh with smoke. Bring back the Wall if it meant the end of bastard tourists gawking and bastard Russians taking your work. At least Communists didn't ponce cigarettes.

Max no longer wanted the beer. It stood beside him, untouched, while the barmaid watched him from behind her bleached frizzy fringe. That fringe was older than reunification.

Maria moaned, 'You're just not interested in people.' It wasn't true. He was interested but not in the way she wanted. He liked to watch but at a distance. Maria demanded attention. She wanted him to sit by her while she bathed. She wanted him to come to bed when she did, even if he would then lie awake for hours while she slept. She wanted him there. That, to her, was love. He should choose to eat his meals facing her. If he wanted to eat in front of the TV, with his bare feet up on the stool, the television was more interesting than she was.

It had hurt his parents when he sat, silent, at home. He would bat off interrogation. His mother would smile at his humour but her eyes were sad. Yet they did not reveal themselves. He could see that his mother hated his father's lewd comments on Erich's girlfriends, their young bodies. He saw her wincing at the table but she'd die before admit it. And if Max pushed her, she would clam up, turn it around, snap at *him*. He did not want to upset her and, even more strongly, he did not want to upset himself.

He opened his eyes to find the barmaid with the ersatz fringe shaking him. How could he have fallen asleep, upright on a hard wooden bench? The woman ushered him out. He put up no resistance. He was thinking about the dream he had had. Erich had asked his advice about Russian coffee. It was a nightmare.

VII

At first sight he may appear a trifle rough, even vulgar. But you must remember that he spent more than half a century in Berlin, where there lives a species of the human race so bold that little can be gained by treating them with nicety; on the contrary, you have to bare your teeth and resolve to be brutal yourself if you don't want to go under.

GOETHE, 1827, Eckermann's conversations

It was in the evenings that Erich was most aware of how his life had changed. The routine closing up of the gallery – switching off the lights, locking the door – felt valedictory. He walked back up the street and into the café alone. Inside, the room was filling up with people talking, and all of them, he assumed, unconsciously, were happy.

As he entered, Barbara was coming out, wearing a black silk shirt, a black skirt revealing too much thigh and long black boots parading unexpectedly dainty ankles. When she blinked after greeting him, her eyelids flashed a silver that caught the setting sun.

'Is Éva on already?'

She understood. 'Erich, I've been working here three years. I don't just walk out of the door when six o'clock comes and leave the customers to raid the till.'

'Sorry.'

She had spoken with a hair slide in her mouth. Now she grabbed her blonde hair and jammed it into the slide and clipped it shut. It had a plastic lilac orchid attached. 'Which they would of course.'

Erich did not want to dwell on this unpleasant truth. He smiled at her, he hoped benignly, but this failed, for it made her stop and look up at him with concern.

'Are you all right?'

He changed the subject loudly. 'Where are you going?'

'Chad's friend is serving cocktails in this new leather club.'

In the vicissitudes of her romantic life, Barbara found a useful friend in Chad. Except for the occasional fraught fortnight when a man would enter her life, and, for that short, delirious period, seem to answer every need (down to an appreciation of Caspar David Friedrich and Dépêche Mode costume parties). Then, ashen-faced, Barbara would come into the café in the morning, wearing the dark glasses that signified the end. Invariably these men turned out to have unspeakable sexual urges. The reality could not match imagination, but she could never tell, only shudder. Her silence frustrated Chad. If she had such a nose for rooting out the rotten apples, she should at least let others take advantage. Chad, whose boyfriend air-stewarded on long-distance routes and was thus often out of the country, had a flexible approach to monogamy. He and Barbara complemented one another. On any particular evening, one would pull and the other would beard. Depending on the club.

'Do you wanna come too?'

Erich laughed. 'Don't be silly.'

She gripped his arm. 'People of sixty go clubbing these days.'

'Only skinny desperate ones with long white ponytails and baseball caps on back to front or women with no hair at all, wearing Goan smocks.'

Barbara smiled and shrugged. He watched her diminish into the vanishing point, stuck his nose into the café, saluted Éva, turned and sauntered to his car.

This journey took just minutes. Winding through the streets, the old and the new, the falling down and the part built; perpetual change.

His life was full of different locations filled with women and children. Ursula in her small place with Otto. Katrina in the mansion he had never seen. Nina in a chi-chi new Berlin flat – no, she called it a 'space'. The empty rooms above the café where Erich lived alone, and then there was Marlene in her flat in the East. He lived a fractured life. Once he had bought three spatulas in a week.

Across from Marlene's flat lay one of many serendipitous parking spaces opened up in the city when a building came down. It would be swallowed up again soon. So he tried to enjoy it, the wheels rolling slowly over the bricks, the exhaust pipe breathing poison on weeds as the car pitched over the uneven ground. He stumbled across the dereliction, past a motionless goose-neck scraper poised menacingly, awaiting the morning's excavation, and climbed three flights of dark stairs.

Marlene. Talking to Max, Erich called her his 'woman in Mitte' and Erich liked this anonymity. And she was like the city. Impossible to tell fact from fiction. She was a dancer, she'd been crippled by polio; she had children, she had no children. Her husband abandoned her, she was never married, she lived with a woman. She worked for the underground movement, she'd had an affair with a Stasi officer who'd given her the diamond she wore round her neck.

For sure, he only knew the details they had shared. That they had met at an Expressionist film festival, in the days when she would go out in the safety of darkness, before her fear of the city trapped her in her attic.

She was nowhere to be seen when he opened the door. The room was different. Narrowed. The walls seemed to be falling in. As he looked through the gloom he made out two large mirrors propped against opposite walls. A third was attached on a diagonal to the ceiling and adjacent wall. The mirrors' reflections pulled the room in. The effect was so powerful he could not stop his hands shooting over his head to protect him from the collapse.

He peered through the room. 'Marlene?'

The thin blonde, with a face loose but unlined, yet with the experience in her eyes that said she was at least fifty, emerged in the darkness, from behind a black leather sedan. She wore a fitted man's suit with a buttoned-up white shirt underneath. Her haircut was boyish and, with the prominent cheekbones, gave her face an elfin vitality.

With a sharp nod in acknowledgement of her lover's arrival, she walked towards him. The floorboards creaked.

'Darling, you're late. Too bad you weren't here when I was lifting the mirrors. But then, my mother warned me there was no man who would be there when you actually wanted him, only' – she said, returning to the sofa – 'when you didn't.'

She stretched out, one leg thrust on the arm of the sofa, her elbows resting on it, as she lit her cigarette and stuck it in an ebony holder. 'And she should know. Since my father left her eight months pregnant and with the bailiffs knocking at the door.'

Erich coughed. 'I'm sorry, but I've got a lot of work at the moment. There's this exhibition next week—'

'Darling, we're all busy.' She grinned and pointed at the mirrors. 'I've been working on this all week. Don't you love it?'

Marlene never left her flat. She did not have a job. She had no dependants and she did not perform good works. She was not busy. Erich squinted to give an opinion.

Her voice was breathless, young with excitement. 'The set from *Dr Caligari*.'

He nodded.

She was smiling, ready with the words that had worked themselves to a frenzy in her head. 'I'm recreating the same effect in my own life. The perfect combination of mirrors to give the apartment a claustrophobic intensity – expressing my soul and absorbing the stench of the streets. Ironic, don't you think, that the optical illusion shows truth?' She giggled. 'In these dark mirrors the couch is a dying woman; the TV set, a cringing child; my shoes scamper as rats. It is the truth at last, can you imagine, achieved through artifice?'

He put his hand over his eyes. 'I can barely even see you.'

She shrugged. 'The electrics are shot. Only two sockets are working.'

'You need an electrician.'

She grimaced. 'I'm not letting a strange man up here. They all want the same thing.'

This mendacity he let go. 'This place will go up in flames.' He peered towards her obscure form.

Her smile was bright. 'If the end comes, it comes. We live for today, my darling . . . *Sekt*, shall we?' He nodded. She walked, very upright, to a small kitchen at the back of the flat, and brought back two glasses of the sparkling wine. She smiled winsomely. 'Anyway, I saved the good socket for the film.'

Erich looked at the ceiling, slapping his thigh. 'Ha!

That's a relief. At least we'll be entertained while we burn to death.'

She was pulling apparatus across the room. It ground against the floor. The projector, like its owner, was old and cranky, like an old, metal-keyed typewriter, lovable for its obsolescence. Erich had room in his heart for any piece of equipment that had been superseded.

She turned to him, her hand stroking a stack of films that towered to the ceiling. 'So, what shall we feast on tonight?'

He was unhesitating. '*Nosferatu*.'

Her face crumpled into tragic lines. 'My darling, are things as bad as that? I'm sorry, I didn't realize.'

He rubbed his head wearily. 'We can talk about it afterwards. Just hit the button.'

Marlene pulled the film from the pile without looking. She knew *Nosferatu*, the first vampire film, as well as her own face – even the feel of the box and its position on the shelf, stacked among dozens of other dusty spools.

They watched in silence, drawing validation from mutual obsession. There was nothing to discuss. Sound was unnecessary, both in the making of the film and in its appreciation. It was black-and-white.

By a ticking clock, through a dark archway, a lunatic is held in a cell. A woman, miles away, senses the worst; she clutches her head in agony. Though the madman snarls and screams at the dripping walls of his prison, the people cannot see that it is the truth that sends him crazy. The truth is too dazzling, too horrible, to face. His speech is written white on black riddled with exclamation marks. The doctor waves wildly as if he strains to be heard. In his delusion he diagnoses an unknown disease. And people are mouthing, more desperately since no sound comes out, '*The plague is here! Stay in your house! The plague is here! Stay in your house!*'

Marlene shivered and looked out of her own window. She would never leave.

After ninety minutes of darkness, Nosferatu is vanquished by the willing sacrifice of a pure woman. But the woman uses her weakness to trap him; a paradox. The candle blows out, the curtains flap in the breeze. The madman laughs and the curse is passed. The vampire burns up in a thin column of smoke. The dawn light is blinding. The spooling tape wails until it switches to stop.

When Marlene looked at him, Erich's face was frozen. She took the cigarette holder and lit up, blowing the smoke provocatively back in his face. She sat on the chair and, crossing her ankles over his lap, raised a sceptical eyebrow. 'So what's up?'

He did not look at her. 'I told you my brother is here.'

'You mentioned it.'

His voice was slow. 'It's very difficult.'

'The adultery?' She was matter-of-fact.

He sighed. 'Ursula? Yeah, but no. No, it's him. Thinking how close he came to destroying himself, it frightens me. I feel I want to know him better but I'm afraid of what I'll find. We have never had what I'd call a proper brotherly relationship.'

'Who does?' She laughed. 'You're so damn sentimental, Erich. Do you think my brother cared about our relationship when he forced me at thirteen years old to strip in front of his friends while they paid him? No.' She shielded her eyes with her hands. 'My brother would swindle my last pfennig from me – and you know what? Now I thank him. He taught me the value of my naked body. But think, Erich. Do you imagine your brother was concerned about your feelings when he tried to kill himself?'

Erich had no idea what went through Max's head. Max would like him, along with everyone else, to believe that nothing much did. That his mind was MTV, constant images across the screen, random pictures, noise and words. But Erich did not believe that. Max liked to hide.

Marlene was impatient with his silence. 'You don't know how lucky you are. Your parents are dead. Your brother leaves you alone. You should hold on to that. Families are trouble. They expose you. Anyone can seem like an original, until they go back home.'

He spoke before he knew what he wanted to say. 'I don't know. His whole life, Max never cared about anything. He made so much money despite himself, doing a job that he slept through – not' – Erich looked coy – 'that the money bothers me.'

Marlene smiled, drawing her cheeks in. She stroked the back of his hand with a long, slightly ridged nail. 'Darling, you wear your poverty with pride. No-one would doubt your sincerity: you're too scruffy.'

Erich looked surprised and eyed his own hands warily. They were still well shaped, with tapered fingers and slim palms, but the veins protruded. He let them fall. 'Max is a very attractive person *because* he doesn't care about anything. He's easy on the eye. He's junk food.'

'Well, he must have cared about something, or he wouldn't have tried to top himself.'

'Yes. That one's been bothering me.'

She spelled her thoughts out on her fingers. 'It's perfect. The brother who has everything kills himself. The other brother is left to make sense of it all. You hate him because you wanted what he had and he just threw it away.'

'I don't hate him.'

She echoed the words from *Nosferatu*. '*You can't escape destiny by running away. Men do not always recognize the dangers that beasts can sense.*'

'That's very helpful.'

There was other help she would offer. 'So . . . how is my Friedrich Wilhelm?' Her voice was melodic, haunting. Marlene. Spirit of Berlin. As she breathed heavily, her cheekbones stood out still further, her lips grew red and full.

From above, her grey roots were startling against the fake blonde hair that now nestled in his groin. It was a strange agreement between them. She admired the phallus. She wanted one. She liked to control it, to have it answer her command.

But not today. Several minutes later, she looked up, her cheeks red with exertion. 'Darling, nothing's happening.'

'Sorry.' Erich avoided her gaze. 'I'm distracted.'

She took his hand and wiped her mouth. She said, almost tenderly, 'Don't worry.'

'I'm not going to. I can't deal with my physical collapse as well. One thing at a time.'

She walked across the room and pulled back the curtain slightly to look out to the street. 'There's that dancing sheep again. I can see her outside the Hackesche Höfe. That costume must get very hot. Do you think she makes a living out of it?' The noise of people and cars and pleasure rose from the street. Her face, with the streetlight shining, was transparent, her smile ghostly. She walked back to him and took his hand. 'You smell of turpentine. Have you been painting?'

He tussled away from her shadow: 'No.'

She looked sulky. 'You should show me, if you want me to understand. Doesn't an artist want his work to be seen?'

'It's a bit late now.'

'Oh, Erich, don't be bleak. I can't abide it. You're the very last optimist in the whole of Berlin.'

This might be true. Erich had arrived in Berlin with a

naïve zest that enthusiasm was enough. It had pushed him on for twenty years. But the little world he had created was still the same little world. Relationships still ended. The city was still in a mess. His brother still tried to kill himself.

She waved her hand in front of his eyes. 'This'll perk you up. I'll show you the new Kurt Weill number I've been practising.'

His eyes refocused. 'Marlene, he's dead.'

'New to me, fool.'

'How can you sing, in this vacuum?'

She murmured, entranced, 'I adore this vacuum. It's the only place I feel safe now we don't know who anybody is.'

'When did we ever know who anybody was?'

'At least then we'd identified the enemy.'

'Oh, that's right: the people with "Stasi informer" tattooed on their foreheads.'

To his sarcasm she unfurled a taloned hand, as if to humour him, and smiled.

'So you practise songs by dead people,' he said, 'since you know who they are?'

'Darling, after a life like mine, I'm dead myself.'

'Christ, Marlene.' But her melodrama appealed to him; it was somewhere to hide.

Erich looked across the street to the parking space, his car the only vehicle in it. He shrugged off her touch and said something again about the lateness of the hour. He wanted to leave but he did not want to go home. Their fantasies felt different. Max's presence made Erich look around him. And he did not like what he saw.

VIII

Everyone believed it was permanent. Weeks before the Wall fell, in a poll, sixty-four per cent of Berliners thought it would be there for ever. Once it was gone, many people felt displaced.

HANNA MEHNER, historian

At three in the morning Erich became conscious of being awake and running through what he would have felt if Max *had* died. Years passed without a meeting and he did not miss him day to day. Was the fear he felt just the horror of pain that made him want to reach out to every desperate face on the TV news? Erich was a sucker for every hard-luck story, even from the neurotic art students who moped in his café with their sunken eyes and histrionics . . . Well, no, perhaps not them – but everybody else.

Why *had* Max wanted to kill himself? Why did it make Erich feel vulnerable? Surely the one death he need never fear was suicide.

And then he heard a loud bang.

That's it. He's dead. Panic froze his breath. He's dead. I know it. I can sense it. This is the intuition that science can't explain. I can feel it all through my body.

He grabbed trousers and a sweatshirt and crept out. If

Max was already dead, quiet was unnecessary, he knew that, but cold terror silenced Erich.

Dim lamplight came from Max's room. With his index finger, Erich prodded at the partly open door and tentatively entered.

Max's body was slumped on the chair facing the open window. Erich walked across the room and stood behind it. No movement. Erich placed two fingers to the side of Max's neck to confirm that the blood had ceased to pulse.

At the pressure, Max screamed, his body convulsed into life. He spun round with his hands shielding his eyes, alert with terror. 'Jesus! Erich! What the hell are you doing? You scared me to death!'

Erich's skin was ghoulish green. 'I'm sorry, I thought you *were* dead. I was testing for rigor mortis.'

Max put his hands through his hair. An uneasy smile flickered across his face. 'And do I have it?'

Erich's voice wobbled. 'You seem all right.' He looked sheepish. 'I'm sorry. I heard a noise. A loud bang.' He pointed forlornly to Max's laptop, which lay upside down, its leads straining over the edge of the desk, in a desperate and failed rescue attempt. 'I guess it must have been that.'

'Oh, yes.'

'Sorry I woke you up. I was worried.'

'No, that's OK. I never sleep long in an upright position.' He picked up the fallen laptop and placed it back on the desk and peered at the clock. 'Well, not bad. A solid twenty minutes.'

Erich smiled ruefully. 'Will you sleep again?'

'I don't want to start getting greedy.'

'D'you want to come for a walk, instead?'

Max looked at him, over imaginary pince-nez. 'A *walk*?'

'Mm. Some fresh air.'

'Couldn't we just open a window?'

'It's the best time to see the city.'

'Erich, it's four-thirty.'

'No crowds.'

'That's because the shops aren't open.'

'Come on.' Erich tugged at his brother's sleeve. Max looked down as if unable to identify the source of disturbance.

'But why, for God's sake?'

'It'd be good to have a chance to talk.'

'Christ.'

'Max.'

The word was chastising and imploring. It startled Max, who actually searched into Erich's eyes. Erich looked tentatively back.

'Go on, then.' Walks at four-thirty invariably ended in sex or revelatory conversations. And the easier of the two in Max's mind, the former, was unlikely.

They took coats although the night was almost warm enough without. The streets were empty. Their shoes squelched in slowly evaporating puddles from earlier rain.

'Don't tell me, Erich, I bet you take your children to see historic towns on Sundays when all the shops are closed, so they can't spend any money, don't you? Just like Mum and Dad did to torture us.'

'I'm not sure they did it on purpose.'

'Of course they did.'

'Anyway, there has to be some pleasure in child-rearing.'

Max laughed. 'I always wondered what your motives were.'

*   *   *

When Max was nine years old he tied a plastic bag round his head. It was an experiment, he said. He wanted to see how long it took for him to stop breathing. His parents were listening to Erich play Schubert on the piano in the sitting room. His last flourish was interrupted by a loud bang from upstairs. Erich, aged sixteen, decided that if Max didn't die he would always upstage him.

Mary's maternal ear knew the difference between the crash of falling hi-fi and that of falling child. She ran upstairs, where she found Max passed out on the floor.

A child's mistake. He was, at that time, interested in science (later, puberty developed his true passion for nothing). He had a microscope with which he examined dismembered beetles and familial pubic hairs and the cigarette butts of his parents' friends, salvaged from the dustbin.

Erich thought Max had laid his grubby hands on the small but potent pornography collection lurking in the padlocked suitcase on top of the wardrobe and found the article, much thumbed, but never practised, on the erotic possibilities of near death. He had no illusions about Max's innocence. A sibling knows more about the darker side of the other than parents can hope to. No matter how hostile, the controlled have a nexus against the controllers. Erich changed the locker combination.

*   *   *

They walked along the streets of Kreuzberg, fuzzy with pre-dawn. The wind blew thin clouds across the stars. Good to be walking here, with Max by his side. Erich felt comfort, moving in tandem, with the familiar body.

*   *   *

92

On Max's last visit, in 'ninety-five, when Erich threw a brick through the window, he was so ashamed the following morning that he behaved unbearably.

They were two in a crowd, scurrying across the concrete, dwarfed by the giant sculpture, the dazzling shroud, the Wrapped Reichstag. The folds of the material blew smooth and brilliant, transforming the old fussy façade of the then obsolete government building. The translucent fabric that covered it, electrified with aluminium powder, shimmered in the wind.

As they walked, Erich lectured, hectored, non-stop. Flexing his knowledge. Covert criticism of Max's affluent life lay more in the way he said it than in what he said. Tinged judgement.

It was a testament to ordinary people. The Reichstag would shine for two weeks. This finite limit was ideal, so non-commercial. The work could never be sold. It could never hang sterile in a film star's living room. When the silver cloth came down it would lie, deflated, a burst balloon. It would exist only in the memories of the millions of citizens who had come and marvelled at the glitter.

The altered edifice spoke of a city emerging from the ashes of the past, a daring new metropolis, embracing art, modernity and humour in one gaudy swipe. Challenging institution, the traditions and history of both East and West. Christo, the artist, who escaped to the West from Bulgaria in 1956, was a figure of hope. His temporary sculpture was a perfect symbol for the new city.

Max, bristling, knowing precisely the ulterior motive behind this information, pointed to a few metres ahead, where, stood on a small round podium, a couple had bound themselves together in silver foil. A baseball cap was thrown on the ground in front for change. Max said, deadpan: 'Now, I think *that's* a great symbol for the new Berlin: rising unemployment sparking the enterprise culture.'

He was angry at the time, but later, when Max had left, Erich felt loss. And he cursed himself for competing, for playing the old games. Max rose to the challenge but he never initiated. That was the work of the jealous older brother. Even now.

*　　*　　*

They headed along the main streets. The place was largely deserted. Occasionally an old square car would pass and the men inside would wind down their windows and shout as if Erich and Max were a pair of young girls in skirts blown up in the breeze of a passing vehicle.

'Are you sure this is safe?' said Max, walking close behind Erich's shoulder.

'This is Berlin.' Erich smiled. 'Of course it's safe.'

'You're like Woody Allen, saying New York is populated solely by people in turtle-neck jumpers discussing Marshall McLuhan and Ingmar Bergman, with the odd all-knowing hooker thrown in. But that ain't how it is.' His voice trembled.

Erich led them down to the concrete banks of the canal near Hallesches Tor, where the overhanging trees threw strange shadows. The swaying branches startled Max. More than once he twisted to see who threatened them and heard the flick of a blade.

'Isn't this where the heroin dealers hang out?'

'No. Why? Did you want some?'

'Erich.'

Erich stopped and turned to Max, who was still pulling an invisible leash. 'Max, why are you walking so fast?'

'Was I? I hadn't noticed.' He slowed down.

Erich smiled and began to dawdle, putting his hands in his pockets, buoyed by Max's fear. 'What a balmy evening! Doesn't the river look dark in the moonlight?'

'Yes,' said Max, trembling.

'You're not really worried, are you—'

His words were interrupted by a male voice, singing. '*Don Gio-vanni.*'

They both turned to the direction of the sound.

A medium-height, overweight man in his sixties was walking towards them. Neither the scarf draped artistically round his neck nor the large moustache hanging over his upper lip impeded the sound, sonorous and melancholy in the darkness. '*Don Gio-vanni.*'

Max clasped his hands together. 'Perfect!'

Erich eyed his brother with suspicion.

The singer had seen them. In front of them he stopped but continued to sing, the notes full and rounded in the night. Minutes passed before he brought his hands down and acknowledged them. The lining was hanging from his coat, his trousers were frayed and on one shoe a detached sole opened wide enough to display the soggy sock inside.

His elevated speaking voice belied the façade. 'I sang once with the Philharmonic. My voice flew.' He closed his eyes to remember, craned his neck until he faced the black sky and inhaled deeply. 'My mother would say, "It matters not how big your audience, Karl, as long as you are sharing your voice with the world".'

'Ah,' smiled Max, 'how true.'

Erich poked him in the base of the spine, muttering, 'Don't, Max.'

'But what the hell did she know?' In a dextrous tonal shift, the old man rasped, 'The woman was a fish-gutter.' He started to turn away.

'Stop!' Max pulled at the man's arm. 'Don't go.'

Erich dreaded what Max might do next. He closed his eyes, only to see the face of the amateur artist, victim of Max's cruel wit all those years ago.

Max was pulling out his wallet. The old man was transfixed. Max's voice was eager, insistent. 'Here, take this debit card. Take the pin number. There's a few thousand in the account, I think. Take it.'

The man stared at the card, suspicious but clearly interested. 'Why?'

Max shrugged, still holding out his arm with the card between his fingers. 'I don't want it.'

The old man took the card with a feeble grip and looked confused.

'Max!' Erich hissed.

His brother turned to him. 'What? I don't want the money.'

'But you can't just give it to anybody. It's irresponsible.'

'What do you mean "anybody"? I'm sponsoring the arts, aren't I?'

'Max. Believe me, I could spend your money on so many good projects.'

'I don't want to give it to something sensible. I want to give it to this old guy, let him book himself a decent venue.'

Erich shook his head, exasperated. The man trembled. He was torn. He did not want to take the card, but he could not throw it back.

'Go on,' urged Max. 'At least go and get really pissed.'

The man's hand fell to his side. The card flipped to the ground. With dignity, his chest puffed out as he turned to look Max full in the face, he said, 'Young man, I don't drink.' He walked slowly away.

Erich stood behind Max, as he felt he always had done. His brother's bigger frame obscured his view of the wounded man, retreating. Erich was fascinated and appalled.

Max exuded energy. A negative, maverick, alluring energy. Even from behind, his unkempt silky hair and his slightly hunched, remote bearing questioned the world. Over the years, while Erich wasn't looking, Max had deteriorated. His negativity had darkened; what was once funny had become tragic, like the ageing drunk. And Erich watched, helpless, as his brother self-destructed, only now realizing how much it mattered to him.

IX

Here is your world. There in the corner the red dumb-bells, which I painted myself; next to them the big, heavy stone, which I dragged up from the bank of the Sound. Both are a symbol for the absurdity of life, but at the same time also offer advice as to how you can struggle against or chase away this meaninglessness, through weightlifting, knee bends, and stretching. Perhaps tomorrow, I'll paint the dumb-bell and the heavy stone with butterflies – symbols of the brevity of life and of the graceful fluttering over calyces.

GEORGE GROSZ, German-American Cartoonist
Ein kleines Ja und ein grosses Nein, 1955

'Did Chad get anywhere at the club?' Ursula sat at the bar with Barbara the following morning, checking the till receipts. Barbara looked underslept. After some minutes shouting, she was slumped against the bar, like a cow carcass, thought Ursula, who had enjoyed a full, dull, eight-hour sleep.

Barbara moaned under her horizontal arm. 'Chad always gets *somewhere*.'

'OK, did he get to a place he wanted to be?'

'He took a guy with boot-polish hair and atrocious pockmarks home. I don't think they'll be meeting again. Not when he sees his face in daylight.'

Ursula sighed, running her fingers through her hair. 'I do think the whole game's easier if you're gay. Everything's so much more out in the open. Just show up at a club and everyone knows you're up for it.'

Barbara was not in the mood to let things go. 'It's easy to get laid if you're gay, but just as hard to find someone you want to spend the rest of your life with.'

'I'm not that ambitious.'

Barbara sank still further into the top of the bar. Does it ever occur to her, Ursula mused, that she is in fact my employee?

'I'm going for a fag.'

'Hey, Barbara, did you read that story in the paper today about the Berlin woman who died after painting herself an ideal man?'

Barbara's lazy eyelids lifted marginally. 'What?'

Ursula picked up the paper from the rack. 'She painted him, with oils, inside her *own* body. She stuck a brush down her throat and chucked the paint down after it. She wanted an unsullied man and the only way was to have him inside.'

'What?' Barbara looked scornful.

'She left a note. She explained that it was a struggle, because she was painting in the dark and, as you know, flesh tones are inspired by light. So she painted violet and ultramarine. She gave him rounded shoulders to fit inside her own slender frame. Of course she gave him enormous parts. It took her days and at the end she licked the colour off the palette and ate it to destroy the evidence, even the brush, bristle by bristle.'

'Suicide.'

'Of course, suicide. But what a crazy story, huh? True love is final. Either love dies or the lover does. But she died knowing her perfect lover died with her.

They found her, smiling with oil colour muddying her mouth.'

'I don't think that's funny. You and I are not far off that level of desperation.'

Ursula was stung. 'You speak for yourself. I'm not even looking for a new relationship right now.'

'Oh, don't. What about what you said the other night?'

Ursula rolled her eyes. 'Haven't you learned, Barbara, not to take any notice of what people say when they're drunk?'

'That's when the truth comes out.'

Ursula shook her head and pushed her hair back behind her ears.

It was expedient, their mutual solace, but if Barbara ever got into a relationship that lasted more than a month she'd drop the café. If Ursula formed a relationship, Barbara would drop *her*. She only wanted single friends. Women with partners made Barbara feel inadequate, though she didn't read it that way. She decided they had no time for her and turned cold before they had a chance to let her down. Barbara was no kindred spirit. So how did it happen that they were so much together? Ursula remembered when she used to be selective about whom she spent time with. Now, with less time, with Otto and all the work, she saw whoever was prepared to listen.

Barbara's lugubrious voice interrupted her thoughts. 'Anyway, what about Max?'

Ursula flushed. 'It wouldn't exactly be appropriate right now.'

A snort emanated from behind Barbara's elbow. 'Well, it's more appropriate than the last time you went with him.' Barbara enjoyed the torment, safe, she believed, that Max was no more interested in Ursula than he was in her.

Collating the papers with angry jerky movements, Ursula muttered, 'I never should have told you.'

Barbara hauled herself up. No, thought Ursula, not a cow carcass, a hippo. The girl spoke through a yawn. 'Did that dating agency guy phone?'

'Yes, he did, damn you.'

Barbara laughed, excited by this intrigue wrought by her own hand.

'It was really embarrassing. He was asking all kinds of personal questions. What kind of men I liked. I think it's sinister.'

'No, they always ask that kind of stuff.'

'Barbara, he asked me if . . .' Ursula raised her eyebrows and pulled at her mouth in an attempt to communicate the humiliation nonverbally. Barbara looked blank. Ursula closed her eyes with quiet dread.

Barbara's eyes lit up. 'What?'

'He asked me if I liked to be *spanked*.'

Barbara was quiet for a second then scoffed. 'You read too much into things.'

'What couldn't I read into that?'

Barbara shrugged. Ursula swung her legs off the stool and took the papers and filed them in the bureau. She came back breezy. Barbara shuddered.

'OK, I'm off to the gallery. See you later.'

'See you.'

'And, Barbara, try and look like you work here, OK?'

Barbara nodded. 'Yeah, yeah. I'm at the double.'

*   *   *

In the gallery, Max stood in front of an oil. He did not often look at hemmed-in pictures. He would rather stare into space, or at a random snatch of people or buildings.

Something that had not been selected to interest him. He hated to be lied to.

But this was his brother's gallery and he was convinced that Erich chose not to please the visitor, but to please himself. Coming into this room was like staring at his brother deep in the eyes, without the risk of Erich noticing or, worse, staring back. It was quiet.

On a blue background, a brown pointed egg in a white cup with a large white handle attached to the blue with a semi-transparent plaster. He turned his face sideways; what seemed to be stuck-on layers was in reality completely smooth.

He did not hear her approach behind him, just, suddenly, a low voice in his ear.

'Do you like it?'

Max jumped.

Ursula laughed with an open mouth. Dark fillings studded even teeth. 'I'm sorry,' she said. 'I didn't mean to disturb you.' Though she laughed, he sensed anxiety.

'Is it original?'

'Original what?'

He smiled tightly. 'Now you've got me. I don't know – these Russian names are so hard to remember. Twenties, probably.'

'No,' she spoke airily, 'it's original Erich. Do you honestly suppose he could afford the real thing?'

'What is it a copy of?'

She sighed. 'Olga Rozanova. One of a series called "Universal War" that she made during the First World War. That one is called "The Destruction of the Gardens".'

Yesterday, on an ugly stretch of half-chewed grass, broken glass and beer cans in Mitte, Max had read 'Leave our Park alone' scrawled in red paint across a hoarding announcing the erection of another office complex. The tin fence spiked haphazardly round one corner was a rash of flyers; breast cancer competed with Irish folk dancing, Mick Jagger, Sumo wrestlers, Australian acrobats, support Burma, and the Tattoo and body artists' convention.

' "The Destruction of the Gardens",' he echoed. 'Hmm, an evocative title. I named it "Egg in Long Cup".'

She smiled. 'Erich told me that when you two were boys your parents took you to galleries. You tried to guess the names of the paintings from the other side of the room.'

'So we did.' His dark eyes skirted round the picture.

'Only, as the two of you got older, he got better at guessing and you got better at taking the piss.'

'We all have to work with our God-given talents.'

Ursula went to the back and returned with a heavy blue book, reading aloud. 'Olga Rozanova. Belonged to the "Supremus" group, "Proletar cult" and Soviet artists, and made plans to reorganize the Museum of Industrial Art in Moscow. All before the age of thirty-two – that's when she died.'

Max blinked. 'What a joiner. Did she die of exhaustion?'

'Diphtheria.' This came out like a spit pip. From here Ursula could smell him. Slightly sweet. Her eyes enlarged and softened. 'That reminds me. I wanted to recruit you to the Kreuzberg Art Preservation Society. You can buy a life membership if you like.'

He looked suspicious. 'And what does that do?'

'Oh, you know, it's trying to keep a hold of the unique artistic spirit that built up in this area in the Wall years. Supporting artists, raising money, fighting the town planners who want to make it more commercial. Five hundred marks and you get to sit on the board at the AGM. Erich is the founder member.'

Out of the corner of his eye Max could see she had a quizzical eyebrow raised. He did not want to look at her but she was looking at him and he was drawn in.

'No shit.' He sighed. 'But then, Erich always was a tin-rattler.'

'Oh, don't be unkind. Erich's a trooper.'

'I'm not decrying him. It's the greatest scam to believe in something. It can keep you going for years.'

'You don't like anything, do you?'

He was frowning at the picture. 'I don't like belonging. Belonging means rules.'

'I didn't realize you were one of the May-the-first brigade.'

He shook his head. 'I'm no anarchist, I just don't like the instinct to bind people to conditions. Whether it's a harmless little club, like this one, or wider society, where the unwritten rules are even more demanding. And most of them are only there to satisfy a few sour old virgins with nothing better to do than write to the paper every time they hear a child swear. It's too much. If we didn't make rules, people would not be bound to fail.'

She bridled at his unconscious belittling of Erich and, anyway, it was a long way from the aspirations of the Kreuzberg Art Preservation Society, but she was carried away by the picture he painted. As the vision grew wilder, her eyes lit up to see him, as so rarely, engaged.

'I mean, which of us hasn't had an alcohol problem or speeding tickets or a homosexual past or a financial scam? I'm telling you, they'll never find another presidential candidate who didn't inhale, or had other—'

'Extra-marital flings,' she whispered in his ear.

He didn't flinch. 'Exactly. Who's got time to care about that? It's soap-opera material. We should take a lesson from France. You can't *be* in public life there unless you've got a mistress. The health-insurance guys insist upon it, as the only way to relieve stress.'

Her heart was racing and her breath short. She stared at those dark eyes glowing.

He shrugged. 'I never joined anything. Not even the boy scouts. I left art college after a term.'

'I thought you were thrown out?'

Max smiled. 'We agreed my attendance was a waste of all our time. Actually, it didn't make any practical difference, since I hadn't been in after the first week. Still, I sometimes derive false pride from the disgrace. It's one for the CV. Makes me feel more like James Bond – he was slung out of Eton.'

Outside, a man covered in dust pushed a wheelbarrow that jolted over a manhole. Max watched. The wheelbarrow was filled with bags of cement which read: '*Beton, es kommt und es bleibt.*' Concrete, it comes and it stays.

Max turned and continued to walk round the gallery, away from Ursula. She followed, with hurried steps. When he had felt her palpable warmth against him, was he imagining it or, under her shirt, were her nipples erect? She had a packet of West cigarettes and, in flagrant disregard for Erich's art on the walls, lit up.

She loved this. Max was so different from Erich. Erich had listened to her. Erich was patient. He was reasonable. It could never have worked. Erich could never satisfy her need to be neglected by a man who couldn't care less. Oh yes, she'd read all those self-help books, she'd diagnosed her problem: she was insecure, self-hating and didn't believe she deserved to be happy. She knew all that, she was just powerless to change.

So, as she poured some wine, she heard herself say with contrived innocence: 'Max, do you want to go out tomorrow night? There is this great jazz bar that I know in the East. It's supposed to be the East's answer to the A Trane.'

'What's the A Trane?'

He was thrown by this non-sequitur, but still he saw through her. The clever, sexy bastard.

'Uh, well, it's the West's answer to that place in the East . . . So do you want to go?'

He gave her a sideways look. 'I think I'll pass. After all, I have a busy day ahead of me tomorrow.'

She smiled, tried not to whine. 'Come on. It'll do you good. It'll do *me* good.'

Max turned to other pictures, hung at odd intervals round the room. The section of abstract shapes was followed by a line of reproductions of Expressionist posters, black furrows on white paper – anxious faces, leaning city towers, marching workers with hands raised in unity. Unmistakable, now he looked closely: the same sentimental hand.

'Why is Erich hanging his own stuff in here?'

'He's between exhibitions. Which I promise is not the same as between jobs. There's a big thing opening next week.' She lowered her voice. '*The* big thing of the year.'

'Ah.' Max was imagining hanging his professional output on a wall. He couldn't. It was the last thing. Like framing your own shit.

'So' – she rubbed her hands together, *fait accompli* – 'I'll meet you here tomorrow at eight.'

'Uh, Ursula, look . . .'

They were interrupted by the sound of running feet. Otto appeared with a mobile phone, his hand out-stretched. 'Some man for you, Ursula.'

The interruption deflated her but she took the phone and held it tentatively to her ear. 'Hello?'

She said it twice before he answered.

'Is that Ursula?' asked a light male voice.

106

Suspicious, she hesitated. 'Who's that?'

'I want you to reconsider joining my dating agency. I think you want to join.'

'No!' she shouted unnecessarily. 'No!' She threw the phone on the floor and looked round, embarrassed, to where she expected Max and Otto to be.

'Otto?' she shouted. The door was ajar. She looked up and down the street, but they had vanished.

X

The history of the underground mirrors the history of the city. Depending on where one digs up the earth or descends into the depths, one runs into witnesses of the past.

DIETMAR & INGMAR ARNOLD
Dunkle Welten – Bunker, Tunnel und Gewölbe unter Berlin

When Ursula's back was turned, Otto nudged Max. He hissed: 'Run! This is your escape!'

Max smiled, put his hands in his pockets. But then the boy really was running, through the back and out. Max fell at the door. He barked in a whisper, 'Do you expect me to follow you at that pace?'

'Come on!'

The boy was fast, scuttling in short but swift steps along the pavement edge. Max's feet spread across the concrete; his bones crunched dangerously. He tried to walk fast. He groaned. He felt like a right-wing politician dressed as one of the kids. Aching muscles betrayed him. At last, Max panting, bending into a stitch, they stopped at the *U-Bahn* station.

Otto drew a bon-bon from his pocket. He undid the see-through wrapper with a crackle. Nausea trickled through Max as icy mint vapour was released into the air.

Otto looked at Max through the wrinkled cellophane. Max saw the green eye and looked away.

Next to him, almost human, stood an old-fashioned weighing machine. It had metal feet, a slender trunk and, on top, a huge, benign round face with antique numbers. Max thought of the girl and the old Russian painter. He wanted to read more and wondered what Otto would want for it, for he was beginning to sense the way the boy's mind worked.

On the wall across the tracks a concave advertising poster featured a girl extolling the life of a temp. She had been there, Max guessed, from her blue eyelids and pink frosted lips, for twenty years. The city's different pasts, wrapped uncomfortably together, unravelled in layers.

They climbed onto the first train. It smelt of oil and burnt sugar. Warm air wafted across his face as Max, gasping, stood by the door, holding onto a vertical pole.

'Sit down,' said Otto, laughing at him.

'I'll get lock-knee.'

There followed a brief silence, during which Max could not decide if he felt awkward. Children did not need verbal continuity. Interrupting with a conversation already half-played out in their heads, and stopping just as abruptly. This disarmed Max, who was happy enough to disrupt adult patterns.

He pointed at a black-and-white sign tacked onto the side of the tram. 'Look at that. A thousand marks to spray the whole car, but if I can contain my anarchic message in one word, it's a snip at two fifty. I never saw graffiti charged by the word before. How organized – except they don't say how much it is in Euros.'

The Wall had injected graffiti with an iconic nobility; elevated it from the tomcat's territorial spray to a symbol of freedom. The West was a mass of colour, protest and liberalism. Antithesis, the East, a silent grey. But after the

Wall came down, the agenda was not so clear. Thierry Noir's line drawings, his strange bald heads, the idealistic raised fists and the peace slogans were replaced by exhortations by anonymous hands to 'Fuck the English'. The authorities built a graffiti park where *al fresco* scribblers could feed their scrawling habits legitimately; it was methadone in rehab, not the real thing.

From his black, tatty holdall Otto pulled a can of Coca-Cola, pushed it at Max, then burrowed for himself. He opened his can with a seasoned thumb flick and settled back in his seat. Max, recovered now, eased down beside him.

Otto said: 'Oh, don't worry, there's a team of people to handle the Euro conversion.'

Maria's sister's girl was ten years old and still struggled when Max asked her if Prague was a place or an animal.

'How old are you? Eight, right?'

Otto did not blink. He looked down his baby button nose untouched by adolescent hormones that would later thrust it forward with accusing masculinity. 'Well, technically, I *am* eight, but my parents like to think of me as twelve.'

'Huh?'

Otto picked at the pull on the can. 'They like to say I arrived the night the Wall came down.'

Perplexity blanked Max's face.

Otto smiled. 'It's a metaphor. Me, the child, symbol of new life.'

Max stared at him, uncomprehending, the sound of the clanking train in his ears.

'Oh, come on, Uncle Max. You know, artistic parents. Can't fart without Dad appropriating it for the putridity of existence.'

'What are you talking about?'

'Oh, come on, Uncle Max. You can see how it fits.' He

110

smiled. 'You know, you born in Berlin the night the Wall went up, you the symbol of a people divided – and me the great white hope, the night it came down. It's perfect . . . What's the matter . . . ? Uncle Max? You've gone all pale.'

Max had jerked in his seat. His hands clasped his temples. His voice was thin. 'I wasn't born the night the Wall went up. Our parents moved back to London earlier in the summer. I was born there in the October.'

'Really?' Otto laughed loudly, in unfettered childish mirth. 'Oh well. Erich's version is much more entertaining.'

Max did not want to ask. They jolted along together in silence. They changed trains. Max did not know where Otto was taking him, but it was not the most direct route.

Next to him a Turkish woman in Western jeans and orthodox headscarf stared at a baby asleep in a push-chair, while a toddler pulled miserably at his mother's coat. Max stared. The child felt the attention and turned slowly towards him. His eyes were so clear, the whites fresh and irises like melted chocolate. Max wondered how the boy saw his surroundings, whether he already knew a stream of colours, sounds, climate changes and passport-control officials. If home was travel.

'So what did Erich tell you, then?'

Otto was ready. The showman had the jokes, the crowd pleasers, polished. This story had been told again and again. Indelible tracks.

'My grandfather Heinrich and his English wife, Mary, expected a second child late in August 1961. Erich was packed off to boys' camp near Wannsee, deep in the West edge of Berlin. On the vast and tranquil waters of the inland sea he learned to tell a tack from a gybe, and on the wooded land, to hold a skewer to cook *Bratwurst* rather than his fingers.'

'Detailed, huh?' Max crossed his legs in disdain. This hid his fear.

Otto nodded ruefully and leaned towards his uncle. 'Papa only bought a TV when Nina started appearing on it. Before that, we had to make our own entertainment – it was quite desperate.'

Max smiled. 'Carry on.'

Otto was eager to do so. 'Mary Brandt hoisted her swollen ankles up onto the sofa and sank into heavily patched cushions. The modest three-bedroom rented apartment fell just within the Russian sector of the city; the hospital where she was to deliver her baby was in the American sector. She had not thought about this, for soldiers and border signs stood on every corner, as common as bakeries.

'On Saturday the twelfth of August, she woke up and realized the baby was coming early. Gasping, clutching her belly, she staggered to the door. Heinrich followed her, picking up the ready packed bag, pushing her in a straight line, closing the door of their old VW after her as she blew her cheeks into balloons, and they rattled off to the hospital.

'The labour was arduous but quicker than her first. You were born early in the evening. As Mary lay weak in the bed, Heinrich gazed at the sleeping ball in the cot, sandwiched between the day's other arrivals. Then he walked to the window. After the sweat of the day, the night was peaceful.

'Afterwards Heinrich could only imagine he had not listened. How else did he miss the noise of truck convoys rolling to the boundary? It amazed him that the sound of unrolling barbed wire and concrete posts plunged into the earth with jackhammers did not register. He smiled at the sleeping infant and both were deaf to the pneumatic drills that tore through the cobble paving, insensible to the drowning jeers from West Berlin.'

The train juddered now across Gleisdreieck, like a rollercoaster through a bombsite. On either side, stacks of wood, concrete blocks, cement and digging and hauling vehicles littered the dusty brown ground that spread into the horizon. What preconception told Max that this mud-flat was not the centre of a capital city?

'While Mary whimpered in fitful sleep, the temporary fence was erected, separating the couple from their home and the West of the city from the East. In the morning, the Brandts discovered that they could go home but, if they did, they could not leave again.

'As Mary began to focus, for the first time Heinrich saw the barrier, which was already being reinforced with wet mortar and concrete slabs. Such was his pre-occupation, his immersion in the personal, it seemed to him for a moment that the wall must be some kind of external reaction to his experience. It was impossible that, during the night, something else, unconnected, could have happened. Mary woke up to the baby's stomach juices but slept through the sound of tanks.

'Erich returned from camp to meet a red-faced, new-born brother and a wall. And their consequence: the family was moving to England.

'Mary had grown up in London. She had been teaching there when she first came to Berlin on a cultural exchange in the mid-Fifties and met Heinrich, a book illustrator. The parents told Erich that in London there were relatives and opportunities. Life would be better.

'Over the weeks of that autumn they saw the fence grow, on TV, into the first generation Wall, ninety-seven miles long and thirteen feet high, and thanked their baby son on his timely delivery. But Erich was silent and had no gratitude.

113

'For instead of growing up in the grey Communist bloc, Erich grew up in the pink-roofed London suburbs. Max deprived him of Berlin and their parents loved him for it. Sometimes Erich still hears, in his head, the documentary film he wrote as a reclusive teenager, the narration of his fantasy life. The camera pans the ugliest stretch of Sonnenallee, the vast concrete spread. A voice says: "He found in those grey blocks and those chill winds the essence of his inspiration. His was the art of resistance."'

Otto turned with a flourish back to Max, engaging his gaze once again.

Max shrugged. 'Uh-huh.'

'Well, that's how Erich tells it.'

Max coughed quietly, unnecessarily, behind his hand. 'That version of my life is more entertaining, I'll admit. But it's a lie. Erich stole my identity. How many people here know this crock of shit?'

The boy smiled and stroked with a careless insouciance the metal pole that bordered his seat. 'Oh, everybody. Erich's incorporated it into his work on more than one occasion.'

'Unbelievable.'

Otto smiled. 'You should be glad Erich's stuff is so unpopular.'

Max wasn't listening. He was looking at the Turkish boy, who with outstretched hand was studying patterns made in the air with his own fingers.

'It's all completely random out there. We're born by chance and we die by chance. Why can't Erich face that?'

They changed trains again and seemed to be doubling back. It was as if the boy wanted to confuse him and by trying to find purpose in it Max would fall into a trap. So he followed dumbly. Nothing better to do.

A crowd joined at Wittenbergplatz, where in the 1920s the Russians gathered to drink tea and read poetry, and the portal to KaDeWe, 'the Western department store', which boasted one of the world's biggest sausage collections, a lavish panorama of pink and brown edible phalluses that shone through the cold war as a beacon of defiant opulence, a paean to capitalism. And right outside the station, where the ageing Goths groaned was a black square effigy to the Holocaust victims. It bore a simple list: Treblinka, Auschwitz, Stutthof, Maidanek. On a lamppost a metre away a defiant sticker proclaimed: 'I love Palestine.' Max looked at the people who climbed onto the train. Passive, faraway faces, passing through.

In the corner of the carriage a woman in grey uniform was noting on a detailed grid map the numbers joining and leaving the car at each stop. If Max moved seats he would mess up her system. It was not designed to cope with passengers who changed their minds. Tempting. This paperwork trusted that, faced with absolute freedom, human beings took the nearest seat and stayed in it.

Max turned to Otto and said more brightly, 'I met a woman on the Internet who was born in Dallas the day Kennedy was shot. At least, so she claimed, and, at the time, I believed her. She told me that on important anniversaries she gets interviewed in the paper. But what could she possibly say?'

Otto spoke with authority. 'One must exploit every media opportunity. I know what I'd say about being born when the Wall came down.'

Max looked across. 'Oh, yeah? Particularly since you weren't, what, exactly, would you say?'

A finger on his lips, Otto was lost in dignified thought. But he would not hesitate too long and lose his platform. 'I have grown up confused. Certainty that held Germany apart for two generations has disappeared. I have an inarticulate longing for the simpler age but am swamped by the noise and need of the materialistic present. I am, put simply, a modern tragedy.'

Max nodded. He was smiling, though he tried to hide it. '"Inarticulate longing": that's *good*.'

They walked up Unter den Linden, past upmarket coffee shops, the opera house and university and the green-domed cathedral. They saw tourists buying crumbs of the Wall encased in plastic on postcards to send home. They were trying on fake Stasi hats at a Polish street stall and succumbing to the incoherent patter of the salesman's Central European English. Coach-party women were unscrewing layer after layer of Russian dolls in front of a Turkish salesman, who kept his eyes on the women's fingers more tightly than his lips gripped the cheap cigarette.

The xenophobic barmaid had dismissed him as a tourist. He was not. Tourists spend money to substantiate a city. And nor was he, as his brother's world thought, an artist. He would not seek to imbue the barmaid's tatty fringe with pathos to search his own soul. He did not need to imprint himself upon this place, or any place.

Otto was pulling at his hand. 'Uncle Max, did you enjoy that story I gave you the other night?'

Max looked airily at the passing view. His glance was sucked into a dark space, a statue to the victims of war. There was a pause. 'Uh, yeah, I did.' He must play this cool. Otto had an agenda. 'I was wondering if you had the rest of it, actually. I need something to read in the middle of the night.'

Otto's eyes gleamed. 'I thought it would interest *you*.'

Max looked at him sharply. The stress on 'you' disquieted him. Physically, he was a child, but those eyes! Max felt violated. It was as if Otto was looking through, to a self Max did not recognize but seemed more real here than the one he had left behind in London. He stumbled.

'W-well, it's an interesting idea. A girl sublimates her own ambitions by encouraging those of a man whose talent is rich but dead. Futile but interesting.'

Otto turned to him. 'I will give you the rest, but I want you to do something for me in return. That's where I'm taking you now.'

'What are you talking about?'

Otto shifted closer and croaked into his uncle's ear: 'I want you to teach me to paint.'

'Why?'

'Because you can.'

Max sneered.

Otto was persuasive. 'Next week Father's opening his biggest exhibition ever. There will be people there, useful people.' Otto's face was so close, Max could count his curly lashes. He enunciated carefully. Clearly this had been long thought through. 'I want to be bigger than my idiot sister. I've got more to say than that airhead. I need *you* because I know exactly what I want. I just don't know how to achieve it yet, but I can't afford to miss this chance.'

'But, Otto, what do you imagine I can teach you in a week?'

Otto gave a gurgling laugh. 'I'm not going to get *my* hands dirty! No, Uncle Max, I want to learn through watching. This is how it goes. I come up with the concept and you do the work. I'll just sign at the bottom.'

Max was rubbing his neck. 'Uh-huh. Isn't that a bit dishonest?'

A hand wave dismissed this. 'Come on, Uncle Max. You think it's all nonsense anyway, so what's the difference? I'm *going* to be a genius. I'm the same as you, don't you see that? So what's the harm in a little push in the right direction from someone who wasted his chances? You want the story, I want the glory. It's a fair deal. Why the hesitation?'

Why was he hesitating, when it was so clear he should reject this proposal? A deliberate sabotage of his brother's work. The brother who had dropped everything to come and retrieve Max from a self-inflicted mess. Moreover, it was a pointless sabotage, since there was no way, with just days' notice, to smuggle into an exhibition planned months in advance – to the last detail, if Erich had anything to do with it – the hare-brained creations of a weird child and a derailed man who hadn't picked up a paintbrush in years. It was a strictly hypothetical betrayal. The only black cat in this non-existent black room was Max. Like the eternally undiscovered adulterer he must live with the lonely knowledge of his guilt.

Which thought suddenly made it appealing. He was angry about the retelling of his childhood. An eight-year-old had boldly laid out the altered reality. This long-held lie upset him more than he would admit. He should not care about a new version, since he professed no attachment to the truth.

And he had laughed many times over great-aunt Phoebe, mown down by a celebration coach on Armistice Day, 1918, and the body lost by medics in the mass of jubilant villagers waving Union Jacks. *Her* story was brought out for visitors like the best silver. When, years later, his mother admitted that she was not convinced the accident took place on the actual day and that the vehicle was probably the normal twice-weekly bus to Southampton, Max felt no remorse. Her memory was not violated. It was as it should be.

The past was always rewritten; yes, to support the winning side, but even more to entertain the present generation, who wanted their tragedies to be significant. They did not want to know it was a random meeting of madmen and bad weather.

So he should not care, but he did. Perhaps it was the

weakness of his grip that made the reality more precious. When he was so close to losing it. And Erich had, after all, betrayed him. He would not confront his brother: 'Erich, you used me.' He shuddered. No, they would never talk. This revenge was a spray can in front of a white wall but the paint was non-permanent. In daylight it would fade away.

'I guess so,' he said quietly.

They stopped underneath the towering bronze of Emperor Friedrich II, triumphant astride his steed, on an island in the middle of the road. From his rucksack, Otto proceeded to unpack oil paints, brushes, a small folding stool and a large piece of perspex.

Max looked distressed. 'You want me to paint this statue, with all these people here?' he said, sinking wearily onto the plinth of the statue.

Otto nodded, looking over Max's shoulder and winking.

'No way. I'm not doing that.'

A young girl, dressed in a bright blue shirt with a red scarf tied with a toggle, identical to thirty squealing others, bumped into Max and smiled broadly. Next to his face, he felt her sweet breath. She giggled and pulled others around her, until Max was hemmed in by a circle of female bodies and a Slavonic cacophony. He felt moist fingers and silky hair on his face. He pushed at them desperately. The more he pushed, the more they laughed.

His suffocation was both real and imagined. He wanted to scream but could not find the air. The screw turned. 'All right! All right!' he spluttered. 'Take a snap if you like and I'll scrape something together later.'

As if they had been under Otto's control all along, the girls grew bored of tormenting Max and dispersed. The attack left Max angry. People, children, were dangerous en masse.

'Why do you want a picture of this pomposity, anyway?'

'Uncle Max, I told you. These statues are witnesses to history. They see through everything.'

'I'm glad somebody does. Come on, I've got to get out of here.'

XI

The Memoirs of Gerte Mela (II)

When I arrived, as instructed, at six the next morning Poltonov ignored me. But Anna, the housekeeper, let me in.

The dog lay at Poltonov's feet. His master sat in a leather chair by the fireplace. I attached the lead to the dog's collar and said, my voice trembling in the silence, 'Where do you want me to walk him?' Poltonov stared into the fire. There was no indication that he knew I was there. If I believed it possible, I would say he slept with his eyes open. I waited a few moments, in increasing agitation, and then fled. I ran out of the door, the dog, his nails clattering, bounding down the steps in front of me.

Much as the old Russian sitting in those purple rooms frightened me with that shouting voice and dreadful face, often contorted in pain, I wanted to know him. Something drew me. The certainty of his anger. The foreignness, the knowledge of other things. For someone brought up on the pragmatic wisdom of potato farmers, this tantalizing glimpse into the unknown was irresistible. There was power in those watery eyes, there was understanding I did not have, of a life I had never known.

In those first few weeks in Berlin the regularity, the rhythm, gave me a purpose. Without it, who knows, I may have crumbled, like so many others. Then again, I may have fought harder to get back what was mine: the art-school place, the money to sustain me.

Instead I was drawn into a precise routine and the encompassing lustre of my new employer, Nikolai Poltonov. I know now that this was the intoxicating power of genius. But at the time, before I knew who he was, I was smitten with the man who, despite physical frailty, could dominate a room.

From the first day I learned that, to Poltonov, my dog-walking obligations morning and evening meant before dawn and after midnight.

He said it was the way the dog preferred it, but it was clear to me, as I got to know him better, that these were the times that the man wanted companionship. During the day he was indifferent to human company, drifting through the hours, kept afloat with painkilling injections.

But at night he slept little and found the long hours alone almost unbearable. As the weeks went by he would encourage, even coerce, me to stay after I returned from the night walk. I would deliver the dog back into his hands something before or after one in the morning and find Poltonov changed. Suddenly he was inviting, loquacious, charming.

He was not always alone. Often there would be broad-faced Russian friends, intellectuals, artists, revolutionaries, introduced to me in a fog of foreign names. Important people, brilliant people, but they all submitted to Poltonov. It did not matter that I did not know what they were saying. Whatever the language, it is easy to identify the most important person in the room. The person in whose energy others bask.

On those nights, I was a servant but he liked me to sit

122

there, on the footstool by his side. He liked to send me out to make tea or build the fire.

At other times he and I were alone. He spoke of people, art, politics, flavoured with references to the lands of the East that were a mystery to me. On those occasions I was loath to leave him. I did not resent this burden. There was so much he could tell me. I was blessed with a profound ignorance; a young girl brought up in blind rural isolation. I knew so little. It makes me blush to think that I even asked him why the dog was called Raskolnikov. But I knew no Russian literature. Poltonov was the first Russian I'd met.

Not three years earlier I had been taught that the Russians were our enemy. In my tiny school – the biggest building in the village after the white church, with its spire that stood out against the acres of brown field like the finger of God pointing down from the sky – they had told us all we needed to know about Russians. That they had pulled out of the war because their country had collapsed into revolution. These people had a dangerous and subversive nature. They had no discipline. They had rejected their strong Imperial leadership and fallen apart. Then the war ended, the Kaiser abdicated and my schooling was over.

What Poltonov said was entirely new to me. That there were thousands of Russians in Berlin, workers and intellectuals. That the region between the zoo and Charlottenburg was so overrun it was colloquially known as the 'Russian Emigrant Republic'. That refugees came from all over Eastern Europe, arriving in trains at the Anhalter Bahnhof. Employers looking for labourers would go there and pick up a fresh group every week. For a while that thoroughfare was a busier recruitment office than the labour exchange.

There were twenty Russian bookshops, more Russian

publishers, three daily newspapers, countless restaurants, cafés and clubs ranging in quality from the splendid to the squalid.

Berlin, I learned, had many floors and people lived on one in ignorance of the others.

I was ready to hear. I was thirsty for escape from my drab past. Poltonov talked to me, spurred, I think, by my nescience. But while his stories enflamed within me a desire to see, his urge to see was gone. After the revolution and his proud part in it, his being forced to flee, to live in exile, crippled by the people he fought for, had left him bitter. He railed against the world. And, free from outside interference, protected in his purple prison, he railed at me, at what I represented.

'I had never seen such stupidity until I came to this terrible city, this primeval dump!' He glowered at me. 'This is a pit of depravity. You are aware of that, boy?'

I believed every word he uttered. His words were stronger than mine and he said them more forcefully. Next to him, I could only mutter into the beard I did not have. Neither negative nor affirmative, my mumbles seemed to satisfy him to the extent that he shifted his piercing gaze from me to the beloved mutt.

Raskolnikov's intelligent eyes twitched appreciatively whenever he was paid the slightest attention. He had an overlarge, aggressive head, attached to a stringy body, whose balding patches, I was sure, were highly contagious.

Such a dog struck me as a strange choice for an aesthete such as Poltonov. Though I had not seen his paintings, I knew, even with my ill-developed senses, that he was a man who appreciated the beautiful and felt genuine pain when confronted with the ugly.

Raskolnikov, of course, played the biggest part in those early days. Though hideous to look at, I still felt in him some of the dark strength of his chair-bound master. He was equally strong-willed.

Within days I stopped trying to tempt my charge into green and open spaces – the places I thought a dog would like. I remember, early on, stumbling into the Tiergarten. I pulled him in, thinking that a dog cooped up in stifling rooms with an elderly man would long to scamper among the fragrant roots and shrubs. This was not the case. When I took off the leash, instead of galloping with the other mutts he crouched down by a dying camellia bush with his ears laid flat, as if the sound of his artless brothers offended him. He made a piteous whining sound. He cried until I led him back onto the street.

At first, I enjoyed the morning duty more. At least, I found it less frightening. The mornings were quieter, safer. The noises around me were identifiable. They were the comforting sounds of industry: the early trams, the clatter – extinct now – of wooden carts loaded with crates of fish and vegetables.

The street workers were often at their posts before me, so early in the morning I wondered if they ever went home. Like *Glockenspiel* characters, stuck to the spot, striking, with incessant futility, iron hammers on the same block of stone.

There was no need for directions: the dog led the way. He knew the streets, it seemed; he knew where he wanted to go. It shocked me at first but fascination with this new world meant I was happy to explore. The city thrilled me and early in the morning my problems seemed remote.

It was autumn and the trains' steam melted into the hazy air. That's how I remember it, but it was a long time ago; my dreams are distorted by nostalgia.

The evenings were different. In the evenings long shadows waited for me at every corner. The noises were less predictable, both in frequency and in their source.

Some, doubtless, were concoctions of my mind; the green shadows of Berlin preyed on the trusting. Dismal corners of the city that Nabokov would later describe as Berlin's 'little cul-de-sacs where at dusk the soul seems to dissolve'.

There was a man who picked up girls, mainly Eastern, from the Anhalter station and took them back to his house, ostensibly to be servants. He murdered them all. Twenty-three by the time he was caught. The police found a burnt thorax in his fireplace. These girls had disappeared and nobody noticed until a woman who worked in the laundry recognized the clothes of her missing daughter in a bundle of bloodstained washing. The murderer was caught not by his crime but by his fastidiousness. That's the story I remember, but as with so many tales my memory alters it to fit my vision. This is, after all, the work of an artist.

This murderous tale resonated: I was regularly visiting a strange man in the middle of the night, all alone. It scared me but I was also fascinated. Fear was an aphrodisiac. I had long dreamed of the city, real and metaphorical, the wealth and the poverty, the buildings and the rubble. The different faces, the untold stories of people who gathered together to buy and sell. The streetwalkers, the brothels, the noise of the carousing drinking clubs. The thin layer of respectability that made out Berlin was a thriving metropolis like any other – too thin, for the cold winds blew a hole for all to see.

Every so often a bright-eyed researcher hears that a sick but sound-minded German woman with comprehensible English has first-hand stories of Berlin's golden Twenties. Usually I laugh and tell them to dream something up in their own dirty minds. Sometimes, the more persistent or more generous, I invite in. Sometimes I tell the truth, as I see it. Sometimes, as their eyes widen, I tell them what they want to hear. It makes no difference.

It will be clear that my initial preference to walk with Raskolnikov in the morning was down to cowardice. And that soon, as the city infected me, I liked to walk at night. In the evening, Raskolnikov travelled further and we could cover considerable distances.

Poltonov came alive at night. The night gave me my purpose.

The first time I went deep into the East was the night when I felt I had discovered my vocation; when for a short time everything made sense.

It was a few weeks into my employment. I was despondent. Though I was drawn increasingly to the exotic figure of Poltonov, there was little else in my life. I was not studying, I had no creative output and the petty world of my landlady and her greedy son, attempting to seduce me with his black-market acquisitions, interested me not. It did not escape my weary eye that the aimless twice-daily walks were a perfect illustration of my own existence.

We walked for a long time that night, passed so many people and scenes, from Poltonov's wealthy enclave, where chattering ladies, arms linked in new-found freedom, left theatres and bars, fur and foul-mouthed outrages flying behind them. Overfed couples sporting bird's-nest beards and tiaras flitted through the night. As we walked, unseen, East, the faces grew thinner, the drunks less amiable. But still they poured from bars, from the vaudeville clubs with the raucous strains of so-familiar songs. 'Tomorrow is the end of the world,' they hollered. (After the currency collapsed no-one doubted the advent of this apocalypse, and it must be toasted with *Gemütlichkeit*: Berliners go down delirious.)

It was more than an hour before Raskolnikov turned off the main thoroughfares and we were in a part of the city I didn't recognize. It grew darker as the roads narrowed and the streetlights appeared less often and, soon, not at all.

Raskolnikov pulled more urgently. I strained to see what he chased. I smelt a strange cloying scent of dirt and perhaps rotting meat. But no-one would leave this lying around; even the cheapest cut was a luxury out of reach.

As we walked further in the darkness, the ground underfoot deteriorated, the asphalt giving way to mud and detritus. My eyes slowly acclimatized and I saw that the stench was coming not from meat but from dirty bodies. Ahead, the street we walked along was crowded with people wandering out of noisy, crumbling tenements.

As we drew closer, the volume intensified, a cacophony of inarticulate speech. Then a gruff voice, thick with tobacco tar but clear against the muddled background, arrested me. 'Is your dog for sale, boy?'

I stopped and turned round to my right, to an open doorway where a man sat on the floor, dressed in a black robe, with his naked feet, dirty and misshapen, sticking out. His eyes glinted in the light of a feeble lantern that hung over the doorway, swinging in the breeze.

He stared at me. I stared at him. He opened his mouth. 'This soup is as thin as water, needs thickening. Your dog would do nicely.' There was a chorus of laughter. In what I had seen to be a black vacuum, I now spotted a whole group of amused open mouths, with long yellow teeth shining from the black chasms between them.

'I'm sorry,' I murmured and tried to move on. I wanted to run. The man grasped at my coat and examined me closely. I stood petrified. I felt him looking through my skin. I could smell ingrained dirt on him, which sickened me though I was far from scrupulously clean.

'What are you doing here so late and so young?'

He growled with an accent. To me, in those days everything that wasn't German was Russian. Where I came from, the same families had lived and died in isolation for generations.

I stood still. He looked at me with a mixture of pity and temptation. 'Go home to your mother before I'm forced to take that fine suit you're wearing.'

I slunk from his vision and hid behind a door. The darkness that once held fear was now my protector. I felt Raskolnikov's warm body against my legs and, feeble though he was – more a large furry rat than a dog – was glad he was there.

I had stumbled into some kind of a hostel. The air was thick with the smell of foul sauerkraut, stale grease and unwashed bodies, laced with sickness. I walked in. There were people everywhere. Wasted men were lying around, eyes fighting exhaustion and cheap alcohol, venting feral yowls; women were more active, comforting children who would not be comforted. The children, with pinched, lined faces, were too weak to scream, but instead they whimpered, choking the air. And their young mothers looked more like grandmothers, with hair tied up in dirty scarves and their flesh fallen away. Nobody saw me – they were not looking – except a small girl who broke off a splinter of a rotting doorway and felt the air move as I passed in stealth.

She turned round and stared at me. Her face was dirty, her hair stuck out like a chimney brush. Still, but for her cupped hand, which stretched out towards me. Her eyes knew that I had nothing for her, but somewhere within her she was still striving.

It felt like a theatre piece. I felt pity, disgust with what I saw. Disbelief – I had not seen starvation before. But also a growing sense of elation. My exhaustion after the long walk vanished. I had found what I had come here for; in the bowels of the city, I had found a reason for painting.

The walk back seemed to be over in minutes. When I

returned to Poltonov, it was the first time I wanted to talk – before, I listened. Previously, my only efforts at speech strove to hide the secret of my sex – little wonder that he took me for some kind of halfwit. This night I could not hold back my breathless, squeaky pitch.

As I told him my tale, he made no response, except to take longer drafts of the hot honey vodka that sustained him through the night. His silence convinced me that somehow this was what he had intended for me, that all along he had wanted this to happen. It was his plan for me. I was chosen. Tenderly he had released me into a journey of discovery. I must learn alone, but nevertheless he had sought out a disciple to learn from him, to paint in his stead.

'I found a reason for painting tonight,' I gasped. 'I want to paint Berlin. I want to bring the poverty, the suffering, to the eyes of the mink-lined women who lie dreamlessly, luxuriously, on the soft beds of the Hotel Adlon. I want to let the two sides of the city see one another.'

He smiled and winced, shifting his position in the chair. He seldom talked of it, but the tray of syringes and fluids in Anna's kitchen told a story of constant pain.

He put the vodka glass down and let his hand drop. 'Gerhard, you're a noble boy. And youthful zeal is a wonderful thing. But a city has more than two sides. A man has more than two sides. And those two sides brought together will splinter. Do you really want to learn what the city and its people have to tell you?'

I nodded, rapt.

Again he winced, but this time at me, I think, not his own agonies. 'You are asking to be disillusioned. The destitute are not the innocent. Nor are the rich so ignorant that you can tell them anything they don't already know.'

'But surely', I said, astonished, 'you yourself believe that. You believe in the revolution?'

'I believe in dreams,' he said. 'I still believe in dreams. I believe in the power of the anaesthetic. But I no longer expect anything from reality.' He banged the useless arm with the other. 'I believed in the revolution, yet the revolution left me a cripple. Now I live as a stranger in a depraved city where I can eat Baltic caviar while the poor leave their dead on the streets. Why not?' He shrugged, a slow and pathetic gesture in his ruined torso. 'It fills the holes in the road.'

There was silence between us. I stared into the fire and watched the miraculous flames that burned freely in these airless rooms. Such quantities of coal was luxury beyond imagination.

He turned his head and smiled with a sneer. 'But you could try it,' he said carelessly. 'Go on. Germans have strong stomachs. They revel in horror. Try it, bring out the dying. Much good may it do you.'

'It is not for my own sake that I want to do this,' I protested, roused by his response.

He scoffed: 'If it is for others that you wish to paint, then you are more of a fool than I took you for.' He sniffed. 'And if you recall, I was not much impressed from the start.' He banged his chin on the withered arm. At the same time he banged the chair with the other. 'That's where philanthropy gets you, foolish boy. You little idiot. To think that I entrusted my darling Rasko into your doltish hands!'

But, for all these words, I felt no great disappointment. For something in him changed. He regarded me with a stronger gaze. It was as if, destroyed though he was, his own youthful ambitions smouldered within him still and, though he tried to deny it, a part of him grasped at the chance to rekindle those desires, in me.

That night, once his anger abated, he kept me up longer. After nights of the general, the political and the

131

societal, on this night, for the first time, he talked about himself.

He admitted what I had already learned from Anna – an inveterate gossip, it turned out – that in St Petersburg Poltonov had been an artist. Not any artist, but one of the most precocious, the most talented. That his family was aristocratic, land-owning, favourites of the Tsar; but still he wanted change. These political beliefs, and his giving of assistance to his own peasants fleeing from the burning, ravaged estate, the incident in which he injured his arm, had initially seen him held as a hero of the revolution, prepared to sacrifice his talent to the cause. But less than three years later, his intellectual associations and his overt criticism of the Artists of Revolutionary Russia made it impossible for him to remain. He fled, with others, but not before receiving the thrashing which finished off the weakened arm, saw to his legs and left him with internal injuries that, with the journey to Berlin, reduced him to his current feeble state of health.

Until that night, I had ended each day down on my knees beside my bed. In my prayers I had painted my life: I would be an artist; I would marry; I would grow old and die. But I would die satisfied.

All that was now challenged. These new visions filled my heart with hope and despair at the same time. I was in a state of fever as I listened to him. I was too tired to answer but it did not matter, he kept speaking. Some sentences made sense, some didn't. He said that all his work had been lost. Many of his paintings had been burned when the family estate was torn apart. What he had with him in his studio in St Petersburg he had carried with him as best he could, but they had rotted on the long journey. His jewels, and a stash of money, which he carried in a locked box, and which supported him now, were all that he had.

I sat on a stool by the side of his chair. I drifted in and out of consciousness and each time I woke he was still there, talking softly, dropping to incomprehensibility, his eyelids drooping.

XII

Traditional machines risk the human touch and results can vary, rendering quality dependent on the night-life of the staff on duty. But coffee from push-button machines, on the other hand, is consistently poor.

MARCO ARRIGO, *Illycaffe*

Max stopped reading and the air still felt heavy. For a moment the words made sense. He felt, not uplifted, but resonance. He flicked back through the pages. 'I believe in the power of the anaesthetic . . . In those first few weeks in Berlin the regularity, the rhythm, gave me a purpose.'

This was why his brother loved the city. It gave him the illusion to live by. A rhythm, an artificial importance. The girl, Gerte, was deceived in the most intoxicating fashion. The old man too. Everyone was lying to survive. Maybe, Max needed Berlin too.

If ever a place knew about self-invention, it was Berlin. 'Tomorrow is the end of the world,' they sang. And so they had something to live for. It brought out the heroes and the enemy.

He was vulnerable. Like a day-old duckling, ready to attach itself to the first moving object. He felt both guilty and embarrassed that even he could be seduced by Berlin's easy tragedy.

And they made Berlin in a couple of centuries. Families divided, kids shot by soldiers, soldiers shot by soldiers, child prostitutes, mothers turning their families over to the police, ruin. No wonder there was no museum of the comfortably off in modern London. No display cabinets of puy lentils, drizzled spinach and raspberry coulis. No shrines to Max's snowboard, his scuba-diving equipment, the thirty-thousand-pound kitchen he had never cooked in and his 'Zen' walls – in any other language, grey.

He could see why Erich liked this story. A girl, a mediocre artist with ambition that overreached her talent, hopelessly in love with the ethereal beauty of a devastated city and a man who had destroyed his life. It might have been Erich's own story.

And if Otto wanted a painting of Berlin, Max would do it. He was the family genius after all. Or he used to be.

Max sighed. He walked across to the computer in the room. It had an Internet connection. He switched it on and, his other hand tapping impatiently the side of the keyboard – what was his hurry? – accessed a search engine. He typed the words 'Nina Brandt'.

1) Nina Brandt Amores single CD published by Pfingsten record.
2) www. frw ca gov/legal/hgk/71-amw-105.psh. The state of California in the first appeal of Jonathan and Nina Brandt. For Appellants: Holly Brinkman, Attorney at Law. For Respondent: Merl D. Buck . . .
3) blmnolanotherworld/ Following Maya-salaam Chapter 11.
   . . . Nina looked where Brandt pointed. The ebony forest . . .
4) Brandt, Nina, born 1982: German artist. Arrested on Potsdamer Platz. Naked Nina wows . . .

A random gathering. Which had been born the night the Wall went up? Who had something to say about the confluence of East and West? He double-clicked on number four.

An image of a naked woman standing on a crowded city pavement. The woman, the girl, was Nina. Max felt uncomfortable. He fixed his gaze on the words.

Art is seeing. Seeing is judgement. So, we dress to persuade. My face, my clothes, my words, I play with. My signifiers, my labels: Feminism, Marxism, Prada, *Pravda*, Miu Miu, Mau Mau, Miaow Miaow, Mao Mao, BMW, BSE. These are the ways of seeing. Choices we can wear.

Oh God.

Five years ago Nina was something that belonged to his brother. At that age, she had sought out her exotic uncle. Flirting because she had learned how. And she was precocious. When Erich had mentioned Kandinsky, Nina looked up from the chair she slouched in, and opined: 'Ah, good old Wassily. Impure Materialism, prescient, don't you agree?'

Then Nina made not just herself but everyone look ridiculous, showed that they all held absurd postures. Until that moment, Max had unconsciously enjoyed being a missing figure. His pleasure dissolved.

Now the role was reversed. His niece was absent, too busy. The power had shifted. The only way to see Nina was inside a machine.

Max would not be curious, at least not out loud, because this was how her business worked. He knew that, like perfume, the image and reality were unrelated, but he would still desire.

Max clicked on an icon: Where I came from, where I am going.

Nina's Black Hole (video installation). In darkness, an animated image, a camera, was swinging close up and pulling back to the edge of a barely discernible circle. Underneath were black words.

I gave up the study of art. I realized that by learning I would know less. Learning is exposure to pre-existing prejudice.

I know little and I seek to know less. I am the artist. The artist sees. The politician interprets.

Art is that which is not functional. My sexual intercourse is without function. I will never have children. I am a channel not an incubator.

Black and white are shades, opposites of feeling. Hate and love, pain and pleasure. Grey is the confusion in between. The city is grey.

The streets on which I live, the dirt on those streets. This is what I am. This is art. I use no paintbrush. I use myself.

My body is a fetish, a product, a living instrument, a transitory thing. I am the city. The city has no function. The city is art.

Max yawned and clicked on an icon labelled 'Nina's arrests', denoted by barbed-wire handcuffs. It opened to a Disney Siberia. Rolling white desert, a line of chained prisoners digging at the barren land. At the bottom a shot of his niece being led away, naked, by two armed police officers. A man, also naked, followed her. Angry horror on their faces.

My art has attracted much attention. I was arrested in Paris and London for public displays of gross indecency. The open state wields transparency like a glass shield to deflect the light and distort the truth.

'They created a wasteland and they called it Peace' – Tacitus.

Max's face palled.

I am the satire of the wasteland. I am the satyr of Berlin, the God of satyriasis, of uncontrollable desire. As they try and stop me, so the people clamour for more.

At fourteen she had wanted to be a waitress. Her adolescence was fresh then. She wobbled on newly coltish legs. She wore too much make-up. Gaudy rings on hands

137

swollen to adult dimensions with baby dimples round the knuckles.

Five years on he was her voyeur.

He recalled a series of postcards he had made, lucratively, of many women's breasts. The mammary snaps were sold across the tourist world stacked on revolving stands. Across the cleavage the message read 'Welcome to London!' '*Willkommen in Berlin!*' '*Isten hozta Budapesten!*' Tits spoke an international language. This meant something to people. This was profundity.

He did not want to be alone.

Downstairs, Éva was still working. It was a little before two and the café was empty except for the Brothers Dostoevsky singing '*Je ne regrette rien*' in the corner.

The thin, dark waitress leaned against the open flap of the bar. She was reading, her face frowned in concentration. Her elbows propped her up on the wooden surface. She took occasional drags on a cigarette. Her slender body rose from its hunched position at the sound of his arrival. She looked up at him with a heavy head.

He smiled, for once a ghostly effort. 'What's the book?'

'Hungarian photography.' She held it up half-heartedly.

'André Kertész.' Max nodded. 'He used a thirty-five-millimetre Leica to capture random moments on the street with unaware subjects. He wanted to show that ordinary scenes in the city were as interesting as anything artificial.'

She smiled. 'I thought you didn't know anything about photography?'

'Well, no, I don't, but he's really well known.'

'Not that well known.'

'Well, perhaps not universally well known, but I *am* a photographer. So I suppose I know more than average.'

138

'Hmm.'

Her eyes rolled and she shifted irritably. He enjoyed her rudeness. He saw a clarity in her that was missing in others, especially himself. There was something compelling in her slim fingers undoing the bottle, picking up the glass.

She handed him the drink. He sat on the high stool up by the bar, looking at her. She almost went back to the book but first, her hand on her hip, she said, 'Aren't there people in London who are wondering where you are? You've been gone two weeks now.'

His mouth moved as he thought. 'Probably it has struck a few people that I'm not there any more. But I don't suppose they think about it for very long.'

'You don't have a girlfriend, right?'

'Correct.'

She nodded. 'Well, what about your friends? Won't they be worried about you?'

'I doubt it. I'm sure people would be delighted to see me but they're not going to notice if I'm not there. When my friends don't receive a card from my ex-girlfriend on my behalf at Christmas, I expect they'll assume we split up.'

'*Christmas*? How long are you planning on staying here?'

Max shrugged.

When it was clear no response was coming, she shook her head. 'So you can just uproot, leave your life behind without a second thought?'

'I prefer it that way.'

At this Éva emitted a cluck of ridicule. Her constant disapproval made him want to shock her pale face. 'Maybe you like the idea of it. Dropping your life. Leaving no ties. But everybody's got to be attached to something.' He didn't speak. So she said, 'Tell me what happened to the girlfriend.'

'She left me.'

'Why?'

He laughed. 'You don't hold back, do you?'

Éva yawned. 'You come to talk to me, you take what you're given.'

'Fair enough.' He bit his lip to hold back laughter. Not because it was especially funny, it was more a surge of relief. She wasn't afraid of him. Alternatively, she had been warned. Stories preceded him. To tell her that these were exaggerations, that he was normal, would confirm her suspicion that he was covering up. It was better to play along and let her untie the slander slowly. Discover that he'd made some bad choices. He'd been charmed by the fragile smiles of beautiful women, mistaken them for sensitivity. He'd equated blind lust with a true communion of souls, who hadn't?

'So,' she opened the dishwasher and pulled out shining glasses in a hot fog, 'you were telling me why she left you.'

Max hadn't been, but he let this pass. 'Oh, you know, the usual thing. She wanted commitment. I wanted sex. Normal story.'

Éva laughed. 'I never believe a word of what you're saying.'

'Very wise.' He smiled at her.

She looked into his eyes for a second too long. 'What?' she demanded.

'What, what?' he retorted. He stroked the metallic edge of the bar with his fingers. He was trembling, he noticed, and she had stopped her task, one glass held in mid-air, to watch him.

'Hmm,' she said again.

He looked up at her. 'What do you mean, "hmm"?'

And she felt annoyance that his eyes softened her. She hid behind a caustic smile. 'Oh, don't ask me what I'm thinking.' She jumped off the stool. 'Come on, I'm closing up. Let's go out.'

* * *

They wound through narrow streets. Her arse was slim but well defined in tight jeans. They ended up in a small courtyard of bulb-lit entertainment, hidden from the road, down a narrow alley.

They walked up a broad staircase rich with damp and arrived at a makeshift cash desk, behind which a white man – or, to Max, a boy – with a sheaf of yellow hair knotted like old rope, was working turntables and taking cash in a deft juggling act.

A wool curtain led into a dark room. As they entered, lights flashed on and Max saw that they stood, with five others, on a small stage looking out over rows of empty chairs.

And they continued to stand. At first Max assumed that somebody knew what was going on. He expected at any moment to have one of these people shout in his ear. He feared that he would be forced to sing.

But nothing happened. The others looked as confused, especially the suited man propping himself urbanely against the edge of the stage with a feigned smile. Max fought the urge to talk to the others, to make some glib comment. But that would be playing into their hands. Then he realized he didn't know who *they* were and, in any case, this was probably exactly what *they* had planned: that he should be stymied by his misconceived notion of what they were thinking. Either way he was trounced.

They stood there for maybe fifteen minutes. Along with calculating the conspiracy, Max snatched glimpses of Éva. A flash of dark eye, or her waif arms entwined at the wrist. She was more tantalizing for being barely visible. Her stance was not awkward. She never looked uncomfortable. A person less concerned about what anyone else thought he could not imagine. He could watch the just discernible outline of her denim legs against the blackness for hours without boredom.

Then, lest they grew comfortable, noise: a single male voice, accompanied by a synthesized bass, repeating the same sound. He was planning to tell Éva afterwards that he had not heard anything, that his mind had wandered, but he noticed he did not want to lie to her. Then the noise penetrated his brain. The word '*schleimig*' – slimy – endlessly, synthesized, slurred, oddly Sean Connery to Max's ear.

And with no more warning, it was over.

Éva smiled. 'Did you enjoy it?'

Max rubbed his face, narrowed his eyes against new light. 'I didn't realize it had started. I was still waiting for the ads and the forthcoming features.'

She nodded. 'Drink?'

'Where?'

'There's a room upstairs.'

They sat in old armchairs patterned with a browning apple fabric. Pink and blue dots of light revolved across the ceiling, walls and scuzzy floor. Music thrummed. The barman looked remarkably similar to the man on the door earlier but Max would make no assumptions.

For a while she closed her eyes and nodded her head in time to the music. He felt night air seeping through a hole in the wall. Through jagged concrete he could see people walking in the street below. He gripped the sides of the armchair. That would help when the building collapsed.

Instinct opened her eyes with the arrival of the drinks.

He grimaced. 'What the hell's that?'

'Camomile tea.'

'It looks like urine.'

'Well, it will be soon.'

Max smiled. Éva tapped her foot and looked round the room. Opposite, a man in a hooded top was zonked out on a tatty armchair. His mouth was hanging open, his eyes were closed, but he was still keeping rhythm with a pendulous chin.

'Erich said you're Hungarian.'

'Yeah, but I've been in Germany most of my life.'

'So what do you feel, German or Hungarian?'

She eyed him with suspicion. 'I guess I feel German, well, Western, now. But I was quite young when it all changed. My mother is very different. She thinks it was better in the bad old days, when the rent was cheap.'

'Your father's dead?'

'No.'

'No?'

She rolled her eyes. 'When the Wall came down my father ran off to the woman from the West he'd been having an affair with. We just thought he had a hell of a lot of conferences in Leipzig but it turned out he was screwing some woman from Frankfurt.'

'Ah.'

Éva threw back her head. She sat up, dragged her knees up to her chest and encircled them in her arms. 'I don't know much about it.' She smiled.

He stumbled for the next question. 'And do you have, uh, brothers and sisters?'

'There's just me. My mother fell ill – MS – not long after I was born.'

The pieces, the piles of used bricks, that do not fit smoothly together.

He took her hand. 'You're very beautiful.'

She was, then. The puffed-up cheekbones, the thin

143

eyebrows that fell so low and ironic they seemed almost to graze her eyes, the ill-fitting full mouth.

She smiled wanly. 'Is this the famous seduction technique?'

His eyes widened. 'What did Erich say?'

'Not Erich,' she said, hanging one leg over the edge of the window into the air, one bent into her body. 'Ursula.'

'Ursula?' he said in alarm. 'Ursula?'

Éva shook her head. 'Don't worry. She didn't say anything specific. I watched her, that's all. And I watched you. You're good with women. You always look interested.'

'It's a curse.'

'Right.'

He sat forward, closer to her. 'I love your sarcasm.'

'I'm not sarcastic. You're sarcastic. You read things into my face. To suit yourself.'

'Everybody does that.'

'Possibly.'

He stretched towards her and stroked his hand across her cheek. It was so soft, yet she stiffened, looked distraught. Her voice was low but stern. 'What are you doing?'

'Sorry.' He retreated, shamefaced. 'I thought maybe you wouldn't mind.'

'Well, of course I do,' she said. 'You're a self-centred, misogynist depressive – you think that's tempting? Exactly what kind of idiot do you take me for?'

He looked blank, sitting back in his chair. He was exhausted.

She sipped her tea and winced. 'You're right, it is urine.'

XIII

She was without shame. She appealed to me like an innocent child. Suddenly she stopped the crayon, with which she was painting herself chalk white, in mid-air and said: 'You can sleep with me if you like.'

FRED HILDENBRANDT, Arts Editor, *Berliner Tageblatt*,
on Anita Berber, *c.* 1923

Ursula stood in front of her Thursday-morning class. Eight old ladies sat on wooden stools behind easels, straining short-sighted eyes towards her. Their mouths hung open. Such was the power of authority. Fools, she thought.

In between the teacher and her pupils, placed on a white sheet covering a small table, a collection of limes, lemons and oranges were arranged on a wooden plate.

Ursula had woken up in the night, sobbing. She walked angrily to the college, every grinding step building her determination that she could not live like this any longer.

The Thursday beginners' class comprised, exclusively, of women. It always did. Men would not risk failure.

Ursula walked round the circle of students as they strained over their pictures. Frau Werner, sitting at the far left of the semicircle, found no good reason each week to mention her age (seventy-three) and her childhood membership of the Hitler Youth. She had loved the picnics and sports days. She had never been interested in politics. But, ever since, she had forced herself. She gave interviews to local newspapers and spent afternoons at the Turkish women's support group, explaining that she was not, that no-one was ever, innocent. That ignorance was guilt.

Growing up in West Germany, Ursula had had history lessons of perpetual penance. It must never happen again. Ursula supported peace organizations, social welfare and divided her rubbish into plastic, paper, glass and organic matter. She still hated herself and not because of her nationality.

Ursula didn't hear Frau Werner's confessions. She concentrated on her own. She was a fraud – as a teacher, a mother and a human being. She lived with the agony of exposure. But now she was aching to tell, to take away the constant fear, the painful prayer that no-one would ever find out.

Next to Frau Werner sat Frau Keil, whose dull lemon picture was outshone by the riotous clothes draping her body. Green and navy-blue silk swirled round her neck and dripped down over a flowing peppermint top. The effect was heightened by the powerful fragrance sprayed with excessive liberality into Frau Keil's drooping cleavage.

Ursula swallowed away the clinging mint flavour. Next Frau Plessner, the visual equivalent of tone deaf; next to her, Frau Winckler, who emitted strange chewing noises when concentrating but never spoke; then four women whose names Ursula always forgot. They all looked the same, with square-rimmed gold glasses and white, cropped hair with intermittent specks of dark colour.

Ursula looked at the plate of fruit. She was filled with

jealousy. She thought, what an easy life being a lemon must be. *Tell them*, she thought. *Tell them.*

Citrus was big in Berlin, ever since an abstract artist had one afternoon abandoned the conventional companions of the post-modern – the corrugated iron, the neoprene, the spray paint – and produced instead a pair of lemons in yellow and green oils curving towards one another flirtatiously on a rich chocolate background. It sold immediately. He painted another pair. They sold too. He painted hundreds of sexy lemons. Day after day, they dried in his studio. A semi-celebrity now, the newspapers lapped up the feel-good story that everyone wanted to hear and believe might happen to them.

'Ursula,' cried Frau Plessner suddenly, 'this looks like a tennis ball not a lemon. What's wrong with it?'

Nobody heard Ursula murmur, 'What's wrong with it? Never mind it, what's wrong with me?' She cleared her throat and raised her voice. 'You need to give the background more substance. Your image looks flat because there is not enough separation between the fruit and the space behind it. Try and think of the space as a flattened shape itself. There is no emptiness, the space must be filled with its own identity.'

Taking the brush, she encouraged the two-dimensional Frau Plessner to be bolder with her edges, painting thick colour round the contour of the lemon. While she did so, she wondered why this woman painted. Because her father was no longer alive to tell her she couldn't? Because her husband was no longer alive to belittle her? For the sheer joy of drawing fruit badly instead of washing it and peeling it and cutting it up for other people?

She sighed as she walked across the room to the window. Immediately below her the view of municipal children's play area, where the bouncing horse, the tiny

147

slide and the octagonal climbing frame were all cemented to the workplaces. An androgynous, middle-aged woman pushed an empty wheelchair round and round.

She looked further down the street. From the fourth floor of this 1960s educational building, the view was long. She could see Friedrichstrasse, open now, stretching north. From here could be seen no scar of the Wall; she noticed only that she no longer expected to see it. The streets and buildings merged into grey, dotted with the yellow of cranes. She saw the faces of Max and Erich swimming into her mind's eye. Erich's face was a comfort. It was something solid. After two years apart, she was almost nostalgic about their arguments, that level of intimacy. Screaming at someone who cared. She had not relished the period since her marriage, being alone again. The embarrassing conversations, tasteless dinners, the calculated box-ticking, looking for love in a few hours a week. Her mouth turned dry.

Her image of Max was more nebulous. She could not picture what he looked like. It was easy to project her desires onto his washed-out face. *Tell them*, her tongue was itching, *tell them*.

Ursula walked back, bent down to her case and brought out a large cardboard tube. 'We discussed last week the reason for painting fruit, why it has been a tradition for so long.'

Eager eyes looked up as she turned the tube on its end and tapped it against her hand. Rolled white paper eased out. She unfurled it and held it to face the women.

'I want you to look at this painting. It's called "Basket of Fruit". It's held here in the Staatliche Museen and it's by an artist called Balthasar van der Ast, painted in 1632.'

'I've never heard of him,' gasped sagging Frau Werner. She feared the unknown. She liked the painters she had been told to like, preferably by that soft-voiced American Bob with a California beard who appeared on late-night German TV.

'"Basket of Fruit",' said Ursula more loudly. 'Still life was hugely popular in the seventeenth century. Apart from appreciating the attention to detail that rendered the objects so lifelike, apart from that, what every educated seventeenth-century art fan would love was the symbolism – what could be said about the nature of life from this simple thing.'

The women stared. Abundant fruit overflowed from a lattice basket onto a table. Cascading green and purple grapes, red-stemmed foliage so fecund, it was still growing. Oozing pears, blushing apples and apricots spread across the space. The sheen of ripeness was balanced by fruits that had fallen to the ground and, spotted with warts and freckles, begun to decompose. A curled lizard sucked at a rotten fruit and a lacy-winged dragonfly let its legs sink into sweet decay. Yellow and blue butterflies flew around the haul with little concern for entomological truth.

'There aren't any lemons in it,' Frau Keil pointed out.

'The decaying fruit basket', Ursula's stridor drowned the objector, 'is a parable. Its message would be clear to the contemporary viewer: that they should turn away from the overindulgence of the royal court to something more holy.

'Like the skull, which was a constant reminder of death, the butterflies represent transience. The abundance of overripe fruit is a lesson that we all must die, that underneath our bright exteriors we are all corrupt and deca-ying.' Her voice cracked over this word and, when she attempted a recuperative swallow, tears came into her eyes. The heads of her group were bowed. 'Your true nature will come out in the end.'

149

They thought she was still talking to them when she opened her mouth, paused and then said, 'My life is a lie.'

Slowly, they lifted their heads.

Ursula's head was held highest and her straight hair seemed more rigid. Her words were clipped, her voice too strong. 'For two years I have pretended that I had a wildly sexual affair with my ex-partner's brother. I convinced Erich that I was screwing Max when he and I were still together . . .' She gulped. 'This was untrue. I don't know why I did this. Perhaps it was some kind of cheap thrill at the time in a life that had become trapped in routine and domesticity. Christ knows what I've done to Erich. I think I probably destroyed his childhood, to say nothing of his self-esteem. But I didn't really mean to; it just got out of hand. It's a tribute to my creative powers really. I even convinced myself.'

She was breathless, but the words fell out of her, unstoppable. 'It might not have mattered, it might have faded into nothing, but Max has come to stay with us, something I believed could never happen. I mean . . .' Her tone became confidential; she sat down, rested her elbow against the top of the desk, and her chin on her palm. The ladies shifted, looking less startled, bent towards her, intense curiosity barely masked in their stiffly powdered faces.

'I mean, they were hardly even in contact. They disagree, oh, about everything. But then something happened to Max, something bad. His life collapsed, I suppose you'd have to say. I don't know why. And it seemed there was nowhere else for him to go. So he's here. I'm seeing him every day. And Erich must be looking at him and thinking, how could you do that, screw your own brother's wife – well, sort of wife. I'm the mother of his child after all, for what that's worth, which doesn't seem to be much any more. I know Erich's looking at me. And all the others, you know, in the café, are wondering why Max doesn't pay me more attention. I can't pretend it's because he's preoccupied with his own misery for ever. People are getting suspicious. I'm living in fear. I can't keep up the pretence to him or the others. It's too much. I panic in bed at night. I'm sweating in the dark.'

This last comment seemed to rouse the most sympathy in the fastidious females. 'Sweating! You poor darling.' Ursula did not know who said this. It could have been any of them: they all pulled the same face of revulsion.

Ursula smiled at their earnest faces with new-found appreciation. The dear old things, they seemed genuinely concerned.

'Of course, added to that, I still feel for Max. I'm still filled with an unhealthy obsession. It's like unfinished business. I've spent so long thinking about what it would be like with him, I've built it up in my mind. It occupies a large part of every day. I know it's unhealthy and very wrong but I've lured him out tonight. It'll make things worse but there's a part of me that just has to see him naked.'

She fell on her chair and her forehead hit the desk with a bang that rang round the room. She lifted it up and slammed it.

There was a momentary silence, then Frau Winckler, the woman known only for her nauseating mastication noises, growled, 'Sleep with him. I would. While you still can.'

Everyone stared at her, shocked because until now no-one knew that she *could* speak.

'I agree,' put in Frau Keil hastily. 'Remember Gertraut Biedermann.'

'Don't!' said Frau Werner, covering her mouth with a

151

handkerchief, quaking. 'That poor woman! Let her rest in peace.'

'Well, it can't hurt her now, surely?'

'Oh, the things that man made her do.'

'And poor Gertraut was so wrapped up in the Church. Those women spread gossip like the good news. It was dreadful.'

'Everybody knew.'

'Filth gets around.'

To the bobbing heads of the circle's consensus and the clicking of their false teeth, Ursula's head was spinning. She gripped the sides of the table. 'So, uh, what are you saying, what should I do?'

The newly vocal Frau Winckler pulled at Ursula's sleeve. Her chewing lips were working hard as she gathered strength. 'Do it. Before it's too late.'

Frau Keil looked solemn. 'Gertraut had a chance. That pig's brother, a wonderful man, a florist, would have taken her away from it all, would have offered her a beautiful life. But she wouldn't desert that dirty *devil*. Misguided loyalty. Don't be another victim.'

Ursula shrank back, shaking her head. 'Uh, you know, I don't know that the situation is that similar. Erich is a wonderful person. It's me that's the bad guy. Sometimes I think it's his understanding nature that pushes me on. Like I want to test the barriers.'

She stared out of the window. The woman below was still pushing her circles. Ursula turned cold.

'So.' She released a breezy smile and wiped the tears from her cheek. 'So. Perhaps you can be thinking about our lemon paintings. The motifs are not so clear in modern painting. There is much more . . . confusion. We are not given so many clues, or perhaps we are given too many. Uh. We'll talk about it next week.'

XIV

I constantly saw the false and the bad, and finally the absurd and the meaningless, standing in universal admiration and honour . . .

ARTHUR SCHOPENHAUER, *The World as Will and Representation*, 2nd Edition, 1844

Returning at eleven o'clock at night, and seeing no-one on duty in the café, Max was surprised to find the normally dark upstairs sitting room lit and full. Barbara sat sulkily in a corner. He had to push past Éva, who was near the door, arms folded, dubious. Max inhaled the cool air that seemed to surround her. Erich stood in the middle of the sitting room. Around his ankles, Otto threw a ball. A large, clear marble that smacked monotonously against the wooden floor. He did not look up, even when Max prodded him.

For the first time since his arrival in Berlin, the TV was on. After an absence, advertisements: panting ecstasy is a peculiar response to strawberry yoghurt, unless one sees it five times a day.

'Hey, Max! You said you wanted to see Nina.' Erich was smiling, through bared teeth. 'She's giving an interview about her latest exhibition.'

'Ah,' said Max, 'excellent.' There was a space left for him, next to Ursula.

The ads ended and the programme continued. A previous guest was walking off the set, waving. The camera spun round as he exited and zoomed between the cackling audience and a featureless young presenter who stood, shirt cuffs over her fingers, clutching beige programme notes. She was a thin blonde, swathed in black; only from her toenails colour shone – vibrant peacock blue.

After some seconds the noise abated.

'And now – thank you, Joachim . . .' She turned and gave a flirtatious, three-fingered wave to the semi-clad departing guest, who was still receiving catcalls from the audience. She reeled back on tottering sandals to face the camera, raised her voice to command control. 'And now, and now, we welcome back an old friend of Subkultur, our favourite controversial artist, described in a leading magazine as "an offence to women, art and Germany".' She paused for indulgent laughter. 'Her medium is her body' – she lowered her voice intimately and the camera moved to close up – 'and I mean all her body [more laughter]. She has sex in public, on screen; she does things that my mother told me nice girls didn't [more laughter]. So . . . [pause, the voice descends into a sexy crackle] here for an exclusive interview before her first exhibition since her arrest in November, Nina Brandt!' The interviewer's voice rose at the end to a climax and the crowd whooped.

'"Exclusive",' Barbara scoffed. 'What rubbish. She's given interviews to all the papers, she told me.'

Barbara had seen her? In the café and he missed her? Max felt consumed suddenly by this manufactured excitement. And this hurt. If he had to be a part of it (who did not?) he wanted to be a manufacturer.

To the notes of a bass guitar and a Hammond organ, her hips led, then the shimmering thighs wrapped in gold, catching the studio lights. As her face came closer, the sudden familiarity turned the studio into an extension of Erich's living room.

The chubby adolescent was a long-limbed, gaunt-eyed waif. Her genetic sandy hair was platinum blonde.

The blonde interviewer withered. She looked duller. 'Nina, welcome back.'

The goddess acceded magnanimously with a tip of her head.

Max looked at Erich. 'That's your daughter?'

Erich nodded, smiling, enjoying his shock.

Otto continued to drop the marble. Max looked at him as if weighing one child with the other. He missed much of the early exchange, switching his gaze from the girl on the television to the boy on the floor, as if he were seeing them both for the first time.

'And so . . . the exhibition's called . . .' The interviewer hesitated over the notes.

Nina bent forward; the top of her head blurred, as the camera could not adjust in time. Max jumped, expecting her to walk through the screen. 'It's called: "Accidental sex in the German living room".' She settled back with a precocious smirk.

Now the camera went close up on a small statuette, a model of an elfin man with stick arms and legs. A fuzzy mop of red hair clashed with a green felt tunic. He had unpleasant half-moon eyes, a nose like a stuck-out tongue and a wide malicious smile. Bending slightly on his haunches, his knees pointed outwards, one east and one west, to make room for a corkscrew. The screw went through his legs and out behind, like a curly tail, and the large, kite-shaped wooden handle thrust forward, held at a forty-five-degree angle from the floor by the little man's hands.

There was an amused murmur from the audience; baffled silence in Erich's living room.

The interviewer turned round, losing her camera for a moment, her black jacket a little crushed, and, etched on her face, the smallest sign of panic that she was lost. It was just a few seconds before she found her public face and sighed. 'Uh, OK, Nina, perhaps you can talk us through this one.' She flashed a smile now the camera was back on her face, where she liked it to be.

Nina's disembodied voice, professionally deadpan, was swift in response: 'I call it the Elf's Enormous Penis.'

Laugh.

'I see. Uh, and how did you come across the little fellow?'

'I just went knocking on doors. It didn't take long to find.'

The camera was now swinging between the two women. Nina played the cooler card; as if she did not care if it landed on her or not.

The interviewer resented competing not just with a taller, thinner and more expensively dressed girl but with a novelty dwarf act as well. She was bored. She needed more attention. She pulled back her shoulders and sucked in her stomach, eyeing the camera. 'I see. And did you tell the donors what the purpose of your request was?'

Nina smiled that canny smile again. 'You mean, did I say to some old *Hausfrau*, "Can I look round the house to see if any of your ornaments are actually representations of human genitalia and you never noticed?" [Laugh] No, I did not tell them that.'

The other girl was sour. 'So what did you tell them?'

Nina's voice was calm. 'I told them I was collecting for a charity junk shop.'

'But that was a lie?'

This was what Nina wanted. She smiled sweetly. 'Are you saying I should not lie?' (Uncertain laugh) 'Western society is founded on lies. It is inherent in the nature of competition that we are brought up, by the family, the media, and society, to fight. I should say I *deserve* to be on your show more than anyone else. That is a lie. We both know that I am here because I can talk about sex. It would be dishonest of me, as an artist intent on portraying society, to tell the truth.

'In fact,' she leaned forward on her elbow, cupped her hand over her perfectly decorated lips, 'it was perfect. A lot of the doors I knocked on were in the East. These people wanted to believe that some of the old values were still there – the scrimping and saving, the making the best of nothing. That I was lying was actually a perfect representation of the cruel new world they have entered.'

'Well,' the interviewer was terse, 'you must have a point here. Why don't you tell me what it is.' By the end of this sentence, professional that she was, she had recomposed herself. Tilting her head to one side, she unzipped a smile for the camera – wobbling like a jack-in-the-box one – best profile presented.

'What interests me,' said Nina, 'is the denial. We like to think we are an open society and yet in a million German living rooms there are these phallic and clitoral charms, bought in apparent ignorance.'

'Apparent?'

Nina nodded. 'There is no such thing as ignorance, there are only closed eyes.'

The conversation was flagging. There should be no more than five minutes without nudity, according to the programme brief. The producer growled in the presenter's ear and she duly quickened her pace. 'So, Nina, there are, what, twenty of these found objects?'

157

'Nineteen. I'm very much against round numbers, pre-set notions of what ought to be.'

The interviewer coughed. 'Now, in case your fans are disappointed that there is not enough . . . flesh [indulgent laughter] in this work . . . Don't panic! Next to each object, you have a blown-up photo of a real human being holding the same position to show just how X-rated these little ornaments really are.'

'Yes.'

'Can we get a close-up on that, camera one?' The picture zoomed forward. 'Can we get it more in focus?'

The audience, which had gone rather quiet, cheered. 'Wa-hoo!' They sounded as instructed, like a Friday-night beer-hall crowd.

The interviewer rode it. 'I won't ask you, Nina, where you found a man of such proportions.'

'He's a friend.'

The interviewer gave that confidential look to the camera that said she was the viewer's friend. 'We'll put his phone number up at the end of the programme.'

Laugh, penis, laugh. It was the winning formula.

'This collection seems upbeat for you, Nina – almost, dare I say it, humorous, compared with your last work.'

'Yes.' Nina nodded carefully. She tucked her hair behind her ear, rested her head on one side and lifted her left foot over the right knee. 'Yes, last year's stuff was quite black. I had come out of a very damaging relationship. I was punishing myself with drugs and self-abuse.'

The other woman arched a highly plucked brow. 'Some critics suggest that you spend more time making art about your experiences than you do living them. It was a matter of weeks, the relationship, was it not? And your drugs hell, too, seemed over as soon as it had begun. I believe you exhibited your rehab art before even the *tabloids* knew you were in trouble. That must be a first.'

158

Nina twitched and swapped her legs over. 'The drugs problem had been building for a long time. The relationship was short but very violent.'

'Well,' said the blonde interviewer, her pupils swelling at the camera like for a lover, 'there you are. We're taking a break now. Don't go away.'

The programme disappeared in a trail of bubbles. A girl in a black bodice and a blonde ponytail lay on her back on a bed holding a bristly hairbrush. Her legs were open wider than her eyes. She looked into the camera. 'Call me. I need you. Call me.' Her number flashed onto the screen.

A *faux* Eighties discotheque. A large glittering ball hung from the low ceiling of a dimly lit room. A man in a peaked studded cap, naked to the waist, extremely tanned, bobbed up and down to a drumbeat and synthesizer. The camera panned down to his leather trousers. Two girls, one with a blonde mane, one brunette, both dressed in leather thongs and high heels, tugged at his ankles and rubbed at his calves and they writhed on their knees, plump buttocks bobbing.

'Mega fun, mega sex, mega girls!' English words spoken in a heavy male German accent.

Erich flicked the volume off. He looked at his brother.

'Is it a porn channel?' asked Max.

Erich shook his head. 'It's a twilight channel. Some sex, but more applied sex dressed up as pseudo-documentaries – and "culture" shows, of course.'

'Astonishing,' said Max.

'Revolting,' said Erich.

'Well, perhaps.' Max was thoughtful. 'But the funny thing is, despite all the bullshit, she does make some sense.'

'It's a monkey at a typewriter,' scoffed Barbara. 'By the law of averages she has to string some sentences together.'

'Hey!' protested Erich, 'that's my daughter you're talking about!'

Barbara's eyes were sleepy. She yawned. 'She's still a tart.'

Erich raised his eyebrows at Max and folded his arms. Max expected more from Erich but he had realized since being here that Erich could be passive, letting those around him operate the situation. Max had taken Erich to be more assertive. He had retained the unconscious belief that whatever he, Max, was, Erich was the opposite. It wasn't true.

'I'm going back downstairs,' murmured Éva. 'Somebody ought to be there.'

Erich pressed the volume button. The teasing voice of the interviewer resumed: 'And so we're back with controversial Berlin artist Nina Brandt, who uses pornography to push back the barriers of art. At least, that's what she says.' She gave Nina a faint smile. 'Now, Nina, everybody wants to know what happened on Potsdamer Platz. You were arrested for having sex . . . What about the juicy details?'

Nina smiled and recrossed her legs. 'I was making a statement about wrongful arrest and the denial of artistic freedom. It was not about me engaging in a sexual act.'

'Mm-hmm. Do you think the crowd interpreted your work in the right way? Or did you view them as the newspapers did – and I quote [a blown-up extract from a newspaper flashed onto the screen]: "The night three hundred teenage boys licked their lips".'

'Inevitably, with a piece like that you get jokers. But I think alone, late at night, the point will have gone home.'

The interviewer gave a wily smile. 'Well, we have some footage from your own recording of that infamous night coming up right now.'

'Oh God,' said Barbara. 'Enough.'

Max looked away. Erich, he noticed, had done the same. What could this feel like? Max would have done anything to keep this quiet. But Erich had wanted Max to see.

Max heard uneasy laughter from the screen. He looked back when he heard the blonde move on. 'And so . . . Nina, what's next?'

'It's a meditation on death, on transience,' said Nina.

'Not filming yourself in the act this time, I hope?'

Nina looked gracious, rather tragic. She paused. 'I was profoundly shaken by the suicide recently of my uncle, Max.'

'Were you close to your uncle?'

Nina left an exquisite gap. 'It's still very difficult for me to talk about. You see, he was a very talented guy. He had something, you know?' Her voice broke audibly. 'He could have been a great artist. But he never used it. He deliberately threw all that away. It meant nothing to him, he said. His meaningless end left me with so many questions. What led him to despair? Was it the realization that ultimately he had wasted his gifts? I believe my uncle's life was lost a long time ago. I wanted to look at that idea of wasted life. In an era where the emphasis is on achievement and personal fulfilment, there is someone who had so much, but threw it all away. It's a very powerful image of our society.' Her voice tapered off. There were tears in her eyes but her make-up was too expensive to run.

'So,' the interviewer turned away with a conclusive voice, 'next time we hear from you, Nina, you'll be knocking on the door to see if there were any suicides in the family, huh?'

Nina smiled an enticing smile, cheering up. 'Something like that.'

'Thanks, Nina.' The blonde whispered this intimacy.

'Any time.'

The interviewer swung round to another camera, a light background drumming started and green lights flashed. 'We have to end it there. Thanks for watching. Join us next week, for more tales from the cutting edge of Subkultur, and remember: if it's underground, it's over here. Now we finish with DJs Bastard and Abgefuckt spinning us out, accompanied by performance artist Mastiff Mareike, who will be shouting abuse at the audience. Goodnight!'

Erich switched the TV off. Nobody spoke.

XV

Take a big pencil and cover a sheet with vigorously drawn
straight lines . . . Let yourself go – free, uninhibited, and
without a care in the world . . . What really matters is that
tomorrow hundreds of young painters, full of enthusiasm,
throw themselves into this area of expression . . . The
Metropolis has to be painted!

> LUDWIG MEIDNER, *An Introduction to Painting the
> Metropolis*, 1914

German film theorists compared these films, with their
Gothic towers, vertiginous staircases, to the tunnel of the
female form.

Late at night, Erich climbed the long flights to his
lover. This tunnelling had started between them only
because Marlene possessed a near perfect collection of
German silent films. Prints unavailable on the commercial
market, films Erich had only read about. She had antique
equipment and a screen that took up an entire wall.

He did not love her. Yet she provided an antidote to
the fearful pace of change around him. The Berlin he
believed he remembered. A little deviation in a new world
of straight lines.

She felt safe under the roof, clutching the key to her

chambers. The workmen on the ground were operating their machines of torture, erecting scaffolding that so far had not reached. She looked through her window and saw these articulated monsters who swallowed bricks and let sand dribble through their teeth. She clung to her tower.

Twelve years ago, more than a dozen families lived in these few huge houses. Marlene's building was one of several residential properties that lay in this small business area of Mitte. The offices were derelict, abandoned, though some still held Seventies furniture, stationery, filing cabinets and antique computer paper, reams of single lined binary. Anything of interest was long gone.

The families were relocated, most further out of the city centre, as their long-term secure agreements ended and new private rents in the area were set at three times the price. The houses were slowly torn down. Now weeds grew out of the walls and rain ate the rusting drainpipes.

Squatters moved into Marlene's building – the best preserved. A tatty banner was hung out of the second-floor window: over a large green cannabis leaf were daubed the words 'Freedom from the money chains! Rent free into the new millennium!' The front door was secured with nailed planks of wood, attached to the wall with a bicycle chain. The original lock was missing.

The squatters occupied the first two floors of the house but left Marlene in peace. In truth, they were afraid of her.

Erich knew this fear. Even Berlin, which revelled in its eccentricities, had a code. Norms which Marlene failed. He wanted the fear. When he was with Marlene, he was someone other people would not recognize.

She was alone but for the doctor who saw her, an energetic young woman with no taste for gloomy attic apartments. The doctor lived in a spacious glassy new building in a gleaming courtyard three streets away, where the dust of building work still lay on the cobbles. She worked in an efficient new practice off Monbijou Park. She bought her lunch in an American sandwich bar. She sat inside at a high round table, her legs dangling, and stared through the huge glass window at the stage show outside. The doctor had left her sleepy Bavarian town to witness this metamorphosis. Her predecessor retired to the country to leave the noise and constant upheaval of Berlin. He wanted to cycle through the forest with his elderly wife and stop at a tiny *Bierstube* that had been there for ever.

Erich walked up the stairs, past the squatters, who nodded at his familiar face through a fug of smoke and dub music. Nina lived not a hundred and fifty metres from here. In an apartment in a sparkling new building with a twenty-four-hour concierge; every evening Nina swam in the private glittering pool with its mosaic floor of aquamarine and lilac. Nina could scarcely believe Marlene was real. But, Katrina, in the tone she reserved for her ex-husband, said, 'Darling, if your father had the imagination to dream up a lover like that, he wouldn't be where he is today.'

Tonight Marlene chose *The Other Side*. The hero, a wanderer down dark streets, is infected by a malign power which convinces him that behind the ordinary lies the sinister. He enters a teashop and sees the waitresses as wax dolls controlled by mechanics. The other customers sit around him, thick with conspiracy. He knows they are not human but children of Satan.

The shadows, chaotic chiaroscuro, draw together the tortured hero's mind and the apocalypse outside. Only the permeable membrane of his skin separates them. In the future not even thought will be safe.

Max did not sleep. Nina's words spiralled through his mind. He was dead. He was an entry in Nina Brandt's biographical index, his tragedy a minor influence on her work. He could have been as big. Instead he would die nothing. 'Be a dustman, as long as you're an educated dustman,' his grandmother had said. Of course, his parents disagreed. Surely it was more Christian to hide his light under a bushel. Even though he was an atheist. Was modesty really his incentive? Or was he just inert? Or, option three – suggested to him by women over the years; first his mother and, most recently, Maria, by which time he was considering a Ph.D. in the psychological cliché – option three: he was scared. Of what? *Of what?* Maria, you self-proclaimed expert, tell me what I'm afraid of. She had looked at him with those amber eyes once perceived as cool beauty but now as persecution.

'Of being alive.'

'Do you know how stupid that sounds?'

When she smiled he recognized it as his own. She stole everything.

'Why, Max? You're doing the same, safe shit you were doing ten years ago. You keep yourself hidden away behind this bullshit façade. You don't give anyone anything. You won't have children.'

He narrowed his eyes. 'Funny how you drag every conversation back to that. Would you really give a damn, Maria, about my artistic talents if I offered you my procreative ones?'

'Fuck off, Max.'

'I'm thinking about it, Maria, I'm seriously thinking about it.'

But while he was thinking, she was gone.

*   *   *

It was three a.m. He stared at Nina's site. Her teenage certainty saddened him. Since he was a child, he had found Erich's solid purpose reassuring. But now Erich seemed to be faltering.

Erich kept his car keys in the top drawer of the hall bureau. Max walked to the basin, splashed his face with water and brushed his teeth again. He smiled at himself. Christ, you look sick, he said, almost aloud. The dark ovals under his eyes looked not like shadows but black eyes, hanging, haunting from his face. He corrected himself: You *are* sick. The Subkultur programme had, in one way, achieved its aim. Sex is infectious.

He parked in an alley off Oranienburger Strasse and walked up to the gleaming onion dome of the New Synagogue. He nodded at the police outside, the men in green, the twenty-four-hour guard, stroking the guns on their hips. They did not nod back. They watched him pass and he knew he should come back another way, knowing what a man on his own on this street at this time in the morning wants but he should not be seen to be doing it.

The two girls, in black leather boots reaching above the knee, walking in step, as if to a dance, up the road, lingering under lights, turned to look into passing cars. A flash of fishnet thighs, a triangle of black leather that covered the area from the hips to the very top of the thighs, and black Puffa jackets not unlike the officers' in shape, were topped with that long flash of blonde hair hanging pendulous down the back. They were rightly renowned as Europe's best-dressed whores, he thought, with an unaccountable glow of pride.

'Two hundred marks. And in euros—'

'Just take the money. I don't care how much it is.'

'Here, or in the car?'

'Car.'

'Car's extra.'

'Fine, I don't care. What about your friend?'

'That'll cost you—'

'No, I mean will she be OK on her own?'

'Yeah,' drawled the girl, her blanched face twisted into a bemused smile. 'I'm sure she'll be fine.'

She balked at the car with its ageing denim paintwork and rusting hubs. It was the first time he'd been embarrassed to show a girl his car since about 1982. Nostalgia threatened. With the cash transaction over, he could forget what this was.

'How's the suspension in this thing?' she said, looking worried.

'Rigid.'

'I have back problems, you know.'

The front seat would not shift. She was forced to scramble over. Her exertion wafted sweet perfume and stale nicotine.

'If I ladder my tights, you pay.'

'How about some music?'

Deep sarcasm. 'Sure, honey, a little atmosphere in a beat-up Beetle: what could be more romantic?'

He switched on the stereo. There were a few moments of crackling, then shocking estranged notes exploded at full volume from the speakers like springs from the worn-out back seat. Max yelped. 'Christ! Erich's fucking Schoenberg!'

She was wincing with her hands over her ears, shouting, as he turned it off.

'Is this really your car?'

'Yes. Why?'

'It just doesn't fit with the Prada trousers. Which I love, by the way.'

168

'Take them,' he said as he clambered into the back seat to join her.

'What?'

'You can have them.'

'What? You mean, take them away with me afterwards?'

'Yeah.'

'What about you?'

'I have a coat.'

She removed his trousers and folded them now with extra care. 'Mm,' she said, with feline appreciation, 'gorgeous underwear. Makes a change, I can tell you. You should see the shit rags I have to contend with.'

'I'd rather not.'

He turned his head away as she removed the bottom half of her clothing and eased herself on top of him.

As she began her well-oiled routine he found himself feeling further and further away from the car and the woman milking his dick with expert rhythm. He was distracted by the sound of his own voice in his head. Slow and easy, urbane chat, like Nina in the interview.

I've always been a prostitute man. Mm-hmm. Oh, you know, the usual reasons. Less hassle. Always available. You don't have to talk. Doesn't want to go shopping for sofas on weekends. Do I feel *bad* about it? Oh no – you see, I've always got laid for free so easily. I have no self-esteem issue. It's just, you know, more honest. No-one's pretending to be something they're not. Yes, I do think that's a problem. I see a lot of it. More and more, in fact. You'd be amazed; frankly, I'm amazed. (He gives the camera a knowing smile, better than Nina's.) I've discovered a lot of deception since I've been here. Not that I'm singling out Berlin, of course. Only in so far as it exemplifies everywhere. And it's easy to see here. Berlin has always been a city of façades, of reputations. Of fear through secrets. Where was I?

He *used* to get laid easily. But he had been surprised at the resistance Éva put up – he thought he'd seen interest. Perhaps he was losing it. Decline hit everyone sooner or later. Even eighty-five-year-old Texan billionaires.

Had Erich ever used a whore? He must remember to ask him. Funny the things brothers don't share.

'Aaargh!' Suddenly dragged from his reflections into excruciating ecstasy, he was winded; his heart beat wildly and there were tears in his eyes. At last he looked up at the girl, trying to focus. 'My God, that was effective. What the hell did you do?'

She winked. 'A trick they taught us at graduate school . . . I wanted to speed things up – you were taking too long – I've got other appointments.'

He was still biting his lip, bending forward to contain himself. 'You must tell me how it's done.'

She shook her head as she pulled her clothes back on and levered her knees back together, then put a hushed finger to her lips. 'Never share recipes. Golden rule.'

'You have rules too,' he murmured.

He thought she was leaving then, for she veered towards the front seat, but instead she stopped and pulled a small colour photo tacked to the outside of the glove compartment.

'What's this?'

'What?'

'I recognize this picture.' She screwed up her eyes and held the photo nearer. 'The girl in the McDonald's queue. I saw it in an exhibition. It was wonderful.' She stroked the paper between her fingers.

His body, after spasm, in a warm glue of relaxation, was beginning to petrify. He had not noticed the picture

170

stuck there last time he was in the car. But then, he didn't notice much on that journey.

'Did you go to the exhibition?'

'No.'

She wiped her mouth and settled, upright against the door, stroking her hands against her thighs. 'So why is this picture in your car?'

He quailed. 'I don't know.'

'I wish I could remember the artist.' She drummed long nails on the dashboard. She held the picture closer. 'I can't read it. Can you?'

He held the paper in front of his eyes without looking. 'No.'

'That exhibition really inspired me. So . . . negative. I use a lot of photography in *my* work.'

Warily: 'What do you mean, your work?'

She was combing her hair without mercy, ripping through knots. She looked at him. 'Yes, honey. Have you got a problem with that? I have two boys. Do you think I can afford the Bayern Munich strip every season selling art?'

With a mirror from the pocket of her jacket in one hand, she carefully reapplied lipstick with the other, mopping up the spread of the last application before colouring her mouth once again. She reached her hand to her head.

'No!' Max begged. 'Keep the wig on. I like it. It makes you look like Britney Spears.'

'Hey, do you mind! I have some professional pride.'

'Whaddya mean? I like Britney Spears. Everybody likes her. She beat Jesus in an international poll of inspirational figures.'

The girl yanked off the wig, revealing tousled stringy copper hair.

*

It is very easy to lose three hours in the early hours of the morning after the existential experience of banging an art-critic whore in a twenty-year-old car. At least, so it seemed to Max, who had little recollection when he walked through the doors of the café at seven a.m. of where he had been in the interim. At deserted traffic lights, he gazed at a hoarding on which advertisements for a Robin Williams film and cheap flights to Majorca fought for space, the papers flapping in the breeze. A couple kissed in the full light, her leg curled round his thigh. He heard a pair of American guys, big, one of them with a T-shirt with DDR written on it. There was a man, he thought, urinating against a tree. But this could have been any night. He had meditated on the whore's astonishing finishing technique; it went against everything he had believed about bought sex being less satisfying than the 'real' thing. The real thing? Whose definition was this? Shouldn't a society that deemed an expensive pair of trousers better than cheap ones believe that expensive, paid-for sex was best too? And he thought about Nina, who'd been, disarmingly, in his head throughout.

When he walked into the café, he must have looked rough, as even Barbara took pity on him. For once, she allowed him to make his own coffee, waving him through with her eyes closed. He passed by her to the machine with averted gaze and poured a handful of coffee for a double shot into the grinder. He enjoyed the noise. He poured cold milk into a small bowl, guided the wand slightly into the liquid and released the steam into it. At a variable point between ten and fifteen seconds, the milk is perfect. The moment after its peak it quickly declines. It must be watched constantly for the moment of perfection. The moment the eyes wander, the milk is spoiled.

This time Max stopped a fraction early. He was

nervous, trying too hard, not yielding to instinct. He sighed gently. This froth was not poetry but nor was it a disaster. With a spoon he lapped it into the coffee and carried the full cup to his seat.

He felt a sleep-deprived high, a red-rimmed ecstasy that suddenly anything was possible. Turning to the German paper, and finding nothing there, he felt strangely let down. 'Contrary to report, non-achiever not dead, insists Chancellor Schröder, who cut short his Tuscan holiday to handle the crisis.' But no, nothing.

Erich walked through from the back, clasping a bunch of papers. He sensed something and looked up at the spectre of Max. Erich's face crumpled in empathy. Max saw and was glad. When they were young and just for once Erich beat him at chess, Max would feign anger to seal his brother's pleasure. Sometimes he let him win.

Erich walked over, with a coffee in his hand. 'You look terrible. I take it you didn't sleep after last night.'

Max smiled. 'Well, it's a tad alarming to be announced dead on cable television, but, you know, if it helps the cause . . .'

Erich shook his head. 'I'm so sorry. Sometimes I can hardly believe she's my daughter. She's become so ruthless since she got successful. She'll use anyone. Well, you saw for yourself. We've all been through it, in one way or another. Don't let Nina get to you.'

'Like you don't, huh?'

Erich laughed. 'Well, obviously, the fact that we have virtually no relationship and she despises everything I stand for distresses me. But she's my daughter. She's nineteen. She's *meant* to hate me. But there's no need for you to suffer.'

'Nice of you to say so.'

Erich was already elsewhere. 'The real trouble is, Nina represents the future. If you want to make it in Berlin – as an artist, or, let's face it, in any way – then you need, what's the word . . . I don't know.' He swallowed coffee, closing his eyes to concentrate. 'Savvy, I suppose. Media savvy.'

Max raised his eyebrows. ' "Make it". I hate that phrase. It implies there's a finishing line you reach or you don't. It's so artificial and yet it's accepted as truth.'

Erich nodded. 'That's the way it's going. We all compromise, manipulate, misuse others. I'm stooping pretty low these days myself, I tell you.'

Max demurred. 'Have you ever used a prostitute?'

Erich barely took a breath. 'Listen, I've even asked Nina, my own daughter, to show up at the opening of the exhibition next week because I know it will attract some attention. With her as the bait, a few reporters and a paparazzo or two will show up. I'm using her notoriety. I've never done that before. You see, I've sunk to the lowest level. That's how bad things are.' Erich looked back at his brother. 'What did you say?'

XVI

I am not a myth.

MARLENE DIETRICH

When Nina was young, and Erich was painting, the girl used to watch her father at work. Erich remembered the feel of her hand on his neck. The warm, soft, slightly moist, childish hand was artlessly sensual.

Nina, with shiny dark hair and tight little features, would run up to customers and declaim proudly, 'Papa's a painter!' He would run after her and drag her away, apologizing, though he did not mind.

She used to love the café. It was a child's paradise with its waterfalls of chocolate and frothy milk. She liked to watch him make a cappuccino and he let her lick the top. Katrina, for reasons he never fathomed, did not approve, and so when she wasn't there Erich steamed the milk into froth especially for Nina – or was it for him, since he took pleasure in her pleasure, their shared wickedness, in watching the flash of her naughty eyes? She would hold the bowl in both hands and bend her face in and lick it and look up at him, knowing that he would be looking at her.

Nina sat on top of the bar, her legs dangling, socks round her ankles. He missed badly elasticated socks, or a time when Nina was not deliberate.

Nothing was unconscious now. Her hair still shone but in so many different colours. She was still sharply pretty. Her cheekbones, lips and nose cut precisely across her face. To these, she later added delicately angular breasts and pointing hips that gave her slim figure a feminine tang. She spoke more pointedly too. The childish acceptance of the world vanished. She no longer believed her father. She stopped drinking coffee.

He joked about it, because that is what fathers do. How funny, Nina on TV, arrested for you know what, with that web site of pornographic persiflage – should achieve fame and wealth unimagined because of it. How ironic. How like life, huh?

She did what was necessary. Reputations were ruined these days only by keeping quiet. Silence, once so big in Berlin, was out of favour. Erich could not conscionably wish the old days back, but a nagging inner voice said that his own life then, with the Wall intact and his daughter a child, was better. Since the Wall, the gallery's viability had slithered downwards. The state and tax subsidies, the competitive bolstering that poured money into Berlin from both East and West, drained away. The new investors wanted returns.

He had, at first, embraced change. This was what they fought for. What they wrote on the Wall: FREEDOM! BREAK DOWN THE BARRIER! But now it was gone he missed something solid to blame.

*   *   *

Ursula stood under the stairs, in the space that contained only a bureau. There was a small window into the dark backyard. The Berlin courtyard enclosed by towering six-storey buildings with identical winding staircases leading to flats, jewellery-makers, techno-artists, PR advisers.

The courtyard was concrete-paved. Inevitable bags of building materials in one corner gave the erroneous impression of work in progress. She listened to her own breathing and thought she heard a clock tick.

Then came the sound of footsteps as Barbara, reassuringly habitual, walked past the skulking Ursula, through the door and into the courtyard. She sat on a bag of sand and lit a cigarette. Barbara liked this first smoke of the morning, after the essential tasks.

Ursula sprinted into the bar, muscles taut. She screeched to a stop in front of Max and tapped him on the wrist. He looked up from his paper, puzzled, and, when he saw her face looming, would have shrieked, but for Ursula's cupped hand over his mouth. She felt the warmth of his breath; his dark eyes. She kept a chastening finger over her lips. 'Tonight?' she hissed.

'Wha—?'

'We were going to go out and talk.' She almost choked in urgency.

His voice rose in pitch. 'We were? Well, the truth is I didn't sleep that well last night.' The small pale face, the tiny nose, pale brown eyes and lips looked so sad, he could not cope. 'We did, huh?'

She nodded.

'Well, sure, then.' Easier just to say yes.

She began to breathe again. She took her hand away but she could still feel the impression of his lips. 'Don't tell Erich.'

Relief is a cruel pleasure because it obscures the worse torment that is to come. Max knew this and still he allowed himself to sink into his chair, nose skimming the coffee aroma, when Ursula had left.

'Mex!' The avuncular, confident tone was unfamiliar, but he turned cold. Professor Lucas Froniel was dressed in an expensive, slightly trendy suit. His short dark hair was flecked with grey. He was the guy in the ad, meeting good-looking colleagues with a firm handshake in empty airports, with a golden-haired daughter waiting at the end of the phone. Masculine, corporate sexy, in control, non-existent. 'Mex. We met the other day. I run the institute across the way. We talked about the commission of some pictures.'

'Oh.' Max frowned.

'May I?' He pulled out the chair opposite. 'I haven't long. I'm taking a thought-reprogramming class in half an hour.'

'Oh yes?'

'I'd be delighted if you'd like to come along to some of our sessions. I think it could help you. I don't know if you're aware of it, but your language pattern is very negative. The effect of this repetition of negative language on your psychological self is profound.'

'I think it's more that my psychological self has a profound effect on my language patterns.'

'Exactly! And that's where we can help.'

Max smiled. No matter what his problem, Froniel's treatment would be just the thing. You did not pay good money to be told there was nothing they could do.

'What is your professorship in?'

'Uh, sure. Geology.'

'A-ha.'

The man smiled broadly. 'There's a lot the human mind can learn from rocks, huh? Stoicism, weathering storms . . . My students love it, all that metaphorical nonsense. But seriously, Mex,' (overuse of the first name, a by-the-book trick to establish early intimacy) 'seriously, Mex, I've been working in the psychotherapeutic field for fifteen years. I went through therapy myself. That's how—' He looked at the clock above the bar. 'But still, save that, let's talk about the photos.'

Make the photos real, a given, so that, as Max hesitated, he was already letting the man down. Cunning.

'No, really. I'm here for a rest.'

Christ. Froniel was bringing out sketches on post-it notes. He was breathless. 'I'm thinking of women's heads. Gorgeous girls. All with their mouths open, talking, in fact. The beauty of communication – clever, hey?'

He was painting grand visions in the air with his fingers and Max was not hearing the words but watching the broad evangelical jaw, chomping through oxygen and spewing out bile. Max blinked. He was feeling light-headed. He had sunk in his seat and was about to cave in just to stop the torture, though he knew it would come back: 'Yes, yes, with luck, before we next meet either you or I will be dead—'

But then he was reprieved.

'Hey, Froniel!' Wielding a bright-red dishcloth, Éva was at the table. 'Leave him alone, can't you? Didn't you hear him? He doesn't want to do it. He's here for a rest.'

Only Froniel's slightly higher pitch betrayed a loss of nerve. 'But, Éva, I'm paying him for it. He's a photographer. What's wrong with asking? I'm a great fan of his.'

'Then have a little respect and shut up!'

He didn't. Rather, he set off again, pulling at Max's arm. With sudden violence Éva lashed the dishcloth across his face. Its wetness added force. Froniel leapt back, letting out an out-of-control, unmanly yelp of injured shock. His cry ricocheted around the room as people turned and stared.

The professor gingerly fingered the stung cheek. It was numb. He looked up at her in amazement. 'That's assault! Where's Erich?'

Hands on her hips, Éva was defiant. 'Call him. He knows what you're like.'

Froniel breathed stiffly and stood up with an aggressive scrape of his chair. 'I'm boycotting this café, *Fräulein*.'

'Oh, like that'll make a difference: three cappuccinos a week, right? Get lost.'

With an ineffectual slam of the door, he went.

'Thank you.' Max was flushed and felt exhausted. He stared in bewilderment at Éva, whose face was glowing with adrenalin.

He wanted to grasp and inhale her strength. Instead he tugged the cloth. At this tentative friendship, she closed her lips but her eyes were still smiling.

Statue: Friedrich II, 1851, restored 2000
Granite and marble

I'm back. After all the waiting, the frustration, the hopes, the tears, I'm sitting atop the old steed once more, my chiselled profile staring imperiously (how else, kids? It was their words, not mine) down Unter den Linden.

The media turnout for my return was fabulous. If the headline 'Fritz rides back!' makes me sound like a porn movie, part *zwei*, I don't object. Not after all those decades of being shunted from pillar to post. Surviving the Second World War unscathed only to have my arse unceremoniously kicked into some crappy little park in Potsdam. There's gratitude. Then, thirty years later, when Erich Honecker has a bit of a Prussian thing going, I am brought back and stuffed six metres up the road and expected to be pleased about it.

Finally, I'm back where I started – between the university and the opera house – and accorded due respect. Yeah. But you know the funny thing? I've lost the taste for it. Sure, all the bowing and scraping was cool at the time. I dare say I played up to it, waving that old stick and dressing in my three-cornered hat and military uniform. Can you blame me? The skirt really went for it.

But now, well, I've been dead way over two hundred years. Even by the end of my *life* I had lost interest and was living as a recluse with my dogs in Sanssouci. I let my kingly boots go dirty. (Why does everyone remember that?) So, how do you think I feel *now* about the daily knuckle fights of power? It bores me rigid. So they found cocaine in the Reichstag toilets. So, a bit of dodgy money passed into a few backhands. Yeah? Big deal. It's just not interesting, objectively. I should try to get a little perspective, if I were you. You're all going to die! Focus on the important stuff. Take me; I built the Brandenburg Gate, right? Stuck that damn winged chariot on the top to celebrate the unbeaten war record of the Prussians? Yeah, well, quite. Let it go, man. If I had my time again I'd see the dogs a lot more and clean my boots even less.

But here's the irony. All this, power, infamy, immortality, it means nothing to me now. But I still can't let go, because I'm even more afraid of the alternative. The abyss. I guess the survival instinct is in all of us and it gets a little out of hand.

I shudder when I think what happened to poor old Hindenburg. Never had a man worked so tirelessly for his country. Rightly was his statue twelve metres high, hewn from Russian alder and erected with glorious tribute in 1914.

I remember the opening day. I had a pretty good view from this height down to the Tiergarten. I saw the crowd all done up in barely afforded finery. Uniformed guards, standing beneficent with their hands behind their backs. Women stiff-faced under huge-brimmed hats piled high with flowers. Gloves sewn up for the occasion. Hordes of deferential little folk. Life doesn't come much sweeter.

The statue was monumental. Hindenburg's mighty moustache – that most Teutonic measure of stature – curled away from his nostrils with a flourish. A mighty staff he held rooted to the ground, by which the people might know that Germany's foothold was solid.

What happened to it? Nobody really knows. Times were desperate. No-one was looking. Rumour had it the stripped bare statue had been carted off to a warehouse.

Even the wooden steps inside were stolen for firewood. Hindenburg's head was found on a dump in 1938. Oh, the indignity! It makes me wobble.

I'm standing on this five-metre-high pedestal with a relief of female figures – representing wisdom, moderation, justice and strength – under my feet. Well, I tell you, they don't bring me much relief. Not the way I like it. I'm looking down the most picturesque street in the world, watching skirt lengths rise one year, fall the next, witnessing perpetual change while I stand still, but it doesn't make me feel any less temporary. I won't last. Fifty years I give myself, a hundred, tops. That might seem a fair old whack to you, and probably it is, given your chances of survival in this dangerous world, but let me share with you the benefit of some of that wisdom: the years skip by a lot faster after your second century. And you just can't enjoy them.

XVII

Night! *Tauentzien*! Cocaine!
That is Berlin!

Song from Tauentzienstrasse, centre of Russian
cabaret, 1920s
Cited by Andrei Bely: *How beautiful it is in Berlin*, 1924

He waited for her, as she had told him to, in the gallery,
knowing she would be ten minutes late.

On a shelf on the back wall was an A3 bound file. The
laminated pages held black-and-white photos – elegiac
prints of Berlin buildings, knocked down, it said, since
the Wall. A lifeless high-rise, a hundred tiny windows
trapped in concrete; a railway signal box, rusting, sprout-
ing weeds from all sides; a warehouse that once housed
hospital equipment, a flat-roofed eyesore. Ugly in life,
monochrome gave these buildings faces like Forties Hollywood publicity shots. No pore marks. No pigeon shit.

Seeing angles struck heavy with Fritz Lang cool, Max
felt a stab of sadness for the lost Berlin. Fictional Berlin,
a grainy image between Wim Wenders and John Le
Carré.

This was the catalogue of a previous exhibition. A
fluorescent orange sticker next to a picture denoted a

sale. He found the sales interesting. What governed the decision? Buyers needed to believe they had made a personal and intelligent choice but Max believed all these pictures were the same.

He imagined that, once settled on the 'favourite', a mind justified its choice by bestowing the picture with false meaning to maintain the illusion that it was special from the start; that it was somehow reminiscent of Venice at sunset, or evoked the smell of peaches or one's first successful copulation with a woman more good-looking than oneself. Conviction was a sign of ignorance. He was no longer a Catholic.

Max liked to play this game. A picture editor wanted artfully crossed bare legs for a (frequently German) Sunday supplement women's health special. She demanded twenty rolls of snapped legs. On receipt, the editor then spent hours choosing. Discerning infinitesimal differences, staring at each frame through an ovoid lupe. Max would come into the office to discuss. Finally she found the perfect pair. She trusted him to tell the art desk and he took pleasure in betraying her, passing on not her choice but one of her early rejections. No-one ever noticed.

This game could not survive the digital revolution, where human flaws of both photographer and model could be removed by science. Thank God he quit.

His skin crawled at the touch of her hand on his shoulder.

'Don't tell me I took you by surprise this time.'

*　　*　　*

It was raining. He held the umbrella like a regular Forties hero, while Ursula clung to him. The sound of traffic in the wet was welcome. She had long made him nervous.

That night five years ago, after Erich threw a brick through the gallery window, Max did not sleep. He heard a loud slam. He sat up and looked into the darkness. He could make out that his door was open, though he remembered closing it. He got up and padded a few steps towards the dim light. He saw Ursula, in the kitchen, dressed in a thin shirt. It was unbuttoned and she held the garment together near her navel with one finger.

She was fetching a glass of water, she explained. Then she made herbal tea while he waited. It helped her to sleep. She wouldn't normally bother, but since there were two of them . . . She urged him to join her. Refusal was difficult.

He took the tea, said something pointless and tried to return. She blocked his path. She was going to the studio, she said; she found the smell of the materials calming. When he did not join her, her disappointment was tangible. The air cooled.

He did not speak of it afterwards, not to Ursula, not to anyone. Perhaps Erich had a right to know, but why cause trouble over mere suspicion? He was not surprised that they later split up. When was he ever? It was good that they stayed amicable. It showed an ability to address failure that Max lacked. Maria left the same evening; he did not expect or want to hear from her again. And there were others, too. He let them go. It was easy.

The rain strengthened the scent of Ursula's perfume. A fresh light fragrance, though he liked perfume only because of the woman who wore it, never the other way round.

She walked in step with him.

'You'll love this place.' What would he love? If *he* didn't know, how did she? She hesitated but her voice was bold. 'It normally plays world music – mainly South American bands. They're very big here at the moment.'

'What's on tonight?'

'I'm not sure. I meant to get a *Zitty*, but . . . I didn't,' she finished lamely.

He liked Ursula. She had an appreciative (though rarely generative) sense of humour. She was attractive in a rather tired way and it would not be the first time he had slept with a woman because it was easier than not – but the problem was Ursula was not going to disappear afterwards.

'Where is it?'

'Prenzlauer Berg.'

His mind was scanning its patchwork map of the city.

She prompted him. 'This place is meant to be for the East what the A Trane is to the West.'

'Oh, yes, you said. What does that mean?'

'Uh, I don't know – cool jazz spot, I guess.' She spoke the words slowly, with pleasure. '"A smoky dive". That's what people say.' She turned her head with a flashing smile and the thin straight bob followed her.

'And what do you think?'

Hesitation. 'Well, I've never actually been.'

'Ah.' He smiled and looked at her sideways.

She cleared her throat. 'It's difficult with a child and the café. I don't get time. You get out of the habit.'

'Oh, sure, sure.'

She bit her lip.

The tram stopped at Senefelderplatz, next to the Jewish cemetery. She mentioned it and Max wanted to look. She trotted to keep up. He held onto the iron bars and stared into broken tombstones thrust back into the ground after the war.

'The jazz place is further along, on the other side of the road.' Ursula shivered.

They were walking for some minutes, with the rain throwing mud on their ankles.

Ursula's voice was almost swept away. 'This place is really great. Apparently a lot of music-scene people go.'

The street was wide and empty. A taxi driver bought cigarettes at a kiosk and returned to his cream cab, throwing them a university-of-life-has-taught-me-better-than-that sneer at their soggy enterprise. Max looked at the taxi's warm interior wistfully as it sped away with a splash of wet rubber.

'What number?'

Ursula pulled out a ripped page of the listings magazine, sodden at the edge.

'A hundred and thirty-five.'

Max held his hand over his eyes as he surveyed the building. 'This is a hundred and fifty-one. We've come too far.'

'But I didn't see anything likely, did you?'

Max didn't answer but he was backtracking, past stony-faced fronts. Ursula stood motionless, getting wetter. He shouted back: 'This is number one three seven.'

She ran towards him, splashing miserably, calling through the wind, 'So what's next door?'

He strained his neck. 'Uh, it's a kebab house.' He couldn't laugh for her tragic face.

'But look,' she said desperately, 'it says number one three five.'

'Well, maybe the jazz is in the back somewhere.'

The entrance was wide enough for two people, but unlit and crowded with bicycles, bins with bursting lids and the escaping stench of rubbish. They tottered over the uneven ground to the yard, which was dripping and dark, and surrounded by spattered black windows. Ursula heard the rain against the plastic dustbins.

'I can't believe this.'

'The best places are the hardest to find,' Max said staunchly. 'This must be just great.'

188

They walked back more slowly; past the entrance to the *U-Bahn* and beyond, past a café with life-size fluorescent cows hanging from the outside wall. Past shop windows gleaming with bottles of olive oil and champagne truffle vinegar. The regeneration of the East.

Ursula clamped her jaw grimly. They looked through the window of one empty bar. Inside were orange walls and metallic tables. Max looked hopeful.

She shook her head. 'There's no-one inside and no music.'

'Nice place, though.'

She looked at him incredulously. 'Katrina designed it. They *all* look like that.'

They stood now at the corner of a large square. Houses and bars surrounded the bushy green in the middle.

'Kollwitz Platz,' said Max slowly, reading a sign way above his head.

'Käthe Kollwitz's statue,' muttered Ursula, hooking her wet face towards an iron mound as they traipsed through the sodden grass. A huge bulk of dark stone had a head of a woman on top. Sad eyes stared bleakly out of a broad face.

Max stopped. 'She did all those miserable pictures of starving children in Berlin backyards, right?'

Ursula spoke monotonously through the rain. 'Kollwitz lost her son in the First World War. She left satire to the others. She said she didn't find life funny.'

They rejected several bars on the other side of the square. One promised jazz on the window, but inside there was only one man, who sat next to a bare wall. The piano lid was up but no-one played. It was the emptiest city. Something about Berlin was all dressed up with nowhere to go.

'It always seems to be raining in her pictures,' Ursula said. 'Across people's faces.'

As their steps grew wetter and heavier, the point came when unspoken agreement pushed them into the next open bar simply because it was dry.

The sudden glare of tropical neon was dazzling. On the walls, bleached-out girls on white beaches sucked fruit cocktails through straws. Sunshine pop assailed their ears.

'Oh, but this is fantastic,' Max breathed.

Ursula looked up at him through her dripping hair. 'I think I preferred the kebab shop.'

Max laughed. He found Ursula funnier when she was miserable.

The underground jazz crowd was as elusive as ever. Instead a group of boisterous Australian business-men toasted the end of a trip, blasting endless sagas of drunken antics past, all involving an outrageous absent character called 'Jiff'.

The women on the wall peeped over their sunglasses and let the breeze blow open their sarongs. Painted legs towered flawless above the tables.

Ursula prayed that her make-up had washed away completely and was not running now in patches down her face. She looked at the beach scene. This was her city yet she was a foreigner in the East.

They were still two places. The East, cooler, rawer, more elusive. The West, wealthier, older, with less tension, the Mövenpick restaurant and the crowded sleaze of a Western city centre. Where the art shops were full of rich oil reproductions and drunks leered at fat middle-aged women in mink hats. The West, where you catch an Andrew Lloyd Webber musical and buy American sweatshirts proclaiming 'I love Berlin!'

'I'll have the Hemingway special,' said Max cheerfully to a yawning barman in a Hawaiian shirt. 'What about you, Ursula?'

Her menu lay untouched on the table. She inhaled in the affirmative, then looked down. 'I'm very, very sorry. And embarrassed. I wanted you to see something German and modern.'

Max shrugged. 'What the hell. This is better. It's symbolic. You know, the city changing day by day. Blink and you'll miss it. It's perfect that you and I should end up in a cheap tropico-Cuban theme bar. How fast changing could the place be if a single mother who never goes out and a layabout foreigner could find the hottest spot in town?'

She sniffed heavily and tried to push a clump of sodden hair behind her ear, but it slapped back across her face. 'I hear it happens a lot. Places closing before you even know they're open. And that kebab shop did look new.'

'Yes.' He pulled his chair in. 'The sign was gleaming. There was no scum on the tiles. I think you could even have eaten there.'

She smiled weakly. Her skin felt soft to the back of her hand.

'Maybe,' he said brightly – farce broke the tension – 'the kebab shop did jazz in a dark room out back.'

'That's not what happens in the dark rooms out back Chad tells me about.'

He laughed again.

The barman scrawled the prices of their drinks in a teetering line on a beer mat, to be totalled at the end of the evening. The German system of trust brings out the honest in people.

'So-o . . .' Her word staled. A drip of rainwater trickled down her steaming neck and evaporated on her chest.

It was easier from a distance. His wet form sat across the table from her. He was looking straight at her – an action somehow less intimate than avoiding her gaze.

There was so much she wanted to say, it was a struggle to open her mouth.

She swallowed. 'Are you enjoying Berlin? I mean, do you miss London?'

'No.'

She didn't know if this answer applied to both questions. 'I'm sorry we never visited you in London.' She coloured. 'Sorry, that sounds like you're never going back. I didn't mean, I just assumed, well, I don't really know what I assumed. I . . .' Her words tapered off.

'That's all right. I may not go back. One day my bank account will drain away. I'll have to sort that out some time, but not for a few months.' He sipped and put his glass down. Sweet, sickly. He could not taste alcohol; it must be deadly.

'Did it bother you about Nina – on the TV last night, I mean?'

'Yes.'

'She's very young. She thinks she knows everything.'

'Yeah, I know.'

'Not that I'm standing up for her. I can't abide her. Other people's adolescent children . . . God.'

'Otto will be an adolescent one day.'

'I don't think so. Otto's about thirty-five already, a far superior specimen, and I'm not just saying that because he's mine.'

'Yes, you are.'

'No.' She laughed. 'I'm really not. I know everybody says that, but Otto's so mature. He's more grown-up than I am. He looks after me. I was dating this guy, a violinist at the Philharmonic – well, a reserve, it turned out. Still, he was gorgeous. Very intense. Russian. Deep voice, wild hair.'

'Good.'

'Mm. That's what I thought. But Otto hated him.

Wouldn't even shake his hand. The next week I found out Vlad was still seeing the second oboeist. Now, how many eight-year-olds would you expect to have that kind of insight? The rest of his class is reading Harry Potter; Otto's reading Nietzsche.'

'That must make him popular.'

'Oh, Otto gets on much better in adult company.'

'I can imagine. The kids probably spit on him.'

'Max!'

'Well, I should think it's true. The only thing you can hope for at his age is to fit in.'

'He's very well adjusted. He's wise. I've learned so much from him. He knows the secret of happiness.'

'Not from reading Nietzsche, he doesn't.'

She looked steadfastly at Max. 'You're so sarcastic.'

He held his breath. 'You want me to ask what the secret of happiness is?'

'Very insightful.'

'Go on, then, Ursula. What's the secret of happiness according to an eight-year-old nihilist?'

She looked at him intently over her cocktail umbrella. 'Keeping busy, routine, repetitive tasks . . . you don't have to think.'

'So Erich's happy?'

She looked at him, trying to see where he was leading. 'Yes, I believe he is. And as long as he has stuff to organize, he will be.'

'And what keeps Otto busy?'

'His music, the freedom we give him, his intellectual curiosity.'

'And you're happy?'

'Y-es,' she hesitated. 'I work very hard. I have no time to worry about it.'

'A-ha.'

She drained her glass. 'You don't believe me, do you?'

He looked at her. 'Not really.'

She looked away to order another drink. Sucked on her straw, taking gulps, filling time.

Max was changed this evening. There was an edge to him that she had not seen before. It scared her. She could not articulate, but produced conversation that, as a girl, listening to her parents entertaining downstairs, she would make for her own phantom guests.

After sipping his drink Max said, 'If someone pointed a gun at Nina and said, "Die now and be Germany's biggest artist of the twenty-first century," do you think she'd agree? How much of a celebrity whore is she?'

'Have you got a gun?' drawled Ursula, her chin now sunk almost into her drink.

Max laughed.

Encouraged, Ursula ventured: 'Nina is unbearable, you know. Even now that she's hardly around. She makes Erich so sour.' She waved a shaky finger at the barman. 'I'll try the Cabana Cup.'

'Eternal fame for the small price of untimely death . . . If she hesitated, they could throw in a full-size statue in a square of her choice.'

'Hasn't this city got enough statues?' Ursula could see, or imagine she saw, the Käthe Kollwitz bronze, buffeted by the wind and rain. The normally pitying stony face condemned.

Max's voice was flat. 'By the way, did Erich ever tell you I was born the night the Wall went up?'

She looked at him. 'Yeah, sure he did. Why, wass wrong with that?'

'It was a complete fabrication. He made the whole thing up.'

'Oh.' And, probably because she was nearly drunk already, she laughed. A sniffling giggle, that annoyed him.

'Why would he do that?' Max's voice was insistent, even aggressive, incited by her feeble response.

She smiled. 'He lives in a fantasy world.'

Max nodded.

'Like all of us.' She drank some more. 'Max, listen. I've got something to confess.'

His jaw tensed. 'What's that, then?'

'Erich thinks you and I slept together . . . four times.'

Max's face wrinkled. 'Why would he think that?'

She took a deep breath. 'Because I told him. When you came to visit last. You know, when I met you in the kitchen . . .'

'I remember.'

She added in a coaxing tone, touching his arm, 'I told him you were great . . .'

Max pulled away. 'I don't believe this.'

She looked down like a child. 'Sorry.'

He breathed again, released his muscles. 'Yeah.' He waited for her to say something. Something pertinent.

'I'm going to the loo,' she said, touching him again. 'OK?' She dragged her leaden body from the stool and walked away.

Alone, Max fiddled with the edge of the beer mat, on which the line of prices now tottered precariously under its own weight. He didn't get angry; maybe that was a problem. He felt a familiar freeze inside and stared at the two-dimensional women on the wall.

And then he followed her. Across the restaurant, through the door at the back, past the telephone and the stand of free postcards selling clubs, drink and TV. He pushed against the door of the women's toilets. It fell against the inside wall with a loud bang.

She was standing, gripped to a basin, gasping. She noticed his face in the mirror and looked up. 'Max!'

He was not shouting, but it was still shocking, because

195

he never raised his voice. 'Why does everyone make up all this crap about me?'

'I don't know,' she whimpered. 'Maybe we all need something to believe in.'

'But nobody here knows me! Nina doesn't know me. You don't know me. Erich barely knows me.'

'I'm sorry.'

He grabbed her. She was trembling.

'Max!'

He started pulling at her clothes. 'Come on, then. Since you've wanted to so long, why don't you see what it's really like, what a letdown I can be. Come on.'

'I don't know!' She was breathless as his hands felt her skin, moved from the small soft breasts, across the curve of her waist and to her small, dimpled buttocks. His hands were warm and her skin was cold. She was bent backwards over the basin. Feeling the taps digging into her back, she winced, and he stopped momentarily when he saw the pain on her face.

He dragged her across the small space and held her against the tampon machine. She stood placid while he fucked her. Ashamed because she was excited. And though this was never what she dreamed of, it felt like a dream.

They were silent and she didn't know whether she was enjoying it or hating herself. Any decent, self-respecting woman would have slapped his face and stormed out. He would have let her go.

But he too was ambiguous. What other bastard in this scenario would stop to stock up from the condom machine? He was banging away at her but she was aware that he was checking all the while that he had not gone too far. His aggression was half-hearted.

The rain pelted the skylight. She looked down at the ground, her arms folded, embarrassed as he withdrew.

'Maybe I should fuck Erich and Nina while I'm here,' he muttered, straightening his clothes. 'Do you think that would work? And Chad too? He's told me he's ready.' He washed his hands.

She let out a sort of laughing sob. 'Chad always is.'

He turned his back on her and felt for the door.

She stretched out her hand. 'Max! Don't go. Not just like that.'

He hesitated, his head bent.

'Come on, Max, you're not just going to walk away, are you?' He didn't say anything for a while. She was perched on the basin, trembling. 'Please, Max.'

And slowly he turned round and she saw the misery in his face. 'I'm sorry,' he said. 'We— I shouldn't have done that.'

XVIII

The 'New' museum was closed after the war. It stayed a wreck during the DDR, a palatial nineteenth-century shell. Ten years after the Wall came down, it was opened up to house an exhibition of Berlin architecture. The rooms simply had grey panels tacked over the old walls. Leaving much ghostly evidence of the old museum underneath. Faded arrows pointed to long-disappeared Babylonian rooms. That is Berlin. Plasters over the wounds.

ELSE BLANKEMAIER, Berlin artist, 2000

Sunday morning was the busiest of the week. Groups met for leisurely discussion over coffee. Filling up on rye rolls, sunflower rolls, multi-grain crackers, wheat toast, black bread, sliced fruit, freshly squeezed juices, *Sekt*, muesli, bio-yoghurt, herb quark, rich fruit jams and translucent honey, hams, and eggs, soft-boiled in a glass, scrambled, cooked as an omelette, or fried in a glistening trio.

For impact, Barbara waited until two, when the rush was over. By then Max, who had struggled in late looking dreadful, had loped back upstairs to lie down and she and Éva were sitting in the yard, smoking cigarettes. Barbara spoke confidentially, low, as if she was merely confirming

Éva's suspicion. 'You know about last night, why Max looked so rough this morning, don't you?'

Éva took the cigarette out of her mouth, sifting through her mind, and raised her eyebrows.

Barbara butted the air with her head. 'Ursula and Max.'

Éva released smoke through puckered lips. Her back straightened. 'How do you know?'

'She can't keep anything from me.' Barbara smiled, her voice enjoying the words. 'Last night in a toilet.'

'Really?' This single word was not quite a question, not quite an expression of outrage, nor fully a noise reflecting the salacious nature of the information she had received: it fell somewhere between them all. Éva let out a half-laugh and looked down at her coffee. 'God help him.'

Barbara watched the girl's face for chips in the marble. If she could not find pleasure for herself, she could at least enjoy misery in others. But Éva showed no suffering.

Only when they were back in the now almost empty café did Éva speak again. 'Was Max really so great an artist?'

Barbara smiled. She walked to the bureau in the dark hallway, behind the stairs. From the middle shelf, she pulled out a large black scrapbook. She beckoned to Éva. 'Here, honey, look. Brandt brothers, early works.'

Éva took the book from her, walked into the light and opened it. The book was ring-bound, holding grey pages, rough to the touch. Glued to them were white sheets of paper covered in children's drawings: pages of early struggles with animals and buildings; a lorry, with the wheels contorted like dislocated ankles, travelling up a vertical road lined with lollipop trees to the top of the page; a two-legged horse. A one-eyed rider, one arm twice as long as the other, grasped string reins. His upper body was taller than the horse. The clouds ruffled his hair. The sun, with thick yellow deck-chair stripes, hung below a narrow strip of blue sky.

Then the pictures changed. A rabbit's skull in pencil. The object was turned slightly so that the jaw faced to the right of the page. By its side was a shiny iron hammer. The two objects lay on top of a cloth-covered table. The texture was created with tiny woven lines. The perspective was almost perfect. Almost, but even the slight skewering gave the picture a menace that could have been deliberate. The eye sockets were hollow to the back of its skull.

She could hear Barbara's impatient breathing behind her, grating her attention. Barbara said, 'They were the same age when they made those pictures. Can you guess who did which?' She put an index finger up against her lip in a gesture of mock cluelessness. Éva didn't answer. She started towards the kitchen. Barbara grasped the side of her arm. 'Don't take it away. You don't want Erich to catch you with it.' Éva obeyed and went back to the bureau, from which she retrieved another book.

The pictures had developed. The first hand drew more adept horses and trucks. Perspective was applied rigidly. The orthogonal lines of the roads converged into rule-book vanishing points. Painstaking effort yielded slow progress. The other hand had only two pieces, she discovered, in this whole book. Darker, alarming juxtapositions, dream-like visions that resisted dissection. Black and grey. They looked abstract yet she saw things in them. She closed the book quickly and sniffed.

She walked back into the café, where Barbara rested on a stool. Éva spoke. 'How did you know about those books?'

Barbara's voice was casual. 'Ursula showed me.'

'Why?'

Barbara smiled. 'There have to be some perks to my

working such long hours.' She clicked off to clear a table, her breasts bouncing self-righteously.

* * *

When Ursula had first woken up, she had forgotten. Then she felt the weight in the bed. There had never been a solid form in the morning. In her fantasy, after the conjoining the man melted into liquid form and flowed out of the door.

She blinked and swallowed. Her stomach heaved. She grasped her watch from the bedside table. Ten o'clock. Oh God. Class to teach.

She stumbled out. Her efforts not to wake him magnified every footfall. She tripped on the lamp flex, landing heavily on her ankle, and stifled a gasp of pain. Max groaned, but did not seem to wake. As he rolled over, she felt a rent inside her; whether it was caused by him or the drink, she did not know.

For a few seconds she stood still in fear, a raised pulse at the side of her head, her dry mouth open. She looked at the lump of Max in the bed and felt a nauseating panic. What now?

Ursula was not such a fool as to think that anything would come of this. She could not even say that she would want it to. In the morning, grey light showing cracks in his face, Max looked distinctly, unappealingly human.

If she had been fascinated by Max it was because Erich told her to be. Erich believed it more than anyone. He had always been both resentful and desperate for Max's success.

The first time she met Erich, he talked about Max. Nearly eight years ago, at the private viewing of one of her former pupils and one of his former deck-hands. She had gravitated towards Erich as the only normal person in a room full of funeral-parlour employees. (The art world still divided into the 'ares' and the 'are-nots': the 'people in black' who dictated terms, what was good and what was mere amateur scratching, and then the lesser beings whose lowly status was compensated by a freedom to wear any colour they pleased.) Besides, Ursula needed someone to hide behind while she poured her pink fruit beer into a plant.

He was funny and self-effacing. Moreover, he seemed prepared to go to any length to assist her waste-disposal needs. It was right that she had asked him, he told her, with only a slight smile. For he had, years ago, spent an adolescent summer as a dustman, in the macho days when real men still hoisted the huge bins onto their bare broad backs and warned their colleagues of impending trouble by shouting 'Shit *hole*!' in front of slut houses with dirty nappies, untied, brown side up, piled in the front gardens. Why hadn't he stuck with that profession? she asked him with a glimmering smile he could not fail to notice. Oh, he said, the profession lost its soul when they introduced those wheelie bins to reduce back injuries. She was anxious to seem witty. Don't you mean backbone? He smiled appreciatively. Perhaps. The thrill had gone. Besides, he moved back to Berlin, where he didn't like the uniforms. Too orange.

Funny: she had finally nailed Max and all she was thinking about was Erich. But *Erich* always thought of Max. From that first time they met: 'Did you see those pictures of Lise Weiss in *Stern*? The black-and-white ones? They were taken by my younger brother. They won some Spanish award.' In some way it compensated for his own disappointment. Erich, more than anyone, was in love with Max.

In the dark hallway, as she loaded materials for the

class into the large leather bag, she could not guess how Max would react. It was another of his talents. For a moment she felt responsible; Max was in a weak state. Fuck it. How tough was it for a man to have sex?

Yes, she sighed, then straightened her hair in the mirror and tilted her face to examine the lines. Yes, it was humiliating. As she exhaled, there was pain in her side. Appendicitis! In hospital, people would bring her flowers and feel sorry. She sighed again, more heavily. Max could afford to be ill.

With masochistic flourish, she pictured in her future a trail of similar humiliations, more sordid and less pleasurable as life went on. Until, at last, only age saved her from herself. When men stopped succumbing to the easy lay and she, like an actress, had pulled off her last face-lift.

She must pretend last night had never happened. Rescue a little dignity. Surprise him with her indifference. It would surprise her too.

She remembered reading in a magazine (for thin women with beautiful children, offshore investments and perfect teeth) a piece in which famous, thin, beautiful women revealed their most embarrassing moments. The article nestled between lower-leg exercises for long-haul flights and the rise of the live-in housekeeper among the middle classes. The ensuing list of celebrity catastrophe – the broken heels, the flashes of accidental (but exquisitely toned) nudity – didn't strike Ursula as all that hideous compared with her own. Yet the message was clear: a real woman transcends disaster. She smiles, laughs a little, waves away the flies and moves on. It was so loathsomely girlish to assume that *she* was humiliated. They had both succumbed. Perhaps it was she who patronized *him*.

By the door, Ursula looked back to her bedroom and the body in the bed. She belched and was hit by a malodorous return of the Cabana Cup. She'd get some breakfast at the café en route to work. For once she looked forward to distraction. For two hours she could take comfort in the problems of drawing citrus fruit. The tonal contrast, flat and form-hugging curved lines, how to blur the linear edges, which in reality do not exist. She could reveal that cobalt blue, with its warmer mixture than Prussian, produces riper fruit. Walking round the class, she would think that it was a pity human interaction could not be predicted so accurately as colour theory.

*   *   *

The moment the front door shut, Max opened his eyes. Let out a low moan. Yet he wished the hangover worse to leave him incapable of thought. The value of crises: everything else becomes trivial, temporarily forgotten.

It was of some consolation that Ursula had left without speaking, that there was no loaded morning kiss. Some consolation but not enough. The regret was directed towards his brother. He pushed it away but it returned, simmered and swelled.

Strangely, of all his brother's women, Katrina was the most tempting. Katrina, the perfect Darwinian, thrived on change. She had no intransigent beliefs, no awkward little moral stances that got in the way of her progress through decades and changing political climates. When it was useful, Katrina was a hippie. Now she was a thrusting entrepreneur. Max appreciated her honest hypocrisy. She was not a bad person, just a realistic one.

He wanted coffee. Please let it not be Barbara this morning, scraping crumbs off the tables so hard, as if they lay around on purpose. Let it be Éva standing at the bar, her fingers wrapped round the handle of the coffee tamp, the power of relief in her hand. Éva would not speak. He would mouth his request and she would read his lips. He felt the creamy balm coating his tongue, the bitter panacea travelling down his throat, its curative vapours steaming up to his distended brain.

*　　*　　*

Erich had laughed. Ursula hated jazz. Particularly modern, experimental jazz. It made her jump. When they were together, she vetoed any evening involving trumpets. He understood what Barbara meant him to know.

En route to Marlene, Erich sometimes chose to walk along Auguststrasse. He passed the yard with an art gallery and café, built on two four-metre-wide glass cubes, one roof transparent, one opaque. Once this was a margarine factory, employing people raised to expect permanence, raised with the Wall, who knew nothing else and afterwards joined hapless attempts to block parts up again. To keep the old life.

Now the area was injected with an air of artistic anarchy, which ran down arterial roads that led to small theatres, workshops, hip bars of glass and metal, their windows decorated with live fish. Further on, black, imperious graffiti read: ' "Out of the crooked timber of humanity no straight thing can ever be made" – Immanuel Kant.' Someone else had added: 'Eat more bortsch!'

*　　*　　*

Nothing happened. The more she rubbed and teased and nuzzled, the more ridiculous he felt. Him sitting there, massaging his aching temples, her, on her knees. His skin was ghostly white in the darkness, gleaming next to the pile of trouser round his ankle. An old woman in a three-piece suit groping on the floor. What if there *was* an afterlife and his parents were watching? His mother thought oral sex was blasphemy and, son or no, she would tell God.

Marlene relaxed on the floor beside his chair, lit a cigarette and said casually, 'I had an affair with my sister's husband.'

'What?'

She smiled. 'Poor man! They'd not slept in the same bed for five years. He was desperate. Men have needs, you know.'

He hated her medieval aphorisms. By implication, he was included. 'Did your sister find out?'

'Not until much later. After he was dead.'

'Did you tell her?'

'No!' She drew back, shocked. 'She came across some letters. He should have destroyed them but he was never very bright.'

'And what was her reaction?'

'She didn't want to see me again.'

'Oh dear.' Erich was only partially engaged. He was staring away from her, into the shadows. The wood-grain floor: its pattern seemed to fall into the features of his brother. Max looked ill. Sat in bed, resting on one elbow, his chin down, skeletal.

Marlene waved her cigarette hand. The smoke trails lit up a swarm of floating dust particles. 'Oh, I wasn't bothered. She was twenty-five years older than I was anyway. I'd hated her for years. Since we discovered she'd been an orderly at Belsen. She told *us* she was a military nurse. Her idiot of a husband let the secret slip. He was desperate for my reassurance. Etta'd been with a Nazi lover and she told him they were great lovers.'

'Really? I heard the opposite.'

'Well, quite! And that's what I told him. Not that I wanted to make him feel better, but I couldn't let a travesty like that stand. "No, Norbert," I told him, as he lay in my bed, covering what he had tearfully dismissed as pitiful privates with a sheet, "it works the other way around. Those anaemic blonds have party sausages, two-inch weanies like the ones you enjoyed in your pea soup, in the revolving restaurant at the top of the media tower" (he hadn't much imagination). "You want good – I never screwed a Turk who didn't leave me gasping for air. It's a cliché because it's true. You go to the sauna," I said, "take a look for yourself." But he never would. He had a complex about it and it was all her fault.'

'How many Turks have you screwed?'

She put a finger to her lips.

'Where is your sister now?'

Marlene shrugged. 'Mouldering in a geriatric home, I believe. Blocking her arteries with afternoon *Kuchen* and slowly forgetting the rules of *Skat*.'

'Why haven't you mentioned all this before?'

'It's hardly something to be proud of. Pass us the schnapps, would you?'

Erich was silent, examining his fingers.

'Oh . . .' she nodded knowingly, 'I'm sorry. I shouldn't have said all that about male inadequacy.'

Erich laughed dryly. 'Marlene, with what's going through my head, it'd be strange if I was functioning normally.'

She looked at him. 'Maybe you *should* talk to him.'

'Max doesn't talk. We don't talk. You just said yourself you would never have talked to your sister if it hadn't been forced on you.'

Marlene eyed him blithely. 'Yes, but, darling, I didn't give a damn.' She stared too into the darkness and in the wood grain saw herself. Young, upright, singing, more beautiful than ever.

'He's always been withdrawn. When he was younger he couldn't hide it so well. I don't know, he was too clever and the other kids resented him and they were scared too. He asked weird questions. He became very disruptive, especially when he was bored, which was most of the time. The teachers hated him because he undermined them. When he was eleven, the school said he should see an educational psychologist. I don't think it did him any good, except he learned one lesson: to keep himself out of trouble if he wanted to be left alone. No-one told me what happened, naturally. I looked in my parents' filing cabinet.'

'You naughty boy.'

Erich smiled. 'They trusted me.'

Marlene lit another cigarette. 'What did it say?'

'She described him as intellectually and emotionally isolated. She said, "He fears he is not normal but nor does he want to be."'

Marlene smiled back at him. 'So he's stuck really?'

'Yeah.' Erich looked up. 'But of course when I read that I wanted to be him more than ever.'

XIX

The Memoirs of Gerte Mela (III)

Stefan Zweig called our world 'rotten, greasy like the polish on old furniture'. This I painted, oh, so much, in those euphoric days when I first found my calling – to paint the poverty and ironies of Berlin, where the caviar-scented thoroughfares lay next to tenements in which eight shared a bed.

I did not need sleep. I left Poltonov's in the morning, my head burning with the images of the night. He found space for me to work in the studio of a friend of his. I looked from the skylight onto ragged children playing with mud and stones. I worked on two, sometimes three, pictures a day. My frenzy came from an internal belief that these dark scenes, like a dream, if not pinned down, captured, would soon fade.

They were happy, those months before I realized that I did not have the creative power to reproduce my visions on paper. That dismal frustration soon came. Let me enjoy, while it lasts, the memory of hope.

Raskolnikov's nose sought out decay. One morning we passed the back door of a popular hotel dancing establishment. I could never go in the front, where the wails of the

'Black Bottom' echoed onto the street. A place where respectable middle-aged women took tea and often one of the 'dancers' home with them.

The back, where the bins stood and the staff came and went in the polished uniforms – the only good clothes they owned – was a dowdy grey square, richly redolent of bad cabbage. The back door led straight into the kitchens.

I could not see far inside but the best view was through an air vent, to the left. I clambered on the top of the giant bin and peered through the tiny slats. My eyes adjusted and I was looking into the yellow larder. All I could see was a huge bowl of fruit. It burst with ripeness but, from the underneath, a blue fur crept. The surface of plump pears and apricots, of violet grapes, was false. The fruit was rotten.

This image of waste moved me. I knew that when the kitchen staff arrived, with the sun already piercing those narrow slats and eating at the fragile skin, they would have to throw this feast into the bins. By then, flies would have found the apples' sweet decay. The grapes would have spread together, shedding their skins in morbid warmth.

Max put the pages of the memoir down beside him on the table and picked up the small notebook. The pen felt strange in his fingers. 'I am reminded of a picture Ursula showed me of a bowl of decaying fruit. She said it was her favourite. At the time I wasn't sure but after last night I think I understand. Do I also seek empathy in words and pictures, because there is no human being? Why else am I reading? Finding personal meaning, interconnection, in a text that has nothing to do with me?'

Around the Gedächtniskirche stood many cabaret theatres and busy restaurants, where wide-eyed men walked too quickly and women, arms linked, strutted long-hidden ankles, laughing in unison, heads thrown back, coats open in all weathers, revelling in the new liberty. An area of 'ill-repute', as Frau Kellermann read aloud in delighted horror from the morning papers. Georg, her repellent (though well-connected) son, offered with his libidinous leer to take me there.

Raskolnikov was a safer guide. He pulled away from the main road and down a dirty, narrowing alley to the back door of the Green Glass Theatre, as I recall.

The dog nuzzled against the unlocked door. It was unguarded and he led me up the stairs. We walked into an empty dressing room. Empty is wrong. There were no people in it, but the room itself was overflowing. Every surface was covered. The walls were a mumbled mosaic of gilt-edged mirrors, pictures, small intimacies, postcards of girls in top hats and bow ties, bare breasts and high-legged knickers. Clothes lay strewn across the floor.

The smell, strong and sweet, led to tables of powder cakes and beautifying unguents. I could not resist. I sat on a stool before a mirror and grabbed one of the shining pots. It did not matter which. The richness, the oily colours, I wanted to touch them all. I held up a pot of cream rouge and put my fingers in. Shaking (yes, with excitement, but also the stool lurched on the uneven floorboard), I rubbed the cream into my cheeks. My inexperience showed. My face, with two greasy red circles shining brightly, resembled a clown's. But I had more idea than my accomplice, who was vainly licking the side of a perfume bottle.

The smell of alcohol led my own nose to a silken shawl. I whisked it away, like a magician's tablecloth from under crockery, and rejoiced to find open bottles, labelled Veuve Clicquot, abandoned, half drunk.

I took one of the bottles and put it to my lips. The liquid

tasted sweet, slightly sticky. But since it bore the hallowed name champagne I would never have admitted that the flavour was anything other than superb.

'What are you doing?'

The voice came from nowhere. I jumped in fright and looked around, my guilt already smeared across my face. The dimly lit form of a woman was propped up against the doorway, one leg crossed over the other, hands on her hips. She was maybe thirty but her skin was drawn hard and her expression tougher.

I smiled, to hide. 'I don't know.'

'Are you looking for someone?'

'No,' I stammered. I was not a natural liar. I needed a script.

She heaved her chest. 'Everyone's gone. The show's over.' She looked at the bottle still in my hand.

'I'm sorry,' I said. 'I'd never tasted champagne before.'

She snorted. 'Nor have you now, my love. That's lemonade and schnapps.' She looked at me piteously. 'Are you looking for a job?'

'No!'

As she laughed at my consternation, she swayed and spotted my bedraggled companion, his muzzle now coated in oily lotions. She shrieked. 'What the hell is that filthy animal doing there? Is this yours?'

'Yes, no, not mine exactly.' And in my fluster, I blurted out the truth. As she listened, I saw cynicism and pity in her face. I realized that though I might deceive a failing old man with a reason to believe, this woman had seen straight through me. The fake fur stuck to my upper lip. The tweed jacket of Georg's better brother Heinrich could not hide my femininity.

'Come on,' she said, 'I'm locking up. You can't be a dancer here – all the girls are trained – but there's places for a girl like you.'

'I'm not lookin . . .'

She put her finger to my lips and smiled at me. 'Of course you are. Better than dressing up for the old man's sick fancy. Have a little self-respect; don't live in the sewer all your life.'

She smiled. And I was moved that, despite her own hardships, she still had sympathy behind her immutable skin. Humanity showed up in strange places. We walked together into the street and she put her arm around me to protect me from the eyes that preyed in dark alleys. Only later did I notice she had stolen my wallet.

Frau Kellermann thought I was a prostitute too. I was out all night and always had my rent money – what other explanation was there? I suspect the only reason my mother's unscrupulous cousin did not propose that she and I go into business together (Georg's connections providing an endless list of clients) was because she was convinced I had started my own racket elsewhere.

In a way I was a whore. When inflation pushed the price of food beyond my reach, Poltonov provided unlimited delicacies. When Heinrich's cheap suits finally wore bare, Poltonov lent me clothes, of luxury fabrics I had never known.

Supported at this level, paid for by a man, I was able to watch the circus revolving around me with the eyes of an artist not a victim.

I learned to live with my subterfuge. My guilt faded. And by the time I read, at Poltonov's insistence, 'Russia's greatest novel', I no longer accepted Dostoyevsky's assumption that, once a sin is committed, guilt must grow, always, like a living thing, like rumours in the city.

'No. Guilt is all-consuming. It pushes me to greater atrocities. Perhaps Erich has nothing to apologize for.' Max's assumption that the words he read were beliefs of his brother went unnoticed. He *did* notice that he was putting self-indulgence to paper, though. He despised diarists. 'When I am alone, the room is entirely empty. There is *no-one* there. It is very frightening.'

Everyone was hiding, to keep up appearances, to keep up morale. Like others, I painted over the holes in my stockings. I cheated the tram system – abusing the loophole which meant that after paying for one journey one could travel freely all day. I wrote elaborate letters to my mother to tell her the progress I was making in my art classes. I even described the new people I had met, the rosy-cheeked greengrocer, the young bartender from the country whom I took watery soup with on Sundays – every one a fiction. I did not tell her about the only real person in my life.

I *was* a prostitute. I created illusions. And I did it because I had to, and because, in the painting, I had purpose. 'Art justifies existence,' said Nietzsche. It shields reality; it is 'the genius of untruth'.

In Berlin, the images were always perfect. So *frameable*. Each scene, self-conscious, waiting for a viewer. Falling apart as people smoked wrapped cabbage leaves in lieu of cigars.

A genius for untruth. They call it the golden Twenties. Gaggles of girls, laughing, gripping their hats and clinging to one another in the muddy streets. Laughing in despair.

Before I knew the depredation of Berlin, I had known the stagnant German countryside, with its thinking unchanged for centuries. Little wonder that Russia stole my heart.

I have said that sometimes my nights with Poltonov were shared with old compatriots, smoking heavily in his purple room. There were still rarer occasions when, after my return in the early hours, he would want to go out.

214

From nowhere, a starched white shirt was produced, shining collar studs, and a velvet black dinner jacket. Then, Anna and I carried his ruined body down the few stairs, her unfortunate daughter (who was never allowed to sleep through the night) running behind with the bath chair. I would then push him in the chair the short walk, jolting along broken pavements, to his club.

Of several thousand cabarets in the city, just a few were Russian. They were fiercely protected and hugely popular. Poltonov frequented only one, a discreet, obscure place, lurking behind a small black door next to the bankrupt accountants Tritschler & Marx. According to him, every man in The Black Bear, as it was known colloquially, was an intellectual, a celebrity, a hero back in the Motherland. They had, to a man, escaped through a storm of gunfire.

We descended the badly lit staircase into the small cellar below (the thuggish Ukrainian who sat inside the door seemed to relish carrying an old cripple down after carrying so many old drunks up). The Balkan cigars stung my throat from the top of the stairs. The twang of the balalaika was carried on waves of smoke.

Poltonov insisted I keep quiet so as not to betray my nationality. The only words I knew of Russian were 'vodka' and 'njet'. (Frau Kellermann swore that vodka covered most eventualities.) Anna tried to teach me to say 'Happy New Year', but I never was understood, not even on the thirty-first of December.

So, the men in the club took me for Poltonov's dumb boy. I enjoyed playing up to it by casting him intimate looks periodically and rubbing his crumpled knee. He did not object.

What a contrast was this darkness to the bitter dark I saw on the streets with Raskolnikov! The lines of reed-thin children in dirty pinafores waiting for the shops to open, in the vain hope of food, knew nothing of this smoky hideout.

Since I couldn't talk, I ate and drank and the flavours burned my taste buds. Pickles and sauces that were entirely new to my provincial experience. Entirely new colours.

Eight or so men would sit with Poltonov round a small, dark, highly polished table. He was always the centre of attention. Newcomers would stop at his table first, nodding their respects.

We would eat, drink (alcohol and, just as often, interminable pots of tea) and always smoke. Sometimes Poltonov would whisper in my ear as the conversation progressed so that I could follow. Other times he was too involved and I let the words run through me. I saw shapes in it. I almost believed I understood.

They reminisced about the creative atmosphere of St Petersburg in the first decade of the century – all the sweeter since it was now gone for ever. They celebrated yet more brave escaped Russians who had overcome Bolshevik repression and Slavonic heathens to find uncertain haven in Berlin. Gregor Piatigorsky's escape was cheered all night. His arrival in Berlin with bullet holes in his cello, wading across the Spree with the instrument above his head, brought tears to the eyes of the stoniest face. He now slept on a park bench in the Tiergarten, or crept into the concert hall. Fate would pay the debt of his tenacity with greatness.

They toasted the memory of Kulbin, who, some said, beat the Italians to uncover the principle of the 'art of noise', that music and fine art were inextricably linked.

This was one of countless excuses to break into song. Poltonov assured me that all Russian artists excelled in more than one discipline. 'Naturally,' he whispered crossly, 'I played the violin. One had to endure the winter somehow.'

As the inflation crisis worsened, Russian morale was

maintained by the strength of the rouble against the valueless mark. Foreigners could buy up whole crumbling streets for their monthly wage in American currency. In the comfort of the club the stories of German destitution sounded so ludicrous, we laughed at them.

Poltonov repeated the story of an upstanding professional (a watchmaker, as I recall, from a long and illustrious line of German watchmakers) who had forbidden his daughter to turn a trick. They should rather starve, he said, before stooping that low. Later, walking off his bitter agonies with a solitary stroll through neglected alleys, he felt a tug on his thin sleeve and turned to see a grubby street girl. He flinched but she promised that her younger, more beautiful and untouched sister was waiting upstairs for a pittance. Such precious flesh, they dared not let her walk the streets herself. Up the broken spiral staircase to an attic he climbed. He barely had his clothes off, panting at the curled young virgin on the mattress, when he saw in horror it was his own girl.

Everyone knows this story or one like it. The pleasure was the irony: that the hypocrite had stumbled across an honest operation. Lucky chap! The Russians screamed with laughter. By a million-to-one chance the promised untouched virgin was under sixty years of age.

We stayed until dawn at the club, where I received more education than the Volksfeld Art Academy could offer. I did not feel tired. I was never bored. I loved to hear the music of this meaninglessness and I loved to watch Poltonov – the oldest probably, the weakest for sure, but still the most alive. His words were listened to most attentively, provoked the wildest laughter. People came into his presence and felt warmer; I could see it. His angry energy, fuelled by deformity. His eyes, bloodshot and yellowed, could pierce the heart of men half his age.

Of course, I was learning to love him: love for what he

should have been. I think he felt that and came to like it. Though he rarely talked of his former life, he left clues, drops of blood on a handkerchief that I held to my cheek.

My vanity! I began to believe that he had, from the beginning, picked me out; that he saw potential. He would make me great. Does the guru want a disciple to replace him? I thought Poltonov did. He fed me scraps of wisdom, tantalizing pieces, from his hand, the way he fed Rasko little pieces of raw meat. Meat better than any other I had tasted, but just scraps. No matter how much I ate, I was always left hungry.

XX

'By the way, what has become of Trawley? I have quite lost sight of him. He was hot on the French social systems, and talked of going to the Backwoods to found a sort of Pythagorean community. Is he gone?'

'Not at all. He is practising at a German Bath, and has married a rich patient.'

GEORGE ELIOT, *Middlemarch*

I *was* a prostitute. I created illusions. And I did it because I had to, and because, in the painting, I had purpose. Art justifies existence, said Nietzsche. It shields reality; it is 'the genius of untruth'.

Max read the words again. They echoed. He looked at his hands and he started to cry. He shook, alone on his bed, febrile, his head burning. Images ran across his eyes; ideas raced through his head. Ambitions he did not want to face. People he did not want to remember. He pulled Otto's half-sketched picture from behind the wardrobe. Through wet vision, he looked at it and laughed mirthlessly.

*   *   *

Erich sat at the back of the gallery, in the alcove office, staring at the white wall ahead. He was hunched in front of his computer on the revolving plastic chair, with its sienna white seat. But the chair did not revolve. It turned only two hundred and seventy degrees before striking some invisible blockage and turning back to the start. Typical.

The chair was 'self-assembly', which did not mean, sadly, that it assembled itself. After an hour and a half straining over a wordless instruction booklet, Erich settled for seventy-five per cent of the promised rotation. By most standards this was good. Giant corporations assume that only fifteen per cent of its workforce functions. He read this in a book of essays on globalization, jacketed with a photo of trees in mist, to reassure people like himself that, though they had no share options, they were alive. Alive but powerless. Like a tree.

Fifteen per cent of any workforce, claimed the book, is dead wood. Sixty per cent is ruthlessly self-serving. Ten per cent means well but is incompetent. Ergo: only fifteen per cent works.

A seventy-five-per-cent chair function was excellent. In comparison to *his* workforce, it was astounding.

For this, their biggest exhibition in years, Erich had done everything. From the germination of the idea, the development of the concept, the logistics, to the execution, the after-sales support and, doubtless, the cleaning-up afterwards.

The women in Erich's life assuaged their apathy by colluding with the suggestion that he enjoyed moaning.

Katrina never had done anything. They both made a lot of noise but, looking back, it was always he who was banging in nails while she shouted ineffectual instructions. She deceived him. When Erich met her, they had dreamed together of a better world. She didn't tell him her dream entailed running off with a wealthy Belgian aristocrat. Nor that it meant taking Nina with her and implanting her with all the rationalized values of an ex-socialist artist who rechannels her energies into interior design. But it wasn't so bad. Dirk could be relied upon to bring his aristocratic cronies. Erich felt cheered at the thought of flogging bad art to some thick, rich people.

Ursula, oh Ursula. He smiled. He couldn't criticize her absolutely. She put in the hours. She was always there. But she was easily distracted. Like now, she should be running round but instead was suffering an existential crisis (with vomiting) following ill-advised sex with his younger brother.

See, who said he took life too seriously? It was the day after discovering that Max had betrayed him once again and he was already back at his desk. What a professional.

Max. On a piece of paper to his right he began to doodle his brother's outline in pencil. The likeness came easily, his hand familiar with the shape. The face he drew was probably from five years ago. Max at his best.

And he found himself thinking: if *I* was going to fuck one of *Max*'s women, which?

Mary Taylor. Even for one of Max's girlfriends, she looked great. Long, lean legs that seemed to flow straight up to her disproportionately large breasts. Comic-strip beauty. That severe fringed long blonde hair – she was part of the mid-Eighties, Sixties retro thing. She had a *top-ten hit*. A relentless, irritating pop jingle called 'Baby, You Make the Sun Shine'. Max had rung Erich when her song hit the German charts.

Erich saw her on the TV. Mary Taylor was dressed in a fuchsia and emerald mini-dress with polka-dot hoops in her ears the size of dinner plates. She wore pink frosted lipstick and huge false eyelashes. She danced to a remorseless beat and a backdrop of spinning pink and green spots.

Erich didn't find it funny; she was not the person they had dressed her as. He could see it in her eyes. This woman was miscast and it was killing her. We become what other people think we are.

A postcard: 'Erich. This'll be late, so Happy New Year. Thought you'd want to know, all over with MT. Very disappointing. Turned out not to be a twenty-year-old good-time party chick at all . . . She's thirty-*seven*. (She has some kind of hormone-related excess-oil problem – she doesn't wrinkle.) For fifteen years she has been producing experimental assaults on the ears. She lives in a one-bedroom hovel in Brixton that stinks of damp and roll-ups. Most of the time she writes poetry about death. Horrible. "Baby You Make the Sun Shine" was an ironic statement on the parlous state of modern music but nobody got it. The record company rejected her follow-up single, "It's All Just Bollocks". Ho hum. Regards to Katrina. How's Nina? Does she still dance to "*Neunundneunzig Luftballons*" in that tutu? Tell her, if she's still going to be a pop star, to trust no-one.'

It was the first card Max had written. The handwriting – he had never noticed before – was like his own.

Erich wrote back, saying he'd like to read MT's death poetry (he was rowing constantly with Katrina then), but there was no answer. Mary Taylor was forgotten. Max had moved on.

But enough, he had an exhibition to launch. Erich screwed up his fists and punched the air. The eye of the tiger! Go, go, go! He looked at the phone to his left and crumpled.

Ringing in his ears already were the voices of the half-dead journalists. 'Yeah, right, yeah, mm-hmm, I'll try and be there . . . what was it again?' And then the artists – a lazy and resentful bunch – must be rung. Most had careers so perilous that even a minor gallery like Erich's should matter. But it inspired no commitment. In the big show last year, one artist delivered a week *after* the exhibition, only to threaten Erich with a court action for giving him the wrong dates.

They might be the artists but Erich was also creative. He could imagine a world of nothing but chain restaurants selling a hundred dishes from plastic cartons delivered by the same lorry. One day Berlin would wake up with all the cafés swallowed by Starbucks and all independent art ventures owned by BMW. Too late, they'd be sorry for all those meetings of the Kreuzberg Art Preservation Society they'd never attended.

He trailed a finger down the list of names in his notepad. Seventy parasitic freeloaders had committed themselves to the opening. Impressive. His previous record was fifty and that included Chad and his three visiting Taiwanese air stewards.

He sniffed disparagingly. They would come to an exhibition called 'Berlin: Myth Exploded'. Did even one of these lightweights show up for 'Jejune Commitment' – the splendid satire on the depoliticization of the avant-garde by a group of Ukrainian immigrants that he ran last year? Like hell they did. But give them a bit of artistic narcissism and they couldn't wait to get their chops round his hors d'oeuvres. Pah!

Razed, bombed, raped, deracinated, cut off, starved, depopulated, repopulated, carved up but always reinvented, Berlin nurses images of appealing cliché: Marlene Dietrich with that knowing smile and her suggestively cocked leg swathed in black stocking; tin-hatted soldiers leaping barbed wire; the black sense of humour forged in the fire of disaster.

Why was Berlin more interesting than Munich? Because it was a tear-jerker. A tragic, brave city, with human tragedy at its heart. We want tragedy. We need hyperbole, within cities, within people. Yet as he read the title once again, 'Berlin: Myth Exploded', Erich groaned, for the idea was appealing to him less and less. Dissipating over time and talk, it was itself a cliché.

After two decades, Erich still did not know what sold a picture. He even doubted his ability to judge a work of art. Instead he had gained small truths. That blue squares sold better than red circles.

*　　*　　*

Later – how much later, he did not know: the afternoon had stretched way out of shape – there was a rap on the door. He gave no answer, but Max entered, stooped, and sloped across the floor like a rueful dog.

'Hi,' he said slowly.

Erich smiled and spoke with disingenuous briskness. 'Hi. Just sorting out the order for the opening.'

Max, despite his canine demeanour, still managed to look elegant with his hands in the pockets of expensive black trousers. He scratched the back of his head, hovering a metre short of Erich's workstation. 'Uh. Yeah. I knew you were busy. I thought I'd offer my services.' He took his hands from his pockets and rubbed them together.

Erich's brow crumpled. 'It's not necessary.'

Max stood back. 'There must be some lowly job. Some heaving and hauling or running around that I could spare you?'

'Not really!' Erich's tone was unnaturally light.

'Driving, hanging stuff, chopping vegetables, emptying the bins. Anything!'

Erich screwed up his eyes and applied his concentration to the phone list once again.

Max sat down. 'Actually, I've got a couple of things to say.'

Erich turned and said tightly, 'I'm working.'

'No, you're not. You've been drawing that bridge on your notepad for at least the last ten minutes.' Max smiled, craning his head to look. 'Pont Neuf, isn't it? And is that me on it?'

Erich looked at his notepad sardonically. 'Very possibly.'

'Look, Erich . . .'

'Mm?'

Max sighed. 'This is new ground for me. Confrontation's not my thing. All that "let it all out" self-help bullshit makes me feel very . . . uh . . . uncomfortable. You know, sitting round in a circle and telling a bunch of strangers that you have an alcohol problem.'

Erich looked up. 'You have an alcohol problem?'

'No, Erich, that's not what I'm trying to say and you know it.'

'I don't, Max. How can I? You haven't said anything.'

'I'm sorry.'

More loudly: 'I said you haven't said anything yet.'

'No, Erich, I'm trying to say I'm sorry.'

'What for?'

Max was going to remain calm. This was a test of nerve. Outside the gallery window there was a peal of laughter, a flash of red, as two women passed, reminding him of the streetwalker. He felt like low life. He *was* low life. His instinct was to flee, joke, give his brother some money, anything to get beyond this moment unscathed. But he must speak. 'That unfortunate incident with Ursula last night.'

Erich bit his lip, stacked papers. 'Yeah. Heard about that.'

Max leaned forward, clasping his hands in front of his lips. 'What I think you don't know is that it has never happened before. Uh, I think Ursula might have told you otherwise.'

Erich put the paper down. 'Yes, she did.'

Max swallowed heavily. 'Well, it's not true. She made it all up. I know it sounds odd, but I knew nothing about it until last night.'

Erich looked puzzled. His eyes darted. He inhaled, covered his mouth, pressed his cheekbones, considered some more and then let a stream of air out through his teeth while Max, biting his top lip, waited. The response, when it came, was not what he expected. 'And you screwed her after *that*?'

Erich put no value by the moral certainties he enjoyed. It did not occur to him that other people might be in two minds on this one, that a woman who deceived you was still a viable sex option. He felt no relief that he would never face such a dilemma, since he did not know it existed. Though they both knew the other was different, still they made assumptions. But in fact it was in these undetected attitudes that the difference lay; in other ways, they were more similar than either would believe.

Max faltered. 'Yeah – I know. It was a weird thing to do. I don't really know why. Tension, probably. You know how it is.'

'Tension?' Erich did not know how it was.

'Mm.'

'That's a rubbish excuse.'

'Yeah,' his fingers went through his hair, 'but it's honest. If I made something up, I can assure you, the story would be much better.'

'But why should I believe you?'

Max thought about it. 'I don't know – because I'm your brother? A poor one, in most respects, but I don't think I've lied about anything major.'

'But why would Ursula do that?'

'I don't know. I don't really know her. But, she strikes me as a bit . . .'

'A bit what?'

'A bit lonely.'

'You reckon?' Erich's voice was harsh. He felt challenged – illogically, since he'd asked – by Max's diagnosis of Ursula.

Max sensed the hostility and backtracked. 'Well, like I said, I don't know.'

'Are you going to have sex with her again?'

Very quickly: 'Definitely not.'

Erich bent his head over his earlier doodle. 'Poor Ursula. Why not? What's wrong with her?'

Max looked at him incredulously. 'Erich, is there no limit to your empathy?'

'What do you mean?'

'I mean, why aren't you angry? I'm angry with her myself.'

'Because she must have been desperate.' *He* could dissect Ursula; Max must not.

Max was staring at him. 'Christ, you're a nice person. I never realized. I always used to think you put it on to impress women.'

'Didn't you wonder why I wasn't more successful?'

Max laughed and, for the first time since he entered the room, his body relaxed. 'Now, what about those bins I was going to empty?'

Erich smiled tentatively. 'But I don't want you to sleep with her, all the same . . . Max.'

'I won't.' And he was aware that Erich had the moral

high ground and that he still had not confronted him about his own lies, the mass-market fantasy about Max's birth. He could not confront him now. For it was even harder to show his own anger than it was to face Erich's.

XXI

The Memoirs of Gerte Mela (IV)

It was my unspoken hope, when Poltonov first showed an interest in me, that he would wield his influence on my behalf. He seemed to know so many people. It is easy to believe in the power of others when you have no power yourself.

In a flush of enthusiasm I had produced many works over the months. The endless lines: the bread queues, the meat queues, the rigorous symmetry of the Prussian tenement blocks, four floors up, six windows across, each divided by two perpendicular lines. The rolling drunks. The potato hawker working in darkness to hide his rotten offerings. Black-marketeers' children showing off their new rifles. The food stands where the hungry consumed their daily ration of a glass of Berlin beer and the optimistically named 'sausage' in bread.

I wondered sometimes about my motives, whether my desire to expose poverty and suffering was philanthropic or self-seeking, that rather than helping these people I was just using them. What possible impact could my obscure scrawling have? Perhaps these concerns pushed my desire for Poltonov's opinion.

By the summer of 'twenty-two I knew far more of Poltonov's theories of art. On the nights when we were alone, pain permitting, he would talk for hours about the possibilities, what art should be doing.

Formalism, which the Communists hated so for its flagrant disavowal of Socialist Realism – or indeed any trace of tonality – was only half an answer, Poltonov said. Schoenberg's insistence that 'art belongs to the unconscious' was progress. Abstraction in art and music was a necessary development but the social side of art should not be neglected. Abstraction should not be so elevated that it could not move the general viewer.

Relying on the unconscious: there was another mistake. The unconscious was slave to our worst prejudices. Consciousness, rational thought, morality (albeit artificial): these were the only protection against our instinct to hate.

I never tired of listening to him. He was everything to me. And so, terrifying though the prospect was, I had to show him my own impressions of Berlin. I carried some of the pictures from the studio, wrapped in a dirty sheet. I could see the bundle shaking in my arms.

My anxiety was wasted. It was inevitable that he would loathe them. They espoused just the kind of youthful enthusiasm that he deplored. The grimmest scenes, the heavy lines, the careworn faces, appealed to the viewer in such a simplistic way, were such an obvious show of humanity. My transparent politics vexed him sorely.

I remember to this day the look on his old face as his eyes cast through the pictures in front of him. It was horror, to look at such mediocrity. It hurt him physically. His round, lined face, ashen from lack of sleep, was well suited to expressions of disgust. The slightest downturn of his mouth – what signified mild displeasure in a less sculpted face – could leave me aghast. But now, his reaction to my poor little sketches was a horror I hope I shall never see again.

'Oh my God!' he sneered. 'Gerhard, my boy, are you trying to kill me? This is the stuff for vaudeville. For the baying masses, who would cheer at executions if such were put on a stage. Dear God, you'll be hung above the bar of every *Bierkeller* in Berlin with the dear old Frau Landlady weeping into her coarsened hands.'

Though stunned by his repellent expression I did protest. 'But I thought you said that art should not put itself out of reach of the ordinary viewer.'

'Yes, but my God, Gerhard, there's a limit! There's only so far one should condescend. One can stoop too low. This is roiling in the filth. This is hysteria.'

Never mind the message, he hated the style. It was dated, already. The year before I arrived in Berlin, the school of New Objectivity was founded to attack the grip of Expressionism, the Gothic style that the Germans had so long embraced. But I was still clinging to it. I painted the murky grotesque shades of heightened emotion. The black magic, the spiritual, the fantastical, the intensity of the mind, claustrophobia in the city, all elevated by Utopian dreams of the modern metropolis. Nothing new: I could only hold up a distorted mirror.

My ordeal was long. Poltonov held on to the pictures and insulted them individually, for hours, working himself into a frothing fury. He dissected them, indicating with a shaking finger scenes and images that particularly offended.

'Listen,' he sniggered, 'your infants are so angelic, I can hear their farts whistling the Hallelujah chorus. Poverty, Gerhard, is not synonymous with virtue. Beggared children embrace crime not God.' He inhaled testily and, as he did so, perspiration beaded his forehead. 'Oh, the sky so brooding, it makes one weep!' he mocked.

I felt close to tears myself, saved only by the constant undertow of fear of feminine exposure.

As the hours passed, Poltonov railed less in words and more in a series of contemptuous snorts and groans. This was not, however, because he was losing interest in abusing me. His rage grew delirious and was ended when, in a final frenzy, he began wheezing and coughing in some kind of attack. The noises grew louder. I stared at him with desperate impotence, until, after I don't know how long, the sound roused the sleeping Anna, who came running into the room, armed with a prepared syringe, and injected him with some kind of sedation, whereupon he fell into a startled paralysis.

Anna said nothing, did not even acknowledge my presence, but turned immediately back to her room as if this were a normal occurrence.

I watched the sedated Poltonov, who even now looked far from peaceful. Then I fetched the leash from its kitchen hook and took Rasko for his morning walk. I had never felt less sleepy and I wanted to think.

I was filled with despair but also with awe, for though I was disappointed for my own ambition I felt no anger towards Poltonov. If anything, I felt greater respect and more emotionally bound. The more he insulted my work, the more I believed in his words. His wisdom was culled from bitter experience. Of course my response to the poverty of Berlin was naïve. I had seen nothing of the world; he had seen everything. That he raged at me was not surprising in a man who had had to watch fools take over when he was left a cripple.

I watched the dawn rise over the tenements. A weary mother unleashed the rusty door hook, inhaled the foul air and looked at the opal sky. I wondered again, and more bitterly, if she would thank me for committing her image to paper. She would not.

On that walk I thought I must give up painting. As I moved through the strangely quiet streets – even Raskolnikov was subdued – I also became determined to see for myself what remained of Poltonov's work. By seeing these jewels, I hoped, I could finally lay my own ambitions to rest.

He only once told me outright that none had survived. After that he would only imply it with a dismissive brush of the good hand when I brought the subject up. He would turn his head to the wall.

In the end it was Anna who gave away the fact that, despite everything, a picture had indeed survived intact and was here in Berlin. In an exaggerated whisper, she talked to me in her own room, at the far corner of Poltonov's apartment. It was an unnecessary precaution, but one that added to the thrill of revelation.

The greater part of his twenty-five-year collection, which was held mainly at his family estate and, some, in a museum in St Petersburg, was plundered in the revolution. What was not lost in the fire was presumably finished off later in vindictive fervour by the authorities. Much of the artistic avant-garde was silenced by strong-armed persuasion to produce work more palatable to the new regime. Careers were built on politics, not merit. We will never know the 'real' history of art, what would have happened had all players in all places and all eras participated with their hands unbound.

But though he had to abandon hundreds of paintings to their fate, Poltonov had escaped, Anna thought, with more than twenty; among these were some of the best, the most important.

Inevitably, in the long and often hazardous journey through Moscow, Minsk, Warsaw and the desperate peasant-populated regions between, most of the remaining masterpieces were lost, damaged, or stolen (whereupon they were used, no doubt, by the thieving philistines for firewood, for none of the missing gems has ever resurfaced).

Poltonov arrived in Berlin with one picture. One picture left of a lifetime's work! It was heartbreaking.

Anna's smile that accompanied her denial told me that she not only knew where this painting was, she had the key. Since he had not expressly forbidden it I persuaded her to show me.

I rarely now returned to my lodgings at Frau Kellermann's between the evening walk and the morning one. There was little point, since I would regularly be up until three or four, listening to Poltonov and sometimes his companions, and then would need to be back at my duties in just a couple of hours.

It was a straightforward business, then, to snatch a few moments when Poltonov had finally slipped into stertorous slumber. I had to wake Anna. Though it was three in the morning I felt no remorse, since she so regularly slapped her poor daughter into action in the early hours and sent the stumbling child on some unnecessary errand. It was far more important that I accomplish the job before Poltonov awoke.

Nor did Anna seem surprised. She took me into the bedroom, her eyes gleaming. She was clearly excited once she had got over her initial misgivings. I have no doubt that she wanted me to see. The painting meant nothing to her. She had no feel for art. She was, however, of an atavistic mould in revolutionary Russia for the esteem, almost sacred, in which she held the power of her master. I have no doubt that she would have laid down her life for him. I suspect she had a weakness for hero worship, judging by the glow in her eyes at the mention of a screen idol. (She loved the cinema. At least once a week she drank in those silent stories. That Poltonov funded these trips confused her admiration, I think, rolling the screen and the master into one.)

She wanted the vicarious pleasure of watching me, an expert in her ignorant eyes, see for the first time.

We tiptoed, even out of his earshot, into the nominal bedroom. (He preferred to sleep upright: it was less painful.) In an alcove at the far side of the bed, she drew my attention to a locked leather trunk draped in a cloth of fading purple velvet. An elaborate iron candlestick holding a long, white, unsullied candle created the aura of an altar. Such an image in a dark corner sent my already heightened nerves into spasm.

With a dramatic flourish most uncharacteristic, Anna removed the candle and whisked off the velvet. She then extracted a key from her apron pocket and crouched down to unlock the box.

I cannot swear it opened with a creak, but that's how I have heard it ever since. Then followed agonizing seconds as Anna pulled out a rectangular parcel, loosely wrapped in a grey sheet and tied with wool.

In all that I had seen since my arrival in Berlin, nothing came close to the excitement I felt at the moment of seeing Poltonov's only remaining work. I gasped. It was a portrait. I recognized the face at once. Though she looked much altered, it was Anna. She was sitting by a window in a tall room with a view of a city behind her, a concentrated image of steeples and cupolas that seemed both set on a hill in the distance and transported into some unfamiliar world of the mind.

Anna's face seemed to look into the eye of the painter with a deep consciousness. The face gave off a blue sheen, unaccountably made, as one looked closer, of streaks of purple and silver. The face expressed so much.

It had the pathos of a Malevich, yet the musical intelligence of Kandinsky, who notated his growing abstraction like a sheet of music. There was an unmistakable bold form, the yellow of the wooden floor-boards, and the plain chair on which she sat had a Fauvist energy. Yet the bright colours and simplification of form also reminded me of the Bubnovii Valet, the progressive Russians who dared to look to the West.

But all these comparisons are inadequate. There was nothing derivative about it. The associations I made betray the limit of my own judgement.

It was old, universal and at the same time so new I could not look at it and breathe. It was instantly, irrevocably, smote on my memory. A work of genius that would be with me for ever.

The incomprehensible tragedy, I felt strongly. I clutched my heart. From my mouth came an almost feral sound. Anna's alarm, that I might wake the master, was I think challenged because she could not believe I had made such a noise. I crumpled, bent with a great pain in my stomach. I began to cry.

Is this a great painting? Its immediate effect? Its ability to reach down inside me, for no reason that I could account for. An apotheosis?

If I had fallen in love with the despot in his purple throne room who drew nightly audiences, I was now more in love with the dead painter inside. The dead painter I would never know. I had always felt his pain but now I knew what was within his grasp.

When I got back to Frau Kellermann's I cried again – no longer, I am ashamed to admit, for the extraordinary beauty of the painting, but with the knowledge that he would never paint me. The painter and the painted: the greatest of bonds.

Seeing this picture, I now understood his livid frustration with my paltry brushwork. And I was in some way consoled. I had seen his raw self.

From now on he made little attempt to hide it. There were times when his face bulged so with rage at fate and folly, I was afraid for his health. I found no words to comfort him, but sometimes he allowed me to stroke the thin hair on his perspiring head. My touch, when the rage was spent, seemed to reduce his sobbing.

Of course I did not, as I had resolved that empty morning, give up painting. I did not have the strength. However, I did stop striving. I found my limits and used – and still use – what little skill I have to provide for my existence. Poltonov was right. My poor sketches sold well enough in certain circles, but I never flourished. My income was always supplemented by teaching – a reality which I am glad Poltonov did not live to see.

It has interested me, in latter years, to think about my early beliefs: that by working harder, grinding away at technique, spending hours studying the opinions of great artists and great thinkers, I would finally achieve what I wanted. Now that age and illness have eaten away my vainglory, the pain of failure has eased too.

Was my effort less than that of Käthe Kollwitz for the fact that her work endured? Did I deserve less reward? We hear the voices of the successful, the celebrated. We believe they have an insight that others do not. But perhaps we are mistaken. How much more of the nature of existence can we learn from one who has tried and failed? Is the voice of the mediocre not important?

Posterity has been kinder to my canon than was Poltonov. Critical reassessments of the period are wont to say that my work was committed and touching, if lacking the acerbic eye of some of my better-known contemporaries. But all the critical vindication in the world cannot compensate for the ill opinion of the man whose approval was the only one that mattered to me.

XXII

Reality has long been a shifty bastard . . . Let's not pretend we live in terms of it.

EDIT deAK, New York *ArtForum* discussion, 1984

Max stood in a small green break in the concrete at the edge of Kreuzberg. The object, the third that Otto had assigned to him, was a twisted modern sculpture soaring over both of them. It was an ambiguous shape: a curlicue, a dollar sign gone awry, hollow female curves embracing a long masculine pole. Its dark-red-painted metal made a stark silhouette against the dusk sky, where a glimmer of evening sun still glowed. Otto was lurking somewhere behind the structure, out of sight. Max contemplated the sculpture with his head on one side, then lifted the camera to his eye. It still felt strange to hold.

The previous quiet made the sudden noise more shocking. From nowhere came a wild cry, piercing the dark. Max leapt, dropping the camera. It fell on the grass with a thud. Unable to make out the boy behind the metal, he groped towards the noise, which had now become an incessant screech.

'What! What?'

Otto at last noticed him. 'Sorry. Did I disturb you?'

It was laughter, uncontained laughter. Otto was ecstatic, uninhibited, bloated with humour.

Max's voice was shrill, angry now that the fear was gone. 'What the hell are you doing?'

Otto peered round, surprised at his uncle's outburst. 'Sorry, Uncle Max. I was listening to the statue.'

*　　*　　*

Max painted the picture in Otto's bedroom. Otto watched, sometimes standing behind him, sometimes engaging in conversation, but mostly sitting silent on the bed opposite, toying with marbles, playing elaborate, invented games. Max was loath to admit even to himself that he was enjoying the task: the smooth feel of the brush, thick with paint, against the canvas; the warm breeze blowing through the open window; the peaceful regularity of the work that let thoughts, good and bad, flow tolerably through him.

He could relax while he was painting here, knowing Otto had checked beforehand that Ursula would be at work during his visit. Erich's translation filled his head. Wrapped up with it were complicated plays of deception. Max was drawn to read it because on some level it gave him an insight into his brother. There was a reason Erich was working on this. Something had changed in Max that he wanted to know. Yet he also knew Erich would not want him prying. He would not have continued reading (he told himself) except for Erich's lies.

He did not understand why that made him angry. It shouldn't matter that half a dozen people in Berlin had a false story. Who cared? Max had always ignored his past except when it was demanded from him at the video store or the doctor's surgery. And yet it bothered him. It bothered him that it bothered him. He did not, as every fourteen-year-old whines, ask to be born, but since arrival in the world was forced upon him the subsequent details were his: his to use, his to ignore, his to throw away. It was something solid. It was all he had, lately, all he was.

Otto crawled from the bed to look at the picture. He made no comment. Max could hear his soft breathing in his ear. The child's strange patience was unnerving; it broke his thoughts.

'Otto, uh, don't mind my asking, but do you have any friends?'

Otto considered the question. 'It's difficult.'

'Is it?'

'I don't fit in.'

'You surprise me.'

Otto scratched his forehead, in confusion and, perhaps, a little sadness. 'I'm not a swot, so I can't hang out with the geeks. But my superior intellect makes hanging out with the hard cases just too boring. Snot-shooting competitions suck. Anyway I can't bear the thought of joining the gang with the nickname "Brains". Then I'm forced to play in the orchestra but those kids are so wet. I hate team games and as for all those boys who think they'll be footballers "when they grow up", *please*! You see, there is no gang for antisocial, misanthropic, precocious misfits . . . by definition.'

'Do you talk to your parents about this, uh, problem?'

Otto looked a little put out. 'My *parents*? We don't really talk much. I'm not in their gang either – not that I'd want to be.'

Max felt he had inadvertently patronized the boy. Otto was already embarrassed about having parents. Children always grow up faster than they used to. 'Are Erich and Ursula in the same gang, then?'

'Oh yeah. No doubt about it. They both want to do

things all the time. Erich thinks quality time with me means a trip to the Pergamonmuseum. They never just hang around.'

Max laughed. That annoyed him too. That hanging around was deemed an inferior leisure activity required an apology. Nicola, it was, he cancelled one time because he wanted to watch TV. Two weeks later she dumped him. She came up with some other reason – he was an 'unfeeling, commitment-shy bastard' (really, there was no originality when it came to ending relationships) – but that was the trigger.

'Erich and Ursula have their idea of who I am, what they want me to be. They'll say they just want me to be happy, but that's rubbish. They want me to make *them* happy. That's why people have children, isn't it?'

Max shrugged. 'I don't know why people have children.' He put his brush down.

'Have you finished?'

'Yeah, for the moment.'

The canvas was now crowded with images. The modern sculpture was still glistening, Friedrich II standing pompous behind.

Otto examined the work, turning his head on one side to get a better view. 'What's that boat doing there?'

Max cleared his throat. 'I was going to tell you, I've been enhancing the overall cohesion of the piece by adding some of my own symbols. I thought it needed something. That's the boat from *Apocalypse Now*.'

'What's that got to do with anything?'

Max rubbed his greasy fingers against a cloth from his pocket. 'Uh, mm, human celebration of horror, myth of war, you know, it all links up to the sick nature of human existence.'

Otto nodded sagely. 'Oh, right. I've never seen *Apocalypse Now*.'

'You should, it's the greatest film of all time – and it's about the obliteration of the human spirit. Ironic, huh? An anti-war film that makes it look like the biggest blast. I've got it here on DVD, if you want to take a look.'

'I'd like that.'

'We can watch it on Erich's computer.'

'No, that's OK. I've got a DVD player with surround sound and a forty-inch screen. I bought it for my birthday present. It beat the luxury oils set I got from Erich.'

'I can imagine.' Max hesitated. 'Otto, can I ask you another question?' It was easier to be direct with an eight-year-old child.

'Sure.'

'Where do you get all this money from? Do you sell drugs?'

Otto blushed. 'Hash; nothing big, only what I pinch from Dirk – he's too stoned to notice. It's a very small operation.'

Max smiled. 'I know this is a really irritating thing to say, but in a lot of ways I was like you.'

So this was what Otto looked like when interested. Suddenly the moody insolence vanished. His green eyes glowed. His mouth twitched. 'Really?'

'Well, I was selling cigarettes and pornographic magazines, but it's the same principle.'

Otto nodded appreciatively. He swung back to the bed, picked up a marble and aimed it at the small round bin by the door. It missed. He picked up another and tried again. Max sat down next to him, picked up a marble and also threw. The game rules were reached by wordless agreement. Otto could not hide the small smile on his face.

'What are you thinking about?' he asked.

Max glanced sideways at him. Women could never get away with such a line. But Otto had no agenda. Or, rather, he had an agenda that Max could sympathize

242

with. 'Nina's website earlier this evening. Um, the blood. It's stuck in my mind.' A blurred figure of a woman had crouched over a large floor. The picture was distorted but she was clearly naked – and drawing an image in falling menstrual blood.

Otto smiled. 'Don't worry. It's not real.'

Max frowned. 'What?'

'Fake-blood capsules, stuffed up the appropriate orifice when the real stuff ran out. That's just for the video performance. Trained eyes like yours will spot at once that half of the picture is a distinctly different shade. I believe she wasted most of the genuine article getting the camera angle right.'

Max's aim was deteriorating. Otto watched the flailing marbles. The noise changed from the sharp clash on metal to a heavy crack against the wooden floor. 'Of course, technically, it was quite good.'

Otto waved his marble-free hand nonchalantly. 'Yes, well, she pays them a hundred marks a day.'

Max stopped throwing and turned. 'She doesn't make her own stuff?'

Otto laughed at the question. 'Of course not. Nina's more your celebrity chef who pulls a finished cake out of the oven with panache, but everybody knows she hadn't had anything to do with the cooking. Hard-up art students actually bake the thing.' He paused, enjoying Max's agitation, then whispered emphatically: 'Nina wouldn't get a job in a decorating firm. She can barely draw a straight line – like her father, only' – he winked – 'with a little of her mother's entrepreneurial flair.'

Max's voice was faint. 'She's a complete fake?'

Otto smiled. 'Oh, no . . . she does her own publicity.'

'How come you know all this?'

'I have sources, good sources, carefully cultivated. You know, people usually want to talk.'

Max laughed incredulously. His eyes rolled and he shook his head. Otto looked hurt. He jumped up and yanked Max's hand violently.

'Ow! What the hell are you doing?' Max could not have held the boy back; his whole body felt limp. This shocked him. He had recovered almost no strength since leaving hospital. 'Where are we going?' Max panted.

'I told you I know what's going on. I know everything about this place. I don't like it when you don't believe me.'

They left the house and hurried away – Otto always hurried – only stopping abruptly at the *U-Bahn* station. The entrances were stranded in the middle of the road where traffic streamed past in the dark in a cloud of noxious fumes. Max was sweating. Summer was coming.

They walked down and along to the very end of the platform. The few bystanders did not look, wary of unusual movements, unconsciously expecting crime or insanity every time in the underground system. Only one of a group of teenage girls, hair gelled into tiny pigtails emphasizing her chunky frame, looked round as Otto and Max flurried by. She pulled a lump of gum clenched between her teeth into a long string and pivoted back to the group. She did not see as, just before reaching the train tunnel, Otto deftly vaulted with one arm onto the track.

'Get back here!' Max's voice rang hollow. He did not believe in his own authority and so it couldn't work. He turned cold. First his niece pronounced him dead; now his nephew was trying to kill him.

As the figure retreated into the darkness, with a dry mouth Max tipped himself onto the track, shielding his eyes from the wind. 'Otto!' His voice, weak, shrunk in the darkness. 'I'm not sure this is such a good idea.' He stumbled forward. It was cold and dark. This is it, he thought. He felt a calm at yielding into death's soft arms, when he was shaken by a sharp grab at his coat.

'Here,' shouted Otto and pulled him into a side tunnel. The boy switched a torch on.

Max screwed his eyes at the impenetrable face of his nephew. 'I don't know what the plan is, but so far I'm not having a good time.'

Otto pulled a look of horror. 'You look awful when you panic.' He relented. 'This is a dead track, out of use. Don't worry.'

'But the other one wasn't, was it?' Max heard his voice strain.

'That's why we shifted. Anyway, I've not been hit yet.' Otto reached into his pocket and put a metal hip flask into his uncle's hand. 'Here, have a nip of that.'

Max took the flask.

They began walking again. In the darkness, Otto took Max's hand. Max was glad. The torch threw little light across the tunnel and the track was uneven, broken in places.

Max cursed the drips that landed irregularly on his face and neck.

'Otto, is this legal?'

'No, Uncle, of course not, but it's a very quick way of getting around. Moreover, it's safe. No-one can see me down here. And that's something when there are six hundred cameras in the *U-Bahn* alone. There's surveillance material everywhere. New stuff, old stuff, and much of it in the wrong hands. All that cold-war equipment didn't just vanish, you know.'

'Yeah, right, Otto, and who would want to tag you?'

'You'd be surprised.' Otto looked affronted, his elastic face sulky.

Max smirked. 'I read that it was a far more common problem that, after years of waiting to see what Stasi had

245

on them, people suffered the ignominy that there was in fact no file on them at all. Couldn't even rouse suspicion. A far worse fate, nonentity.'

Otto sniffed.

'I'm more worried about getting out again,' Max grumbled. 'Have you any clue where we are?'

'I have a great brain for spaces.'

They walked in silence. Max was not consoled. Particularly when, without warning, Otto piped up: 'Uncle Max, am I going to have a little brother?'

Max's throat tightened. 'What?'

'You and Ursula.'

'How did you know about that?'

'I told you, I have people everywhere.'

Max thought: Otto *is* going to kill me. He's brought me all this way to plunge a knife in my throat.

'It disappointed me,' Otto continued. 'It was not what I expected of you.'

'I'm sorry about that. If it's any consolation, it wasn't what I planned.'

The torch grew dimmer. They had been walking for perhaps twenty minutes. A faint thumping sound grew louder. Then Max heard music. Not a psychopath, then, but some satanic cult that Otto's fallen into. His initiation celebrants demanded a human sacrifice. Who better than the incestuous uncle, his father's usurper? Perfect.

Otto stopped. Max offered no resistance. 'Watch out,' warned Otto: 'we're going up steps.'

They turned right. The steps were few but steep. Max felt a rough metal banister. The stairs stopped at a door. Otto pushed under Max's arm to force it. It didn't budge. Max pulled a 'what-did-you-expect?' face. Otto frowned and pulled a bunch of keys from his pocket. He held them close to his face under the torchlight, then shoved one into the door. Unwilling, the door at last gave. Max looked at the boy in surprise.

'Skeleton key.' Otto grinned. 'I told you I know everything.'

The door opened into a cave echoing with metallic music. Blinking in the red light, Max looked around. He saw people, young people, not one dressed in any kind of cultish leather, but wearing evening clothes. Sparkling, clinging fabrics cut away, exposing flesh. No sacrificial altar, but a bar selling drinks. As Max adjusted to the possibility that he might not be ritually executed after all, he focused on the foreground. And he saw her holding a bottle to her indolent lips. Nina.

XXIII

This is where it happens. At least, people who live here believe that, because it is a sexy thing to live right where it happens. Other people who live here and whose prime desire is not to live a sexy life watch the sexy ones believe that this is where it happens. Those who watch have lost their belief when the country they believed in, obeyed or resisted ceased to exist ten years ago.

ROBIN DETJE, journalist, *Children of Berlin*, 1999

Three hours and three bars earlier, Nina was searching a glowing orange room for anyone she knew, anyone she wanted to know. This was not a good evening.

Lise followed her. Lise, her pale assistant, who seemed slightly overweight next to her emaciated employer. Lise, who was two years older than Nina, but did not look it because Nina had control in her eyes.

In the darkness idled a meagre number of badly dressed people in thin huddles. Nina, perfect in skin-tight silver trousers with the smallest ankle kink, grimaced. She stood alone, while Lise bought drinks from a bar so crowded with mirrors it was hard to tell where the reflection ended.

In terms of sex appeal, a new place lost it roughly

two days before opening. When it became official, the sexy moved on. The perfect bar was like perfect sex. Anticipation. Best when half-built. And afterwards, in the memory, once the bar was closed, when sexy people told the others what they'd missed.

When the Wall came down, there was a period of liberated hedonism. In the vacuum of the East, people made their own bars and clubs, in abandoned spaces and squats without a licence, often without lights. There was usually a choice of two beers kept in boxes in the yard, drugs in a smaller box and the cash in an old sauerkraut tin. Looking back now, people forgot the cold, the damp, the smell and the boredom; they forgot that there was no toilet or the toilet was rendered unusable by people too drunk to distinguish it from the surrounding walls. These anarchic times took a hold of the collective consciousness of a generation of young Berliners. It was *raw*. It was real. It was 'Subkultur'.

Any evening you could pay for with a credit card was just not the same. When planning permission and interior decorators moved in, free spirit squeezed out. What was left was driven further underground. Only the very few could ever know. And they were not going to talk about it. Nina believed that somewhere a truly sexy evening was taking place. But not even she had yet found it.

Nina's belief in the myth of Subkultur was all the stronger because she was too young to remember the original. When she was of an age to look for the bar to die in, those who knew were already saying that nothing was as good as it used to be.

The few thin clusters turned to look at her. This mild thrill was ruined by the misery that she was alone, that she was the person everyone would go home saying they had seen.

A tall man walked in front of her eyes. He had long,

lean legs, encased in a pair of indigo jeans and black stilettos. He pushed his hand towards her. Alarm turned to relief when the hand held a small microphone, barely visible in the darkness. She lifted her head and her hair followed in a spray. When she smiled it was dazzling.

'Hi.'

He smiled back. 'Hi, yes, it's Kabel 4. I'm covering this club launch for the Entertainment Show weekly round-up. So what can you tell me?'

She looked blank. 'What can I tell you?'

He continued to smile, for too long. 'Who's here this evening?'

'Uh.' The blood drained from Nina's face. She could feel it creeping down the back of her neck. Her mobile phone rang. She answered, aware that he was waiting. It was her mother calling, but she did not give this away in her conversation.

The interviewer hovered, smiling. 'So is anyone else coming to this thing, or is it just you?'

Lise returned with glasses of champagne. Nina shouted at her: 'I need the loo. You talk to him.' She started running. She pushed through a smooth fake steel door, almost fell into a cubicle and only then breathed again.

Pulling down her trousers and pants, to expose smooth olive buttocks, she crouched over the bowl, her legs bent but rigid at forty-five degrees to the seat. She never let her skin come into contact with a public seat. To cope with the muscle strain of Nina's hygienic decision, her trainer had devised a series of eight exercises for the Abdominizer to develop her psoas and thus an unusually strong hip tilt. One day she would not be expected to piss along with everyone else. Julia Roberts always got her own floor.

Opening the door of the cubicle, she almost ripped a nail on the tiny lock bolt – an obvious design flaw – this

250

renovation had been done on the cheap. It annoyed her. Nina had her mother's eyes.

Lise was waiting for her by the toilet mirrors. Nina pulled lipstick from her bag and used a tiny brush to reapply the orange pink. She stopped to feel redness on her cheek. A pimple? The creeping sensation returned. There was an emergency spot-freezing kit back home, used by models in New York, allegedly. It didn't seem to work on German skin.

Standing back from the light, the shadows squashed her face and she looked like a little fiend. Like Otto, she thought in terror.

She looked back at Lise and raised her hands in despair. 'Where is everybody? I thought at least Abbie Corinth was supposed to be here.'

They found a table too easily. Nina fell weakly into a seat. She picked up a laminated card lying on the table. The chair she sat on, it explained, came from a new Berlin design co-operative. They were anti-waste and all their furniture was reclaimed from dumps, the street, abandoned houses. Nina put the card down and rested her champagne glass on it.

The man with the camera sat next to her. Nina looked as though she had smelt something bad. Her lower lip jutted with distaste as he leaned towards her and muttered confidentially: 'I'm thinking of making a documentary about people making documentaries of the Berlin scene. An independent project, you know, multi-tasking. What do you think?'

Nina turned to Lise, hiding her face. 'I thought no-one was supposed to know about this place? I thought this was strictly word-of-fucking-exclusive-mouth.' She swallowed, trying to bring moisture to her throat, which was unbearably dry. 'I'm leaving.'

*

They were in a cab, streaking across the city. The traffic was slight, as always. Jams were only caused by road-works. All the new buildings – the glittering high-rises, the sparkling shop fronts, the embassies shell-shaped in marble or towering post-modern in brilliant white that vied with each other in daring design – they were all silent. The crowds still thronged through the tatty Sixties buildings that housed the cheap shops and piled-high restaurants.

Nina was furious. 'And where was Jörg? I thought he was supposed to be there?'

Lise, arms folded, snapped. 'No. *We* were supposed to be at The Mound.'

'The Mound?'

'It's new, but I heard that nobody was going to be there.'

Nina pushed the phone at her. 'Can't you call Jörg, see where he is?'

'Call him yourself: he's your boyfriend.'

Nina fell back against the seat, put her fingers through her hair. 'I hate it here. This is a ghost city. Nobody goes anywhere any more. We're all afraid of being alone.' She pressed redial. This time the phone rang. 'Jörg,' she breathed, 'where the hell are you?'

'Treasure,' the voice at the other end was cool, 'how can you expect me to be there if you won't tell me where you are?'

'We were at some shit place. I don't know. We're going to the Tunnel, like I said. We're late. But you're even later.'

He laughed. 'Just wait there. There's a show later . . . you can be in it. You'll love it – it's being filmed.'

'What show?'

'Hey, my coverage is going, I'm out of range. See you later. *Ciao*, baby.'

He always got away first. The phone fell dead in her hands.

The car streaked softly past Weinmeisterstrasse. This station closed during the Wall years; the entrance was blocked like rags stuffed into the mouth of a corpse. Now people walked in and out, oblivious.

When the new venue proved hard to track down, Nina's mood improved marginally. At last, next to an old hairdresser's still indicated in faded paint, they found a peeling door that matched the description whispered to her on her cell phone. The door opened onto a tatty corridor. They walked over dead pipes. It was wet. Nina worried about her calf-skin boots.

'Champagne.' Lise pressed a glass at her mopish employer.

A woman was walking towards them. Nina squinted. She tugged Lise's sleeve. 'Who's that? I know her.'

Lise shrugged.

She had a thin face, a pointed chin and vivid red, short, spiky hair. Familiar. Strangers always looked like people she knew. The young woman was feeling in a bag. Nina caught her breath. Out came a notepad, spiral-bound, and a pen. The woman gave a smile. Nina did not reciprocate.

'I'm writing a feature for *Art & Application* magazine about fatuous conversation. I'd be interested in your opinion.'

'What?'

'I am testing a hypothesis that modern artists seek out situations with loud noises so they don't have to speak. I want to ask you a few questions.'

'What?'

The woman laughed and scribbled. 'That's very funny.' She sucked her pen. 'No, I'm thinking of the interview you gave at your last opening, here in Berlin. Some people said you deliberately organized a techno party of the loudest legal decibel so that you would only have to give one-word answers.'

Nina's expression fouled.

The woman seemed unconcerned. 'But I think I know what that was all about. Were you at that Radiohead concert at the American forces old radio hall where Thom Yorke, the famous anarchist, summed up his entire philosophy in four words?'

Nina shook her head dumbly. 'No.'

The woman seemed surprised. 'Well. Yorke stopped between songs and he looked at the audience and he pronounced: "American money markets." Silence. Then he said: "Empire."' The woman laughed thinly. 'A-ha-ha-ha! Wasn't that perfect? Critical, penetrating and, above all, short. The crowd, as they say, went wild.'

'Oh, really?' Nina took a large swig of her champagne.

The woman nodded. Searched Nina's face for response. 'I'm not saying this is a bad thing. Wasn't it Adorno who said that the artist should object to society on principle but had no business trying to persuade an audience? They should just express their outrage.' She paused, accepting a light for the cigarette that had all this time been lodged between her fingers. She raised her eyebrows enquiringly.

Nina did not respond. She was trying to look casual, but she was failing. Her pretty face pouted vacant.

'Am I right, then,' said the interviewer, 'that when you give those funny, stupid interviews I've read, that this is *your* point, Ms Brandt?' The woman dragged on her cigarette.

Nina stared at her, wildly, looking for traps. At last she stammered, 'Ye-es. Mm-hm. Absolutely.' And then she turned and started leaving the room. She could hear the journalist laughing again and she had almost broken into a run, when she bumped into a male body.

There was something indefinitely familiar about it, a scent perhaps, even in the smoky atmosphere, that made her look up before moving on.

Max looked down at her, no less shocked. They sprang back.

'Nina?'

'Max?' She bit her lip.

Max stared at her. 'Hey.'

'Uh, I was just on my way out.' She smiled desperately and tried to move past, but Max held her wrist to prevent her. He felt anger.

'Don't you think you owe your dead uncle an explanation?'

'*What!*'

Acute embarrassment, Max realized. She was embarrassed of *him*.

'Hello, Nina.'

She was shaking her head and at the same time desperately surveying the room.

'What are *you* doing here?'

'Uh,' Max looked around but Otto had vanished, 'I'm here for a drink. Would you like one?'

'*What!*'

He had no reply. Her expression of stunned horror gagged him.

A man tapped her on the shoulder. 'Baby.' A young man, tall, dark, with close-cropped black hair, a humorous mouth. He was wearing a suit with a purple shirt.

'Jörg!' Nina's face lit up.

The highly fashionable black suit snuggled over Jörg's pumped body.

Nina turned to Max, stronger now. 'Look,' she snapped. 'You've got to leave. You shouldn't be here.'

'Why not?'

Shaking her head in disgust, she led Jörg away. Jörg's backward glance seemed almost regretful in the shadows that loomed and flickered. As they disappeared into the crowd, Jörg winked and mouthed, 'Women, eh?' Max flashed an absent-minded smile.

Surrounded by strangers, completely alone; no clue where he was, no idea how to get home; noise flowing in and out of his ears, hypnotic. Max shook himself. Where the hell was Otto? He wasn't going to look for him.

A chair. He saw it in the corner behind him, near the door. An incongruous wooden-backed chair with a split seat and functional metal legs, defiantly ugly school furniture. This venue was until very recently something else.

He sat down. There was a time when he sat alone because he was hipper. The most attractive woman and her entourage would look him over. Eyes still trawled him but now they belonged to the woman on her own. By the code he didn't understand, he no longer cut it. He was not invisible. He was making an ageing fool of himself.

Like somebody's father, he attracted the same pity as those students hanging round the café to save on their heating bill gave Erich. Except Erich *was* somebody's father. His two children were somewhere in this room. Whatever else, Erich had produced two human beings, whom he must love and who must, on some level, love him. Max wondered what it felt like. Or if Erich had forgotten: if the miracle was blanched by the gaudy everyday – fights over breakfast cereals, TV channels and underwear spawning fungus on a bedroom floor.

To be good with children, like to be good at sleep, Max assumed, a man must switch off. Be in denial, not think.

XXIV

A woman who has got what she wants and is still unhappy . . .
are you surprised? Isn't that what you came to Berlin for?

ERICH KÄSTNER, *Fabian*, 1931

The lavatory was a regular foil, Max's social boredom
escape route, his haven, but he had rarely fled in fear.
Now he retreated to it, smothered by Nina, the heat, the
relentless anonymous music, by old age.

A white sheet of paper was attached to the rusty door
with tape; on it, roughly sketched in pencil, an upturned
set of male genitals. Max shuddered. This boded ill. Yet,
on entering, he was surprised by the hygiene levels. Only
a mild urine tang and, yes, toilet paper Jackson Pollocks
decorating the floor, but unused anyway.

'Hey.'

Max turned. But the low voice behind was addressing
a tall blond male slouching in the corner by the far
basin, with his back to Max, staring at the window, an
opaque pattern of small ridged diamonds. The blond
recognized the voice, was waiting for it; he turned at
once, the muscles of his oversized jaw melting in pleasure.

'Jörg!'

The bulging suit. Jörg walked past Max, oblivious to

him, unbuttoning his jacket and the purple shirt underneath.

'Jörg!' Such a stodgy syllable was never pronounced so tenderly, from the lips of the strapping, rough-jawed blond, who looked like a Hollywood Nazi.

Jörg walked slowly closer, arms outstretched. On contact, he slipped his hands inside the other's shirt. The blond let out a delirious sigh, rocked his head back, displaying a prominent Adam's apple, then pulled forward again and planted his lips on Jörg's mouth. He closed his eyes but, as he did so, Max saw the whites roll upwards as if a deep thirst was finally quenched. As his hands came to clasp Jörg's buttocks and pull him into the mould of his own body, Max felt tears forming. Had he ever felt such a kiss? This was no sanctuary. He left them.

Outside, Nina was walking towards him, imperious. 'Have you seen Jörg?'

Max pointed a finger back across his shoulder. 'In there.'

She started to push him out of the way.

Max recoiled. 'Uh, Nina, he didn't look like he wanted to be interrupted.'

In the washroom, things had progressed. Hesitating only momentarily, Nina marched up and shook Jörg by the shoulder. He looked round bleary-eyed, smiled benignly, freed himself from his friend and pulled up his trousers.

'Hey, Nina, how's it going?'

Nina, though her body was shaking, remained mute. She merely gesticulated, her hand striking the air, palm up, in an expression of incredulity.

He mimicked her. 'What?'

She shook her head. 'Jörg! What's going on?'

Jörg looked at the blond, who was looking at his shoes. 'What, him?'

Nina nodded.

Jörg turned his head a little, as if confused, and then half laughed. 'Nina, baby, come on. You know what we have is strictly business. Aren't I allowed a little time off? Thorsten loves me. He lets me hold his hand in public. He baked me a birthday cake. What did you ever do?'

Her smooth face crumpled. 'What are you *talking* about?'

Jörg flipped a cigarette between his lips. He was not angry, just disinterested, which was somehow more humiliating. 'Look, baby, it's late. I'll see you tomorrow. Ten, yeah? We need to talk outfits for the Braunfeld opening. OK? *Ciao.*' He pecked Nina on the lips and, circling his arm round the blond's waist, whisked him away.

Max smiled apologetically at his niece.

Her eyes were screwed up in disbelief. 'What do you want?' Her voice cracked.

His resolve collapsed. 'Come and have a drink.'

She shook her head. 'People will see me, like this, with you. There's a reporter here.'

He gripped the sides of her skinny frame. He could feel her shaking. 'Well, let's go somewhere else, then.'

Another moment, another bar, minimalism-vacuumed throughout. Fifteen or so low tables were positioned in front of groups of cream leather armchairs. Three others were occupied. Shielding her face, Nina made for the furthest corner and slid into a seat against the wall.

Max bought champagne. The bartender, woken from his late-night torpor by the flash of generous notes, trotted behind with an ice bucket and stand.

Nina, slumped in her seat, pelvis scooped upwards, legs open, trainers on the table, was talking down to her knotted fingers. 'I was suspicious, you know, all the time.'

Max poured champagne into her glass as she held it.

'Fobbing him off was just *too* easy. We went away for a week to Milan and he didn't pressurize me to do anything.'

'Why would you want to fob him off?'

Behind the apposite clothes, the lip gloss and the Berlin hair, he glimpsed a nervousness that looked, suddenly, like Erich.

She spluttered. 'Well, God, you know, sometimes you've had enough!'

'Right, right.'

'The thing Jörg needs to understand is that I'm the one using *him*. I'm the one laughing here.'

'Who is he?' Max asked questions he didn't care about and gave support, when he wanted to shake her and drag the answers he really wanted from her vapid lips. She had said he was dead.

Nina was staring into her drink. 'He's useful to me, that's who he is. He runs underground clubs and he DJs. He writes style columns, shit like that; he's *always* in the papers. He was named one of the ten hottest people in Berlin – that's *before* I started with him, you know. He's great for my image.'

'So you're not in love with him or anything?'

She laughed and lit a cigarette. Her hand was still trembling. Her hollow eyes looked right through him. 'Christ, what are you, fourteen?'

The image from the TV, the PC, was now in front of him; in all those circular thoughts he had never moved beyond this moment. Beyond the meeting. He had no idea what to say.

Conversation was overrated. To speak was to be misunderstood. Politics – an attempt at constructive dialogue by people suppressing their natural urge to throw things at one another – surely proved that. Maria –

a magnificent failure in domestic politics. They spoke less and less and only then they came to understand each other. He recalled the sound of his five-thousand-pound James Bond chair being slung at the door. He understood that. And so must she. Anti-materialism was one thing, but if that baby had so much as a scratch on it, Maria must pay, every penny.

Swathed in silver, like angels (maybe he had drunk more than he thought), two girls at the bar walked over to them.

'Are you Nina Brandt?'

'Yes.' She flashed an enchanting smile and Max saw himself.

'I think what you do is dis*gusting*.'

Nina let her eyelids fall before looking up like ice. 'Thank you, that's very sweet.'

The heavy lids – Max recalled this tic from the TV show – were a defence, not the provocation they seemed. Unfortunate. It made people want to hit her.

The girl was jabbing her finger into Nina's chest. Her friend folded her arms. 'You ought to be ashamed of yourself. You little tart. And you,' she squared on Max, 'pimp! We all know what you want.' She spat at him; the hit splayed down his chin and neck.

Max rose abruptly from his seat, poised with menace, enough to send the two scurrying away. Silently, he sat down again, took the paper from underneath the plate of complimentary rice snacks, greasy and thin, and dabbed his chin delicately.

Nina leaned forward and held her head in her hands. 'For fuck's sake.'

Max folded his arms and frowned. 'Why did they spit at *me*?'

Nina looked at him unsympathetically. 'I get this all the time.'

With distaste, he folded the tissue and transported it, between fingertips, to the table. The champagne's frenetic early energy had subsided to a feeble vertical trail. The music shifted, to a slothful dirge.

She put her fingers through her hair and sighed. 'Have you any idea what it takes out of me, playing the role?'

Max frowned, bewildered.

She gazed into space, the blurred upholstery and floor. She opened her mouth, curled with a slight smile. 'You know where my money comes from, Max? Crockery. Mugs, plates, oh and calendars of course and those woolly hats with the star-shaped tassels. They do very well. My apartment is full of spin-off merchandise from my designs. That's what people want: a little piece of me, a taste. They want my lifestyle, my cool, my choice of wallpaper. That's what I've become: a commodity. Do you know, at night I switch the lights off and look at that shit pile and I cry. Christ, Max, I make mugs for a living!'

'Nina, that girl just spat on me.'

She looked at him coolly. 'So? Does it hurt?'

His eyes widened. Why did he not just leave, as he had left less atrocious behaviour before? Yet he recognized this self-indulgent misery. It sounded foul from her mouth. He did not believe in her. Something was wrong. He spoke awkwardly. 'So if you hate it, why do it?'

'That's easy for you to say.'

His lips puckered. 'Oh yes, why's that, then?'

'You already walked away.'

Max tried to sound normal. 'I didn't walk away. I just didn't fancy the trail my brother blazed. Achieving mediocrity takes far too much work.'

'Yeah,' she said with a sigh. 'Mother was very anxious that I shouldn't turn out like Papa.'

'She specified?'

'Mm.' Nina stretched fetchingly, her movements, as

ever, ostentatious. 'Specially after Dirk came into her life. Dirk doesn't care what she says. Papa used to shout back, but Dirk just cracks open the beer, so she gets worse, outrageous.'

So she had not denied his mediocrity. Nina's opinion should not matter to him. 'You like Dirk?'

She smiled hazily. 'He put up bail for me when I got arrested. Mother was all set to let me stay there, teach me a lesson. Papa has no money. Dirk didn't care. He's old money – family full of criminals and drug addicts.'

He had never thought about this before: 'So you weren't cut up about the divorce?'

'Fuck knows. Probably.' She shrugged. 'My Feng Shui consultant says my "incessant need for attention" comes from being neglected by parents obsessed by their own shit. But' – she lit another cigarette and exhaled heavily – 'it's never enough, is it? The camera always stops rolling and the audience goes home.'

He rested his feet on the chair.

Her lips gripped with resolve. 'I'm never having children. I plan to burn out and kill myself by the time I'm forty.' She covered her mouth with her hand. It was the first time she had looked at him straight in the eyes. 'Oh. Sorry.'

He smiled rigidly. 'Let's go.'

'All right.'

Out in the street, in the darkness, craning for cabs, Nina swayed as the drink hit her. She grabbed his wrist to steady herself.

They walked most of the way back in their hunt for a taxi. The evening began to impact on her, the conversation too big to breezily tuck into her clutch bag. She grew tired and irrational. He cursed her. She had started out the evening rude and was deteriorating. The air felt chill. They passed few people along streets of silent buildings with blackened windows, boarded-up windows, broken windows, new windows, dirty windows framed in peeling paint. Watching.

'Look!' In an alcove, set back from the street, Max had been drawn to a pile of objects, lit by a light from an inner stairwell. A filing cabinet with white stickers jamming the drawers was propped up against the wall. In thick black pen scrawled across it were the words 'Faked Info'.

Nina walked up, the heels of her boots grating against loose stones. She crouched down and her hands sifted through broken pieces of laminated plastic, long lengths of strip lighting and a leather office chair, oozing yellow stuffing. She looked back at him. 'No name on it.'

'"Faked Info" by anonymous.' Max smiled. 'How appropriate.'

She frowned. 'What do you mean?'

'What?'

'What the hell do you mean, Max? Why is that "appropriate"? What are you saying, that I'm a fake?'

'No.' His voice displayed disbelief. 'I— I was talking about Berlin.'

'Bullshit!'

'Nina!'

'I know what you think of me!'

'Nina, *I* don't know what I think of you, so I don't see how you can.'

Such convolution was too much for her addled mind. She shook violently. 'How dare you, *you*, Max, call anyone a fake?'

'Nina, you're tired and drunk.' He moved towards her, obeying some instinct to hold her, unsure whether he would console or stifle her. And the two possibilities were too close.

'Get off me!' She ran on, away from him, and tripped,

264

her ankle smacking against the ground. She crumpled. 'Shit!' Tears formed, pinpricks floated down her cheeks.

He bent down towards her. 'Are you OK?'

'My ankle!' She did not look up. She sat sobbing, her head in her hands.

'Is it hurt?'

She shook in silent misery.

Max tried to disguise his weary impatience. 'I can't help you if you don't talk to me. Is it broken, do you think?'

'There's a rip.'

'What?' He saw that she was pointing at the trousers not the skin. This evening was too long. 'It's barely noticeable,' he snapped. 'Get them repaired.'

Nina wept. 'You can't *repair* Yoshi Yanamake pants.'

'Well, burn them, then. I don't care.'

She drew her knees to her chest. Her forehead sank to rest on them. He heard only a sodden murmur. He arched his head up to the sky. His neck was aching. The stars blinked through a break in the clouds, a lucid moment.

'What?' he said.

She sobbed again.

'Nina, I can't hear you.'

She lifted her head an inch or two. 'You know, don't you?'

Christ. Guessing games. 'Know what?'

'You know it's all a lie, don't you?'

'Well,' he spluttered, 'I heard some . . .'

'I *am* a fake.'

He tried to smile.

She blinked through silver tears. 'Have you met anyone before who didn't know her boyfriend was gay?'

He crouched down. 'Yes, several. Happens all the time. Why?'

Her back straightened. She was almost calm now and

265

her words were at last distinct. 'I'm a virgin.' She raised her chin. 'You knew it, didn't you?'

'What d'you mean?'

'What do you think I mean? Take that smile off your face, Max. This is a big deal for me, so give me a break.'

The expression he had hoped resembled one of sympathy slumped. 'Nina, look, I really was talking about Berlin – just a pointless metaphor . . . I don't know anything about you . . .' Her words sank in. '*Really*, though, are you *sure*?'

She smiled bleakly. Her revelation seemed to numb rather than distress her. 'At the beginning it was an inconvenience, bad for my image, so I blurred the truth a little. Now it's too late: I can't do it, even if I wanted to. Any guy would see through me straight away. And he'd go running to the papers. I'd be a laughing stock.'

Max looked at her. 'I'm not laughing.'

Nina checked his eyes for cruelty. Satisfied, 'Thank you,' she said. For the first time she sounded sincere.

He offered his arm. 'Can you stand?'

She nodded. 'I think so. But my heel's broken.' She held up the snapped-off stump.

Max examined the damaged boot. 'We'll *have* to find a taxi now.'

Nina held out her hands and he hoisted her to her feet. 'No, I'll be better walking it off.' She unzipped the broken boot and then the other and threw them on top of the filing cabinet.

Progress was slow. For some time they were silent. Max chewed over this new information. It made sense in a perverse way. 'I think you could turn it round, you know. Make a feature of it. Say you were holding back all along, for your art, as a deliberate mocking of a sex-obsessed society.'

She smiled weakly.

'Anyway, what about that guy in Potsdamer Platz?'

She closed her eyes, shook her head. 'It's easy to fake it – they do it in movies all the time. I paid him to keep his mouth shut.'

'You paid a guy *not* to have sex with you?'

She shrugged. 'Not as desperate as paying *for* sex, huh?'

Now he felt cold.

'Look, don't walk me back. I'll just crash on Papa's sofa.'

Max frowned. 'I don't think that's a good idea.'

'Why not?'

'I don't want him to know that I met up with you this evening. I know it upsets him how little *he* sees you.'

'What?' Her sleepy red eyes looked curiously. 'Don't worry, Max; he can't say a word since I'm showing up at his exhibition for him.'

He smiled uncomfortably.

Lying under blankets, she grasped his hand. 'Thanks, Max. I feel like you of all people can understand.' Her eyes held open only to add a coquettish coda: 'Aren't you going to read me a story?'

He sighed. 'Goodnight, Nina.'

Flitting through roles, the artist, the victim, the cynic, the flirt – she excelled at them all.

XXV

And so I now use as models the faces of people . . . whom
I know inside out, so that they torment me almost like
nightmares, to build up compositions showing the struggle of
man against man, their contrast of one with another, like the
contrast of hate and love, and in each picture I search for
the dramatic accent that will weld the individuals into a higher
unity.

OSKAR KOKOSCHKA, 1917–18

'I've seen you at night, undressing. You shouldn't leave
your curtains open. You've got a great figure. Who could
have guessed you'd had a child?'

Ursula closed her eyes, with slow dread, the telephone
receiver still by her ear. He called her at least twice a day.
When he did not catch her in person, he left snake-like
messages. His whispers chilled more than shouting.

Rational. She tried to remain rational. She never un-
dressed with the curtains open. Anyway, how could he
know where she lived? Barbara swore she'd only handed
out the telephone number. (Though Ursula could not
push it, since Barbara was struck with guilt and so
aggressive on the subject.) He was probably a harmless
fantasist. A skinny man with hair falling over his ears. So

he guessed she had a child. There was a fair chance. He did not know what she looked like. She looked like anyone. She was safe in the city. This happens to every woman. Like the pullover that shrinks in the wash, one of life's caprices. Stalkers were feeble individuals, not the good-looking psychopaths who haunted fiction. Her perception of danger was formed and skewed by bad telemovies.

Her real fear was more sinister: identification with the caller's motives. She saw a similarity between his behaviour and her own. Her careful scheming, her Max-driven fantasies. The hours she spent thinking about him alone in her bedroom at night. She had slept naked since his arrival in Berlin and it was not because the weather had warmed.

Apart from what it must be doing to Max and Erich, the horror was that she was shaping into the figure cut out for her. The unfortunate Ursula, her name always prefixed with two adjectives: 'poor' and 'old'.

Her older sister, Sabine, had never cried at two in the morning. She got married young to a solid tax adviser and had three children sensibly spaced apart. In Ursula's family, there was a right way to live. Having an eight-year-old child with no sibling was not it. Being unmarried to Erich was inexcusable, their subsequent separation inevitable. 'What did you expect?' her mother said. Teaching art was a disappointment. Sabine had a management job in a bank, which paid her well – part-time after the children were born. No-one doubted that Ursula would always be single. Now, Ursula suspected, she was growing into the wreck they believed her to be.

No-one talked about her younger brother, who lived rough in Amsterdam and only ever came home to rip off the parents for drugs money. He stole the car stereo, his mother's jewellery, the PC and even the electric tooth-brush. Her parents bought a safe. But they didn't talk about it. Some disappointments were too big. Let poor old Ursula be the disappointment. Everyone was comfortable with that.

'I'm coming for you, Ursula.' His words washed over her, like a passing street conversation. Her lack of response broke his tenebrous gravity. His voice became reedy, petulant: 'Ursula! Are you listening to me?'

She jumped. Lost, she had forgotten him. 'I'm sorry, what did you say?'

Her fear was his lifeblood. The phone went dead.

*   *   *

Erich woke up in a nightmare. He had dreamt that the gallery door jammed; during the opening speech he looked down and saw nothing but his underwear; a rejected artist had overnight smeared excrement over the other works.

Six thirty. His habit was to head straight downstairs in his blue towelling robe and switch the coffee machine on. That began the day. He needed to feel the control flick under his fingers and the rich, dark aroma fill him with quiet pleasure.

Today the lift was short-lived. He peered into the sitting room. On the sofa, tousled, stirring, lay his daughter.

'Papa?'

'Nina?'

She sat up. Rubbed her aching head, her hair muddled and there were traces of smudged make-up on her face. Still, he had forgotten how fresh her face looked first thing.

Nina smiled, interpreting his silence as expectancy. 'Uh, I ran into Max last night. It got late. We were talking. Uh,' she blinked at his falling face, 'he's good to talk to. I feel a lot better.' She stroked her soft hair across her drawn face. 'You know.'

Erich's voice was mechanical. 'If you want a shower, there's stuff in my room. You still coming to the opening tonight?'

She looked perplexed. "Course I am.'

'I'll see you later, then.'

'Oh. OK.'

He looked at her, the nineteen years of indolence stretched out under a blanket, sleepy eyes appealing to him.

'We'll go out sometime soon, huh, Papa?'

'Sure.'

Alone again, Nina scratched her head.

* * *

Ten o'clock and Ursula arrived at the gallery, biting her lip. She rushed across to Erich. 'How are you feeling?'

'Better than you, by the look of it. What's up?'

'I was just anxious that you were OK, after, you know, the whole Max thing.' Saying everything was better protection, for the fragile self underneath, than saying nothing.

'Yes, I'm OK.' He looked pale, his face drawn.

Ursula pulled up a stool and sat next to him. She picked up sheets of printed paper that lay aside in disarray. Two-dimensional plans of the exhibition layout. Quadrilaterals, pyramids, tetrahedrons, endless computer graphics. There was nothing left to do. This was another work of art, without function. Procrastination, intellectualization, masturbation.

'Couldn't you give yourself a break until this evening, Erich? Is what you're doing strictly necessary?'

He turned slowly to her. She felt fear. His eyes were dull. 'None of this is strictly necessary,' he said.

These conversations, when they were together, left her feeling so impotent. She wanted someone to tell her what to say that wouldn't make matters worse, that might help him, but there was no-one else; she was the expert.

Her voice quavered. 'What do you mean?' She knew what he meant.

Erich sighed. He picked up the papers, ripped them in pieces and tossed them in the bin. 'We're struggling to keep this place afloat. Nobody's interested. We're swimming against the tide—'

'And you're resorting to water metaphors.'

'Take me seriously, will you?'

She went over to him. Held the edge of his fingers. He looked at her hand, uncomprehending. 'I am, Erich. You know I do. It's just we've been here before.'

There was colour in his cheeks. He felt anger at her faintly smiling face. Ursula had no grip on reality. He was alone.

Very soon, Ursula told herself wryly, he's going to begin a sentence with 'Twenty years I've struggled . . .'

Erich sniffed. 'Twenty years I've struggled to make something of this place and it gets harder all the time.'

God, I'm good.

Erich stared into the middle distance, spinning a pencil in his fingers. 'So why keep sweating? My stupid, tin-pot exhibitions. If it's such an effort to drag people along, what's the point? No, I mean, really, Ursula, I'm not just being miserable. I'm being practical. Bottom line: Max wouldn't waste his time doing this.'

She laughed. 'Max wastes his time on far more pointless stuff. But what does it matter what Max thinks?'

'You should understand that.'

Now she blushed. 'Look, I'm really sorry about Max.

272

It was all my fault: he was just too embarrassed to say no.'

'What a gent.'

'If it's any consolation, it wasn't up to much – only in the imagination, beforehand.'

He grimaced. 'Spare me. I have a headache. First thing this morning I found Nina sleeping it off on the sofa.'

Ursula held her hand to her face, horrified. Erich looked at her in surprise, then laughed and patted her on the shoulder. 'Calm your lurid imagination. They'd only been for a late-night talk. But Max made her feel "much better", apparently. And you know he's off all hours with Otto, who looks up at his uncle close on adoration.'

She knew this pang; when total possession was lost, when children found other people. Otto was lost to her. Her voice was palliative. 'Max has novelty value, that's all. It'll wear off.'

Erich shook his head. 'I'm not criticizing Max. He's a nice guy. It's me. I let both my children down.'

'Oh, come on, Erich.'

'I've made too many sacrifices. Tell me, when did I do anything for either of them?'

'You're too hard on yourself.'

'That's the fashionable theory, isn't it? Alleviate your guilt; don't look for a reason behind it. We're all good people, plagued by the needless guilt of wealth and good fortune; it's not our fault. Well, what if that's wrong, Ursula? What if guilt is the get-out clause? I must be an OK person because I feel guilt. No need to do anything because I feel bad already.'

'You *have* done things. You started the gallery and the café, to help people.'

'Bullshit, Ursula. I'm not going to comfort myself with that. I started it because it might have made something of me, *for* me. Meanwhile, my children are running wild, neglected, because I'm too preoccupied with my egotistical gallery, an entirely self-gratifying sex life and whether or not my brother is a better lay than me.'

When Erich had first moved to Kreuzberg, life was as black and white as those movies he watched with Marlene. He thought his life universal. He saw a pattern, that Max and he could represent the West and the East. It was neat. Max with his empty money, Erich with a baby daughter in a co-operative nursery. Now he was older and Communism was dead. Disappointed when the Wall came down and all the Ossies wanted to do was spend their welcome hundred-marks gift, he didn't mind now. He needed a new car.

Ursula lifted up both Erich's hands, which were now sweating, and perched on his knees to hug him. 'You old hippie.' She smiled. 'You're too nice.'

Then the phone rang. Erich rolled his eyes. 'That'll be someone important cancelling.' He picked up the receiver. '*Ja, Brandt.*'

Ursula folded her arms and walked across the gallery to the window. She stood close to the pane, feeling the cool of the glass near her skin. A group of teenagers in woolly caps and outsize sweat clothes illustrating American bands with cartoon skulls and guns, hands in their pockets, scuffed a stone between them in an apathetic game of football. They were not interested in German community art. Perhaps Erich was right.

She looked back. Erich was speaking English but mainly he was listening.

Finally he hung up and looked across at Ursula. 'That was Maria.'

'Who?'

'Max's, er, girlfriend, um, ex-girlfriend.'

'What did she want?'

Erich sat down. 'It's hard to say exactly.'

'Well, what did she say?'

Erich winced. 'She said I could tell Max she's had the abortion and she hopes he's satisfied now.'

*   *   *

'I'm going to a wedding.'

'Dressed like that? And it's the middle of the day.'

Éva was wearing a pair of black flared trousers with a diamanté silver halter-neck top, which made her pale shoulders so delicate as to snap in his hands. There was a small gap between the two garments that revealed a sliver of creamy stomach.

She laughed. 'Max, you know, you'd make a great mother. They're friends of Chad's. I'm only going to the reception, but they like to get started early, these boys.' She paused at the door. Something in his eyes prompted her. 'You can come too, if you like.'

The groom and groom wore matching Las Vegas show-girl outfits. Max and Éva arrived during a speech. Roberto's hirsute and adipose body strained his Folies-Bergère costume. Heavy make-up could not disguise the squashed face of a pug dog, yet as he professed lachry-mose gratitude for twelve beautiful years, the emotion was palpable. Max felt his eyes moisten.

Joy was overwhelming. Radiant fabrics and gleaming flesh spun under flashing white lights. The world was a benign place, where every peccadillo was embraced by a populace of disco lovers. With whoops of delight, squeezing cheeks with other sweating dancers for the omnipresent cameras, the group threw back sparkling wine and believed in the future.

Max stood by the bar, looking on, his hand over the lower half of his face, like the child who believes the world will not see him if he closes his eyes. But, surrounded by day-glo, sequins and fake fur, Max, in plain black, was attracting attention. Exhibitionism is an evangelical religion and scowling Max was begging to be converted. He couldn't look up for sequinned eyebrows raising dance invitations. Instead he stared into his drink.

Exuberance was difficult. To let go required a belief in innocence – your own. Dancing could not be ironic. On some level, you meant it. Like sex.

Éva was seduced onto the floor by a friend in a pink furry thong. The man extended his hand and she laughingly took it, pulsing into the bouncing crowd.

Twenty minutes: Max was counting. When at last she reappeared, panting, the broad splash of pleasure painted across her mouth annoyed him. He frowned.

Éva took the drink he had lined up for her. 'When did you get so miserable?' This was probably rhetorical. She wiped the sweat from her forehead and turned to face the dancers. Leaning back with her elbows resting on the bar, she propped one leg against the wooden base. Uninhibited. He was facing the bar, shielding his gaze.

He said, 'I've devoted a lot of time to it.'

She looked at him, still panting slightly. The room was too hot and the music too loud. 'Did you think I was being funny?'

'No.'

She waved at a face he could not see, flashing that disarming smile. He suspected the face was imaginary. His would have been. He stared at her.

She pointed at the heaving mass and shouted in his ear. 'They all have problems too. Why can't you let go?'

He swallowed some beer and shouted back, 'It doesn't distract me. It doesn't feel real.'

She looked at him. 'What does, Max?'

'I don't know.'

Authenticity crises are natural enough in a room full of

men in G-strings rotating to Ricky Martin. But his inadequate answer irritated her and she shrugged. 'It's hard to feel sorry for you.'

'I never asked for sympathy.'

'Why doesn't painting make you feel better? Why doesn't working at something satisfy you?'

'I can't suspend my disbelief. I can't pretend it's important.'

Their conversation was staccato, cut up by the sounds around them. It forced boldness.

'What is it about "important"? You're not important, nobody's important; you just have to get used to it.'

He stared at her. 'I'm not denying that.'

'Yes you are,' she smiled. 'What do you think all this suicide shit is?'

He balked. The silence this struck in him made her feel powerful, strangely high. Urged her on.

'What was that stunt you pulled in London if it wasn't the biggest attention seeking cliché? You pretend you don't need to feel important and then you stage a dumb trick like that so everybody's thinking about you? Christ, it's even over-used in fiction, Max, never mind real life.'

Max frowned. This argument made perfect sense, he would use it himself, if he did not want so strongly to slink into the shadows. Deflect.

'I'm not a cliché. Froniel's a cliché, pushing his pathetic little therapies on people. And you know the saddest thing about him?'

She smiled as if she looked through his skull to the squirming thought processes inside. 'What's that?'

'That he thinks he's helping people when actually he's confirming that they have a problem. He's fucking them up. Whatever else you say about me, at least I haven't done any harm.'

'I'm not sure you *can* say that, Max.'

She looked at him and he looked back. Her face was shining.

He smiled. Attack. 'Beautiful Éva what do you care anyway? You want to unearth something sensitive deep inside me to account for your physical attraction. There's nothing there. Stop trying to understand me and face the fact that you're as shallow as I am.'

Éva shook her head. She struggled as he pulled her face towards him. His lips felt cool against her heat. She cursed her lack of will.

XXVI

The Memoirs of Gerte Mela (V)

I now come to the section of my story that is the hardest to write: my separation from Poltonov and the despond I fell into as a consequence. I can only state the facts as they happened. To embroider renders the events as more pathetic, more farcical, than I could bear to contemplate.

Since I had seen the portrait of Anna and since he discovered I had seen it (I confessed to him one night) – since then, we had grown closer. My feelings for him grew more vivid. In short, impossible though it was, I knew I wanted to be with him. That his affections were so hard won made it all the sweeter.

I thought, and I began to know, that he cared for me. He could not say so but it became clear – through his softening expression, when he caught my eye.

My urge to tell him that I had seen the painting – with such urgency that he laughed at my candour – stemmed, I suppose, from the fact that I could not tell him what I really needed to say: that I was not who – or what – he thought I was.

We spent more time alone. He wanted to talk. I encouraged him, insisting that, just because his artistic career was over, his critical one need not be. He was scornful; a man of over sixty did not want to start again. But I think he liked to be told.

My mind had developed. Through much reading, long discussion and contemplation, I was no longer such an ingenue. I could ask intelligent questions.

We grew together. Something had to happen. Love is not static. But what happened was without dignity. I wish it could have happened differently. It made a fool of both of us.

I had wheeled Poltonov earlier in the week, as usual, to the Russian bookshop on Wittenbergplatz. There, after he had nosed through some émigré journals, he bumped into a dyspeptic poet reduced to writing books on the occult for the black-market press. They discussed the scandalous quality of modern translation.

We were about to leave, when his eyes fell on a book propped up on the centre table. He let out a noise of satisfaction. 'Ah! I've been waiting for this.'

It had an olive jacket, so dark the Fraktur was barely visible.

'*The Rhythms of the Line*,' I read haltingly. On the inside cover, elucidation: '*The Rhythms of the Line*: Analogies in Colour, Form and Music.'

The day was frozen, I remember that. When I returned with Raskolnikov after midnight, the fire in the grate burned wildly. To my red cheeks, the room was thick with heat, but Poltonov's sick body needed warmth.

Poltonov began to talk about the book, which he had read that evening. There was something narcotic about his words. The combination of vodka, abstraction, colour and his mellifluous accent and argument melted my soul.

The book had moved him. The dour expression that swamped his face in mid-discussion was replaced by an eager, almost youthful energy.

At some point, some word, some magic, made me groan. I swooned with the power of his words. He closed his mouth and looked at me. He smiled. He never smiled. I did not think he *could* smile. I had dismissed that part of him as being paralysed as surely as his limbs. Yet now he smiled. The room grew warmer.

'You're a sensitive boy, Gerhard. That means a lot to me now. It gives one hope.'

I moved towards him, just to touch the dear face, miraculously transformed. I knelt in front of him. I kissed him on the cheek. He kissed my lips. Tentative at first, his kiss grew stronger when not rebuffed. He stroked my face tenderly with his functioning hand. I held the other.

It was a touching moment. But this was Berlin. There had to be a pay-off.

Perhaps it was my fault. I pushed it forward. I touched the baggy reptilian neck, an object of such fascination that I could not stop myself. In turn, this encouraged him. He moved his hand from my cheek, down my young neck, over my collarbone, the sternum, the top of the ribs. His fingers moved very slowly. So acute was my pleasure, I didn't stop him. But then, of course, he found something.

His fingers squeezed the unexpected fleshy mass in silence. There was a moment of delay. Then he screamed. He screamed so loudly, in such abject horror, that in seconds Anna burst into the room, still in her nightgown, her long hair splayed across her shoulders, terror on her half-conscious face.

She understood at once. With her better eyes and simpler vision she had seen through my disguise months ago. She had anticipated this.

Poltonov was shrieking, 'Get out! Get out! Get her out!' and shielding his eyes with his hand to dispel my repellent countenance.

Anna threw me a wild look and ran to fetch his sedation. I stared at him, saying nothing. Poltonov turned his face away.

There it is. I left him.

I was stunned, defeated, thrown into despair, all the more acute for the briefest glimpse of what intimacy there could have been. Poltonov was my life in Berlin – in fact, everywhere, for after all I had witnessed I could never return to the country and my mother.

Yet I was banished. I sank. For many days I stayed in my bed, so hollow-eyed and listless that even Frau Kellermann looked up from her self-interest and brought me thin cabbage soup and the hard rolls that Georg left. She pursed her scrawny lips. Nothing surprised her. 'Well, my dear, the conditions in Berlin *are* very hard at the moment.'

I dreamed of Poltonov. His face, rich with life, filled my vision. I even yearned to stroke the rough hair of that ugly dog. Then, as lonely days passed, my thoughts grew confused. Muddled selves competed for my attention. Who I was. Who he thought I was. Who I wanted to be.

Gerhard was dead. The clothes of Frau Kellermann's dead son Heinrich, my drag act, lay deranged at the bottom of the cupboard. I did not exist; not to Poltonov, nor to the authorities since the arrival of my dark doppelganger, Grete Milach, the day before me at the Volksfeld Art Academy.

I was grappling with delirium. The world around me, in front of my hand, grew hazy. This was not unusual in the city at the time. But, unlike others, I did not see an answer in pleasures corporeal.

All around me, while Berlin teetered on the edge of oblivion, the people succumbed to increasingly debauched *Lebensfreude*. Since the end was coming tomorrow, pleasure in the present was pursued with salacious fervency. The joy of life was never so sweet as when it was under threat.

But I did not believe I was alive. Gerhard had inhabited my body. Now Grete robbed my thoughts. Yet I felt like the impostor.

In my madness, I felt that Grete was all that remained of my aspirations, and that only by finding her could I re-establish myself.

I tried to be rational, to believe that, through bureaucratic ineptitude, two females with close to identical names who apply to the same school at the same time become confused. These things happen in the city; people's lives blend together.

(Later I met a man who had received cards lamenting the suicide of his wife. It was a shock, not least because he believed his wife was holidaying in Baden-Baden with her mother. It turned out that there was another Anke Stressert in the same apartment block. This Anke Stressert threw herself out of the fifth-floor window. It made a short report in the papers. But then, two years later, his wife *did* fall out of a window. Investigation revealed a morbid preoccupation with her namesake's tragedy had led to drink and risk-taking. Herr Stressert and I became friends, searching, in each other, for sense. We fell astray. We were chasing different ghosts.)

I was not rational. I came instead to believe that Grete *was* me and that everything else was pretence, at the very least vast distortion – the stories in the newspapers, the people on the street. Nothing in Berlin seemed believable.

Grete was alive. I must find her.

I went, then, to the Volksfeld school, for the first time since my last, ignominious visit. It looked different or I was changed. I walked carelessly over the black-and-white mosaic floor. They said it was eighteenth-century, I no longer believed them.

The class, *my* class, *her* class, was held in the internal courtyard on the ground floor, straight through from the entrance hall. They were working on grisaille, grafting sculpture onto paper, in the inner circle of the room. Standing behind one of six Doric columns that formed a concentric passageway round the edge of the room, I was able to see but not be seen.

The group sat in a semicircle facing a bust, a man with a wig of preposterous curls. At the front, an elderly tutor barked military instructions and sneered when a pupil had the effrontery to utter comment. Their canvases were propped up on bare wooden chairs. Old last-century chairs, they reminded me of Poltonov. I felt loss.

There were just two women in the group of ten and, since early on the other was mocked by name for her choice of pencil, I had no difficulty isolating my subject. Grete Milach could only be the girl diagonally opposite. With stealth, I crept round the courtyard, keeping to the darker further edge, until I had reached the column behind her and was within touching distance.

It was peculiar to look at her, so close that I could see her chest rise and fall and hear the tiny murmurs of her concentration. More striking was her beauty. Her face and body had perfect anatomical proportion. I wanted to paint her myself.

Her skin was a creamy yellow and exquisitely soft. Her lips were almost too full and the result was that she looked at the bust with a false but irresistible petulance. Her eyes were deeply liquid like freshly washed black grapes. Her nose was straight and fragile.

This girl was conjured by some devil to spite me. Her beauty was too complete. Straight ebony hair, parted in the middle, was modestly tied at the nape. Her legs were delicate and well shaped. She had breasts so perfect a child would want to reach out to them for the sheer tactile joy of feeling their fat softness.

There was serenity about her as she gazed at the marble perfection in front of her and committed the image to the page. While the other students rubbed their grubby fingers over their sketching paper and fought yawns, she, I could see, did not lose concentration for a minute. It was evident in the tension of her facial muscles.

After three hours the session came to an end. The cantankerous art master shuffled round the students to examine their work. His wordless grunts indicated whether he held a student in total, or just partial, contempt.

Finally he came to the stool of Grete Milach. He stopped, gazed for several moments and then let out a rapturous sigh. She responded with a quiet smile. An artist does not need words.

The class broke up. Grete moved with grace as she put her materials away. I was now visible but she did not see. After the first weeks in the city, when my newness, my naïvety, lit up in the dark, I was inconspicuous. It pleased me, though it should not, for it meant I was slipping surely into the Berlin sand.

She left and I followed, fired by a desire to know more about this beautiful thing. She was too lovely to hate. Too soft to fear.

It was lunch time. The girl moved quickly. This was not a local meeting. I knew the streets better than she. Several times she hesitated at a corner; once, she completely retraced her steps.

She moved east. After three turns of the circumference of Bahnhof Friedrichstrasse, dazed by train steam and the shrieks of a thousand travellers, she looked up at the heady glass-and-steel curved roof and faltered, colliding into a flea-ridden cabby's nag. The horse snorted hot breath on her face, the driver cursed her and she fell to the miry ground. When she pulled herself up, wiping the dirt from her clothes, it was me she stopped, to ask the way. I had allowed it. I wanted to enjoy my invisibility.

I concealed a smile as I gave her the information. I also hid my surprise. For the place she sought was a notorious slum.

Her expression was different from the one that had entranced me earlier. Fear in her eyes made her more human. I believed that the class was a three-hour reprieve from what really occupied her mind.

I followed her now at a more discreet distance, though I doubted even then that she would have recognized me, such was her preoccupation.

She followed the route, her lips moving as she tried to remember my instructions. There was reluctance in her step despite her hurry. I knew she would not turn back but she dreaded her destination.

She turned into a tall grey building. The outer door was open and beyond it lay a large grim yard with stone staircases on either side. It was a bleak arrival. The building was laced with large cracks, the ground was squalid with weeds and refuse, the stench of unwashed bodies and human excrement. The windows were broken. This was nothing unusual, but I had grown used to the windows of Poltonov's rooms, which gleamed from Anna's cloth so that the purple curtains were visible from the street.

A minute of muffled conversation and she was received. Now I climbed the stairs after her. I peered through the crack in the door and saw a man surrounded by pointed instruments, dirty weapons.

'It keeps the economy going,' I heard him say, with a foul laugh. 'You earn money in the getting and I' – he paused as he slid the palette between her legs, like a man cutting meat – 'earn money in the taking away. Who's the loser?'

I bit my lip rather than let out a scream.

'This is the last time,' she said.

'Don't say that,' he replied. 'I might take it the wrong way. I'd like you to know that not a single girl's come to harm at my hands.'

'What about the married ones?' she taunted grimly.

He slapped her round the jaw. Hard. 'None of that, young girl. Remember what you are.'

'My father was a general,' she said with unconvincing dignity.

'Means nothing, my darling. We're all the same now. I should know, I get all the fallen mighty here. I tell you, I never moved in better circles since I got into this line of business.'

Her face was tinged with green. 'Watch what you're doing.'

'You ought to watch your mouth too, my sweet love. You'll be back in a month and I might not be so happy to accommodate you.'

I felt ashamed to be a witness. I turned and retreated. I was searching, but Grete Milach was not the answer. I felt sorry for her, but not that sorry. It was just another story. These were the Golden Years. Later there would be sex on the streets and girls would not be paid.

I fell into a bar, of a kind I had never frequented. Everyone was drunk. Women were dancing naked together – for whose benefit, I could not be sure. But I knew that round here the criminal gangs operated, their clubs dressed up as wrestling venues. Toothless men sat round decrepit tables, drinking from dirty glasses. Their eyes followed me round the room. Who did they think I was? I did not care, for I did not know myself. Let them place their fantasies on me. At that moment I did not care. I had found Grete, the girl who had taken my place. Every fortune was balanced.

XXVII

We must become conscious that there are puzzles around us. And we must find the courage to look these puzzles in the eye without timidly asking about 'the solution'.

SCHOENBERG to KANDINSKY, 19 August 1912

Three photographers slouched outside the gallery, waiting. Cameras hanging limply round their necks informed the incoming guests that Nina Brandt had not yet arrived.

Eight in the evening and thus far only two celebrity sightings: a large, bearded old guy, the cult Greek patriarch in a German soap opera – of interest for this reason, but actually here tonight because in real life he ran a taverna, art gallery and an appeal for Kosovan refugees; then there was the girl who became a local radio DJ after someone heard her voice over the *U-Bahn* tannoy.

Inside, Erich, dressed in a grey suit over a thin black turtleneck, was refilling bowls of peanuts with unnecessary vigilance, every sense alert to the soft sound of the opening door. Max watched Erich warily. He was filled with a sense of dread.

At half past eight, Erich stood in a free space in order to introduce the evening. It took some time to silence the room, particularly the queue for the wine.

Max began to sweat. Erich seemed to clear his throat so slowly.

'Ladies and gentlemen,' he said bleakly. 'Thanks for coming.' He paused. Inhaled, reflected for a moment and began. ' "The Myth of Berlin". It is an appealing phrase and one we all believe we understand.'

Max's tension eased. His brother was functioning, albeit in monotone.

'It is this very comfort which the exhibition seeks to challenge: the danger that in the new century the history of Berlin will be entirely shrouded in the glow of reputation. By yielding to myth – the easy route of tourism and popular culture – we yield also to easy conclusions, the cliché and the stereotype.'

Feet shifted. Swigs were taken.

'Berlin is not one green and leering Otto Dix prostitute, nor one Blue Angel, one stoic airlift, nor yet one multi-coloured Wall. If one thing has identified this city, it is its continual change.'

In the street outside, a noisy group of teenagers passing the gallery knocked on the window. A few heads turned; the group outside jeered. Erich ignored them.

'It is fitting, then, that a new generation of German artists should take on my brief – to look at the nature of myth, its desirability, its seduction. Why the world craves understanding in the form of a postcard or a decorated mug. Modern artists defy the public's desire that art should be containable, should always hang over a sofa. I hope that in a small way this exhibition will similarly resist the categorization of Berlin.'

Tentative clapping (not, Max suspected, spontaneous support but, rather, premature belief that the lesson was at an end) stopped when Erich continued.

'To this end: the work here displayed is hugely diverse – in medium, form and content. Many of the artists, I am pleased to say, are here tonight. It is my hope that good will come of this unique gathering of artists and opinion-formers. The future is in our hands. Thank you.'

Enthusiastic applause.

Max exhaled long and silently. His fears so far unrealized, his brother's dignity was intact. The speech was hardly ground-breaking – Erich hadn't really said *anything* – but it was thoroughly respectable. At least it was short.

Erich, who had backed off, returned to the front. 'Oh, forgive me; before I leave you all to enjoy the evening, I am obliged to thank Danish Airways for its continued support of the work of quintessential Berlin artist Renate Schmitz. Her video piece of an Alsatian dog chasing its tail under the Brandenburg Gate, you'll see it in the back room, is called "Copenhagen".'

He paused, his eyelids lowered. 'It's wonderful to see corporate sponsorship playing such an unobtrusive supporting role in contemporary art.'

Max smiled. Good. Erich even won a laugh at the end. His brother was immediately surrounded, mulling in conversation. The crowd swarmed into movement. Max downed his drink, and queued for another, wiping his dripping hands on the tablecloth. He looked round the room.

Éva and Barbara, dressed in black, carried large oval trays of savoury delicacies, pastries and blinis, lifted aloft and then lowered as they negotiated the space. Max caught Éva's eye. He smiled at her. She almost smiled back. She sauntered over.

'Hi,' he said. 'How are you?'

'There are a lot of people here.' She snatched his glass from his hand and swallowed a draught of cheap Chardonnay. She then handed it back again. 'Good for Erich, bad for me.'

He laughed. 'Are you working all evening?'

She wiped her mouth and straightened her shirt, her low-cut shirt. 'No, just till the food's gone. And that won't be long at the rate this lot are getting through it.'

'Good. You must come and talk me through some of these masterpieces.'

She grinned. 'Right.'

Éva moved across the room. Max watched her. He was pleased at her acquiescence. Then he sniffed and held his hands behind his back and looked at the first exhibit.

Alone against the white wall, a white sheet hung. On it a bloodstain, a long streak, stronger at the top, fading towards the end. He had seen the image before, or one very like it, on a mug in Erich's kitchen.

And then he spotted Otto, mute in front of the work.

Max bent down and said in his ear, 'What do you think?'

Otto answered loudly, severely. 'Nina is a German artist. Not in the manner of a Kiefer, a Baselitz, an Immendorf, nor yet a Beuys. That is to say, neither the characteristic tropes of twentieth-century Germany avant-gardism – expressive, shamanistic – nor the characteristic dramas of twentieth-century German history are inscribed across the surface of her work. And yet she could not be anything other than German. Her work is *of* that history, enabled by its peculiar conjunctures, and in particular its vantage on the modern.'

'Uh-huh,' said Max. 'Where d'you read that? I had a photographic memory too once, you know. Enjoy it – it fades.'

Otto turned round slowly, scowling. 'Where's my picture?'

'What?'

'My picture. I've been through this whole pile of junk twice and I can't see my work anywhere.'

Max smiled. 'Otto, you didn't really think—'

'What didn't I really think? I thought we had a deal. I thought you kept promises.'

'Keep the noise down, Otto. You don't want to cause a scene.'

Otto shrugged sullenly. 'People don't see me.'

Max looked over his shoulder. 'I can see them looking right now.' He pushed Otto through the crowd, into the corner by the desk and computer. In a stage whisper, he said: 'Do you really think I could shove some picture in here and Erich wouldn't notice? Moreover, that for one minute he'd think something I'd done was by you?'

'We had a deal,' snarled Otto.

'What the hell would Erich have thought if I'd tried to muscle in? I'm in enough trouble with him as it is.'

'That's not my fault, Uncle. Nor is it a reason to renege on our arrangement.'

Max rattled fingers through his hair. Looked again around the room. His tone was exasperated. 'Otto, it was a bit of fun. Those chapters weren't yours to bargain with. And if you want to get professional about it, you surely never imagined that an hour of my time came that cheap?'

'I'm going to tell Papa.'

'Don't, Otto. Don't cause trouble.'

'Why not? You do.'

'Spot the difference', 2000
Brandenburg sandstone, wood and painted polystyrene

Side by side on a narrow shelf were two bricks, broad and pale yellow. Both riddled with shell holes. Only on careful examination was it possible to tell which was real.

Max hurried after him. 'Otto! Come on! Be realistic. I don't believe you really want to destroy what relationship I have left with my brother for the sake of hanging a picture on a wall.'

Otto pointed at the bricks: 'See how this sculpture places together the fictional and the .real, evoking the banality in both. Beuys freed non-objectivity from design and this, to me, is a natural inheritor.' He turned to Max. 'I hate you. You lied to me.'

Max did not know this, a child's intensity. The rawness of Otto's emotions, the sudden turn from the game he thought they were playing to this acute pain.

'Sh-sh,' he hissed, his embarrassment no less sharp than Otto's feelings, glancing round the room. 'What do you want?'

Otto looked up at him, the corners of his mouth drooping theatrically, his cheeks turning impassioned purple. 'I want my painting on display. You *promised*.'

The boy's voice was growing louder. Max felt weak. He foresaw the scream that would silence the room, and himself waving the impotent, hopeless hands of Stan Laurel when the piano fell down five flights of steps.

He crouched down to Otto's level, convinced that eyes were burning into his back, and muttered, 'How about fifty marks instead?'

In the child's hard gaze, the startling porcelain features, the bold green eyes, Max saw his own reflection and shuddered. He dismissed the memory of the Otto he knew; in his place stood a symbol: a beacon of purity in a dirty world, a righteous pillar, a transparent innocence. And he, Max, had crossed him.

At last the seraph spoke. 'I want a hundred and fifty and I want your *Apocalypse Now* DVD right *now*.'

Max felt colour return to his cheeks. 'OK, sure. The

DVD is beside my bed. I think I have cash in my wallet.'
He fumbled in his back pocket. At the same time he
caught the look of Erich. He tried to feel for the money,
with his hand behind his back. Otto was staring at him.

'I'm trying to do this subtly, OK?'

'Just give me the cash.'

Max yanked two notes out, twisting to avoid Erich's
gaze, and Otto snatched them. Max watched the righteous pillar's bottom scampering through the crowd and
out of the gallery door into the night.

Max sighed and turned back to the still suspicious
Erich. He raised his glass to him and mouthed, 'It's going
great!' Erich responded with a tired smile.

The room echoed with the conversation of minor art
people and small media figures. A crowd scanning who
was and was not there, calculating a personal position
within the hierarchy far more carefully than they looked
at the works on display. A vacuum. Max left behind
similar, self-vying circles in London. This was his life.
Like he said, irony did not exist. If he lived it, he meant
it. Secret disdain was a ruse.

As he stood up, a hand burst through: tapered perfection. A violent auburn bob. The perfume. The tinkling,
croaky voice, half coquette, half ashtray. Katrina.

'Max! God, can you believe all that guff he came out
with in the speech? Change? Erich! *Herr* Status Quo
himself! You should hear what he says about my lovely
new bars. They're a symbol of something appalling. I've
forgotten what.'

Max frowned, stepped unconsciously back.

She sighed, a light, sexy, worked sigh. 'You would not
believe how patient I am, how *unreasonably* patient I am,
constantly, with Erich's little ways. But there is no reward
for keeping quiet.'

Max kept quiet and was duly unrewarded.

Katrina grasped his sleeve. 'Oh but, Max, darling. I heard you nailed Ursula.' She prodded him in the ribs with the polished chocolate index finger of her free hand. 'Delicious! Wish you'd asked me.' She winked.

Max could stand only so many assaults. And at this he turned aggressor. He moved in and put his arms round her waist. He squeezed. She squawked.

He whispered, 'Well, what's stopping us?' His voice was dark and her patter paused.

'Oh, you.' The tone was less strident.

'We'll bring Dirk in on it too.'

She nodded, disentangled herself and popped a prawn ball into her mouth, mopping up a stray globule of sauce with the curvaceous nail. And since she was now almost sure that he was joking, she switched the charm back on. 'My libido *has* gone through the roof lately.'

'Oh, really? HRT?' Sometimes he felt as if someone else was speaking for him, throwing in phrases of the day, while he hid behind.

She pulled at his collar. He tilted, like a statue. 'Empowerment, darling, empowerment.'

'Empowerment?'

She nodded. 'Success is *the* great aphrodisiac. Dirk doesn't know what to make of it. As far as he was concerned I didn't even have to work. He doesn't want more money, can't understand the thrill at all. But God, Max, you know what I'm talking about. After all those years with Erich, desperately adding up the black and the red at the end of the month. Lining our pockets with the scant moral comfort that without our efforts the Kreuzberg Art Preservation Society would cease to be.'

'Ah, yes.' Max nodded darkly. 'Money, the great consolation.'

She grinned broadly, all teeth again. 'Come and talk to Dirk.'

'Later, Katrina,' he whispered, trying to play the game enough to keep her quiet, while fighting Erich's gaze. 'I have to go and relieve myself.'

'Liar.'

He smiled uneasily and slunk away, through a corridor of chatting bodies. It was true he couldn't deceive anyone. It showed when everyone else here seemed so adept. Lied to themselves, lied to other people. Convincing or otherwise. No wonder they were happy to talk.

Max walked through the rooms, glancing at the works on display, listening to people. Surrounded by strangers, he was safe.

'A squid always has one leg longer than the other.'

'Surely it's artistic licence?'

Max wound around unnoticed. Listening in.

'Yeah, I've been with the Hochtief team investigating Beirut's international airport – why it overran schedule by two years.'

'And why did it?'

'Oh, you know, usual story. The architect's grand vision, rebuilding after the war, put the place back on the map. It gets talked up, the government gets overexcited, the scheme gets bigger and soon it's out of control. But let's face it, it'll be a while before the Lebanon is back on the package-holiday map.'

Éva was standing by the picture that Erich had executed. Max broke his own rules to sidle up to her. To breathe.

'Fine Coat', 1999/2000
Oil on canvas

A penguin dominated the foreground, its yellow and white coat puffed out against the cold. The bird stood at a Berlin tram stop, his comrades in waiting – a man in a suit, a young woman holding a cello case, a short swarthy man eating *Bockwurst* – all apparently oblivious.

'Why'd he draw that?' said Max folding his arms behind Éva.

'I don't know,' she said.

Max stood silent as a woman tottered, oblivious, in front of him. He could no longer see Erich's picture, just the woman's dyed yellow hair. A very thin man in a sleeveless jumper and translucent trousers accompanied her.

'What a cute penguin!' she said too loudly. 'So refreshing to see a picture that's actually *of* something for once.'

Max would have dismissed the couple as satirical performance art if the action man was not already in motion. Dressed in a green military uniform, with a moustache so broad he had to squeeze through the door sideways, this man had been shadowing guests all evening, scribbling notes. Stretching, Max could read only one line: 'The misplaced brother of the curator tried to see what I was writing.'

Éva stood in a darkened corner where a film ran.

'Two minutes in 1989'
16 mm continuous loop

Ordinary people performed the ordinary. Spliced in was footage of the night the Wall fell. A woman buying apples complained about a bruise. The barrier at Bornholmer Strasse opened. It was eight thirty p.m. A child in a small kitchen cried and stamped because she wanted to sit on a stool occupied by her older sibling. Radio Sender Freies Berlin announced that fifty thousand people crossed into West Berlin. A man smoked a cigarette in a café, empty but for a dour woman washing up. Victorious cheers rose as the Trabbis drove past the Soviet War Memorial. An old woman lay dying in a Berlin flat.

Éva raised her eyebrows. 'I like this one.'

Max thought about it. 'The mundane process of living and dying is something big.'

'Isn't it wrong to use all that pain and suffering for artistic amusement?'

He smiled. 'Absolutely. But Schopenhauer reckoned that's the best way to keep cheerful. Stand on the edge and watch. By watching you get a sense of the universal and timeless, over-awed by the beauty of the patterns, and can forget the individual pain.'

Éva looked at the film again. 'Doesn't console me much.'

Max grinned. 'Me neither.'

Éva smiled.

'But still,' he sighed, 'it's good news for Berlin. Because although anywhere is a microcosm of everywhere, in Berlin it's all been more concentrated. And people will keep coming.'

Unconsciously, she stroked the side of her glass. 'How do you know about Schopenhauer and art?'

He was a little awkward. 'Why not? It's interesting.'

She sensed she should not probe. So she nodded as if he had given a full and enlightening answer. Her next question was almost inaudible. 'What art do you like?'

He looked at her quizzically. 'Are you afraid to ask?'

She laughed low. 'You don't exactly encourage personal questions. Erich says that you think pornography is more important than art.'

Max laughed. 'It serves a more useful purpose to more people. Even its stigma is important – to both the stigmatized and the stigmatizing. They both need to know that it's there. But, personally, I don't happen to like it.'

'You don't?'

He screwed up his face. 'It's done so badly. If they could only use people who were halfway attractive. But it always seems to be some five-foot stocky guy with a huge moustache. Bit like our performance-artist friend, in fact.'

'You didn't answer the question.'

Max glanced at her. 'Art. Hmm. I like inconsequential things. Stuff that trounces the aesthetic theory that something is either art or it's not. I like to think there's no dividing line.'

'I wonder if you'd like what I do.'

He looked into her eyes. 'Well, we won't know unless you show me.'

Her mouth quivered. 'Why would you want to see?'

'I'm interested.'

She smiled wanly. 'Oh, really?' She tossed her head and strode onto the next exhibit. He hurried after her.

'What's the matter?'

She looked at him with her eyes glazed. 'I feel so personally about what I paint. You believe that trying at anything is pointless.'

A tint of indignation rose in his cheek. 'Well, yes, sure, that's what I say.'

'Yes!' She looked at him imperiously. 'Yes!'

'Yeah, but you know that's bullshit.'

'No, I don't,' she said.

'OK,' he conceded, 'but I take heart. You wouldn't have mentioned it if you didn't want me to be interested.'

'Cabaret'
Oil on canvas, wood, glass, white and alcohol and diverse fragrances

A hastily scrawled sketch of a bawdy nightclub scene from the Twenties. A woman dressed in a black bodice with red stockings, a monocle, top hat and cane crouched on a tiny wooden stage with her legs open and arms akimbo. A small dog yapped and jumped in the air. The woman's legs were odd, one at least twice the size of the other. The audience, dotted anonymous heads, shouted '*Bravo!*' and '*Schön!*' in balloons. The picture rested against the wall on a waist-high table. It was partially obscured by a dark-green perfume bottle. There were no instructions. But unwritten art gallery rules had inhibited bystanders. Éva, though, leaned forward and took the entire bottle off the table, lifted the stopper and inhaled fearlessly.

'God,' she grimaced, 'smell that.'

Max smelt the wet contents of an ashtray, stale beer maybe and a low-light of urine. 'Put the lid back on, for God's sake,' he said, grabbing at her wrist, which shook the bottle precariously.

Éva's attention was pulled to a noise at the door. She looked away from the bottle. Shuddered. 'Watch out, the star's landed.'

Max looked across the room to where a just arrived Nina was standing by a blood-stained sheet. She looked radiant, shimmering in a silver dress that fell from spaghetti straps to the floor.

A scruffy man was asking, 'But, Nina, this work is a surprise. I thought you said painting was dead?'

Nina smiled beatifically. 'I believe in reincarnation. Daniel Richter said – and I think he expresses it so well – that painting has something that films and videos don't: you can look at a painting as long as you like. That's a precious commodity in our throwaway culture. Now, excuse me, I need a drink.'

She tottered to the drinks table. Her expression soured at the mediocre red and white wine. She looked up. 'Max! Max! I'm so glad you're here.' Nina rushed to join

Max and Éva (the latter only briefly acknowledged). 'This dress is so hard to walk in. I only wore it to cheer Papa up.'

'And has it worked?' put in Éva, caustically.

'Oh, I doubt it.' Nina looked across at Erich. 'Everything I do pisses him off.'

Max shifted on his feet. He wanted to move but couldn't. He could hear Éva twitching next to him. She smiled, waved him farewell unobtrusively with little fingers held low and headed to the next room. He was trapped.

Nina touched his arm. 'I wanted to say thanks for the other day, and sorry, about everything. I felt bad.'

Not wanting preferential treatment, Max avoided her gaze. 'Don't worry about it.' He felt the collar of his shirt. It was expensive, Egyptian cotton and new tonight, but still it itched. Erich was watching again, from across the room. Damn him. He didn't miss anything. In fact, worse than that, he found things that weren't there. Max tried to pull away from Nina's grip.

She held tight. 'You put things in perspective for me. I want to thank you.'

'That's quite all right.' His eyes cast down; he wished she would leave him alone. But she was gathering momentum, her eyes sparkling, her hand movements becoming more exuberant, more noticeable. Other guests were looking round as Nina showered extravagant praise on her reluctant uncle. They were silently fighting, Nina for attention, Max for invisibility. Nina was bound to win.

'I could walk away tomorrow, just like you, if I wanted, couldn't I?'

'I told you, I didn't walk away.'

She pulled a little closer. Max began to sweat. He felt her soft skin, but, more strongly, he felt Erich's eyes. He broke away from her and started chattering absurdly loudly, bringing the people around them into a circle, to water the intimacy.

Waving a foppish wrist, he sounded like an up-market coffee-table book. 'You know, I've often thought of starting an artistic movement. I was going to call it "Abandonism". All the members of the group would renounce artistic endeavour for ever. Throw in their brushes. Fuck off.'

While others nodded politely, Nina's eyes gleamed. 'That is a brilliant idea.'

'No, it isn't.' He shuffled, dropped the act. His new shoes pinched. People laughed.

A woman in black with a long black bob and a cigarette artistically poised between her fingers said, 'But your idea would be self-defeating, surely? I mean, you'd be doing yourself out of a job.'

'Oh, right,' said Max. 'Of course. I didn't realize.'

'Hold on a moment.' Nina rushed to put her glass back down on the table. Then she smacked the table several times with the back of her hand. The large brown stone on her ring clattered, the noise rang. 'Ladies and gentlemen!' she roared. 'I have an announcement.'

Instant hush. Max felt sick. He saw Erich peering across heads.

Nina dazzled, her platinum hair caught under the lights. 'Uh, ladies and gentlemen, some of you may have heard me on TV the other day mention the untimely death of my uncle, Max. This came as a great shock to all of us, not least the uncle in question.'

The guests murmured.

Nina continued to smile. 'I want to set the matter straight. My uncle is not only alive and well, his brilliance continues to radiate. Like I said on the show, he is a huge talent.' She gulped. Pushed past a few people to get to her blood-stained sheet. In the silence, her heels clanked against the stone floor.

An astonished cry went up when she yanked it off the wall. Faces drained as she held the sheet between her hands and, aided by her teeth, ripped it in two.

Nina, however, was flushed with excitement. 'What is art,' she panted, 'but self-promotion? My Uncle Max has, this evening, created a new artistic movement. He calls it "Abandonism". We, the self-seekers, should join him in turning our backs on this sick collaboration of ego and greed.' She held up the two pieces of sheet. 'Let us destroy this evidence. Let us give up art. I renounce my former ambition. I invite you to join me.'

The woman with the cigarette shook her head, took a sceptical drag and raised a highly arched brow.

Glowing, Nina beckoned to anyone to come and help rip. There was no lack of volunteers. Many artists in the room had wanted to sabotage her putrid and inexplicably successful work for years. Whoops and cries of glee rang out as the cotton gave into a hundred pieces and the dusty fibres floated upwards. Some even stamped on the shreds for joy. The rest of the crowd watched, laughing in astonishment, drinking the energy. With his head now in his hands, not even Max saw Erich slip out of the back door.

XXVIII

Whoever cannot find a hotel room goes to the steam bath. One night costs twenty marks. For this price, one can, as it were, sleep oneself clean and sweat it all out. They should put a motto over the steam bath. Something like: 'Through sweat to the light!'

JOSEPH ROTH, 1920, *Joseph Roth in Berlin*

Erich resisted the easy pathos of looking back and seeing the party glow without him, though he did wonder if anyone would notice his absence. Yellow pools shone onto the pavement and lapped against the cornerstone as he blinked.

In his mind his brother was always as he was just then: surrounded by people; each face illuminated, laughing at his words. It didn't seem to matter what he said. People warmed to Max's presence. There was Nina smiling.

Max meant nothing. Yet the uncalculating conqueror had worked his charm on all of them. Even Otto. Even the cleaner.

What did he feel about Max? Did he . . . The words clung like phlegm in his throat. He said it quietly out loud. It hung heavy in the moist air. 'Do I . . . love him?'

Would he care if he wasn't there? Would he be *glad*? If

he died. Or had never lived. He *had* almost died and Erich had been unable to shake the feeling of terror since. The incalculable terror of being alone. It was ineffable but he needed to know Max was there. Love. It was selfish. It had to be selfish to affect him that deeply. The threat of its removal could chill him, could fester inside him, a cold pool of poison, parasitic, sustaining. And it did not fade, but grew stronger as he grew weak. That was his love of Max. No good for anybody.

*   *   *

When Max was born, he stole his elder brother's talent. This was impossible, yet it happened. On the right-hand side of his head, Max had a small, extraneous lump of skin. It might have passed unnoticed but that Erich, in exactly the same place, had a hole. A hole, he was convinced, that had not been there before.

The parents called it chance. They liked to point it out to friends. Erich did not say it was the scar of his brother's theft. But he knew. For shortly before his brother's birth, Erich enjoyed his first and last artistic triumph. And as Max grew, it became clear that it was he who had the instinctive feel for pictures.

It went like this. The father of one of Erich's kinder-garten classmates was an artist – a Communist. In a fit of goodwill – the man had agreed to judge a class competition and present the winner with a prize.

Fear was then an unknown to Erich. He drew as naturally and as carelessly as he threw his ball in the square across the road. Unhampered by performance anxiety, the small boy drew the view from his window in the flat in Mitte, unaware then that the world watched too. He drew a new high-rise building he could see across the city. He loved its straight lines. While other things around him – his bed, the basin, the dinner plate – got smaller, the block seemed to grow as he did. He carved its gleaming sides onto paper in grey and brown.

Immersed in the task, he forgot the competition. Until he won. The other children stared as he stood up from the floor to accept his prize. Warmth spread through his face as he heard clapping in his ears. The artist bent down to shake his hand and thrust a tin of pencils at him. Erich opened it in wonder. The colours spanned the rainbow and shone under the electric light. At lunch time Heiko Weiss wouldn't speak to him. Heiko, who had a merit badge for good behaviour, turned his back in the playground. Erich stared in wonder. Jealousy was new to him then; he was an only child.

* * *

Erich walked tonight because he wanted the city to hold him. The car was sterile. He wanted the fresh air and brash clichés that he had scorned earlier; the tall men with tiny black glasses, impersonating philosophers, the smell of frying pork and of beer, the cranes, like winter branches against the sky, the overhead train crossing two hundred bridges, the laughter from late-night bars, and the scars on concrete, proofs of the present, proofs of the past.

And so Erich had reinvented his brother. Given him a better start in life. Shifted the story by a matter of months. Polished it; wasn't that what art was for? And wasn't this a perfect Berlin story? With the poisonous twist that saved him from one horror Erich was consigned to another. He was encouraged to tell the story of the family's narrow escape from East Berlin, the early arrival of the *Wunderkind*, who from the start had won the game of chance. Erich craved reflected glory.

Walking in Berlin was not an exercise of cartography but the mind. It should give him the reassurance he needed. But it didn't. For tonight Berlin was vapid.

Light drizzle cooled his head. The street lamps transformed it into falling powder but no-one stood underneath – nor in the darker alleys or cavernous *Hinterhöfe*, though Erich lingered, searching, sniffing for empathy. He walked, impeded neither by predators nor the crapulent, walking on their tightropes.

The prostitutes vanished, stealing their light of swishing blonde. The police outside the synagogue just nodded. There were no pictures tonight. Or his mind had closed to them. The city had betrayed him or he expected too much from it.

Maybe he'd craved Berlin because it was the last thing, before the birth of his brother, that was his and his alone. He had moulded it to suit him, while the world changed. A romance, like all romances, so much more in the mind than was possible in reality. He was not alone. West Berlin was the haven of Lou Reed and David Bowie, the inspiration of all those Eighties pop songs about nuclear war. It was not original. Even JFK was a 'Berliner' for a day.

He has built this world around him, it gives him a reason. No different from the people who climb Everest, collect cars, build muscle groups, learn to dive or have children. Filling their lives with equipment and certificates rather than sit in a room alone. Join in. Love Schoenberg, Marlene Dietrich or Britney Spears rather than face the vacuum of what you really are.

They do not talk, he and his brother. Max *can* talk. Nina told him that. Max and Erich skirt around each other. One is always leaving as the other arrives.

It is not a hostile gesture. He does not feel the need to talk to Max because he knows that underneath their chosen defensive positions, they think the same. They justify themselves by disapproving of the other. They are symbiotic.

He follows Max's mind behind those eyes. Just as Max does not say what he means, nor does Erich. Erich understands obfuscation.

The streets were so empty that Erich had the familiar suspicion that the rest knew something he didn't. That chemical warfare would be raining down within the hour. Right now, Berlin was stacking tins of food, candles and battery-operated radios in the cellar. When they were not laughing at him.

But at last, under a railway bridge in the dark, he saw a skinny figure: a wet-nosed kid in huge trousers was spraying on a wall. The kid stopped when he saw Erich but he didn't bring his arm down. He was poised, sizing him up. The boy was judging him not in terms of who Erich was, but in how Erich was likely to judge *him*. As an antisocial delinquent who should better learn manhood with a few years alone with a gun in the wilds? Or was this man a liberal, pleading the necessity that the anger of poverty should have a vent and repressed creativity be brought out in non-violent means? Erich's suit, to the kid's scant view, could dress a lawyer, an accountant or the long-term unemployed's first day at the call centre. Erich was a prat in a suit.

'You suck it!' The boy wrote this because he read it on another wall. Because his hand moved. Because there was a shop that sold spray cans. Because. His reason and his message suited the vacuum. Poignant, thought Erich, in its pointlessness. Said it all.

Tonight Erich wanted Marlene as a thumb of easy comfort. He wanted to curl up in her. This was what he always wanted but it had never before struck him so sharply that he fled to her, away from the rest of his life. She was his breathing Berlin.

More than an hour later, he climbed the stairs to Marlene's apartment. The wood creaked more loudly in the silence. A little short of breath at the top, he slowly turned his key to her door. Though she was used to his erratic hours, proudly ascribing them to latent artistry, this might alarm even her. It was very late.

But she wasn't there.

At first he was casual about it, drawing his finger along the dust on the furniture as he whistled through the apartment, confident that she was sprawled in some corner. He then became curious, then worried.

He left the door open on his way back down the stairs to the squatters on the floor below. For the first time, he peered right into the fug. Bass and drums throbbed, the only movement in an otherwise airless room. The dope heads showed no surprise at his appearance.

Three bodies, Erich made out in the darkness, reclining on ugly furniture. Two at least were partially conscious; the third was slumped face down, arms hanging, fingers scraping the floor.

'Sit down, man.'

The sofa was ugly. Cadmium yellow medium stirred into burnt umber. Colloquially, shit-brown. Badly sprung and damp. Erich perched on the edge, his eyes wide, expectant.

One raised his eyelids in Erich's direction. 'All right?'

Erich spoke slowly and loudly. 'Do you know what happened to Marlene?'

Blank.

He said, less surely, his voice sounding thin, unconvincing, in the husky darkness, 'The woman upstairs?'

The man drew out the syllables. 'Mar-len-e?'

'Well, she may have gone under other names.'

A silence, a long silence. Erich waited while the moisture seeped through to his trousers. The one youth's flaccid mouth chewed the words and he sniffed noisily. At last he spoke in a hushed whisper. 'That old bag was *Marlene Dietrich*?' Erich shook his head dumbly but no-one noticed. The man nudged his nearest companion, who roused with soporific jerks and murmured, 'But Marlene Dietrich's dead, isn't she?'

'Did you ever see the body? She was a recluse, Steph: they probably just *said* she was dead.' He whistled. 'Marlene fucking Dietrich. Fuck.'

The other shook his head and looked up. 'Who was she? And who are you, man? I don't know who you are. Who are you?'

'I'm Erich.'

'Who's that? Who the fuck's Erich?'

Erich smiled. Good question.

The man had the slow deliberation of a permanent drunk. He held one finger sententiously aloft; his eyes were so unfocused, it could have been a squint. He had devoted years to convincing himself that sitting on the sofa, smoking, had anarchic purpose. And all the time, Erich had thought he should recreate the cafés of the past, of Brecht and Weill, Nietzsche and Wittgenstein, to encourage debate. The world had moved on.

'Who the fuck *are* you, man?'

The key questions were not disseminated via public lecture or published in close-type print any more. They came out of drooling mouths, from ad hoardings, a computer virus spreading malicious love or a graffiti tag under a railway bridge. It must be short. 'You suck it.'

'I have two children,' Erich ventured.

The man inhaled deeply. 'Genetic fascism. Human pollution. Cultural terrorism, imposing your world on someone else's. Pure greed.'

'Right.' Erich nodded, thinking fast. 'I love my brother.'

Afterwards, he was not sure how much of the conversation had taken place outside his head.

The other man, watching the TV all this time and unconsciously nodding his head to the music, took the joint. 'You talking about the old girl upstairs?' He dragged on the cigarette. 'Frau von Schoenecker?'

'Er, maybe, yes! Yes!' Erich grasped at anything.

On the TV an avuncular artist with round, greying beard was talking through trees' reflections in water, daubing ripples on a jigsaw puzzle. Bob. Drawling California, three a.m. calm. 'You can find any colour in a reflection. Look at the red I'm using here. Splash it on. Don't be afraid.'

The man kept his eyes fixed on the art class. 'Uh, she's gone. Ran away.'

'A-ha. Do you know where to?'

The man shrugged. 'There was some big bust-up with her family. You know, the old woman was an informer in the past. The daughter was something in the underground. There was always trouble. The old woman split. I used to hear them screaming through the ceiling.'

Without warning, he leapt up and sprang his long-underused body against the ceiling. He grabbed at it and crashed back to the floor with a piece of plaster in his hand, never once taking his eyes off the screen. He held up the fragment. 'This place is not what you'd call soundproof.'

'When did she go?'

He shrugged 'Couple of nights ago.'

The first guy on the sofa wrinkled his brows, stuck his finger in the air. He stared into space. 'No, Karl, that's wrong. Two people left together, a man and a woman.'

The TV guy nodded. 'Yeah, the old girl and a cab driver.

312

He was speaking some foreign language, Ukranian? Something she understood.'

The first one scoffed. 'How could it be a cab driver, man? She doesn't have a phone.'

For the first time the man slumped against his lap spoke through his swinging arms, in a tone of morning-after Janis Joplin. 'That guy was no cab driver. They look after their own, you know.'

Erich looked bewildered. 'Who?'

*   *   *

Katrina and Dirk returned to their room at the Four Seasons. The staff at this hotel is trained not to laugh at middle-aged females who arrive without their shoes demanding a Sea Breeze. The concierge just smiled. 'I'll just arrange that with room service, madam. If you'd like to go up, I'll have it sent over right away.'

'Where is my room?'

Dirk was pulling at her elbow. He handed the man a ten-mark note.

'Christ, my feet are killing me,' Katrina whined, loud enough to attract the curious looks of two expensive Italian children sitting on chairs across the vestibule, swinging their legs. 'What are you staring at?' she shouted. 'And what are you doing up at this time? Don't you have beds to go to?'

In the room, she retreated into the palatial bathroom. She re-emerged some minutes later, wearing more lipstick and fewer clothes, and stood with her arms draped round the doorway like Elizabeth Taylor in a Tennessee Williams play. But only the vodka winked at her, from its glittering ice cubes. Dirk had fallen asleep.

*   *   *

Burning, Nina left her father's gallery.

As her cab rode home, her head was filled with pictures of herself on television giving up art, the scenes of people, en masse, destroying their work. She saw it taking place on the anniversary of the book burning for impact. That would make the main news, if she could pull that off. Abandonism – she loved the word already – would surpass Dada or Fluxus. The twenty-first century was waiting for a new artistic force. And she would be the leading exponent. It was the big idea. She could meet Yoko Ono and hand her a one-word message, such as 'Burn', like Yoko wrote 'Breathe' to John, and it would go down in history.

She rang Jörg. As soon as he answered, her charged patter started. He groaned.

He said when she had finished, 'There's a guy in Cologne who rejected art.'

Breathless, 'Bluebeard? Yeah, OK, he objects, but he makes wooden models of Bluebeard to prove it. Don't you think that rather spoils the effect?'

'A man has to make a living.'

'But this could be real, Jörg. Can you imagine? This could be huge. I think we should talk. Shall I come over?'

'I'll call you tomorrow.'

'Jörg!'

'Stay cool. We'll talk about it tomorrow. *Ciao*, baby.'

'Are you fucking that hairy-chested tart again?'

Click.

Deflated, Nina sat back in the seat. The cab driver had parked at an angle under a street lamp at the side of the road to look at a map. The car's inside light didn't work. The man was peering at the folded book. He asked for her help. The rain fell softly on the windscreen. Nina slammed the headrest.

By the time she was finally back at her flat, she was losing clarity. She grabbed paper and a pen, but, confronted with space, no words came.

* * *

'You can go now, Barbara. It's so late. We can finish the rest off in the morning.'

The waitress looked offended. 'It's no problem. We're almost done.'

Ursula smiled a tired smile. 'You're making me feel guilty.'

Not difficult, thought Barbara. They worked in the café kitchen. Ursula was juggling space in the fridge. Barbara gathered remains and stacked dishes.

Ursula said, 'Where did everybody go? It seemed like one minute everyone was there and then the next it was just you and me.'

Barbara shrugged.

'I didn't see Erich leave, did you?'

'He was gone after Nina's little performance.'

'Oh God.'

Well may you pull that face, Ursula. Barbara was bursting with dislike. Ursula was breezy, waltzing round the kitchen as if she were not, after this, also going back to an empty bed. Barbara thrust her chest forward, grabbed the fridge door from Ursula and looked for space to insert her tray. Ursula clicked with annoyance but said nothing.

Barbara turned to her artlessly. 'Oh, and, of course, lover boy's off with our tit-less Magyar friend.'

Ursula held her breath. 'Éva? Max left with Éva?'

'Yes!' The harsh delivery implied that this was obvious, acknowledged, inevitable.

'My,' Ursula was nonchalant, 'he does get around.'

Barbara looked into her eyes, an intimacy Ursula no longer enjoyed. 'Are you all right?'

Ursula stared back. 'Of course.'

Barbara looked sceptical. She did not want to believe it.

'Oh, Barbara, come on. You didn't think there was anything in that, did you?' Ursula let out an assured little laugh. 'Be serious. I mean, Max is fine fling material but anything more than that . . . well, I mean, no.'

Barbara scrutinized the other woman. When there was nothing to see, she shrugged and looked away. 'If you say so.'

Ursula smiled enigmatically. Barbara was nonplussed. Ursula was proud of herself.

For a while they worked in their own thoughts, the only noise Barbara's moody footfalls on the hard kitchen floor and the soft suck of the fridge-door seal.

'Here, look!' Barbara's eyes lit up. 'There's a whole bowl of chocolate fondue left over. Pass us the cherries.'

Ursula searched the fruit bowls and scraped together a couple of handfuls. She put them in a dish and gave them to Barbara. 'Enjoy it. I hate chocolate fondue and I've got to go to bed. Don't forget to lock up. See you tomorrow.'

Barbara scowled and let her mind wallow in the dunking – plunging the cherries one by one, scooping up generous quantities of the chocolate mixture and popping them speedily into her waiting mouth. It was an efficient production line: when one chocolate-coated cherry was swallowed there was always another one waiting.

Graffiti – Berlin Mitte, 2001

Spray paint on concrete

'No person is illegal!' That's what I say. Forgive me, I've a bit of a weakness for a sound bite. We all have. It's the only way to get noticed.

Actually, my end used to read 'except gays and Jews', before the cleaning squad blitzed me. You can still make it out if the sun shines just before midday.

They are cracking down on us. Wiping us out, cleaning us up. Worse, *putting us in galleries.* Arguments rage about the future of the gallery, public funding, private ownership of national treasures, the point, what is or isn't art. Endless talk, but all the while our huge public gallery is being eroded. It's a state of emergency and nobody cares.

Any middle-aged sow, with hair sprayed to concrete, is free to cast aspersions at me every day as she makes her porcine perambulations. But nobody minds that she assaults my delicate senses with her cheap perfume, that the car drivers who shake their fists at the crossroad ahead threaten the very paintwork I lie on, with their juddering filth. No, that's OK, apparently.

I admit there's good graffiti and bad graffiti. But I don't know who should be the judge of this. Except that, just as in every other sphere of life, for every witty, perceptive, original little me there's a great pile of rot. Did not Albert Einstein himself say that ninety-nine per cent of

everything is shit? *Ein Stein*, 'a stone'. No coincidence, I
say, that the greatest human being of the twentieth
century was part wall. At least, I think it was him, but it
might have been Woody Allen. *W.All*en. There's still
brickwork in there.

'Graffiti or scribbling? That is the question.' Thus spake
the SPD Senator for State Development, champion of
'*Null Toleranz*' and a man not above using a good sound
bite himself.

Can you imagine how such words strike terror in the
heart of every Pochoir, every Piece, every last Throw-Up
among us? They even pulled down the Hall of Fame at
Mehringdamm. They mean business.

But they're hypocrites (OK, who isn't? I admit to being
somewhat two-faced myself). They litter the city with
corporate-sponsored bear statues. Well, that's OK. Keith
Haring sprayed all over Berlin in the Wall years and now
they put up those phallic two-dimensional people
sculptures all over the city in his honour! Hmm. There is a
saying round here: 'It's not what you say, it's who pushed
your spray.' Don't forget that.

Commentators noted that the Wall came down at the
same time as the political sloganeering of the
Sixty-Eighters was replaced by an era of the 'me'
generation. Fame over fighting. 'The victory of
egocentricity over public spirit', according to Dr Bernhard
van Treeck, Berlin graffiti expert. Dr van Treeck warns
against those who would indiscriminately wipe out the
street artist. Giotto, he says darkly, started out with
graffiti.

XXIX

She was always late – and always came by another road than he. Thus it transpired that even Berlin could be mysterious. Within the linden's bloom the streetlight winks. A dark honeyed hush envelops it. Across the kerb a passing shadow slinks: across a stump a sable ripples thus. The night sky melts to peach beyond that gate. There water gleams, there Venice vaguely shows. Look at that street – it runs to China straight, and yonder star above the Volga glows. Oh swear to me to put in dreams your trust, and to believe in fantasy alone, and never let your soul in prison rust, nor stretch your arm and say: a wall of stone.

VLADIMIR NABOKOV, *The Gift*, 1937

'Come and see my flat,' Éva had said. 'It's a dump.'

He did not say anything but followed her through the door. He liked her silence, her ease with it. He liked to be silent with her, to calm the shouting inside his head.

After they had walked a few metres up the street, 'My car,' she said, slapping her hand against an elderly vehicle.

'It's a Trabant.' He did not disguise his surprise.

She nodded in indignation. 'We waited fifteen years for

this car. We were hardly going to get rid of it simply because something better came along.'

'It's your family's car, then?'

'Kind of. It *was*. My mother can't drive now.'

She wore a black shirt. It was unbuttoned, so that as she shifted to put her seat belt on he could see she had nothing on underneath. He saw the shadow of a soft and tapering surface of skin.

He liked her breasts, that they were almost too small. After gluttony, refreshment. Small, unshowy and, for that, defining. When she worked, under tight vest tops the large nipples had a profile like contact lenses against an eye. He imagined they missed nothing.

The car's thin engine wheezed into action. They spluttered up the street.

'A Trabant,' he reflected, 'but I thought you were from Budapest?'

'My mother is Hungarian. My father is German. I was born in Budapest but I grew up in East Germany, near Chemnitz.'

'Like Katrina?'

Éva rolled her eyes. 'She's a cousin.'

'Gosh. Not much family resemblance, is there?'

'I wore her handed-down blue shirts for the Communist youth group.'

'How awful.'

'My mother wouldn't waste good money on government propaganda.'

'Quite right. So Katrina's an Ossie?'

'Yes, well, she got out early, of course. She escaped, married Erich – if you could call that escaping.'

Max smiled. 'I never knew that. Why didn't they tell me?'

'She doesn't talk about it. She hates it if she thinks someone can tell that she's from the East. So she goes all out the other way. Because people can spot the Ossies, even now. Or they think they can, or Ossies think they can. It's in the eyes, in the older ones: there's still a dead look. Squashed spirit, like nothing will make a difference.'

'I can relate to that.'

She gave him a withering look. 'Don't. Don't make me despise you.'

Her room was dark, with the hanging smell of wet plaster and damp. He got up, walked round the room, looked out onto the street. Shivered. 'The window's missing.'

Éva laughed. 'You obviously haven't squatted.' She put music on, a whistling accompaniment. Blowing the wind on his face. She returned from an unlit room holding two brown bottles. 'Beer.'

He accepted it, together with the slightly warped bottle opener, which mangled the removing of the lid. He finished the job with his teeth. They sat on the window ledge, looking out. The missing glass was vaguely thrilling.

Some nuance in his face made her stretch her free hand to his head. Her nails were bitten to the quick. She touched his temple. 'You're worried, aren't you?'

'Yes.'

'What about?'

'I don't know,' he said. Then, seeing her frustration at this answer, he relented. 'I have to leave here. I'm driving Erich mad.'

'Are you going back to London?'

He sighed. Pulling at the label on the bottle, he said, 'I don't know. There's nothing to go back to. I don't miss anybody. I don't miss anything. How can I have come this far through life without any, I don't know, attachment?' He laughed glumly. 'I need something. Last week

I looked round the city, all those building sites, men working together, bright orange jackets, safety helmets. That seemed a useful thing to do. Physical exertion, no brooding. But I asked and most of them start at sixteen, apparently.'

'How old are you?'

'Thirty-nine.'

Éva choked. Beer bubbles foamed round her mouth. 'That's funny.' Her giggles were infectious. Black laughter.

She took his hand and with it wiped the spilt beer from her own mouth. Then she took his jaw in her hands and stroked it with one finger. He didn't move. He breathed. The apartment was so dingy. This youthful shabbiness was as calming to him as her thin body.

In her hands he relaxed visibly and shook as she stroked, letting out his breath uneasily. His own thoughts were distracted by her dark eyes and the delicate brows that clung to them and the big, petulant mouth. How could a face help him?

'You're so . . . beautiful.'

She stopped stroking and shrugged. 'You're good with women. You make them feel beautiful.'

'I'm not that cynical.'

'No,' she said, 'I don't believe you are.'

Éva swung off the ledge onto the floor. 'Come and see the rest of the apartment.' She took his hand and pulled him across the room.

Walking in the dark . . . He wanted to hold this moment, the expectation. Those Trabants honking through border controls after so long. The moment of promise. It did not get any better.

The floor felt dirty, tacky on his soles. He noticed it. Made him think of his kitchen floor: the white blandness in the steel kitchen installed at some great expense by a London architect who promised timelessness. Timeless-

322

ness and thoughtlessness, for within a week his feet had forgotten life without it. Which was not to say he craved a decrepit floor instead. Just that floors meant nothing to him.

At the doorway to the landing he pulled her back by the waist. Her body felt cool. She didn't say anything. She kissed him.

Her unadorned face and body, her clothes, made no attempt to attract him. She tasted lean. He saw simplicity. Though he didn't know her and he was imposing his own beliefs on her, still it was soothing to feel in her a lightness that contrasted to his own excess. Knowing this was a conceit did not invalidate its effect. That was a strange thing about the city. For all his awareness of its easy lure, it still worked. Like the beautiful child in the charity ad, with those mammoth eyes and one trickling tear. Didn't matter how many times, he cried too. All children were beautiful. The ugly ones have no photos.

Éva tugged his arm. 'I haven't shown you the games room.'

He rested his chin against the back of her neck. With his mouth, he worked his way under the shirt to her shoulder. He bit. He groaned.

'What's the matter?' She turned her head. 'Have you found something unpleasant?'

He kissed the shoulder lavishly. Her skin tasted warm and sweet and ludicrously nostalgic of more innocent times. Which never existed, by the way, he told himself. But she tasted so clean he felt grubby.

They walked up the stairs, which were partially covered with a thin, sticky carpet. He reached out for the banister, then changed his mind. They turned left at the top of the stairs.

A huge pool table dominated the room. Max started.

323

She grinned. The edge of her smile met the jagged ends of her hair to form a bittersweet curve.

'Where did you get that?'

'We looted it,' she said with pride. 'There was an old *Kneipe* a few doors along the street.' She indicated. He peered out to the grey, featureless back street, light kept out with tall, stern buildings. 'It was one of those dingy brown linoleum East German places. It closed down a couple of years after the Wall.'

Éva racked up the balls. The white was as yellow as ancient ivory. The baize was speckled with burn marks and the table leaned to the northwest on the sloping floor.

Éva moved round the table like an acrobat, perfectly balanced as she leaned to reach for a shot, one leg up on the table like a peeing dog, the regulatory foot balanced tiptoe on the floor.

'I haven't played for years.' Max needed to explain losing to a woman.

She seemed to enjoy his discomfort. Her hands were placed atop the cue. Max smiled at her pleasure. He grabbed the cue and threw it aside, letting it clatter to the floor.

He lifted her up. She curled her legs round his hips. He rolled her backwards onto the table and tugged at her jeans, which zipped tightly over her caved-in stomach. He pushed up the black shirt, like pushing papers off a table. He ran his hands over the U-shaped waist and the knob of her hips. The contours were all so clearly defined. He could feel the air between her curved back and the green felt of the table.

'You're so flexible,' he marvelled.

She laughed. 'Not any more. I'm much too old for us to do it on such an ungiving surface.' Her eyes rolled sideways. 'The bed is next door.'

He scooped her off the table, holding onto her naked waist, while the shirt bunched up and tickled his neck. She had poise; her spine seemed to hold itself.

'Were you a gymnast?'

A wry look. 'Oh, of *course*. Don't you know we were all gymnasts – or spies. It was always one or the other – often, both.'

'No,' he said, focusing his face into a frown. 'I remember distinctly discus-throwers and pianists as well.'

'I can't play the piano.'

A double mattress on the floor covered in a used sheet, a naked bulb coming away from the ceiling, swinging in the breeze from another missing window-pane, the hole draped with a cotton sheet. No furniture, but a small pile of books, on both sides of the bed.

He thought, as they moved together, that all the time she was thinking in a language he couldn't understand. He looked at her and imagined how she saw him, an ageing male, puffing. The bravest people in the world were those over-fifty sex freaks who put mirrors on the ceiling.

He imagined that he could lie his face in her hair and inhale the clean unperfumed smell, but she would not rub off. With time, her freshness would evanesce, like the smell of a fourth rose.

He was less open to distraction when he was angry. With Ursula, for those brief moments up against the basin, he had hated her for wanting him so badly, so inappropriately, without even knowing him; for allowing him to carry on. During those moments he forgot everything. He was blinded by hatred.

Éva responded to him gracefully but she gave little away. She was passive, lying on her back, allowing him to admire her. She seemed to like it, curving closer as he touched. Her limbs flexed softly round him.

Still he was anxious afterwards. 'Was that all right?'

She kissed his cheek. 'Come and paint.' She slipped from the sheet and dragged at his hand. He tried to stop to pull his trousers on but she was too strong for him. This was the tiny hand that could carry a whole pile of plates without strain. Hidden strength.

'Paint what?' he protested. His other hand hung awkwardly at his side, wavering, as if he wanted cover but wouldn't admit it.

'A wall.'

He looked round. 'This place needs a lot more than painting.'

'I meant paint *on* the wall. A *painting*.' She flashed him a smile, intimate, friendly.

Max felt better. He said, 'You know, I can be much more creative with my trousers on.'

The wall in this room was about four metres by two. She turned on a bright light and he gasped. Women exposed a lot less, naked, than men did.

'Here.' She threw him a brush. It spun as it flew. In his self-consciousness, he missed it and it clattered on the floor beside him.

She pointed. He admired the subtle definition in her arm. 'The paints are over there. I haven't got very many, but you only need four colours to paint Berlin.'

'I read that too. What makes you think I want to paint Berlin?'

Éva walked towards him, the light exposing flawless skin. There was a coy smile on her face. 'The picture isn't for *you*.'

She picked up another brush that stood in a jar with others and walked to the edge of the room. 'I'll start this end, you start at that one, and we'll meet in the middle.'

She drew ochre lines, parallel unbroken lines that

stretched her whole body, from a crouch on the floor to a full extension. Her waist sucked in and out, an accordion.

'What are you doing?' he asked, the brush limp in his hands.

One buttock rose up as she twisted to reach higher, like a comma. She turned round to answer him. 'Just going with what feels right.'

'Something feels right?'

She turned and nodded, grinning. 'If it isn't, I can paint it all again tomorrow.'

'Well, isn't that something.'

She stood squarely in front of him, her hands on her hips, the brush handle against the top of her thigh with a thick drop of paint clinging to the tongue. She was demanding to know why he stood there frozen. He wondered if her brutal nakedness was more tempting or less. Or both.

Éva was waiting for an answer to the question she had not posed. He liked this non-verbal language of hers. It made him answer her as he would not others. Now he said inadequately, 'I don't really do this any more.'

She rolled her eyes.

He tried to forget himself and let the brush lead. It was impossible, trying to empty the mind. He would have to forget years of objections. Instead of painting, he was colouring in. He followed cracks in the plaster. Roads that widened and narrowed.

They worked in silence but it did not feel quiet. He thought about the girl in front of him and how amazing it was that, despite everything, someone as beautiful as she would still choose to be with him. Miraculous, how people still liked him.

One trait always endured to the bitter end. Let likeableness be his. His father had held on to grim black humour. After projectile vomiting, he told Max he was redecorating the ceiling. Then, his mother's critical gaze. 'Did you sleep last night, Max? You look dreadful.' Rich, when her body was bloated on drugs and disease, but, with difficulty, Max kept this to himself. He did not want to grow old and lose this physical closeness with other people. As years went by his parents moved further and further into their own corners of the living room.

'*Nein!*' A desperate and plummeting cry from outside preceded a solid thud.

Max threw down his brush, ran to the window, his body taut. 'Someone's thrown himself off the roof.' He peered vainly down.

Éva looked bemused, her paintbrush still at right angles to the wall. 'What are you talking about? It's kids playing football or something.'

Max strained to see in the darkness.

Sighing, Éva put the brush down and slouched across the room. She peered over his shoulder. 'There's nothing there.'

Standing behind him, she took his shoulder and felt the strain in his muscles. He felt the graze of her chest against his back and her pubis against his hip as she leaned in to comfort him. She gripped him and said seriously, 'Listen, the world does not take place in your head.' She stroked his arm and turned her attention to his work on the wall. 'You are decorating after all.' She laughed but he heard disappointment in her voice. His lacklustre abstract lines were not good enough. She wanted genius. She wanted everything that Erich sold.

He said darkly, 'I haven't finished.' Snatching back the brush, he plunged it into the ultramarine pot. On the dry wall remaining he drew a single line, into a profile, a face. Éva.

She smiled uncertainly. 'That's scary.'

He smiled back, relieved that he had pulled it off,

but despising himself for playing into this easy trap. People did not want normality from him, they wanted fire. Very rarely, he succumbed. It was not vanity, it was pragmatism: Éva needed to believe. It would make fucking him more exciting.

XXX

The Pont Neuf Wrapped, Paris, 1975–85
Polyamide fabric and rope

The visual impression made by the wrapped bridge was one of
post-modern, aerodynamic architecture that preserved one or
two anachronistically medieval features. Those who asked after
the point of the exercise were well answered by one of the
Chamonix mountaineers who had been engaged in binding up
the vertical walls and who observed that he really had no idea
why he scaled the summits of mountains either. The thing must
be its own vindication: it is done because it is possible to do it.

JACOB BAAL-TESHUVA, *Christo & Jeanne-Claude*

The fat pale girl behind the counter thought he was a
terrorist. He wanted a ticket to Paris, immediately. She
asked unnecessary questions. He lied for the sake of it.
She had no need to know the truth. He said it was a
sudden emergency, his father was dying. If he seemed
tense, well, who wouldn't? She smiled nervously. He
bought a news magazine and read about the resurgence of
Prussian nationalism.

*   *   *

Otto flipped the remote control and pulled the quilt round him. Apart from the TV, the room was dark. On the screen, helicopters whirled against an amber sky. A voice he didn't recognize was singing 'This is the end'.

* * *

Typically, at least one third of the works in any exhibition needed to sell for financial viability. Even with its three-week duration, selling 'Berlin: Myth Exploded' would be tough. Most of the stuff was unsellable. Still, last night the fist-sized model doughnut with a hidden tape inside endlessly repeating '*Ich bin ein Berliner*' had gone, along with the cabaret table. Not bad. But by what measure should the success of an exhibition be judged?

Sipping morning coffee, paring open soft yet crispy rolls, reviewers were already chewing phrases: 'Naïve. Confusing. If art cannot provide answers, it should at least raise coherent questions.' At least it was being criticized.

Or perhaps success could be counted in column inches. 'Berlin: Myth Exploded' would make an unexpected appearance in the gossip pages. The *BZ* was wowed by the dazzling silver number of bad girl of the Berlin art scene Nina Brandt. The tabloid noted she showed up minus her partner, controversial 'Artrepreneur' Jörg Kraller. It referred to *BZ*'s exclusive story of the previous week linking sexy Nina with Alfie Junker, DJ and rap star ('*Mutter, du Whore*').

* * *

Perhaps it was enough that those who attended had a good time. Art was wallpaper.

Katrina wore dark glasses into the breakfast room of

the Four Seasons. Dirk wore a look of mild amusement.

'I feel like shit.'

'Baby, you look like shit.' He pinched her bottom.

'Get off.'

She scowled and he laughed. He had a wealthy smile, a casual confidence that complemented the tousled hair and unintentional stubble. Dirk was completely at ease in this habitat. He was rich enough to look scruffy. He did not need words to communicate this to the serving staff. Dirk made the world feel smaller.

They sat down at a table, chairs held out by an unctuous waiter, labelled Sergei.

Katrina blossomed with sycophancy. As the dark, sallowly good-looking waiter handed her a menu, recommending the kedgeree, she smiled. 'That's a beautiful accent, Sergei. Are you from Russia?'

Dirk sighed.

Sergei smiled with great professionalism, resting his arms behind his back. 'No. I am from Belarus.'

'Ah.'

Sergei bowed. The actor's smile did not fade until he had left the stage.

'Oh God, Dirk, I don't want anything to eat.'

Dirk read the menu through half-moon glasses. He peered up at her. 'You should eat something, babes. Eggs are good, make or break.'

'I hate throwing up egg.'

'Yeah, but the toilets here are lovely.'

She laughed and croaked, 'Do you remember when I threw up in McDonald's?'

He was perusing the menu again. 'Which occasion?'

'God, did it happen more than once?'

He blew a silent kiss without looking up.

'I'm sure I haven't thrown up in McDonald's more

than once,' she mused. 'Not that I wouldn't. It's the best place. The anti-capitalist mob will be sorry come the revolution, when the number one worldwide cleaned-once-an-hour toilet network is no more.'

Dirk continued to ponder his breakfast choice behind the menu.

Katrina examined her cutlery as if she might spot the germs. 'If you're counting Kuala Lumpur, that wasn't alcohol, it was pollution. The whole city made me throw up. Even hotel-room air conditioning made me heave. McDonald's was the only place I felt *well* enough to empty my stomach in peace.'

The coffee arrived in an elegant, thin-spouted pot. Katrina brightened, looked beyond her belly.

'Where are the others?'

Dirk shrugged. 'I don't know. When Pierre buggered off last night he was trying to work out how he was going to fit that cabaret table in the back of his car.'

'Oh, I didn't know he'd bought something.'

'He hasn't yet. The sale hangs on the dimensions of the rear end of his Explorer.'

'Why doesn't he have it delivered?'

Dirk licked his cigarette paper. 'You know Pierre: instant gratification. He'll have lost interest by tomorrow.'

'Oh, I'm sure it'll fit. That car is huge.'

'I guess, unless it just looks that way in Belgium.'

She laughed and then added, 'You'll make sure he coughs up, won't you? Don't want Erich to lose out because your friends are all idiots.'

'Sure thing, babes.'

The ingratiating Sergei was walking towards them with an apologetic expression on his face. Dirk looked over his glasses, his fringe shaking. Surely they couldn't be out of pancakes? At the Four Seasons, it was intolerable. What did one pay good money for? Invisible until the man was right beside them was the figure behind him.

'Nina!'

Underneath a long, grubby white coat, the silver dress of the night before gleamed tawdry in the light. A large brown stain was spreading across the midriff. Her hair clung to the sides of her face, which was pale and haggard.

'Are you all right, Nina?' Having got over the initial shock and embarrassment about what the front desk must have thought, Katrina noticed that her daughter looked like a ghost.

Nina's eyes were glazed. 'I was remembering that exhibition of self-inflicted wounds. Each photo was a different person, with real blood and pain on their faces. Don't you remember?'

Katrina was unimpressed by the spectral act and thought her daughter should sit down. 'I certainly do not remember. That sounds quite revolting.'

'There was that girl with a rip right down her abdomen and you could almost see inside. You must remember that.'

Katrina tutted. 'Nina, darling, why have you come into the Four Seasons hotel, half dressed, to discuss an exhibition I didn't go to?'

'*I* wanted to feel something too.'

There was a momentary silence. Hovering Sergei – preparing to explain the linguistic difference between Russian and Belorussian *again* – wondered whether this was the moment to take their breakfast order. Nina wobbled precariously and he decided against it.

Katrina was staring at her daughter's abdomen. Through the diaphanous material she saw red incisions. Her eyes narrowed. She grabbed at the dress, almost knocking Nina over. 'What the hell have you done to yourself?'

Nina smiled wanly. She recovered her balance and blew air up into her hair. It felt warm against her cold nose.

'Is that blood on your dress?'

'Don't tell me, Mother, it'll never come out. I know. It's dry clean only. What a waste, huh?'

Katrina looked round the room, as if gathering ammunition from the stability of the scene. Other diners were looking over as Nina's voice had raised. Panic ran across Katrina's eyes. She did not know what to say. 'That's not what I meant.'

Nina smiled strangely. Her teeth seemed yellowed against her bloodless skin. She said: 'What's Max like, Mother?'

Dreading a scene in the starched-linen perfection of the breakfast room, Katrina muttered into her lap, 'What are you talking about?'

Her muteness amplified Nina. 'When were you screwing him?'

'What the hell are you talking about?'

'Max is my father, isn't he?'

Katrina's face, lined with protest, froze. She looked at Nina as if she did not recognize her. '*What?*'

Nina smiled, weak but triumphant. Katrina was dumbstruck. *Her* histrionic requirements were met by explosions of electric satsuma on the walls of Berlin bars. Her daughter needed so much more. She spun bloody Greek tragedies, fuelled by an innate sense of the grotesque and an eye on the media. Now Katrina eyed Nina, who was standing swaying gently, her eyelids hovering between consciousness and unconsciousness. She tutted. Wouldn't be surprised if Nina wanted to sleep with Max herself.

She stood up briskly, her chair stuttering behind her. 'I think maybe we should have breakfast in the room after all. Dirk, darling, order me two poached eggs on toast, will you, and I'd like the toast thick.'

Dirk gave an assenting salute. Katrina pushed her daughter in the back with her handbag, marching her from the room. Nina, her voice growing louder with every sentence, was turning heads like a bride walking up the aisle.

'You haven't denied it, Mother.'

Contempt filled Katrina's voice. 'I don't need to. It's the most ridiculous thing your insidious little mind has ever concocted. How long before this one's on national television, huh?'

'Maybe I should ask Papa.'

'That would be very cruel.'

'You won't deny it, will you?'

Dirk picked up *Le Monde* and gratefully hid.

* * *

Success. Maybe if the works at the exhibition sparked a moment of clarity. Someone stood in front of a work of art and saw something in their own life. An abstract conduit to understanding.

Max woke up with Éva's soft thin form obscured by the tatty white sheet. He shivered. In winter she must freeze. For the first morning since his arrival in Berlin nearly three weeks ago his head was silent. It was too much to look at Éva as some kind of solution. But he liked her. He liked her a lot.

She stirred, sensing his wakefulness, her body twisting under the crumpled cover. He pulled it from her face. She looked at him sleepily, groaned slightly.

'Good morning,' she said.

'Hi.' He looked at her and enjoyed reading nothing in her face, no complication. 'What are the bathroom facilities like in this place?'

'Basic.'

'Ah.'

She didn't move.

He said, 'If I went and checked in at a hotel to clean up, would you come with me?'

She took him to a narrow place near the Ku'damm, where modern urban aspirations were signified by glass tables, lengthening mirrors at the far end and dark-blue uplighting, with limpet-shaped opaque glass shades.

The room was big enough. The bathroom, though, was luxurious. New matte white tiles stretched from floor to ceiling. The fitted surround to the wash basin, a high gloss scagliola, was swooshed with black across the grey and white. The bath lay sunken, shining at the far side. A door of green glass to the left led to a walk-in shower with a floor of rough stone.

Max had a bathroom not dissimilar at home but this felt better. What he wanted all along, he realized suddenly, was not a bathroom like this, but the feeling of walking into this bathroom after being without it.

'Go, get clean,' she ordered.

In the absence of odour in this room, he smelt on his clothes her damp apartment. Unpleasant, but he was reluctant to rinse it off. The lure of the stone-floored shower, though, was stronger. He could walk in and immediately pull the handle with confidence. In Erich's shower, his cautious arm led the way through a crackling curtain where interminable tap twiddling rarely found the tiny space of acceptable temperature between boiling hot and freezing cold. Every day the intrepid limb was scalded. And after only a few good minutes the temperature jumped or fell according to its own querulous whim. Erich's shower held more universal truth, Max conceded, but this smooth calumny was *so* much sweeter.

The water streamed across his face. He bent his head and let the stream saturate his hair, which turned dark and thick. He smoothed it back and applied gel to his hands. A superior brand of complimentary unguents, viscous yet clear, it smelt anonymous.

Then he felt her behind him.

He was not, this time, aware of her reaction. He only knew her as she felt to him. He had an angry energy. It was quick, awkward but powerful. Only afterwards did he kiss her.

'Thank you,' he breathed, and meant it.

He ordered a pot of coffee and breakfast and it arrived quicker even than he hoped.

She sat in the one white gown they found in the bathroom. Max wore the white towel. He wanted the room-service man to see evidence of their early sex. He tipped him heavily to make it plainer.

Max poured the coffee and inhaled the aroma. 'Good coffee,' he said. 'Makes a change.'

She nodded almost guiltily.

'I like this place.' He nestled in the pillow. 'I think I'll stay. Do you think Erich would mind? I mean, I'm sure he'd like me gone but not to a hotel. That might seem like a slap in the face.'

'How long are you thinking of staying?'

'Oh, I don't know. Weeks, months, who knows? You can stop by every day after work. No-one need know.' He put his hand on her neck.

She laughed. 'Yeah, whatever.' She sipped coffee. Looked at him curiously. 'How much money *do* you have?'

'I don't know.'

'You don't know? You don't know how much money you have?'

This was probably the only thing he could say that would shock her.

'No.' He smiled quickly. 'Is that bad?'

'No, it sounds wonderful. I've always known exactly how much money I haven't got.'

He put the cup down. 'Don't get me wrong. I'm not really loaded. I just have enough. I have money coming in anyway. Some of my stuff still gets syndicated. I have investments, property. I don't have a lot of' – he paused – 'financial commitments.' He shrugged. Resting his ankle on his knee, his hands behind his neck against the pillow, he sighed. 'I can do what I want.'

*   *   *

'Shut up, Chad, can't you?' Ursula was leafing through papers on the table. Barbara sat next to her, anxiously rubbing the side of her face. Though it was gone eleven, the rest of the café was empty.

Chad, arms akimbo, looked stung. 'Well, that's charming, when I, with *my* back, have been scrubbing that filthy gallery floor on my hands and knees for two hours. Although you'd have me use my *tongue*, I'm sure.'

Ursula groaned loudly and stored some papers between her teeth, enabling her to search through others and preventing her from answering.

'It wouldn't be so bad,' Chad expounded, glowering, 'if those pigs last night hadn't dropped their butts all over the floor. And spilt their red wine, their satay sauce, with not a thought of mopping it up! Artists, huh? Filthy bastards, more like.'

Ursula looked at Barbara, helplessly. 'Do you think Max might have any bright ideas?'

Barbara stared at her pityingly. Her voice loaded with sarcasm, 'Has to turn to a man,' she said.

'Well, you're not helping, are you?'

'Ursula, it's not my problem. I don't own this place.'

'Not today apparently.'

Barbara whistled.

Ursula smiled. 'It's just that Max was really helpful when Erich broke the window. He can be surprisingly helpful with practical things.'

She treated Barbara like a misbehaving child, with testy patience. This infuriated Barbara, who was finding it increasingly hard to deal with Ursula's new resolve. She was tougher since whatever happened with Max, no doubt about it. Their relationship had changed; Ursula wasn't playing along with their usual exchanges of grim self-torture. She was unbearably sensible.

Max arrived at the café, alone, only a few minutes later. 'Hi,' he said, querying the empty room and the group hunched round one table. 'What's up?'

Ursula smiled nervously. 'The coffee machine's broken and Erich's gone. What are we going to do?'

XXXI

The quintessential experience of late modernity in the West is one of rampant technological development in murderous embrace with social stagnation: half of our sensation is of being whirled down the rapids, half of being stuck in the mud flats. It is less a sense of particular crisis which seems to matter, than of the vision of the future being systematically voided.

PAUL WOOD, *Art has no History!*

Ten years ago, Erich came to London for a show. They ate in a restaurant where lights stayed bright so the clientele could watch themselves – Max's choice.

'I met the girl at the wedding of an art director,' Max was saying. 'She was clearly emotional – the kind of woman who buys it when a movie has the lead guy sit next to a book of Yeats's poems to prove his sensitive side.'

Erich smiled. 'Like Mussolini publishing pictures of himself playing chess.'

'Yeah, but, to be fair, the newly-weds *were* obnoxious. The room was clouded with that collective air of resentment when everyone knows the gifts are a waste of money. The groom fancied himself a comedian: "I knew

Jane was the one for me when my father tried it on with her. He has impeccable taste." '

'Ouch.'

Max nodded. 'And the groom was in full flow when this silly girl suddenly shouted, "Bollocks! Everyone knows you're still fucking Sasha Shadwell." She was slung out, the bride's speech was more outrageous, and the party wound inevitably on to the death. I was shocked by her behaviour. Yes, the whole thing was a farce, but don't we all have to keep up the pretence?'

Erich examined with consternation his newly arrived king prawn which was better dressed than he.

'Anyway, the point is,' Max continued, 'two weeks later – i.e., yesterday – I hear the heckling girl killed herself.' Erich looked up from his plate. Max nodded grimly. 'Mm-hm. She fought insincerity and she lost.'

The more he saw of the casual smiles of the artless diners around him, the more Max saw the expression on the dead girl's face. Fear. And he understood.

'I have no sympathy for suicides,' said Erich.

'I don't suppose she felt she had a choice.'

'There's always a choice.'

'I don't think so.'

After chewing a mouthful of food, Erich looked up, wryly. 'If you commit suicide, I'll never speak to you again.'

Max smiled briefly. 'You can't *commit* suicide, Erich: it's no longer a crime.'

'It is – against the people left behind.'

Max shook his head and said thoughtfully, 'I don't think you should perpetuate personal misery for the sake of others. Besides, people need these moments of drama. It gives life definition. You can bet there'll be people this girl knew who decide to live their own lives more fully after this, or use it as a trigger for future pain. In death, her social circle will expand magnificently as people claim their share of the suffering. Someone I knew with terminal cancer said she'd never had so many friends. And it wasn't support they were offering: they all wanted a piece of the melodrama.'

Erich winced at this bitter reality.

Max shrugged. 'People get over it.'

Erich looked at him icily. 'Not if her parents are alive, they won't. Not if she has any children.'

Max chewed his lip. 'She has a nine-year-old daughter.'

'Then it is disgraceful.'

Max stared at the flame of rage that shot across his brother's cheeks.

Erich said: 'Have you ever thought about suicide?'

'Sure, you haven't?'

Erich looked searchingly into Max's eyes, trying to quantify his seriousness. 'How frightening.'

'Not at all.' Max smiled. 'What difference would it make to you?'

Then Erich decided, or chose to decide, that Max was being flippant. There was no reason to believe him. His life was too good. 'I tell you what,' he said: 'if you ever feel tempted, ring me up. I'll talk you out of it.'

Max pictured this whole story in the seconds it took him to walk through the café door and up to the table where the others sat and from where Ursula had delivered her desperate appeal. How fast even his turgid mind could work.

'Why are you asking *me*?'

Barbara's tone was accusatory. 'Ursula thinks you're good at dealing with crises. Besides, you said you had a coffee machine at home.'

An edgy laugh. 'Yeah, but it's a stupid little thing you buy people for Christmas. It's not like this. In any case,

I've no idea how my machine works. I just press buttons.' He paused for breath and ammunition. 'And anyway, why me? Doesn't everybody have a coffee-maker? Don't *you*?'

Barbara folded her arms accusingly. 'I have a Turkish coffee-maker. There are no electronics. I just put it on the cooker until the water bubbles over the spout. It *can't* break.'

Her eyes bulged. He squirmed with dislike. Since he could afford a more expensive machine he must be responsible for the coffee machine in the café and probably the destruction of the rainforests and the cancelling of the Formel 1 music show as well. She misused the word 'fascist'. Her breasts were malevolent sirens. She was a breathing manifestation of unthinking ugliness. He hated her.

'Uh.' Max tried to focus. Only minutes ago he had been cocooned in hotel towels. Towels which someone else would wash. 'Uh, so, uh.' He rubbed his chin. He'd forgotten to shave. 'Uh, oh God, I don't know . . .' He looked round the room. 'Well, who broke it?'

'Don't look at me,' Barbara bristled. 'It's not *my* fault.'

The room felt slow. Stupor hung over the tables. Max tried to smile. 'I only thought if we knew who worked it last, they might offer a clue as to what went wrong.'

Chad barked smoke. 'Loads of people had their filthy hands on it last night. They came in here to get coffee, they didn't wait to be served. I definitely saw Katrina making her own coffee, the greedy old witch.'

'And it was working all right then?'

'Yes.'

Ursula rubbed her eyes and dragged a tired hand through her hair. It felt dry. 'The first we knew about it was when I got in this morning. I only came in because

Erich rang up and left this garbled message that he'd gone to Paris.'

Max screwed his face up. Flitting images hurt his head. If he *had* rung Erich the night before, two weeks ago, how would he have talked him out of it? This urge filled his head, had for years. Self-destruction floated through his mind with every failed communication, every relationship that left him cold. Like fresh air in a sewer. '*What?*'

Ursula shrugged weakly. 'Paris. I don't know. He's had a lot on his mind.' She raised her eyebrows.

Max looked away, raising his hands pacifically. 'Sure.'

Ursula sighed. This task felt huge. 'Look, can't we just get someone in?'

Barbara raised her hands in frustration. 'Straightaway? It's not a gas leak, Ursula. There is no emergency coffee-machine man.'

Éva rapped on the glass of the door. She had changed into a long-sleeved black smock dress with black boots. Her hair was scraped back.

Ursula leapt up to let Éva in before anyone else could. Her greeting was deliberate. She sought Éva's eyes. Her look was at once knowing and casual. Her voice was assuredly warm, purposefully inclusive. She knew, she wanted to say, and it was all right. She was stronger than they thought, stronger than *she* thought. She pulled Éva in with a friendly arm.

'What's up?' Éva did not look at Max. He was glad. Everything around him was covered in glass. Words sounded muffled.

'Four years I've been here.' Barbara was speaking with low menace.

'Really?' Ursula snapped. 'I never knew.'

Barbara ignored her. 'Four years I've been here and the coffee machine's perfect all that time. That's three years of an old machine and one year of a brand-new one which has functioned just fine since the day of purchase. Now, the one day Erich takes off, it breaks down. Don't you think that's surprising?'

'Weird,' said Éva, her heels clacking as she walked across the room. She called back, 'But then, the two of them are very close.' She disappeared into the hall, behind the bar.

Max heaved himself up. He spoke laboriously. 'OK. Here's the plan: I buy a new one, have it installed in a hurry and, with luck, Erich will never notice the difference.'

'That's what you do with a kid and his dead hamster,' Ursula objected.

'Who cares, if it's easier?'

'We can't afford it.'

'I'll pay.'

Ursula gulped. 'No, thanks.'

She looked at him; he looked embarrassed. She felt powerful because Max was so weak.

Éva clacked back with a manual in her hands. 'Here,' she said blankly and sat down, plonking the pages on the table.

Barbara glared at her. She picked up the manual and thrust it at Max.

'Why me *again*?'

'Take it.' Barbara sneered. 'It's time you did something useful.'

Max accepted the book, his shoulders sinking though it was no weight. The paradox was that he could feel so far away from this scene, so isolated by these people, and at the same time every piece of their throwaway banter had a personal sting. As if he was completely withdrawn and the centre of the world simultaneously.

Expectant silence, when what he wanted was to slink into the corner, bind his mouth with cellophane. Wearily, he read the suggestive words aloud. ' "Machine non-functioning – no power/ electronic control unit unlit." ' He looked up. 'Did it turn on?'

'Oh, yes.' Ursula stood up, went over to the machine and examined it. 'The red light's on. It's just that nothing happened after that. It didn't heat up.'

'A-ha,' he said darkly. 'Point two: "Machine fails to heat or is not pressurized".'

'Yes, that'll be it. Great!'

What did she have to be cheerful about? He flushed. His eyes darkened. Ursula fell silent and watched him warily. She rested sombrely, against the machine, releasing this eager energy from her body. She clasped her hands together, as if to contain them.

'I'll make some coffee in the pot upstairs,' said Éva, wanting no part of this laborious exchange. 'Hands up who doesn't want one.'

Max continued with heavy scepticism. ' "Is the heating element (resistor) powered? Check correct voltage of the resistor." Well, how the hell do you know what the correct voltage is? "Check the exact polarity on the leads of the resistor." Does anyone understand this?' He was scanning down the rest of the page. ' "Check inlet valve open, the anti-vacuum system . . ." What the hell's that? No,' he smacked the book shut, 'it's beyond me.' He slapped the manual on the table.

Ursula glared.

Éva walked back into the room with the jug of coffee she had boiled upstairs. She dumped it heavily. A little of the hot brown liquid spilled.

'So *clumsy*,' growled Barbara, dragging herself to the sink at the bar in search of a cloth. Éva let out testy breath.

Ursula paced across the room, a finger to her lips. 'OK. We don't panic. We *don't* panic. We find an alternative.'

She looked up. 'It'll be quiet for several hours. We can open up and serve this coffee from upstairs if people are really desperate. And we won't charge them. Meanwhile, there *is* a diagram of the machine with all the bits on it somewhere, isn't there? Can't you take a look at the instructions with that, Max?'

Max looked terrified. Ursula didn't understand.

Éva spoke hastily. 'Let me have a go. I used to do a lot of repairs at home.'

Max waved his arm wildly after her. 'There you are, Ursula. There's your best hope.' He slumped back in his seat, staring at the lines on his hands.

*   *   *

'Christ, it's quarter to three. Max, you couldn't go to the damn Art Preservation meeting, could you? I haven't been since Erich and I split up and they all hate me. Erich runs the whole thing.' Ursula's face was flushed. The café had reopened and she had been sprinting ever since. Erich made it look so smooth.

Max whimpered, 'But I don't know anything about it!'

'Just chair the thing. Take down a few notes. It doesn't matter what, but someone has to go. The room's booked. We have the key. We have to be there. Please, Max.'

One more brown Berlin building around a dark court-yard. A maze of artists' studios and designers' work-shops. The meeting room was also used for singing classes. An upright piano filled the far wall. The walls were soundproofed.

Grey plastic chairs were stacked by the door. It was five to three. Max took down a few chairs and arranged them in a circle. He sat down facing the door.

After ten minutes he looked at the clock again. He

peered through the glass in the door. He opened the door and peered down the corridor. Nobody. He checked Ursula's note to make sure he had the right room, though there could be no mistake since the key fitted.

Then he sat down again. He wrote down in the notebook the comments he imagined a person who wanted to preserve Kreuzberg's art culture might have:

Protest against new chain restaurant.
Hold jumble sale for Iranian women poets.
Going Pro with the Didgeridoo bestseller in the anarchists' bookshop.
Should we be worried?

He drew Éva's face on the notepad.

He felt moved, suddenly, by Erich's faith, despite everything. Where did the energy come from?

Ninety minutes later, Max made his way slowly back. The hum of the café was reassuring after the silence. He sat down and picked up the magazine again.

Ursula came over. 'How'd it go?'

'Oh,' said Max, nodding thoughtfully, 'I think I held things together.'

Ursula smiled warmly. 'Thanks, Max. It'll mean a lot to Erich that you did that for him.'

XXXII

The fronts of the buildings were pitted with shrapnel and eaten by rot and weather so that they had that curiously blurred sightless look you see on the face of the Sphinx. Only a very young and frivolous foreigner, I thought, could have lived in such a place and found it amusing. Hadn't there been something youthfully heartless in my enjoyment of the spectacle of Berlin in the early Thirties, with its poverty, its political hatred and its despair?

CHRISTOPHER ISHERWOOD, *Diaries Vol. One*

Erich stood on the Pont Neuf looking into the Seine.

Max. With distance, perspective. It was good if Max could connect with the others. Good if anyone could reach Nina. Good to see Max connecting with Otto. Max was interested in them this time. Maybe the phone call from Maria had something to do with that.

He could not tell Max he knew about the possibility of a child. To mention it felt disloyal, collusion with Maria. But was this what had made him so desperate? Regret that he had wanted her to have an abortion, or regret that it had happened? Did Max even know? He tried to imagine Max talking about it. Impossible.

Pont Neuf is the oldest bridge in Paris. Since 1603 it has been painted and repainted and reinterpreted so many times, by Turner, Renoir, Pissarro, Signac, Marquet, Picasso and more. For the escaped Communist Christo to take on the past when he wrapped the bridge fifteen years ago was either extreme folly or genius daring.

Three hundred people used forty-one thousand square metres of woven polyamide fabric, silken and the colour of golden sandstone. Thirteen thousand metres of rope the giant parcel needed, and twelve tons of steel chains.

In a long career, Christo wrapped oil barrels, naked women and a section of Australian coastline. His biographer called it 'revelation through concealment'.

Erich looked into the water. He breathed. Max. It was all about what they didn't say.

*   *   *

Max first ran away when he was twelve, not long after the psychologist had diagnosed him 'isolated'; it was as if he opted to fulfil her diagnosis. At first, he disappeared for only a few days at a time, but their parents never found out where he went. Erich was away at college and was given scant detail. Max went missing every few months. He returned thinner, dirtier. They had tried to talk to him about it. Erich shook his head. He knew his parents' conversation and why it was lost on Max, who, under the gentlest interrogation, retreated behind a dead-eyed shrug.

When, later, Erich had settled in Berlin, his brother, by then sixteen, showed up at the front door of the squat. Erich was living with his girlfriend (the following year, with the accidental arrival of Nina, his wife) and some

351

slack-jeaned guys with peroxide hair. Erich was eager to practise his co-operative theories. Max could share the cooking. He too could vainly bang the water heater with a shoe. He could deny the health and safety officers access to the metre-wide chasm in the living-room floor. Above all, Erich would give Max space to paint.

But Max didn't do anything, save fix the TV. Still, the others loved him and not just for this. Katrina took to him immediately. Erich would find her snuggled up to Max on the sofa, stroking his hair, his newly chiselled jaw and his long, lean thigh. He saw Max needed physical closeness, to women, while remaining emotionally aloof. Erich was seduced too. He laughed more with Max than anyone.

It was a month later, speaking to his mother, he discovered she had no idea where Max was. Max returned to London. He started the art foundation course to keep his parents quiet, but was thrown out after a term. Two years later, he was living rent-free in some spacious north London flat of a girl with up-market vowels, a Soho photographer who paid him to assist her. The disappearances were never mentioned again.

*　　*　　*

Erich walked into the Pompidou Centre, to visit the library; to bathe in the vast public room, rows of metal bookshelves providing a partition between the two lines of tables that stretched to the horizon.

He wanted to know what Max knew about Schopenhauer's theory of art. He found a book and sat down with today's microcosm of humanity flung together between the Journals of the European Union and the window overlooking the Rue St Martin.

A black Jean-Paul Sartre lookalike worked on his Ph.D.

thesis. Reading French upside down, Erich saw something on Africa's new democracies. The Sartre man was distracted by the new Cameroon football shirt in his bag. He stared at the closely typed paper. One arm sneaked into the bag. Collapse was inevitable. Seconds later the whole shirt was yanked out. The man placed it across his face and inhaled.

Three seats closer to the bookshelves sat a middle-aged man in an obvious wig. He was studying English, staring at a long list of verbs and their slithery prepositions. To search *for*. These betrayed Max's rusty German. Max searched *for* when, in German, he should be searching *after*.

* * *

His parents must have been frantic over Max's missing months. They didn't say. Their fortitude left Erich unprepared for the trauma of child-rearing. Nina and Otto were raised in a mix of thought-through policy and daily inevitable neglect. And that was before they asserted their own agendas, their own distorted visions of how to get through. Christ knows where that came from. But he had little influence. He couldn't stop their mistakes; he could barely ease their pain. He could do nothing except love them. That was easy. Telling them was harder when they did not want to hear.

Schopenhauer lay unread. Erich stood up and walked past the neighbouring tables. Where his preposition exercises should have been, the old man was drawing an inky sketch of the Cameroon supporter. Erich smiled. He was not alone. In Berlin, Paris or Yaoundé, everybody fakes it: tries to play the ideal self, to live inside their myth.

Back in Berlin he would talk to Max. He would listen.

He would put his preconceptions aside. Max was human, whereas Erich had treated him always like an extension of his own psyche, from the time he was the little brother who looked up to *him*, to the present, the stranger who now slept in his spare room. Max was a foil to Erich's life. Erich felt ashamed. From now on, he would just listen. But it was hard when Max didn't speak. *Would* Max not speak, or had Erich allowed him not to?

Erich went through the strip detector and wound around to the pictures, up transparent tube escalators. He had forgotten the pleasure of aimless gallery wandering; in the middle of the day in the middle of the week.

Joseph Beuys: 'Plight', 1985
Felt, grand piano, blackboard and thermometer

He bent his head to walk in. The low ceiling and narrow walls were covered with rolls of felt. A simulation of total isolation. In World War Two, Beuys, a fighter pilot, came down over the Crimea. Local people saved his life. They smoothed tallow over his wounds and wrapped him entirely in felt. Fat, felt and claustrophobia became his signature materials. He wore a hat to hide the scars. His trademark. Concealment through concealment.

What had Max ever tried to hide? There was this belief that Max shrouded everything, but he'd no need to with other people's preoccupation, with no-one looking. Maybe Erich held more confidences. More people, more lies. Max left no trail. Erich pulled a caravan: Nina, Katrina, Otto, Ursula. He smiled. Ursula. Now, *she* couldn't hide a reflex. And what a relief that was.

An exhibition in Berlin the previous year studied twentieth-century German artists' self-portraits. Kirchner drew Kirchner the drinker, one of the crowd. Max Beckmann had seen himself as the urbane sophisticate, critical onlooker, smoking in black. Otto Dix was in his soldier's uniform, the artist interrupted by life. Hitler (who called himself an artist) declared art a mission demanding fanaticism.

But Beuys drew himself as a wanderer: not forming society, not changing society, but passing through, at its mercy. A participant, like everyone else, with nominal control. Pleasure and pain were incidental. Already Erich missed the noises of the café, the smells, the ragged routine of his life.

He stopped for a coffee at an old French bar. Sitting outside at a small round table, he rested the thick espresso cup on a leaflet someone had left behind. When he drained the drink he noticed the leaflet advertised an upcoming Berlin exhibition: 'Marlene Dietrich: Forever Young'. There she was, dusky eyes, soft lips, preserved for ever in black and white. The cheekbones still sharp for her centenary. The icon they wanted to believe in. Marlene! He had barely thought of her since he had left Berlin. For two years he had visited her, his hideout, his lifeless comfort. For two years her strangeness was the one thing that kept him sane. Now she was vanished and he did not care. In fact, he felt easier. He had been living in the unreal too long.

*   *   *

In the middle of the night, she woke, aware that a light was on.

She found him curled in the airing cupboard, cowering next to the wine rack. 'Otto! What are you doing? It's three in the morning!'

A pair of green eyes, whites startling, blinked against

the electric light. 'Mama!' His voice was tearful, years younger.

'Sweetheart, what's the matter?'

He was trembling. Her face softened. She pushed forward, reached out to him; then, by hurriedly shifting the pots and boxes in her path, she managed to lever herself into the minimal space next to him.

'Otto, what are you doing in here?'

'Nightmare,' he whimpered.

'What nightmare?' She stroked him gently on the cheek. She was enjoying this babying. 'What happened?'

A long sniff. 'Marlon Brando had chopped your and Papa's heads off and stuck them on sticks. Uncle Max was running round laughing, taking pictures, and the café was on a huge hill made of water and it was on fire – and –' Otto burst into sobs and hid his face in the folds of Ursula's top.

'What?'

Otto continued to shudder. At his side she saw the DVD of *Apocalypse Now*. Helicopters flew across the orange sky.

'Where did you get this?'

Otto sobbed and shook his head against her stomach.

'Tell me, Otto.'

Gasping. 'Uncle Max.'

She pulled a face. 'Max gave you this?'

It took an hour of coaxing to persuade Otto to leave the cupboard. By which time Ursula's anger at Max was tempered by a sense of her own part in this. She too had forgotten that Otto was a child.

*   *   *

The hotel room was now measured out in physical terms between them. The carpet: not quite soft enough – it

356

burned a little; the bed: too soft. The spacious shower; the too narrow bath. The table, not as sturdy as it looked, toppled, they discovered, under uneven weight. The window-ledge, narrow, but a good height; the view across to another building, with tall, unseeing windows and vertical rows of unused, iron staircases, was suitably anonymous.

They rested, still sweating under the sheet. He liked to put his arm round her shoulders; it produced a comfortable, though disingenuous feeling of permanence.

When he was with her, when he could exhaust his mind through exhausting his body, he relaxed. He was more open to her then.

Éva sensed this and so took her chance. 'Max, why do you pretend not to think?'

He looked at her. 'I don't know. It's easier, I suppose.'

'Easier than what?'

'Easier than trying. Easier than engaging.'

'Don't you suffer from boredom?'

'Oh, all the time.'

'Then, shouldn't you do something about it?'

'Like what?'

'I don't know. Engaging in something that fulfils you.'

'Doesn't stop me being bored.'

'How do you know?'

'I've tried it.'

He frustrated her. She saw glimpses of him but he was not prepared to share further. 'Are you afraid of painting?'

He laughed. 'Oh, doesn't that sound good!'

She watched his laughter without joining him. She had learned this trick of his: to deflect an unwanted question with a slick, meaningless riposte and let conversation then move on. And also that, if she waited, silently, he felt obliged to answer.

So she turned on to her side towards him and rested her chin on his shoulder. And then he spoke. 'No. I'd paint if I wanted to but I don't. When I was younger, I painted and it made me miserable. I didn't find it fulfilling, I found it frustrating.'

'Some people say it gives them hope.'

'Pah. Erich might believe that one day he'll paint a picture he likes, but it doesn't wash with me.' He swept her hair gently from her face. In his eyes, she could see him retreating. 'Well, what about you? What keeps you going?'

She accepted that the subject must change. 'That things change. Things going on in Eastern Europe.'

He didn't notice that his eyebrow was raised in scepticism. 'Oh yeah, and what are you doing about it?'

She took out a cigarette and lit it. 'Don't make fun of me.'

'I wasn't, particularly.'

This annoyed her. She stiffened and frowned. He felt bad. He was not used to her candour. He stroked her hip softly while she looked away. Gradually her bruised expression softened.

She flushed. 'I don't mean I'm going to run for parliament. I just think that talking to people, having an opinion . . .' She trailed off, and dragged on the cigarette. 'I have a Czech friend who was fourteen when Communism ended. Overnight, they stopped teaching Russian in her school. But they couldn't just sack all the teachers, so the Russian teachers became English teachers, even though they were barely better than the kids. They were, like, three lessons ahead in the book. It was funny.' She laughed. He watched her face move.

'Of course,' she continued, 'I'm not saying people shouldn't learn English, but people can't just drop an identity of forty years, and so right now the void is being filled with bad Americana. I want to be part of finding a new identity.' She caught him staring. 'What?'

He held her chin in his hand. 'You don't carry all the shit around that I do,' he said quietly. 'You're straight-forward. I like that.'

She frowned. 'Oh God. Don't turn me into your little anti-Western fantasy, Max. That's so patronizing. I'd much rather you just said I was a great lay.'

He looked bewildered.

She whistled. 'Come on, Max, I thought you believed in delusion? Tell me I'm fabulous.' She leaned into him, her nose close to his, smiling into his dour expression. 'Go on, tell me.'

There was a silence. She pulled away. She sat back against the bed and folded her arms, tapping her foot so that the sheet twitched. She waited.

At last he heard the silence and mustered: 'Look, sorry, I was thinking about something else.'

'Oh, great. Now I feel really special.'

Max frowned. 'No. It's nothing to do with you. It's me.'

She stood up, picking the white robe from the floor, and walked to the bathroom to cleanse herself of him.

He looked up. 'Don't go.'

*   *   *

Two round white tables next to each other. In the centre of each an almost identical foil-wrapped TV dinner. A light shone on each in turn, focusing on one unappetizing choice after the other.

Max remembered this installation, a 'Choice of evils'. He walked back to the café.

Since Erich was away, Max went through the back unhindered. He climbed the stairs. He turned into Erich's bedroom. It was the first time he had been fully inside. Books lined the walls in a bright patchwork of colour against the precise male blues of the paint and bedcover. Under the window was Erich's private work desk. So many desks.

Max opened the drawer at the side and leafed through the scrupulously ordered papers. He pulled out the rest of the Gerte story.

XXXIII

The Memoirs of Gerte Mela (VI)

Just when I had resolved to let go of all that had happened, to move on, I received a letter. It read like a civic order. 'Dear Herr Mela, You have an appointment at Weidestrasse 15, tomorrow at ten a.m. Non-attendance may lead to prosecution.' It was so like him.

Anna let me in. She was wild-eyed, red-rimmed, her face puffy from recent and, by the state of her, prolonged weeping.

'Master has been very ill since you went away,' she cried. 'Now he's been in bed for three weeks. He won't eat or drink and he is rarely lucid.' She looked down at the letter in my hand, which wavered with the breeze and my adrenalin-charged fingers. 'He made me write that.' Her face crumpled and her eyes filled with tears. 'Oh Herr, Miss, whoever you are, what are we going to do?'

Instinctively I grasped her and we clung to each other, found solace in the embrace, though our miseries were not the same.

His bedroom was heavy with darkness. The single flickering candle, on top of his old leather trunk, merely illuminated the strength of the black.

The bed, which I barely noticed on the night Anna and I crept in like infidels to gape at the picture, now dominated the room. It stood on vast iron legs a good three feet tall. The mattress was of double thickness. Pillows, stacked vertically, took up at least half the length of the bed. Sunk in the middle lay the decaying features of Poltonov.

It was so dim, I thought he would not notice me. But then, almost imperceptibly, his hand began to move. It pushed forward and up towards me, with agonizing slowness, until it was within inches of my body.

I shook. It seemed the whole room vibrated. And then he opened his mouth. 'Boy,' he rasped, 'where have you been?' His voice was weak.

I stammered, garnering strength as I spoke. 'Herr Poltonov, what's the matter with you? Have you got flu? What does Doctor Meerbohm say? Have you called Doctor Meerbohm?'

At my words Anna wrung her hands and hid her face from me. She was convulsed.

Poltonov opened his eyes and with the most minimal of neck movements looked me in the eye. 'Alas, Doctor Meerbohm is not a medically qualified physician. He is a prostitute.'

Poltonov's fever was not pure bad luck. Anna revealed with sorrowful eyes the remains of cocaine on his tray. He was severely dehydrated. Again, not without personal responsibility, for, daily, Anna had removed trays of carefully prepared delicacies untouched.

'At the very least you shouldn't do this to Anna,' I said, automatically extracting pillows from under him and pointlessly plumping them although they were already balloons. 'She's worried about you.' He made no objection to my chiding tone. 'I can't believe you did this. What's the matter with you?'

'I was disappointed, boy,' he said. He looked at me without flinching. 'I am an old man. I am a rich man but I have not had a happy life. You lied to me.'

I stared at him. 'I'm sorry,' I managed. And I was. It was true I had deceived him, though he had, in as many ways, deceived me.

Poltonov began to sniff and whimper softly but this did not disturb me. I was possessed with a sudden and altogether new energy.

I spoke briskly. 'And Raskolnikov, I imagine, has been quite forgotten?'

I received no answer, but as I walked to the door I saw Raskolnikov lying at the top of the stairs, dejected, his nose drooping, scraping the floor. The dog barely raised his head when I greeted him. To this call of his name, which before would have had him yapping in anticipation, he now gave only a supercilious glance.

Anna whispered to me as I walked back, 'Don't be too hard on him – he's been wretched.'

At the mention of the hound, Poltonov looked suddenly guilty, traumatized. I shook my head. 'You idiot.' He rested his upper lips over the lower, the effect so pathetic that I could only relax my demeanour. I sat on the bed beside him, all the while Anna hovered anxiously in the background. I touched his face with my hand. When I tried to take it away, his arm came up from under the sheets and he held me fast.

*   *   *

Poltonov made a slow recovery. I stayed with him when it became clear that he would not eat or drink unless I was there to see him do it.

The fact that I was a woman was unfortunate but unalterable. It was too late to let me go. We were enmeshed. If he gave me up and sought another, that young man might, in the night-time smoke of Poltonov's Eastern cigarettes and the richness of the décor, succumb. But there would always come a morning. Others had come, Anna confided now, and always left.

We knew little of each other, Poltonov and I. I knew nothing of his past lovers; he knew nothing of my empty past. We kept it that way. It was better that we enjoyed each other on our respective undisclosed terms, leaving no room for disillusionment. There was some spark between us, some understanding, and this would only be weakened by investigation. The matter was left unspoken, but he did not send me away again and I did not seek another.

As Poltonov recovered, he fired me again with his thoughts. When we talked, I began, naturally, to address him with the informal 'you'. Anna smiled again. I took up the old canine duties. Raskolnikov eventually stopped sulking. After a while, at Anna's instigation, I took to wearing the old clothes. We all preferred it that way. And when I left Frau Kellermann's for good (she sent me off with no emotion, save that she would miss my household contribution, the conditions in Berlin being 'so bad at the moment'), I moved into those purple rooms with no regrets but with, instead, a sack of her dead son's clothes.

*   *   *

1983

I often take the train to the botanical gardens at Steglitz. I like to watch the minute changes in the plants. In the warmer months, I give a painting class. The money left me dried up before his paints did. And though I live alone and simply, I have some expensive habits. I learned a lot from Poltonov.

I sit on a bench in the avenue of roses and watch the petals drop. I pick one up and stroke its softness, look at it until the solid form separates before my eyes into tiny yellow ribs. I wonder why anyone would want to paint a flower. Why compete with perfection? I can think that now.

Late in the afternoon, I will return to my small apartment, close to the spot where he used to live, a tree-lined avenue off the Kurfürstendamm, and I will watch a tape I have of my favourite film. Living in West Berlin (only thanks to Poltonov, who did not live to see the good fortune of his choice), I have been able to buy a videotape machine.

I saw *Nosferatu* for the first of so many times in a cinema near here, by the Romanische Café. I saw it in 1922, at the height of my delirium, abandoned by Poltonov, possessed by the spirit of a woman I had never met. I loved the film, its ominous darkness, the flickering fear. From the first, I felt a peculiar link with *Nosferatu*, as if it was written with me in mind; or, more troubling still, that it was not 'written', not a fiction at all, but spoke some wider truth. 'The evil spirits become all powerful after dark. You can't escape destiny by running away.'

I did not run away and I did not escape the destiny that ordained I was to be disappointed.

I was born perhaps too late. By the time I was eighteen the great years of Expressionism, which had so inspired me, were over. The Great War ended ideals. Before it, artists craved war, even unjust war, to refresh the 'stale taste of the ordinary'. Afterwards, the fog stayed thick.

The *Nosferatu* legend would have it that evil can be vanquished by the sacrifice of a pure woman. It is, like so many stories, appealing but not true. I was, once, pure. I sacrificed all I had, my life and my ambition, but the world

365

did not change. I made no difference, except to one old Russian. Perhaps that's all that could and should be.

* * *

If this little work ever hits the desk of a publisher, he will, of course, push me to write less of the feeble old man and more of Berlin's 'golden years'.

I am of a dying breed. My memories stem from a time which, clouded by so much horror afterwards, glows now. People want to hear about that. To believe in champagne balls and glittering cabaret.

I can tell a story. I can talk about the tennis lessons I took from Nabokov though I never met the man.

I can turn out a convincing tale of the New Year of 'twenty-two spent in Bad Saarow with Maxim Gorky. I can describe the huge and decorous tree, bright with light, that he sat next to. He talked of visiting an intellectual friend banged up in a third-class foreigners' sanatorium, I remember distinctly.

I can tell you about the world's first school of psycho-analysis and its first scientific centre for sexual research. Of course they were both in Berlin. Let me tell you the jokes we made. I still hear them.

Of course, I saw Dietrich's audition piece for the film that made her name. The flirtatious routine to piano accompaniment. I told her to play it straighter – and it was I who told her to lose a little weight. Make those cheek-bones haunt the camera. She never thanked me for it.

I am an expert, if that's what you want. I can describe the metal foot-scooter that Tolstoy's son sped round the Stadtpark on, dressed in his miniature sailor suit, or the afternoon Billy Wilder learned to dance. I was there.

Who, of those frequenting the Russian cafés then, does not have a memory of Anna Pavlova, old, tiny and so humble in a dowdy black shawl, sitting at a corner table? I'm almost sure it happened to me. I have such a clear picture. I see her at last persuaded to perform. She takes off the shawl and gives a silent but so poignant dying swan. On that uneven floor space, so close, I am terrified that she will fall. Did she waver? Or does she toy with us, heightening the drama, playing weak, to let us enjoy the exquisite agony that the legend is broken, then to discover that, no, for one more night she does not fall. She is everything we have heard. When it is over, she retires to her corner and freezes into the scenery like a doll in a musical box.

Sit down, I'll tell you all you want to know. Fetch down the old silver canister embossed with figures. Feel the yelling mounted Cossacks chasing around its girth. Let me make a pot of Russian tea and then I'll tell you all about Berlin.

Max threw the book down. He was trembling. Erich's imagination was the one place where Max still excelled.

He had felt, from the start, that there was something altogether too personal about this 'translation'. The set-up; the girl believing in the old man beyond anything; his powers so effective in her head. And then the details. The coincidences accumulated: the fondness for Dostoyevsky; the bowl of fruit; even the story of the Happy New Year in Russian. It was already too much, but now he knew for sure. Max smiled. Some things only he could know, because of his bond with his brother, their unique shared history. This warmth he felt, it was always over the most mundane things.

XXXIV

In the middle of October 1941, Oskar too began to wallow intensely in mud. I hope I shall be forgiven for drawing a parallel between the muddy triumphs of Army Group Centre and my own triumphs in the impassable and equally muddy terrain of Mrs Lina Greff. Just as tanks and trucks bogged down on the approaches to Moscow, so I too bogged down; just as the wheels went on spinning, churning up the mud of Russia, so I kept on trying – I feel justified in saying that I churned the Greffian mud into a foaming lather – but neither on the approaches to Moscow nor in the Greff bedroom was any ground gained.

GÜNTHER GRASS, *The Tin Drum*, 1959

'He won't speak. He won't eat. Not after last night. More nightmares, I think. He's been like this all morning.'

Otto was sitting on the sofa in Erich's sitting room, in red pyjamas at lunch time, catatonic, eyes closed, his hands resting limply on his lap.

'I'm really sorry, Erich.' Max was standing awkwardly, with one foot propped on the other. He hovered over Erich, who sat next to his son.

'Can you shift? You're blocking the light.'

Max moved. Erich was fanning and nudging the boy, stroking his arm.

'I'm sorry,' Max whispered.

'What?' Erich looked up. 'Oh, don't worry, this is not your fault. This has been building for a while. I, that is, Ursula and I, we've lost sight of him somehow.'

Max nodded pacifically. He wondered how much Erich knew about Otto and what he had a duty to tell him. Otto's plastic picture had been put behind his cupboard, though it was still burning a hole in his head.

Ursula looked out of the window, her fist clenched. 'I was so determined to do a better job than my parents. Nothing was going to hold him back – not my own insecurities or my narrow vision. He wasn't going to be *crushed*.' The fist fell.

'He's only eight, Ursula,' Max ventured. 'It's not all over.'

She turned to him, her eyes vituperative, wet. 'Oh, and what do you know?'

Erich walked over to her and held her. 'Everything'll be all right. He just needs some looking after. We have to stop wanting things from him. He's a child. That should be enough.'

She bent her head onto his chest. 'Clichés.'

'Doesn't mean they're not true. Come on,' he took her hand, 'come and make some coffee while I call the doctor.'

She followed meekly, her voice faint. 'Why are you so strong about this?'

'It's an act.'

Alone, Max stared at the boy. His soft face was white and still. Censorious, unpleasantly reminiscent of one of his damn statues. Max knelt down beside him and hissed in his ear. 'For Christ's sake, Otto, stop it. I'm sorry about the picture, OK? I'm sorry about the film. Look.'

He fished out his wallet. 'Two hundred marks, right here. Listen.' He cracked the notes in Otto's ear. 'Just open your eyes and it's yours.'

The boy's eyes did open and the white face slackened. He looked at Max with hatred and fear, the pupils of his green eyes dilated. 'Leave me alone!' Then he shouted, screamed, 'Papa! Papa!'

Seconds later, Erich and Ursula ran back into the room, pushing past Max, who barely had time to move aside. Ursula grabbed the boy in her arms and he clung to her. Erich grasped him from the back and looked at his brother. 'What happened to him, Max? What woke him up?'

Max shrugged. 'I don't know.'

Patting him on the arm, Erich exhaled slowly. 'Well, thanks. You did the trick somehow.'

Max looked uncomfortable.

*　　*　　*

Since Paris, Erich was more direct – which Max translated as more threatening.

But wasn't it better that Erich should know Max for what he was? How slack, how self-motivated, how numb? That his destruction had been gradual, an invisible erosion, fed on vacuity, until now, he thought, there was almost nothing left.

With Otto asleep and Ursula watching over him, Erich said, 'You know, Max, I've been so wrapped up with the exhibition since you came, we haven't had a chance to talk . . .'

Oh God.

*　　*　　*

They sat in a North African restaurant. Erich's choice, but unusual for him it was modern, deliberately designed. It embraced travesty: cooking styles had been stolen and tempered to suit the German palate. The red and gold paintwork was offset in each corner by plants, all man-sized, with sturdy stems spiked at intervals with vibrant red, yellow and orange racemes.

Max attracted the waiter's attention deftly. He ordered wine without consulting his brother.

'What's that you've ordered?'

'Château Musar. Lebanese. Best there is.'

'Don't you want to try something topical? They have several African wines.'

Max was gnawing the edge of his hand. 'Life's hard enough without bad wine.'

Erich chose the food since, to this, Max was in-different. He ordered couscous with lamb in a sauce of apricot and chickpeas. The wine was poured into large tulip-shaped glasses, two swallowed almost half a bottle.

'Mm.' Erich savoured it. 'Good choice.'

Max looked at the red liquid through one eye. 'So, did you, uh, have a good time in Paris?'

The strain in his voice caught Erich's attention so completely that he forgot to reply until Max was staring at him in consternation. So Erich spoke then, rapidly. 'Uh, yeah, Paris, uh-huh, very relaxing.'

'Good. Very sensible, after all that hard work.'

'Not that hard.' Erich smiled, toying with his wineglass between his fingers. 'It's what my life's all about, after all. Apart from the money, I really can't complain. I'm doing something I believe in.' He looked coy. 'I suppose that sounds stupid to you.'

This annoyed Max, not because it wasn't true, but because it was – a peevish paradox that pushed him to speak uncharacteristically. 'On the contrary, that's what I envy about you most.'

'Most?'

'Yeah,' said Max.

'There are other things you envy about me?'

'You'd be surprised.'

Escape had cleared Erich's vision. Berlin felt cloudy, dense with unnecessary subterfuge. 'How are *you* feeling now?'

Max shifted in his seat. 'Not bad.'

'I'd really like to know.'

'Well, I . . . it's just, oh, I don't know. I'm all right. The time here has flown past. That's a good sign, isn't it? I feel bad about what happened with Ursula. Otto too, of course.'

Frustration filled Erich's face. 'It's always other people, Max. I want to know about *you*.'

Max looked up, his brown eyes weary. 'There's really nothing to say.'

Erich tutted. They ate for a moment in silence. Perhaps if he, Erich, confided, Max could open up. 'My girlfriend left,' he volunteered.

Max blinked. 'I'm sorry.'

'No, that's OK. I didn't love her. It was fun, sort of, but it had no place in my real life. Besides, she didn't exactly leave *me*. She left the area and me by default.'

'Uh-huh.'

'Max,' he said tentatively, 'why do people run away?'

There was no flicker of recognition. It was only at the front of Erich's mind, but Max may have blanked it out years ago – though Erich did not believe this. It could never be more in Max's mind than now, during his latest disappearing act.

'Different reasons, I guess.'

'Well, like what?'

Did Max blush?

'Like what?' he said again, more softly.

Max spoke slowly. 'Maybe they can't take the certainty.'

'What certainty?'

'Being the same person every day.'

'But you're not a different person by being somewhere else.'

Max shrugged. He looked at his wine. 'Then, I don't know.'

Bilious thoughts soured the wine to Max's tongue. He saw where Erich was going with this conversation, pushing, probing him to discover the 'secret' of his miseries. He did not like to be interrogated. His guilt was replaced by resentment. Since Erich thought he wanted honesty, then let him have it. Max said slowly: 'Isn't it running away when you're writing about that girl and the old Russian and pretending it's real?'

'What?'

'Yeah.' He shrugged, more confident in attack. 'Otto gave it to me. He thinks it's a translation.'

Erich rested on his elbows. 'What makes you think otherwise?'

'Come on, Erich. So you put me in a wheelchair and cut off my good arm. Gave my lazy-bastard non-achievement a tragic dimension. Very moving. Just the kind of thing that might happen to a symbolic sort born the night the Wall went up.'

'You heard—'

'Yes. Otto let that one slip as well.' Max smiled simply. 'But don't worry, I like to be useful. And I'm far more effective as a fantasy figure.'

Erich did not know what to say. He bit his lip.

'Don't look so miserable, Erich. It really doesn't matter.'

'It felt real.'

'Yeah.'

Magnanimity was Max's refuge. They weren't talking. Erich realized that Max had slithered away.

Determinedly, he took a corner of the unleavened bread to mop up the oily orange juices on his plate. 'So I do a bit of creative writing in my spare time. I'm not the guy pretending to enjoy a life of tits and take-aways, all the while with Schopenhauer's Theory of Art up his sleeve.'

'I only read Schopenhauer to get laid.'

Erich's hands played with a bunch of keys. He pulled one after another, fingering each crenellated edge. Max's fiddling was more complex. He tore off small sections of the burgundy napkin, scrunched them into balls, arranged them vertically; then he pushed them into a circle. Then, once the circle was perfect, he threw them back into chaos.

'I'm serious, Max.'

'I know. Doesn't mean I have to be.'

'Max, stop! You sound like Otto.'

'No. He sounds like me.'

They matched each other. There was a rhythm to it, something formal, a dance.

'Did you like it?'

'The story? Yeah.'

' "Yeah"?' Erich smirked. 'Since you read it without my permission, I think I deserve a fuller answer.'

Max's eyes wandered round the room as he considered. 'It's like you. Good, for all those uncynical reasons, that you make Berlin seem such an appealing place. But . . .'

'But?'

'Yeah. I wanted to know what happened. How the old guy died. How she kept it all together. Why she never found anyone else.'

Erich shrugged. 'I don't know. It only seemed important that she realized that she had had an effect on him.'

He paused. Max had softened. 'Maybe I'd like to know I could have an effect on you.' He looked up anxiously. 'If you ever got desperate again, would you tell me?'

'Sure.'

This was said so definitively that Erich was entirely unconvinced. Max drowned his mouth in his wineglass. In this position he could not speak. After the delay he could change the subject.

'Good food,' he said.

Erich peered at the plate. 'Mm. Have you actually eaten any?'

Max picked up his fork again and pushed some couscous round the plate.

'I just wish . . .' Erich looked at him. 'I'd like us to be close.'

'What makes you think we're not?'

'I just wish we could really understand each other, Max.'

Max stared back. 'You do understand me. You just won't admit it because you want me to be different.' His tone was chilling. Erich stalled. Max maintained his momentum. 'Hasn't it occurred to you that if I really was so great, I would have been?'

'I should be representing you now, Max.'

'No.' Max shook his head, laughing with his eyes, folding his napkin over his untouched meal. 'No, Erich.' But if Erich could live by this illusion, let him. It was the genius of untruth.

Erich wiped his mouth, seeing nowhere to go but back to their familiar patterns, the side-stepping, the evasion. 'So how did you know I made up the Gerte story? I thought it was quite realistic. I thought I imitated her inter-war sincerity to perfection.'

Max smiled and sucked his lower lip, folding his arms. 'What finally swung it? It was the description of the old tea canister with the yelling Cossacks, which I remember sitting in Mother's glass cabinet at home. Horrible, ugly thing – the canister, I mean, not Mum.'

Erich nodded. He looked at his brother. Something lay in this trivial detail. Only Max had known him this long. He had not *known* Max, but Max had been there. His familiar face, his presence, his memory, they would have to be enough. Max would never talk.

*   *   *

'She'll be all right. The wounds are superficial. I don't think she wanted to hurt herself. She's a drama queen, just like her mother.' Katrina lit up a rare cigarette. She deserved a treat. Though an extra night in the Four Seasons was some compensation for what Nina had put her through. She lay on the bed, enjoying the luxury, in her peach silk dressing gown that perfectly set off her copper hair.

'How did Nina get that idea about Max in her head anyway?'

Katrina shrugged, recoiled on the crisp sheets. 'You know what she's like. She'll come up with anything.'

'There's no truth in it?'

'Why should there be?'

Dirk screwed up his eyes. 'Because you're evading.'

'Don't get cunning on me, Dirk.' She looked at him through half-closed eyes, lying on her side, her vivid bob touching the side of her mouth.

Dirk sat at the side of the bed, with a cigar that he was biting the end off. He looked up. 'Answer the question.'

She jumped at his tone. Dirk didn't care about anything, so she thought. This new gravity scared her. He was a big man but normally too docile to show.

376

'It's highly unlikely,' she said in a small voice.

'But not impossible.'

'Nothing's impossible.'

'Some things are, Katrina. It's impossible, for instance, that she's *my* child.'

She looked away. 'I suppose.'

'But this isn't impossible.'

'Virtually, but not absolutely.'

He raised his hands in disbelief. 'Don't you want to know?'

'I do know. I don't believe it. Anyway, the past should be left alone.' She shuddered. 'Everyone's happy the way it is.' She gathered her knees into her chest and wrapped the silken gown round her so only her ruby toenails poked out.

'Don't you think Nina has a right to know?'

'There are no rights. Not in the past. Many people have no idea who they really are.'

'That's not quite the same thing, Katrina.'

She stuck her lower lip out. 'Stop it, Dirk. Feed me some more of those chocolates.'

His shoulders fell and he relented. They too had concentric circles from which they should not stray. Dirk stretched to the bag on the mini-bar and retrieved a Viennese truffle. He squeezed it between his big and second toe. He hoisted his leg towards her and she sucked it lovingly out.

*   *   *

The coffee machine, which had functioned sporadically and noisily after Éva's intervention, grumbled to its final resting place.

Erich flipped the power switch. The machine buzzed weakly, like a dying fly, and then, with a grunt, it collapsed. He put an ear to its side. He stroked it, his fingers lingering over the shiny red coat.

When he turned round, Ursula was screwed up in the corner, hardly able to look.

'I'm so sorry, Erich.'

'Don't worry about it.' He smiled at her concern. 'I'll just get someone in.' This floored her. 'This machine is almost new. There's no reason for it to break down. Let the manufacturers sort it out.'

She shrugged. 'Right. OK.' She looked at him oddly but did not want to push this new hardiness. 'So, how'd it go with Max?'

'You know Max.'

She laughed.

They sat down together and drank coffee from the upstairs pot. The drink had a rich, dark aroma. It felt smooth in Erich's throat. He put down the cup. 'Mmm. This is good.'

'It's a different blend.' She was nervous. 'Max recommended it.'

'Of course.' His eyes glimmered.

She dragged her finger over the table, collecting grains of sugar. 'I'm glad you're back.'

'I wasn't away very long.'

'It felt longer.' Ursula's eyes were warm, untroubled. 'Oh, by the way. You won't believe it, but someone bought your penguin picture.'

'No, really? That's almost too much. When did someone last buy something I painted?'

'I can't remember. Maybe me, when I was trying to impress you.'

'That was a long time ago.' She nodded, laughing. He took her hand. 'We should celebrate, Ursula.'

She hesitated. 'I missed you.'

'Then I must go away more often.'

378

XXXV

The days rattle by, the trudge of daily business unfolds. If, one hundred years from now, we were to look back, would we have achieved something? Affected something? Accomplished something in our life, in our own, inner, true life? Would we have grown? Would we have opened ourselves up, blossomed, would we have lived? Berlin! Berlin!

KURT TUCHOLSKY, 1919, *Berlin: Voices of a City*

He told her she was beautiful. He took flowers. If he lacked originality, he spent a lot of money. The arrangement was breathtaking, all white with darkest green foliage. When she held it, the top half of her body was hidden. She gasped as the pungent scent of lilies invaded her shabby living space.

She let him into the bedroom – not because she was grateful, but because she found his hopelessness exciting. As a fantasy it was cathartic, a thirst-quenching acceptance of the miserable. He did not know why he bothered, for he could barely feel her. His eyes were open but he could not see her body. As she crawled over him, controlling everything, it felt like fucking Hamlet (and she'd always wanted to). But afterwards, she remembered she must not exalt Max. It was not safe. Afterwards, he was alone.

He sensed the shift in her. Her eyes were cold. He was silent.

She fixed her eyes on him. 'What?'

'What, "what"?'

'What are you going to do?'

'What do you want me to do?' There was a desperate note in his voice. 'Do you not want me to go?'

She half laughed, a single moist note. 'Max, I like you. I'm not even sure I don't love you, although you're so completely impenetrable and negative. But I don't want to be the reason for you to stay. That's too much pressure. And there really isn't any reason for you to be here, is there?'

'Funny, that's what Erich said when I left London.' He sighed and took her hand and caressed it with his fingers. He looked at the pink and olive patterns of her skin. The scratched red knuckles. The fingers tapering to bitten ends, the veins underneath pumping life through. He said wonderingly: 'I think I love you.'

'Do you?'

He murmured, 'But I can't give people what they need.'

Her face turned sceptical. 'How do you know what I need?'

'Exactly.' He let her hand go and opened his own out in five-fingered emphasis. 'You don't need me.'

She was irritated with his self-pity, the cracks in him. 'How can I *need* you? I don't know you. Do you think I was nothing before you got here and will be nothing once you've gone?'

'No.'

She sat up, pulled the thin sheets around her, over her bony knees. He stroked the hair away from her forehead. She pulled his hand away but held on to his finger. She looked at him seriously and his heart sank. 'You know what, Max? I think everyone has the balance wrong.

Everyone feels sorry for Erich, battling for survival with this brother who cruises through life. And isn't it a shame how Erich has never let go, never appreciated himself for what *he* is. But the thing is, Max, Erich's fine with it. It's you who needs him to believe in you.'

He glowered.

She touched his shoulder. 'Doesn't mean I don't love you, Max. Everybody loves you.'

*   *   *

Now Max was leaving, Erich looked back on the extravagance with which he had continued his normal life during his three-week stay. Beforehand it seemed for ever; retrospectively it was no time at all.

'I feel like I've hardly seen you.'

'Still, it's more than we're both used to.'

'Look,' Erich sounded awkward too, 'I'm sorry I didn't make more effort.'

Max dismissed this with his hand. 'You were busy.'

'I don't see why you have to leave right now.'

'Why not? I hate farewells.'

'Uh-huh.' Erich added, self-consciously, 'What about Éva?'

Max let out a short laugh. 'Yeah . . . no.'

'That's a pity.'

'Yeah,' said Max.

'She's a nice girl.'

'Yeah, she is. But she sees straight through me.'

Erich registered this with a sympathetic male grunt.

They walked together towards the door. 'Max, you'll be forty soon.'

'Yep, Erich. Next step after thirty-nine. Thought I'd follow convention.'

'Amazing, think of it, you outlasted the Wall.'

Max sniffed. 'Just as well I'm not an artist. Nina said any decent artist kills herself before forty.'

Erich flushed. He had almost forgotten why Max was here. The words came out in a rush. 'No, Max, no. I meant that we all thought the Wall would last for ever.'

'Oh, right.'

The Wall. It would keep Erich busy.

'Why don't you come back *then*?'

'Uh, maybe.'

The pathetic luggage collection was by Max's feet. The bag caved in, anorexic. Erich chewed the back of his hand. 'Come back for your birthday. We'll do something.'

Max grinned. 'Tell Ursula I'm sorry I missed her.'

Coaxing: 'She'll be back at lunch time.'

'Sorry, plane to catch.'

'I wish you'd let me drive you to the airport.'

'You're busy. It's fine.'

Erich stuck out his hand. Max took it.

'Don't forget what I said.'

'Yeah. See you.'

Max slouched away. Erich missed that limp already.

*   *   *

Berlin was noisy. The percussion of the building sites that the irrational heard patterns in: digging, drilling, rubble falling through chutes, constant upheaval that overwhelmed the meagre sound of motor traffic, pedestrians, the silence and the silenced.

The new city was constructed in the ruins of the old. And the wise did not negate the past, or try to forget, but charged it with meaning, built shrines to its memory to show that lessons had been learned. Did Erich understand that he was right?

Max walked a route, as he remembered, that Gerte had tramped with the dog at night. Winding eastwards, past Friedrich II, remembering with regret that his painting still stood behind the wardrobe. The stone plaque promising eternal friendship with the Soviet Union, the golden cross reflecting off the TV Tower globe, despite all efforts to quell it. They called it the Pope's revenge.

Wandering. Maria called it wishing his life away. It was one of those repeated exchanges that serve to remind both partners how incompatible they are, he taunting her with his misery and she clinging to blind optimism.

'You'll be old soon and then you'll regret wasting your time.'

'I'll top myself before then.'

And she would sob: 'You enjoy inflicting pain on other people.'

'I thought you wanted me to be honest.'

But she didn't really; no-one ever did.

His legs grew tired. Even this suitcase was heavy. On the side of the oncoming train, he saw a whole carriage sprayed with massive white letters. He turned his head to read the word 'Otto'. He smiled. He did not get on but let the trains pass in front of him because the noise gagged the voices in his head.

* * *

Barbara stopped by a round ad hoarding. 'Single no longer with the Berlin over-thirties' party night!' A radiant blonde beauty smiled out of the picture. Wearily, Barbara opened her bag and fumbled for a pen.

* * *

Unusually, Éva had stopped by the glass door of the café. She rarely looked out. A man was roller-blading, in a green go-faster Lycra bodysuit and goggles, up the road. He pulled a small dog along. The dog was attached in a harness to a skateboard. Its ears streamed behind like small furry kites.

She did not hear the man shouting at her.

'Are you deaf?'

'What?'

'I've been calling over and over, you stupid girl.'

She focused back inside, on his dull eyes. 'Well, what the hell is it?'

The man looked round him to an imaginary crowd of outraged sycophants. 'Can you believe *her*?' He pointed a derogatory thumb.

Éva's mouth drew tight. 'Well, what?'

The man looked aghast. ' "What", she says!' He pointed at the plate hanging from his hand at a precarious angle. On it slithered an untouched mess of eggs. 'After an hour of waiting for an omelette, you've brought me scrambled eggs *again*. But, even worse, this is the *same* plate of scrambled eggs you tried to fob me off with half an hour ago. Only colder. You are a *shit* waitress. Where's Barbara? Barbara wouldn't let this happen.'

'Yeah, right,' she spat. 'Ask Barbara. Barbara's in the Turkish baths. Barbara is dousing her tits with healing waters as we speak. You can forget her. Barbara don't own this place, you know, though she acts like she shit the Himalayas.'

Since this was spoken in Magyar, he understood not a word. However, the timbre was unmistakable. The man eyed her narrowly and left without another word.

Éva sat at the bar. She picked up her book again, stared at it vainly, put it down and choked silently. The edges of her lips glowed lachrymose red. She sniffed; wiped her nose on the sleeve that fell below her wrist. Better a waitress than a parasite, living off Max. The tears were falling too fast to wipe them away. She stood up and viciously wiped tables already clean.

*　　*　　*

Ursula sat up against the headboard, wriggled the covers around her and let out a long sigh. 'That was a ridiculous thing we just did.' Erich smirked. 'A huge mistake.'

She felt soft and distantly familiar as he kissed her cheek. 'Good.'

'Where are you going?'

She looked startled as he twitched and stirred from the bed. 'I promised I'd call at Anke Melker's this afternoon to check out some new stuff.'

'Get back in here.'

He submitted meekly.

Her chin jutted out. 'It has to be different, Erich. You have to loosen up.'

Erich looked penitent.

'And I want you to give up the Art Preservation Society. You have too many commitments. There's no time left for anything else. I want some pleasure in my life. And I want another child.' She looked at him belligerently. 'So what do you want?'

What did he want? Confidence in the future, acceptance of the past or just present calm? With his arm round her neck, he dragged her back down to the horizontal. He painted, with his finger, a line down her chest, between her breasts, over her flat belly. 'You know the gallery will probably have to close.'

She sighed. 'You've been saying that all the time I've known you.'

'Doesn't mean it's not true.'

Ursula closed her eyes and delicately massaged her temples.

Erich perked up. 'But I did have a thought in Paris.'

'Oh, yeah?'

'Yeah. For next year, something on cafés. Paris cafés, Berlin cafés, the inspiration, the difference, the past, the future. I don't know, something about cafés and art. I'm not putting it well. Why are you laughing?'

She moved towards him and he squeezed her until she gasped for air. He released her. She sank gratefully back into the pillow.

He said, 'I want Max to know that he doesn't have to be anything.'

The phone rang. Ursula stood up and walked to the landing to answer it. He had forgotten her unconscious nakedness. He waited alone, straightening the sheet she had left rumpled. Footsteps hurrying back. She reappeared, clutching the side of the door. The colour was drained from her face.

'What is it?' The words sounded harsh.

He never forgot her hollow eyes.

'The police. It's Max.'

This was nothing to do with Berlin.

THE END

The first Starbucks opened in
Germany in May 2002.

Permissions

I

'*We live for the most part in closed rooms . . . made entirely of glass*'

From *Glasarchitektur* by Paul Scheerbart (Berlin, 1914). This translation from *Glass Architecture* by Paul Scheerbart and *Alpine Architecture* by Bruno Taut, edited by Dennis Sharp, translated by James Palmer and Shirley Palmer (New York, Praeger Publishers, Inc., 1972).

II

'*The propaganda exercises . . . of his wife's unfaithfulness*'

From the article 'Berlin's The Bummel Town' by David Fish in *Querschnitt* magazine, 1929. Cited in *Berlin im Querschnitt* by Rolf-Peter Baacke (Munich, Econ Ullstein List Verlag, 2001).

V

'*The taste of espresso is bittersweet . . . One false step and you are totally doomed*'

Jeffrey Steingarten, American *Vogue*, November 2000.

VI
'A city is itself a medium . . . yet it also shows one's weaknesses'

Thorsten Schilling. From the catalogue published to accompany the exhibition *Children of Berlin. Cultural Developments 1989–99* curated by Klaus Biesenbach, Director of Kunst-Werke Berlin. Translations: Mitch Cohen, Lucinda Rennison, Andrea Scrima, Ts Skorupa, Claudia Tannhäuser. Published by Kunst-Werke, Berlin and PS 1 Contemporary Art Center, Long Island, New York, 1999.

VII
'At first sight he may appear a little rough . . .'

Johann Wolfgang von Goethe, 1827. *Eckermann's Conversations.*

IX
'Here is your world . . . the graceful fluttering over calyces'

From George Grosz, *Ein kleines Ja und ein grosses Nein,* originally published by Rowohlt Verlag GmbH, Reinbek bei Hamburg. Copyright © 1955 by Estate of George Grosz, Princeton, New Jersey.

X
'The history of the underground mirrors the history of the city . . .'

From *Dunkle Welten – Bunker, Tunnel and Gewölbe unter Berlin,* by Dietmar and Ingmar Arnold, originally published by Christopher Links Verlag – LinksDruck GmbH, Berlin, April 1999.

XII
'Traditional machines risk the human touch . . .'

From *Illycaffe* by Marco Arrigo. Quoted in a feature in the *Guardian* Saturday magazine, 4 August 2001.

XIII

'She was without shame . . . "You can sleep with me if you like"'

Fred Hildenbrandt, Arts Editor of the Berlin *Tageblatt*. Quoted from Lothar Fischer 'Anita Berber 1918–28 in Berlin' in *Die Wilden Jahre – Eine Klatsch- und Kulturgeschichte der Frauen von Birgit Haustedt*, originally published by Edition Ebersbach, Berlin, 1999.

XIV

'I constantly saw the false and the bad . . .'

From Arthur Schopenhauer, *The World as Will and Representation*, 2nd edition, 1844.

XV

'Take a big pencil . . . The Metropolis has to be painted'

From Ludwig Meidner 'An Introduction to Painting the Metropolis', 1914. English translation by Victor H. Meisel in *Voices of German Expressionism* (Eaglewood Cliffs, New Jersey: Prentice Hall, Inc., 1970).

XVII

'Night! Tauentzien! Cocaine!'

Song from Tauentzienstrasse, centre of Russian cabaret in the 1920s. From *Russen in Berlin: Literatur Malerei Theater Film 1918–33* © Reclam-Verlag, Leipzig, third edition, 1991.

XXIII

'This is where it happens . . .'

Robin Detje. From the catalogue published to accompany 'the exhibition *Children of Berlin. Cultural Developments 1989–99*, curated by Klaus Biesenbach, Director of Kunst-Werke Berlin. Translations: Mitch Cohen, Lucinda Rennison, Andrea Scrima, Ts Skorupa, Claudia Tannhäuser. Published by Kunst-Werke,

Berlin and PS 1 Contemporary Art Centre, Long Island City, New York, 1999.

XXIV
'A woman who has got what she wants . . .'

Erich Kästner. *Fabian*, 1931. Translated by Cyrus Brooks (Libris, London, 1990).

XXV
'And so I now use as models the faces of people . . .'

Oskar Kokoschka. From *Painters on Painting*, selected and edited by Eric Potter. Originally published by Grosset & Dunlop, New York, 1971. Revised edition published by Dover, 1997.

XXVII
'We must become conscious that there are puzzles . . .'

Schoenberg to Kandinsky, 19 August, 1912. Quoted in *Die Kunst gehört dem Umbewusstsein* (*Art Belongs to the Unconscious*), published by the Arnold Schoenberg Centre, Vienna to accompany the exhibition *Schoenberg, Kandinsky, Blaue Reiter & the Russian Avant-Garde*, 9 March–28 May 2000.

XXVIII
'Whoever cannot find a hotel room . . .'

From *Joseph Roth in Berlin*, edited by Michael Bienert © 1996 by Verlag Kiepenheuer & Witsch, Köln and Verlag Allert de Lange, Amsterdam.

XXIX
'She was always late . . .'

From Vladimir Nabokov, *The Gift* © 1963 Dmitri Nabokov. Translated from the Russian by Michael Scammell in collaboration with VN (Penguin, New York, 1981).

XXX
'The visual impression made by the wrapped bridge . . .'

Jacob Baal-Teshuva. From *Christo and Jeanne-Claude* (Taschen, America, 1995).

XXXI
'The quintessential experience of late modernity . . .'

From Paul Wood, *Art has no History! The Making and Unmaking of Modern Art*, edited by John Roberts (Verso, London, 1994).

XXXII
'The fronts of the buildings were pitted with shrapnel . . .'

From Christopher Isherwood, *Diaries Vol. One*, edited by Katherine Bucknell (Chatto & Windus, London, 1996).

XXXIV
'In the middle of October 1941 . . .'

From Gunther Grass, *The Tin Drum*, 1959. German translation by Ralph Manheim, translation © Pantheon Books, New York, 1962.

Acknowledgements

I would like to thank my parents and brother for their unfailing enthusiasm.

For advice and information: Joanna Anderson, Kat Barrett, Roger Bennett, Heiko Blankenstein, Angelina Bosczek, Sara Conkey, Maria Julietta Cervantes, Mareike Czybulka, Anna Holz, Alexa Jansen, Martin Lambrecht, Michael Marray, Peter Matsen, Nora Meyer, Jane Morren, Jetta Rudolph, Louisa Schaefer, Rachel Seiffert, Christine Wirrell and many other artists and gallery owners in Berlin.

And for stalwart editorial support, Jo Frank, Bill Scott-Kerr and Sarah Westcott.

IDIOGLOSSIA

Eleanor Bailey

'HIGHLY ORIGINAL AND BEAUTIFULLY WRITTEN . . . A
BRILLIANT IMAGINATION AND GENUINE PSYCHOLOGICAL
INSIGHTS'
Sunday Telegraph

For four generations of women from the same family, madness is a
potent legacy. It tempts, is persuades and it destroys. But it can also
bring a strange kind of freedom . . .

Aggressive, demanding, eccentric, Great Edie curses the
psychological weakness that runs through the family like a fault. No
one would suspect that her psychic powers were anything more than
a business, security for her old age.

Her daughter, Grace, has languished in a mental institution for long
spells of her adult life, after a tragedy years ago. Grace's only child,
Maggie, grew up, working with her father on a fading cruise liner.
But the golden age of ocean travel is over, and a relationship with
the mysterious comedian, Rudi, leaves her pregnant and alone.

Now Maggie's daughter, Sarah, is truly dispossessed and, through
gratuitous sex, seeks revenge on her loveless childhood. She rejects
the world of overused clichés and overpriced coffee but can see no
alternative – except to let go . . .

'RELENTLESSLY BUILDING BENEATH AN ENTERTAINING AND
WELL-WRITTEN STORY THE READER IS MADE AWARE OF THE
RELATIONSHIPS WHICH BIND US, NOT ONLY TO OUR FAMILY
BUT ONE BEING TO ANOTHER'
Daily Mail

'[BAILEY'S] UNSENTIMENTAL BUT SYMPATHETIC LANGUAGE
PENETRATES THE PRIVATE WORLD OF THE EMOTIONS IN AN
IMPRESSIVE WAY'
The Times

'A BRILLIANT ACCOMPLISHED DEBUT . . . SLICK AND CLEVER,
HEARTFELT AND DEEP . . . BAILEY'S OBSERVATIONS ARE
STARTLING AND FRESH . . . THE SORT OF READ WHICH
HAUNTS YOU FOR WEEKS AFTERWARDS'
Sunday Express

'BAILEY IS AN INTELLIGENT WRITER, ELOQUENT ABOUT
MONEY AND WOMEN'S STORIES. HER GRIP ON POETIC
LANGUAGE IS AN ASSURED ONE . . . AN AMBITIOUS
FIRST NOVEL'
Independent on Sunday

0 552 99860 5

BLACK SWAN

EMOTIONALLY WEIRD

Kate Atkinson

'THE LUSTRE, ENERGY AND PANACHE OF HER WRITING
ARE AS STRIKING AS EVER . . . FUNNY, BOLD AND
MEMORABLE'
Helen Dunmore, *The Times*

On a peat and heather island off the west coast of Scotland,
Effie and her mother Nora take refuge in the large
mouldering house of their ancestors and tell each other
stories. Nora, at first, recounts nothing that Effie really wants
to hear, like who her father was – variously Jimmy, Jack, or
Ernie. Effie tells of her life at college in Dundee, the land of
cakes and William Wallace, where she lives in a lethargic
relationship with Bob, a student who never goes to lectures,
seldom gets out of bed, and to whom the Klingons are as real
as the French and the Germans (*more* real than the
Luxemburgers). But strange things are happening. Why is
Effie being followed? Is someone killing the old people? And
where is the mysterious yellow dog?

'BEAUTIFULLY WRITTEN . . . BRIMMING WITH QUIRKY
CHARACTERS AND ORIGINAL STORYTELLING. KATE
ATKINSON HAS STRUCK GOLD WITH THIS UNIQUE
OFFERING'
Time Out

'A TRULY COMIC NOVEL – ACHINGLY FUNNY IN PARTS –
CHALLENGING AND EXECUTED WITH WIT AND
MISCHIEF . . . AN HILARIOUS AND MAGICAL TRIP'
Meera Syal, *The Express*

'SENDS JOLTS OF PLEASURE OFF THE PAGE . . .
ATKINSON'S FUNNIEST FORAY YET . . . IT IS A WORK OF
DICKENSIAN OR EVEN SHAKESPEAREAN PLENTY'
Catherine Lockerbie, *The Scotsman*

0 552 99734 X

BLACK SWAN

LIKE WATER IN WILD PLACES

Pamela Jooste

FROM THE PRIZE-WINNING AUTHOR OF *DANCE WITH A POOR MAN'S DAUGHTER*

'A REMARKABLE NOVEL . . . OUGHT TO WIN PRIZES . . . A GREAT BOOK'
Jennifer Crocker, *Cape Times*

'JOOSTE IS A SENSITIVE WRITER AND A MASTER OF UNDERSTATEMENT'
Isobel Shepherd Smith, *The Times*

The stories and legends of the Bushmen were told to Conrad when he was twelve years old. He was on a hunting trip with his father, Jack Hartmann, a brutal but confused man who 'gave' Conrad an old Bushman to teach him the ways of the land. Bastiaan taught him not only about the beasts and plants and soil, but inculcated in Conrad a philosophy that would remain with him throughout his life.

But at home Conrad learns a different set of rules as he and Beeky, the young sister he adores, huddle together listening to the sound of his mother being beaten and told she is trash. Jack Hartmann, a senator and man of power in the community, hates his wife and daughter as much as he loves his son, and Conrad's mother impresses on him that he must always protect and guard his little sister.

As they achieve maturity, Conrad appears to conform to the vision his father has for him. But Beeky defies her father and the establishment, and goes her own way, yearning for a new South Africa, a new life, tenderness and kindness in place of hatred and derision.

The story of their fulfilment, tragedy and the return of hope is the portrayal of an ancient land fighting towards redemption.

'HER UNDERSTANDING OF CHARACTER AND MOTIVATION, OF THE WAY IN WHICH HUMANITY CAN SHINE THROUGH IN ONE AREA AND FAIL LAMENTABLY IN ANOTHER IS OUTSTANDING. UNRESERVEDLY RECOMMENDED'
James Mitchell, *The Star*, South Africa

0 552 99867 2

BLACK SWAN

KNOWLEDGE OF ANGELS

Jill Paton Walsh

SHORTLISTED FOR THE BOOKER PRIZE 1994

'AN IRRESISTIBLE BLEND OF INTELLECT AND PASSION
. . . NOVELS OF IDEAS COME NO BETTER THAN THIS
SENSUAL EXAMPLE'
Mail on Sunday

It is, perhaps, the fifteenth century and the ordered tranquillity of
a Mediterranean island is about to be shattered by the
appearance of two outsiders: one, a castaway, plucked from the
sea by fishermen, whose beliefs represent a challenge to the
established order; the other, a child abandoned by her mother
and suckled by wolves, who knows nothing of the precarious
relationship between church and state but whose innocence will
become the subject of a dangerous experiment.

But the arrival of the Inquisition on the island creates a darker,
more threatening force which will transform what has been a
philosophical game of chess into a matter of life and death . . .

'A COMPELLING MEDIEVAL FABLE, WRITTEN FROM THE
HEART AND MELDED TO A DRIVING NARRATIVE WHICH
NEVER ONCE LOSES ITS TREMENDOUS PACE'
Guardian

'THIS REMARKABLE NOVEL RESEMBLES AN ILLUMINATED
MANUSCRIPT MAPPED WITH ANGELS AND MOUNTAINS
AND SIGNPOSTS, AN ALLEGORY FOR TODAY AND
YESTERDAY TOO. A BEAUTIFUL, UNSETTLING MORAL
FICTION ABOUT VIRTUE AND INTOLERANCE'
Observer

'REMARKABLE . . . UTTERLY ABSORBING . . . A RICHLY
DETAILED AND FINELY IMAGINED FICTIONAL NARRATIVE'
Sunday Telegraph

0 552 99780 3

BLACK SWAN

A SELECTED LIST OF FINE WRITING
AVAILABLE FROM BLACK SWAN

THE PRICES SHOWN BELOW WERE CORRECT AT THE TIME OF GOING TO PRESS. HOWEVER
TRANSWORLD PUBLISHERS RESERVE THE RIGHT TO SHOW NEW RETAIL PRICES ON COVERS
WHICH MAY DIFFER FROM THOSE PREVIOUSLY ADVERTISED IN THE TEXT OR ELSEWHERE.

99313	1	**OF LOVE AND SHADOWS**	*Isabel Allende*	£7.99
99734	X	**EMOTIONALLY WEIRD**	*Kate Atkinson*	£6.99
99860	5	**IDIOGLOSSIA**	*Eleanor Bailey*	£6.99
99922	9	**A GOOD HOUSE**	*Bonnie Burnard*	£6.99
99767	6	**SISTER OF MY HEART**	*Chitra Banerjee Divakaruni*	£6.99
99836	2	**A HEART OF STONE**	*Renate Dorrestein*	£6.99
99954	7	**SWIFT AS DESIRE**	*Laura Esquivel*	£6.99
99898	2	**ALL BONES AND LIES**	*Anne Fine*	£6.99
99851	6	**REMEMBERING BLUE**	*Connie May Fowler*	£6.99
99978	4	**KISSING THE VIRGIN'S MOUTH**	*Donna Gershten*	£6.99
99759	5	**DOG DAYS, GLENN MILLER NIGHTS**	*Laurie Graham*	£6.99
99890	7	**DISOBEDIENCE**	*Jane Hamilton*	£6.99
99885	0	**COASTLINERS**	*Joanne Harris*	£6.99
99867	2	**LIKE WATER IN WILD PLACES**	*Pamela Jooste*	£6.99
99738	2	**THE PROPERTY OF RAIN**	*Angela Lambert*	£6.99
99977	6	**PERSONAL VELOCITY**	*Rebecca Miller*	£6.99
99959	8	**BACK ROADS**	*Tawni O'Dell*	£6.99
77088	4	**NECTAR**	*Lily Prior*	£6.99
99777	3	**THE SPARROW**	*Mary Doria Russell*	£7.99
99865	6	**THE FIG EATER**	*Jody Shields*	£6.99
99952	0	**LIFE ISN'T ALL HA HA HEE HEE**	*Meera Syal*	£6.99
99819	2	**WHISTLING FOR THE ELEPHANTS**	*Sandi Toksvig*	£6.99
99902	4	**TO BE SOMEONE**	*Louise Voss*	£6.99
99780	3	**KNOWLEDGE OF ANGELS**	*Jill Paton Walsh*	£6.99
99673	4	**DINA'S BOOK**	*Herbjørg Wassmo*	£7.99
99723	4	**PART OF THE FURNITURE**	*Mary Wesley*	£6.99
77107	4	**SPELLING MISSISSIPPI**	*Marnie Woodrow*	£6.99

All Transworld titles are available by post from:
Bookpost, PO Box 29, Douglas, Isle of Man IM99 1BQ
Credit cards accepted. Please telephone 01624 836000,
fax 01624 837033, Internet http://www.bookpost.co.uk or
e-mail: bookshop@enterprise.net for details.
Free postage and packing in the UK.
Overseas customers allow £1 per book.